THE FARSALA TRILOGY

BOOK 2

RISE OF A HERO

Will a champion come
to Farsala's aid?

HILARI BELL

EAN

US $6.99 / $7.99 CAN
ISBN-13: 978-0-689-85417-0
ISBN-10: 0-689-85417-X

9 780689 854170

50699

Read all the books in the Farsala Trilogy
by Hilari Bell:

Fall of a Kingdom

Rise of a Hero

Forging the Sword
(coming soon)

THE FARSALA TRILOGY
BOOK 2

RISE OF A HERO

HILARI BELL

Simon Pulse

New York   London   Toronto   Sydney

SIMON PULSE

An imprint of Simon & Schuster Children's Publishing Division

1230 Avenue of the Americas, New York, NY 10020

Copyright © 2005 by Hilari Bell

Map on pages vi–vii drawn by Russ Charpentier

All rights reserved, including the right of reproduction in whole or in part in any form.

SIMON PULSE and colophon are registered trademarks of Simon & Schuster, Inc.

Also available in a Simon & Schuster Books for Young Readers hardcover edition.

Designed by Greg Stadnyk

The text of this book was set in font Cochin.

Manufactured in the United States of America

First Simon Pulse edition June 2006

10 9 8 7 6 5 4

The Library of Congress has cataloged the hardcover edition as follows:

Bell, Hilari

Rise of a hero / Hilari Bell.— 1st ed.

p. cm.— (Farsala Trilogy ; bk. 2)

Summary: Although the Hrum believe their war against Farsala is nearly over, Soraya has strategic information that will help if she can reach Jiaan and Kavi and their separate resistance movements, but discord and Time's Wheel seem destined to keep them apart.

ISBN-13: 978-0-689-85415-6 (hc.)

ISBN-10: 0-689-85415-3 (hc.)

[1. Fantasy.] I. Title.

PZ7.B38894Wh 2005

[Fic]—dc22   2003025164

ISBN-13: 978-0-689-85417-0 (pbk.)

ISBN-10: 0-689-85417-X (pbk.)

When I tell Lisa she's the best niece I have, she gives me a look and tells me that she's my only niece. So this book is for Lisa, who is not only the best niece I have, but also the best niece anyone could have.

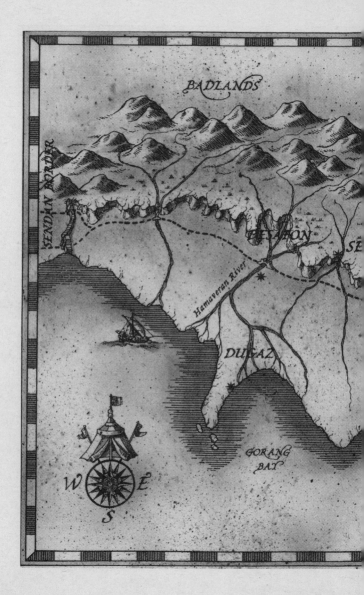

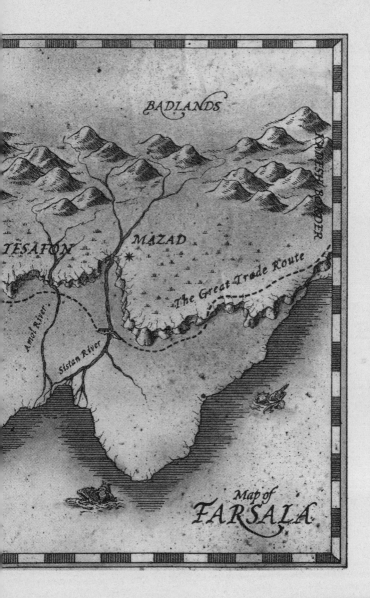

BADLANDS

TESAFON

MAZAD

The Great Trade Route

Amok River

Sisian River

Map of
FARSALA

THUS SORAHB WAS SLAIN, *in all the power and promise of his youth, and all who knew of it grieved. And marveled too, for the God, Azura himself, had descended to earth and taken the boy from the arms of his stricken father, promising that Sorahb would be returned ". . . when Farsala most needs a warrior to lead it."*

But Time's Wheel turned, and turned again. Decade yielded to decade, and Farsala knew no greater trouble than a few border skirmishes with the Kadeshi. Decades flowed into centuries, and the tale of Sorahb became legend, and even the legend grew dim.

Then came the army of the Hrum, the Iron Empire that had conquered half the world with small difficulty, before it reached Farsala's borders. At first, it seemed Farsala would be much the same. Though the mighty deghans who defended the land fought fiercely, they were overcome and slain almost to a man—only a handful surviving to be taken as slaves. The Hrum knew that the peasants of Farsala were not warriors. They believed that the land was now open to them, all its wealth free for the taking, and they rejoiced.

And even among those who knew of it, none gave a moment's thought to the ancient tale, told to wide-eyed children as the fires grew low. But they should have, for the time had come—Farsala needed a champion.

CHAPTER ONE

SORAYA

ORAYA TRIED to urge the iron-mouthed mare to a faster pace, but the mare—who had probably pulled an ore cart before Soraya stole her from the miners—plodded stubbornly onward in the deliberate walk that seemed to be the only gait the worthless creature possessed. The sun was setting, painting the new spring grass that covered the low hills with mellow golden light. Soraya wondered if her home was still there.

She'd been forced to travel at night once she reached the Great Trade Road, for fear of encountering one of the mounted squadrons that scouted ahead of the Hrum army. Her rough, sturdy britches and sheepskin vest could have been worn by any peasant boy, but her straight, black hair marked her as the descendant of a long line of deghans—and the one thing all the rumors agreed on was that the Hrum were taking the deghans' families prisoner. She'd considered cutting it, but unless she shaved herself bald, her hair would still betray her. Though it wasn't a certain indication of rank. Soraya had seen girls with hair as straight and black as hers wearing peasants' gaudy skirts, and her own father had had curly, peasant-brown hair.

The messenger's account of her father's death flashed through her mind. "Shot full of arrows like a . . . It was quick, girl. Um, Lady."

Soraya thrust the memory away. She was a hunter herself. She had seen the death arrows brought. *Forget it. Forget it.* Merdas came first now.

Her father's death and the defeat of the Farsalan army, which he had commanded, left all Farsala open to the Hrum. But they didn't seem to have destroyed much so far. Even when she reached the Great Trade Road, where the Hrum troops were moving, most of the small villages she passed through, and the towns she skirted, were completely intact. Only occasionally did she scent the bitter stench of recent fire, or see townsfolk

4

removing the blackened remains of some building whose owners, for whatever reason, had resisted the Hrum.

Of course, rumors abounded. Soraya sometimes stopped in the smaller villages, where she would purchase dinner from an innkeeper who had no idea that the meal served for her breakfast. There she learned what she could about the road ahead. She never had to ask for the whereabouts or doings of the Hrum—it was the primary topic of conversation: The main army was here, it was there. Setesafon had fallen. Setesafon had defeated the Hrum, and the leaderless remnants of the Hrum army were looting the countryside. The Hrum were besieging the capital city and negotiating with the gahn to leave Farsala forever, in exchange for all the gahn's treasure, for a yearly tribute of taxes, for half the populace to be carried off as slaves. . . .

Soraya cared little for the rumors, except for making certain there were no troops on the road in front of her. With her father dead, and all the deghans perished, Farsala would fall to the Hrum as surely as day fell to the night. The only question was whether she could reach her home and get

Sudaba and Merdas away before the Hrum found them. Or had her mother and brother fled already? Or been taken as slaves, or . . . No, they couldn't be dead. If they were dead, Soraya would have nothing left at all.

She had little enough, in truth. Golnar had left a pack, filled with food, in the house where Soraya had been hidden over the winter from her father's political enemies.

If her father had sacrificed her, as the priests demanded, might he have won the battle and survived? Soraya's heart contracted, and she pushed the thought away. She didn't really believe in propitiating the war djinn. No one did, not anymore. Especially not the political enemies who had cynically demanded her sacrifice, hoping to catch her father defying the gahn's order, hoping to take his command. But her father had outwitted them.

Soraya had gone into hiding, more or less willingly, for her father's sake, and to help him save Farsala from the advancing Hrum. But she would gladly hand Farsala to the Hrum on a platter, or the priests her head, if it would bring him back.

Tears blurred her view of the road, and Soraya wiped her eyes impatiently. She had wept too often in the last few weeks. But after she had wept out her first grief, she had resolved to do what her father would have wanted. *A deghass' first duty is the continuation of the house.* Soraya had to find Merdas and save him. He was only three years old now—two, when she'd seen him last—worth nothing as a slave. But surely even the Hrum wouldn't kill a child. Not out of hand, for no reason. Surely.

In the bottom of the pack Golnar had left for her, Soraya had found a small purse of smaller coins. It was generous of Golnar, the farmwife who had been Soraya's servant in the hidden croft where she'd spent the winter, to have left her any money. Soraya wondered if she'd had to argue with her husband about it. He was a practical man, with two sons to feed—it must have galled him to leave anything useful behind. On the other hand, Soraya's father had paid Golnar and her family to take care of Soraya. Oh, well. They'd left what they could.

It hadn't been enough to buy a horse, so Soraya had hiked to the nearest miners' camp and stolen one. She could repay them someday, she supposed. And she hadn't stolen one of their best horses, though that was more because she feared a good horse would make her conspicuous on the road than out of consideration for the miners. Deep in the mountains, the miners posted no guards. Soraya had opened the door to the shed that protected the animals from jackal packs, and selected a plain, sturdy-looking mare. She had saddled her and led her out without the slightest problem, though her palms had been slick with sweat.

It was only when the sun rose, and Soraya had tried to kick the mare into a canter, that she'd discovered the stupid beast wouldn't run if a lion were on her heels. But Soraya was almost there now anyway.

The lowering sun cast long shadows over the road. The ruts left by the winter's rains were still deep, but the mud only lingered in the lowest hollows. And even if the horse should pull a tendon, or be dragged bodily into the pit by Eblis, the djinn of sloth, it wouldn't matter, for the hills and fields along this stretch of road were as familiar as the lines of Soroya's own palm. She was less than an hour's ride from her father's manor, and after so many days of wishing the mare would hurry, it was sheer cowardice to suddenly wish that her steed would walk more slowly. *Merdas will be all right. He has to be.*

It had taken her two weeks to get home. Two weeks of hiding, of sleeping through the days in the brush, far away from the road. Of lying to everyone she spoke with, and feeling her heart beat more quickly when a man's gaze lingered on her face for more than a moment.

This was the hill that she and her father had so often raced their horses to when she was a child. But her father wouldn't have ridden around it with his eyes glued to the road to avoid the first sight of the house. He would have expected his leopard cub to have enough courage to look. Soraya lifted her gaze, and gasped.

Burned. The good stone walls still stood, but even from this distance she could see black streaks rising above the windows, telling of fire within. Soraya cried out and drummed her heels against the mare's sides. The mare jumped, and trotted for several paces before returning to her determined amble.

"Djinn take you!" Soraya flung herself from the saddle and began to run.

The road was rougher than she'd thought, but it was the growing stitch in her side that finally slowed her. Running was absurd anyway—no fires burned here now. Whatever had happened was long over. The Hrum had come, and gone. All that remained was to learn what they had done.

Soraya walked the rest of the way to the house, plodding as deliberately as the accursed mare, who followed her. She had to learn where Merdas and her mother, Sudaba, had gone. Or been taken. At least Sudaba loved Merdas, as she had never loved her daughter. She would keep him safe. Perhaps she had already fled with him to . . . to where? With the Hrum inside Farsala's borders, no place was safe. No place except with the Suud. But to get her brother to the Suud, Soraya had to find him.

She saw few signs of battle on the tough, outer walls as she approached the house. The ornamental bushes that some long-ago deghass had planted had been trampled, but their flowers still scented the air, warring with the stench of scorched timber. The outer gates that closed the long passage to the courtyard had been wrenched from their hinges and cast aside. A waste of good timber.

10

The stone-flagged passage was dark in the fading light, but it was empty and undamaged except for . . . What were those stains around the ceiling grates? Surely no one had . . .

Soraya walked forward and stood below the iron grid. It was too high for a girl who was small for her fifteen years to reach, so she knelt and felt the floor beneath the grating. Her fingertips came away rough with grit, and slippery with grease. Someone had poured hot grease through the grate as the Hrum soldiers passed below. That was what it had been designed for, in that long-ago time when the house was built, but . . . They must have been possessed! Surely they knew they couldn't defeat the Hrum, and angering them was the madness of the djinn of rage himself.

Still, Soraya found the corners of her mouth turning up. The House of the Leopard had fought to the last. Good for them! She knew that her father would have thought such helpless defiance a fool's gesture, but it lifted Soraya's heart.

She rose to her feet and walked on down the passage. The inner gates were still there, though their latch was broken, and one side sagged crookedly on a single hinge.

Beyond the gates Soraya could see the court-yard. The carved and polished railings of the second-story gallery were dark with soot and had been smashed in places, but Soraya could see that the rooms behind them were intact. Not all had burned, then. The central fountain seemed to be whole, though no sound of splashing water disturbed the stillness. That fountain had been the heart of the house. Its silence spoke of death, more clearly than even the shredded garden around it. Still, Soraya closed her eyes and listened.

No sound of servants cleaning and repairing damage. No scent of cooking. No footfalls. No childish voice, raised in laughter or indignation. They might have been hiding, but some other sense told Soraya clearly that Sudaba and Merdas weren't here. The house was empty, and had been for some days. Did her certainty come from the magic the Suud tribesmen had taught her? Perhaps, but what good were those shreds of domestic magic in the face of something like this?

Sudaba and Merdas were gone—but gone wasn't the same as dead. She needed more information.

Soraya reached out and laid her hand on the

gate, but it was only a gesture of farewell. There was nothing for her here but memories, and she was a deghass. A deghass didn't let grief stop her.

Soraya turned, and walked out of the passage and into the gathering dark without looking back. The village that served the manor was only a little farther down the river road. At least some of her father's servants would have survived. She could get help, and information, from them.

THE MOON HADN'T YET RISEN, so she was forced to grope through the grass around the walls for a piece of broken shutter. Even with flint and steel, she couldn't make it burn without the magic the Suud had taught her. The discipline of meditation calmed her, and perhaps the memory of those months when she'd deserted the mountain croft to go live with the Suud was helping her as well. At first Soraya had regarded the tribespeople as being lower than Farsalan peasants, but once she came to know them . . .

Soraya shrugged off the memory. Missing the Suud was a human thing, alien to the spirit she hoped to reach. Forcing out all thoughts of the present, she sought the bright, still place inside her where Maok had taught her to find magic. Reaching her own shilshadu had become easier with practice, and Soraya had always loved touching the shilshadu of fire. Even the tiny spark struck from her flint was alive with that joyous, hungry dance. Still, it was an effort to yield her spirit to that of the flame, to convince it that this cold wood provided it with the air and fuel it needed. Eventually the wood burned well, and Soraya let the link fade, let herself become only human again.

She felt more hopeful than she had before. Perhaps it was because melding her spirit with the spirit of fire delighted her, but Soraya suspected that the core of warmth in her heart had more to do with old friendship than new magic.

Her improvised torch only illuminated the road a few yards in front of her, and it seemed to take her hours to reach the scattering of houses around the central square. Darkness concealed the garish paint that marked the doors and shutters of peasant homes, but Soraya smelled only the musty scent of the dried dung peasants used for fuel—no burned wood. The village had been spared. Had surrendered?

Soraya had ridden down this street hundreds

of times, and she had no idea which house belonged to the old headman—she'd never had reason to care which peasant lived in what hovel. But everyone had to know what had happened at the manor. The second house on her left showed the dim glow of candlelight around the closed shutters and under the door.

Soraya opened the door and stepped into the dimly lit room. It held a middle-aged man and woman, clad in the brightly embroidered garments of peasants, a table, benches, and two chairs by the fireplace. It was so similar to the main room in the farmhouse where she'd spent much of the winter that a pang of something almost like homesickness touched Soraya's heart. Which was absurd, for she'd hated the primitive croft. And if she'd felt safe there, well, this man and woman, rising openmouthed from the chairs by the fire, weren't Golnar and her husband.

"Lady Soraya!" the man gasped. "Where did you—I mean, forgive me, Lady, but we'd heard you were dead." His head bent in the short bow most peasants used in casual situations. "Enter, Lady, and be welcome."

"She's already in," the woman muttered. She

had risen when her husband did, but she didn't
bow. Her closed face was vaguely familiar. One of
Sudaba's maids? Yes, that was it, though if Soraya
had ever heard her name, she couldn't recall it.

"Hush, Marlis," her husband murmured.

"Well, her father was always knocking," said
the woman rebelliously.

Her father had knocked before entering peasant homes, Soraya remembered. Her mother had
had no patience with it.

"I require information and assistance," Soraya
told them, taking the chair the man had vacated. It
felt good to sit in a chair again. "Where are . . .
What happened at the manor house?" Cowardice
was despicable in a deghass, but she couldn't quite
bring herself to ask straight out.

The man's creased face softened. "Your
moth—The lady Sudaba and the little lord both
live, Lady," the man told her. "When I last saw
them, they weren't even hurt, though the lad was
properly scared."

Relief struck like a hammer blow. Soraya had
refused to admit they might be dead, but now the
painful knot below her heart relaxed, and the
hearth fire blurred and brightened.

16

"Here now," said the man kindly. "Let's be getting you a cup of tea."

Marlis moved without prodding, to fill a kettle and put it on the fire, but her back was stiff with resentment.

Soraya cared nothing for her—all her attention was focused on the man, and she blinked back tears and faced him squarely. "Where are they?"

"Ah . . . well, I don't exactly . . ."

Soraya had come to detest the sight of pity in men's eyes.

"The Hrum took them," she finished calmly.

She had known it ever since she'd seen the stains around the grating. Only Sudaba would have ordered that, and the Hrum only captured those who fought them. So if they weren't dead, Soraya knew what had become of them. And curse her mother for the daughter of Kanarang! Only one possessed by the djinn of destruction would have committed such folly.

The man was talking about the battle at the manor. He'd been too old to take part himself, but many of the village's younger men had been there.

Marlis slapped a mug onto the hearthstone in front of Soraya, so abruptly that hot tea splashed over the side. Soraya opened her mouth to demand a clean mug and less insolence, and stopped at the blaze of anger and satisfaction in the woman's eyes.

If I make them too angry, they don't have to tell me anything.

A chill passed down Soraya's spine. She was at the mercy of these peasants. Oh, they wouldn't dare harm her, but if they refused to aid her, to tell her where Sudaba and Merdas had been taken, there was nothing Soraya could do about it. And even more chilling, there was nothing to stop them from telling the Hrum where she had gone.

The man, sensing her tension, had fallen silent.

"I thank you," said Soraya. Even to her, the words sounded stiff and unnatural. Marlis snorted. Soraya scowled, but she had to go on. "I appreciate your telling me this. Your hospitality." As if hospitality wasn't the clear duty of any house—especially to a deghass! Peasant manners. Her father had tried to teach Soraya about them. Why hadn't she paid more attention?

"That's all right, Lady," the man said gently. "We're glad to be helping you."

"For your father's sake," Marlis added.

Clearly not for hers. But why did this woman dislike her so? Soraya didn't remember being particularly unkind to her mother's maids.

"Ah, he was a fine master, the high commander," said the old man. "We were sore grieved to hear of his death, and that's Azura's truth. He must have hurt the Hrum bad before he . . . um . . ."

"Died," said Soraya calmly. She'd had weeks to face it, but even though her voice was calm, she felt the annoying tears slide down her face again. She wiped them away and picked up the tea. It was scorching hot, and bitterly strong. It helped.

"Well, yes," said the man awkwardly. "But the Hrum have taken Desafon, so they say, and are moving right on to the gahn's city. And they're not bothering much with anything along the way, so the commander must have been angering them plenty, for them to send a squadron this far off the Trade Road just to loot one manor and—"

"And take two slaves." Soraya sipped the tea again. *Alive*, she reminded herself. *That's the important thing.*

"Oh, they took more than two. All the lads they captured, who had helped with the defense, were hauled off with 'em." For the first time, anger stirred in the old man's voice.

Soraya cared nothing for peasant slaves, but awareness of his helpless fury, his caring, pulsed through her. She had been more aware of the people she met on the road, but she'd put that down to fear—and despite the woman's hostility, she didn't fear these people. Was this extra awareness of how they reacted some effect of the magic the Suud had taught her? Or was it just that in learning to see the Suud as people, she had learned to see people in a way she hadn't before?

Perhaps Marlis had reason to dislike her. Either way, it didn't matter.

"Where did the Hrum take them?" Soraya asked quietly. "Do you know?"

"Main army camp," said the man promptly. "Least, that's what we heard. All the slaves, all the loot, goes to the main camp, to be writ down before they ship them off."

"Well, that shouldn't be too hard to find." Soraya finished her tea and set the mug on the hearth. She stood, turning toward the door. The moon would rise shortly, and the road was sufficiently familiar that she could manage until it did.

"Here, you're not going now," the man protested. "It's being night!"

"I traveled nights all down the Trade Road," Soraya told him. "I only came on in the light today because . . . because I couldn't sleep." So near to home, hope and fear had flooded through her nerves. But Sudaba and Merdas were alive. As long as they lived, she could find a way to free them.

"But—"

"I'll be all right," Soraya interrupted. "My horse will have scented the village herd. She'll be grazing beside their pen. She's slow, but sound. She'll get me there. After that . . ."

She didn't know what she'd do after that.

"Lady." It was Marlis who spoke, and for the first time, her voice held something besides resentment. "You're never going to the Hrum's camp. There's an army there. They'll take you too, or kill you, or—"

"I'll have to find a way to avoid that," said Soraya, wry humor prickling through her weariness. "But if the Hrum camp is where my mother and brother are, then that's where I'm going."

The woman's eyes met hers, lighter brown

21

than most peasants—they looked faded. "You're not afraid?"

Soraya's head lifted proudly. "I'm a deghass." A deghass didn't let fear stop her.

"Well, that's as may be," said the man. "But even a deghass has to sleep. You'll spend the night in our bed, if you'd be willing to sleep so humble. It's not what you're used to, but it's clean, and as good a mattress as any the village can offer."

Sleep. In a bed, in a warm room, instead of in the brush beside some stream. It was infinitely tempting, but . . .

"I should go on. I could be a third of the way to the Trade Road by morning."

"Yes, and sleep the day away, and by dusk you'll be in exactly the same place you'd be in if you spent the night here and traveled in the day! Your father commanded an army, Lady. Let me ask you just one question: What would he be saying to you right now?"

The words sounded in her mind as clearly as if her father had spoken them. "That to march day and night to a battle, and arrive too tired to fight, is so stupid that only a deghan would do it."

The weak, foolish tears were flowing down

her cheeks again, but thinking of her father wasn't quite as painful this time. And as always, he was right.

"I thank you for your hospitality," said Soraya. "Truly." She smiled at them, and to her astonishment, Marlis smiled back.

CHAPTER TWO

JIAAN

WHEN THE SENTRIES dispatched a messenger to tell Jiaan that Markhan and Kaluud were on the road to the croft, his first impulse was to flee. But a commander couldn't run from his own subordinates, so Jiaan folded his good arm over the arm his mending collarbone still kept in a sling, and stepped out in front of the farmhouse to wait for them. In the open, as a commander of an army—such as it was—should.

Less than three hundred men had escaped the Hrum on that disastrous day—over a month ago now. And of those who'd escaped, over a hundred had chosen to return to their homes and try to keep the Hrum from learning that they'd ever been soldiers. For the Hrum captured all who fought against them, and sent them off to their own lands as slaves. All who fought them and survived.

Jiaan pushed down the wave of grief. He refused to let Markhan and Kaluud see him weep.

But over a hundred and fifty men, the shattered remains of Farsala's army, had followed Jiaan to the hidden croft. Only one of them was a deghan—the rest were just the archers and infantry who had supported the deghans' mounted charge. And crazy to the last man, to have followed him to this place in the preposterous hope that they could hold some part of Farsala till the Hrum's year was over. And Jiaan himself the craziest of them all. He blushed to think what his father would have said.

It had surprised him, arriving at the croft with his battered, exhausted men, to find that the lady Soraya and the family who had cared for her were gone. The only reason Jiaan had known about this place was because his father had selected him to see the lady into hiding last fall. The lady—she was his half sister, the only blood kin he had left.

25

Not that she had ever seen him as anything but a servant. Jiaan had spent his whole life wishing that his father would call him "son." He knew that the lady Soraya would never even think of calling him "brother."

But the hoofbeats were approaching now—at a gallop, despite the muddy, rocky road. The last of the snow had finally melted, even in the shadow of the trees, but the road was still slick and treacherous.

The sound brought Fasal out of the barn they had converted into a carpenter's shop, to build shelter for all his troops and for the others they hoped might come to join them.

Sawdust frosted the straight, black hair of the only deghan who had survived the battle to follow Jiaan into hiding, and Jiaan nodded grudging approval. Fasal had worked as hard as any of them, gathering supplies on the way to the croft, cutting timber, inventorying and repairing what few weapons they had. Of course, he'd shirked the menial tasks of cooking and digging latrines, but Jiaan knew that was too much to expect. In all fairness, Fasal had worked hard. It was only in every other way he'd been an unmitigated annoyance.

"Who comes?" Fasal demanded. He reached for the hilt of the sword he persisted in wearing, even though it was a hazard to him and all around him when felling trees. It wasn't a tone anyone should use to their commander, but since the question wasn't unreasonable Jiaan decided to overlook it.

"Markhan and Kaluud." Jiaan kept his voice neutral, and only winced inwardly at the way Fasal's face brightened.

"Well, about time! It shouldn't have taken them this long to get here, even from Dugaz."

Jiaan's father had sent them away with a message for the governor of Dugaz, Farsala's violent, fever-ridden port, shortly before the battle. Jiaan wasn't certain if his father had done it to get them out of his own way, or to keep them from making trouble—more trouble—for Jiaan. His father had granted Jiaan far greater rank than was permitted by his birth. All the true-born deghans had disliked him for it, but Markhan and Kaluud had been two of the worst. He had prayed they wouldn't be able to find this place. In fact . . .

"How in Azura's name did they know where we are?" Annoyance gave way to alarm. If the army's presence at this hidden croft became known, the Hrum might be able to find them too.

"Don't sound so panicked," said Fasal. "I sent one of my grooms for them. I knew they couldn't get back to us otherwise. Hiding like rabbits, the way we are."

Jiaan opened his mouth to answer in kind, but Markhan and Kaluud were clattering into the yard, pulling their muddy, blowing horses to a halt.

"Fasal! What in Azura's name is happening? Your man wouldn't tell us anything except that you had survived, and he was to guide us to the army."

It was Markhan who spoke as they slid from their saddles, but Kaluud was the first to reach Fasal. They seized each other's wrists in a warrior's greeting, but it wasn't enough, and they ended in a three-way embrace, thumping one another's backs. Three heads of glossy, black hair shone in the sun. Jiaan, standing with his arms folded, thought of his own peasant-brown curls and regarded them with distinctly mixed emotions.

After only a moment they pulled apart, though

it seemed to Jiaan that Fasal let the others go reluctantly.

"So what happened?" Kaluud asked.

Fasal took a deep, steadying breath. "You know the army was defeated?"

"Of course. The whole countryside knows that, and the Hrum are advancing. But how could we be defeated? We had assembled the mightiest army in Farsala's history!"

For a moment Kaluud looked his age—eighteen, the same as Jiaan and Markhan. Fasal was actually a year younger, but his face was old with bitterness as he replied.

"They had lances. Very long, over five yards. We didn't know—who could have imagined men wielding something like that? They brought them up as we charged, and killed the horses."

He had to stop and swallow, and Jiaan grew cold remembering the sound of the chargers' screams. At least Rakesh was healing well. The high commander must have somehow pulled his steed aside in those last, impossible seconds, for Rakesh had suffered only a deep gash in his shoulder.

"With the horses dead," Fasal went on, "we had no choice but to fight them on foot." He took another breath, but found no further words, and ended with a silent gesture of despair.

In truth, no more needed to be said. The Farsalan deghans were—had been—cavalry, all their fighting methods dependent on their agile, well-trained horses. And the Hrum were the best infantry in the world. The deghans hadn't stood a chance.

Kaluud and Markhan exchanged dismayed glances.

"I see," said Markhan quietly.

Fasal's groom rode into the yard, breaking the moment of silence. Jiaan heard the door open behind him as men began to emerge from the farmhouse that now doubled as the camp's kitchen and the headquarters of Farsala's so-called army.

No, it is an army, Jiaan told himself. *No matter how small and battered. My army.* He didn't know whether to laugh or weep.

He hadn't wanted to command, the night after the battle, as survivors slowly found their way to the fire he had kindled. But Fasal had ordered the handful of injured, exhausted men to attack the Hrum camp, to try to rescue the prisoners. Ridden with guilt for having survived when their friends and comrades had fallen, and trained from childhood to obey their deghan leaders, the men would have tried—if Jiaan hadn't intervened. He had taken command in his father's name, because he knew it was what his father would have wanted. He just wished he knew what to do with it.

Men were coming from the barn too, and the woods where the barracks were being built, as word of the new arrivals spread.

Fasal stiffened his spine, bracing himself for bad news, and turned to Kaluud. "You said the Hrum were advancing?"

"They took Desafon shortly after the battle," said Kaluud. "You've probably heard that?"

Fasal nodded, and but now Kaluud hesitated. "Well, they marched straight to Setesafon. The city guard fought. They fought like lions, the country folk said, but Setesafon is too open. The palace was even worse. You remember. All those gardens. The Hrum . . ."

"They took Setesafon two days before we reached it," Markhan finished harshly. "The gahn is dead, executed in sight of the whole city." A murmur of dismay rippled through the listening crowd, but

Jiaan had expected it. "His wife and his children, the young heir, are in the Hrum's slave pens now— if they haven't been shipped out already. That's why we made such haste to join you. The first thing we must do is free the heir. But your groom found us at Setesafon and it took us over a week to get here, so I hope the army isn't too far off."

He looked around the yard, now filled with somber, listening men. "Is it much farther? Your man said you were with them."

"Markhan." Fasal's voice was rough. "This is the army. All that's left of it."

"What!" Markhan looked at the crowd again—fewer men than a small village could boast. "But that's . . . There were almost seven hundred deghans in the army! Where are they?"

There had been almost seven thousand other men in that army, Jiaan remembered dryly.

"Dead," said Fasal. "Dead or enslaved. The commander is dead. Our fathers are dead. We're all that's left."

"But . . ." Markhan shook his head, as if trying to shake off the truth. Kaluud was gripping his stomach as if it hurt him, his golden brown skin pale. Jiaan felt a flash of pure pity.

"But . . . Who's in command then?" Markhan asked.

"That would be me," said Jiaan. For a wonder, his voice didn't squeak.

"*What*? Don't be ridiculous. By what possible authority would you command?"

So much for pity. "By my authority as High Commander Merahb's son," said Jiaan. He had spoken those words the first time right after the battle, and a few times since, but it still felt like taking off his clothes in the middle of the town square on market day.

"His peasant-born bastard," said Markhan. "The commander may have granted you some rank, but only a true-born son inherits. And high commander isn't an inherited title at all."

"That's true. But since the gahn is dead and can't appoint a new commander, you'll have to make do with me. Peasant-born bastard or not."

The men who'd gathered around them were peasant-born bastards themselves, or the descendants of such. Only those with some deghan blood were trained to fight, even if they only served as support troops. Peasant-born support troops didn't talk back to deghans, no matter how

idiotic their attitudes, but Jiaan could feel the subtle shift of the crowd as those standing nearby
moved to stand behind him, and even those who
didn't move somehow made their allegiance clear.

"But . . ." Kaluud looked at Fasal, who nodded
resentful confirmation.

"There's no one else left."

"There's us," Kaluud protested. "We're
deghans, at least."

The silence was so deep Jiaan could hear the
soft wind soughing in the pine branches.

Markhan gripped Kaluud's arm. He might be
a fool, but he wasn't that stupid. "Very well,
Commander. We've reported to you that the gahn is
slain and his heir taken. How do you plan to go
about freeing him?"

Jiaan tried not to wince. He hated moments
like this. "I don't. In Azura's name, think! What
good would a four-year-old gahn do anyone now?
The best way to get him back, to get back all who
survive, is to withstand the Hrum for a year. Just
like my fath—the commander planned. Or had
you forgotten about that?"

Judging by their expressions they had forgotten,
and Jiaan could hardly blame them. The Hrum's

policy of giving their own commanders one year from the first battle to complete their conquest—and of making a peaceful alliance if they failed—seemed absurd to Jiaan too. But his father had confirmed and reconfirmed it.

If the Hrum hadn't taken all major cities, and pacified most of the countryside as well, at the end of a year, the Hrum would either offer Farsala a peaceful and profitable alliance, or they would leave them alone. And when the Hrum began negotiations, the first thing they would offer was the return of all the Farsalan slaves.

But the Hrum preferred to add the wealth and manpower of other nations directly into their army and tax base. Only if the price of conquest proved too high, would they offer alliance and peace. The Hrum had attacked thirty-one countries in the last two centuries, and there were only three allied states. So clearly, resisting for a year was harder than it sounded—Farsala had ten and a half months to go.

Even the commander, with all the information he had gathered, all his experience, had underestimated the Hrum. Maybe Markhan and Kaluud were right—there had to be someone more qualified than an eighteen-year-old, half-blood bastard to take command. But he wasn't here now, and Jiaan was. He knew what his father would have said about that.

"The Hrum have smashed our army," said Markhan slowly. "They've taken Desafon. They've taken Setesafon, destroyed the guard, and killed the gahn. Just how do you propose to stop them? *Commander*."

"At Mazad," said Jiaan deliberately, and saw all three of them look suddenly, grudgingly thoughtful.

"But Mazad's a tradesman's city," Kaluud protested. "If Setesafon's guard couldn't hold out—"

"Mazad has walls," said Jiaan. "Walls, and supplies, and deep wells, and its citizens are prepared for sieges."

He watched their faces brighten further, and felt something approaching despair. His father had led the deghans like this, offering hope and pride as the carrot—since he wasn't allowed, he'd once commented dryly, to hit them with a stick.

But how could they fail to realize that the Hrum must have conquered hundreds of walled cities? Jiaan was certainly aware of it.

"Mazad is also a city of weapon-smiths," Jiaan went on. "So hopefully they can figure out how to make swords that won't break like dry wood against the Hrum's. I don't know if you heard that, about the battle, but the rumors are true. The Hrum's steel is stronger than ours."

Jiaan's own sword had shattered on a Hrum blade, leaving him at his opponent's mercy. And perhaps he'd shown mercy, for he'd only knocked Jiaan out with his shield. The line of battle had passed over Jiaan when the Hrum advanced, leaving him alive. There were still times when he regretted that, but they were growing farther apart.

"Is that how they beat us?" Kaluud demanded suddenly. "When we heard about the battle, I couldn't believe . . ."

Jiaan sighed. "Not really. They beat us when they broke our charge with their lances. But the swords were the reason they beat us so badly. That so many died."

He knew it was true. The traitor who had lured Jiaan, all unknowing, into revealing the Farsalan battle plan, really had very little to do with their defeat. But he would still die, as soon as

Jiaan found him. That wouldn't happen today, though. Probably not till the land was free of the Hrum. Then there would be time for vengeance. But to free Farsala from the Hrum . . .

"It all hangs on Mazad," Jiaan continued. "We have to concentrate on supporting them. I haven't been to the city myself yet, but I've sent messages to the governor explaining the situation, and he's confident he can hold out till next spring. Our job will be to harass the Hrum besiegers, and for that we'll need more men and better weapons, so—"

"So you intend to sulk in hiding while the heir—our gahn!—is dragged off into slavery, in the hope that one day the Hrum will condescend to *give* him back?" Kaluud asked contemptuously.

Fasal had described Jiaan's plan in exactly the same tone, if not quite the same words. Could none of them see beyond their honor to the facts? Jiaan sighed. "We don't have the men, or the horses, or the—"

"Or the courage," said Kaluud. "Which is why deghans fight and peasants farm, and putting half bloods in positions they can't handle always fails. If the commander had seen that, if he'd had a *deghan* at his back, he might be alive today!"

That thought had occurred to Jiaan himself, in the deeps of the night. If only his father had appointed a deghan, a real fighter, to carry his banner, instead of a jumped-up archer who fell and broke his collarbone when his horse shied at the Hrum's lances. If Jiaan had cared less about earning the others' respect, if he'd had the sense to refuse the honor when his father offered it, would the commander still be alive?

In the morning light, he knew it wasn't true. But hearing it spoken aloud struck him dumb, and he felt his face grow cold, which probably meant it was pale. A fine picture of a commander that presented.

Jiaan opened his mouth to reply, with no idea what he was going to say, but Fasal beat him to it.

"No," he said firmly. "I didn't see him fight—I was in another part of the line—but he was taken out by a Hrum soldier when his sword broke, just like half the deghans who died that day. And the commander survived till the very end. When it was clear that Farsala had lost, he challenged the Hrum to send a champion for single combat. Instead, they sent archers and murdered him. Right there in the circle, Razm take them. There was nothing Jiaan could have done except die, or be captured with the rest of them. Nothing anyone could have done."

He looked up to meet Jiaan's astonished gaze, determination to be fair written all over his open face. How like a deghan to be fair, just as you were set to bid the djinn to take the lot of them.

"It's still cowardice—peasant cowardice—for us to cower here like jackals while the lions plunder at will," Kaluud objected.

At least he was right about one thing—the Hrum were more like lions than the spawn of Razm, the djinn of cowardice, for which Fasal so often cursed them. Jiaan was suddenly tired of all of them. And he was done with trying to be liked.

"It was deghan courage that got us into this mess in the first place," he said coldly. "We need a secure base, a larger force, and a realistic objective before we do anything. You can help, or you can leave. Those are your only choices."

He felt like an idiot, spouting orders that way. But he also felt the support of the men around him—their willingness to uphold his judgment.

Though Azura only knew what he'd do if the idiots chose to leave. Bad enough that the traitor knew where this place was—but as long as no one knew the army was here, it shouldn't matter. Right now the Hrum had no way of knowing the Farsalan army still existed, but if word got out . . . No, they were deghans. There was no doubt how they would choose.

Kaluud's face was dark with anger. Markhan looked at Jiaan intently, but whatever he was looking for, he didn't seem to find it. Jiaan waited.

"Stay," Markhan spat. Kaluud nodded.

Fasal's sigh of relief was audible even where Jiaan stood. "I'll show you where to put your horses."

Both Markhan and Kaluud were glaring at Jiaan over their shoulders as they followed Fasal toward the horse pens, but they went.

He started to sag with relief, then caught himself and straightened his shoulders. At least he could try to look like a commander.

His father had argued with the deghans under his command—it had never left him clammy-palmed, his heart pounding with sick tension. His father had cursed them up one side and down the other, showed them a carrot or two, and they'd followed him like geese flying after their leader. His

41

father could handle them. His father had been one of them.

Jiaan wasn't one of them, and he wasn't his father either. But he was the best commander Farsala had left, so he was stuck with the job. *Djinn take the lot of them.*

CHAPTER THREE

KAVI

KAVI REACHED Setesafon just before the Hrum's new curfew took effect. It was dusk but he had till full dark to get off the street—and if he could show the tattoo on his shoulder, no curfew sentry would be hauling him in. But the house he sought was only a laundry in the suburbs, not some grand manor in the heart of the city. He could get there before dark.

It was the closest thing to a home he had, and part of him dreaded to arrive. If anything had happened to Nadi's family, he'd never be able to forgive himself. He was having a hard enough time with forgiveness, anyway.

But there was little sign of fighting around the

small shops and homes he passed. Nothing burned. No blood stains in the gutters. Most of the blood had been shed over a month ago, in a faraway field, and even if it hadn't been his folks doing the bleeding, it still haunted Kavi's dreams. The thought of the survivors, taken off to be slaves in foreign lands, bothered him even in the daylight. But the Hrum didn't treat their slaves badly, not like the Kadeshi. There was time to redeem himself—to make things right.

And the Hrum hadn't lied about being merciful where there was no resistance. A few broken shutters, already replaced, were the worst damage he'd seen. That, and the wariness in the shopkeepers' eyes as they pulled in their wares and closed up. Everyone still in the streets was seeking refuge now.

No, the Hrum hadn't lied when they promised that his folk would survive, mostly unscathed. Mind, they hadn't mentioned they'd be imposing curfews, but that was supposed to be a "temporary measure."

What was it his old master, Tebin, used to say? "There's nothing as permanent as a temporary tax." But it was the deghans who'd imposed those taxes, who'd broken their own laws with impunity, who had stolen a man's trade and left him to rebuild from nothing. Kavi flexed his scarred right hand as far as he could, not quite fully open, not quite fully closed. The deghans were gone, and he couldn't be too sorry for having had a hand in that.

The laundry was already dark. It usually closed a bit early—and Nadi was the kind who'd let her workers go even earlier, to be certain they made it home by curfew. The house beside the laundry, built by master stonemasons, showed no light around the well-fitted door, but a faint glow around the shutters revealed human presence within.

Kavi took a deep breath, stepped up to the door, and knocked. It was built of heavy planks, and he could hear nothing beyond it—he almost jumped when the door opened, revealing Nadi's worried face.

"Who in the . . . Kavi!"

"Is everything all right?" they both asked simultaneously, and Nadi snorted.

"Get in before the patrol comes by. Don't you know about the curfew? Or are you being reckless enough not to care? Where's Duckie?"

She stood aside to admit him—a plain, middle-aged woman, worn by work and care. She was the linchpin of the small family that Kavi had unofficially adopted. She was his partner in their scheme to sell gold-covered bronze for the price of solid goods. She was the closest thing to a mother that he had.

"I left Duckie in one of the farms outside the city, along with my wares, for I'm not here to sell or buy," Kavi assured her. "Are you all right, and the children? Sim and Hama?"

"We're all fine, lad, and the young ones too. Though we were worried about you, with those Hrum roaming the—"

"Kavi!" It was a shrill, childish shriek, but there was nothing childish about the stout staff Sim cast aside as he hurtled forward to embrace his friend.

"Quiet, imp, you'll wake the little ones." Hama paused to sheathe the knife she held before she followed her brother into Kavi's arms. If anything, she was thinner and more gangly-awkward than she'd been when he'd seen her last. He was the one who had taught her how to hide a knife under her vest like that. And many of the other skills she'd used, selling the gold-bronze pieces Kavi had forged.

"Hama's working in the laundry now," Nadi told him. "They're far too lawful, these Hrum. If anyone has succeeded in bribing any of 'em, I haven't heard about it."

"Well, that's being a good thing, isn't it?" Kavi asked. "In the long run at least."

"True enough," Nadi concurred, but her eyes were worried.

And if Nadi was arming the older children before she'd open the door, there must be more tension in the city than he'd thought.

"They're teaching me to fight!" Sim exclaimed.

Kavi froze, then said casually, "I'd heard they were drafting every man, mule, and dog into the army, but aren't you a bit young?" Sim was eleven, no, twelve now, if he was remembering rightly.

"They're not drafting him yet," said Nadi, laying a hand on her son's shoulder. He was taller than when Kavi had seen him last. "Just starting to train him up for the future." She sounded calm too, but Kavi saw fear in her eyes.

Anger flared. "In Desafon they said they only

drafted men fit to fight, between the ages of eighteen and twenty-three, to serve for five years," said
Kavi. In all fairness, that was exactly what Patrius
had told Kavi before the Hrum invaded—all men
fit to fight. After the battle Strategus Garren—
Governor Garren, he was now—had announced
the draft to all the people of Desafon and given
them three months to set their lives in order before
reporting. Patrius had been astonished when Kavi
burst into his tent and accused him of lying. But
Kavi had *told* him that Farsalan peasants *never*
fought, that that was a deghan's job.

He should have realized that an army like the
Hrum's, that admitted women into its ranks, would
also consider peasants fit to fight. It was Kavi who
had assumed that the Hrum wouldn't consider
making peasants into warriors, any more than the
deghans had.

When the Hrum patrol had captured him,
Kavi's one intention had been to lie fast enough to
survive and escape. It was only after the long,
rainy night he'd spent talking to Patrius, that he
had come to believe that the Hrum would be better masters than the deghans. And they were, in
many ways. But now that the invasion was upon

them, the few ways the Hrum weren't better seemed to be mattering more.

"Is it safe for you to be here?" Nadi asked quietly. "You're nineteen. I'd think you'd want to stay as far from the Hrum as possible. In fact, I wondered . . . We were worried about you."

"Near twenty now," Kavi told her. "But you needn't fear for me." He held up his scarred hand. "This isn't holding a sword any better than it will a hammer." The relief in Nadi's face lightened his heart. There weren't many in this world who worried about him. "But what's this about Sim being drafted at twelve?"

"It's only for two marks each morning," said Sim, with a slightly guilty glance at his mother. "And for now it's just building strength and endurance. They make us lift things over and over, and run forever. But when we get strong enough, we get to start with a sword. Just a wooden one at first, but . . ."

He babbled on, as Nadi went to get a bowl of bean-and-sweet-potato porridge left over from the family's supper, and Hama made up a pallet for Kavi in front of the fire. Hama even managed to push in a few sentences. It seemed working in the laundry was boring after stealing gold and selling fake pots, but her mother was giving her more and more responsibility, and some of the little ones were becoming old enough to help. And the business was doing well, Sim chimed in. Well enough they could spare him for a few marks in the morning. The fighting had shut things down for several days, for folk were afraid to go out. But now, with the Hrum patrols about, it was actually safer on the streets than it had been under the old, corrupt city guard.

The rule of law, just as Patrius had promised. And better for his folks than the deghans' rule, just as Kavi himself had promised. He hadn't been wholly wrong.

Still, he wasn't surprised the next morning, that after Sim went to his training, Nadi sent Hama and the young ones to open the laundry without her.

Nor did Hama seem surprised, though Kavi could tell that her mother's trust pleased her. He waited as Nadi cleared up the breakfast dishes, wrapped the leftover bread in a tight-woven cloth, and finally brought the kettle over to refill their mugs.

"I hesitate to ask for more help, after all you've done for us." She put the kettle down on the hearth and sat on the bench opposite Kavi as she spoke. "No, that's a lie. I don't like it, but it doesn't look like I'm going to hesitate for a moment, does it now?"

Kavi grinned. "I'd be insulted if you hesitated, and you know it too. But what's the problem? The business is doing well, all the children are well and happy—even Hama, for all she says she's bored."

"It's Sim. No, it's not him, it's those Flame-begot Hrum and their draft. I'm not having Sim go off to die in some war. I lost my husband to the accident. I'm not sending Sim off to fight—nor Pesh when he's older. He's already tagging at Sim's heels, trying to fight him with the laundry paddles."

Kavi turned his mug in circles on the table. "They aren't always fighting. They tell me it's the Hrum army that built those stone roads they brag on so much, and other things as well. A stonemason's son should fit right in."

"But they do fight," said Nadi. Her hands, reddened with soap and rough cloth, were clenched so hard the knuckles were white. "I tell you, Kavi, I will not have it. Not my sons."

"The Hrum are pretty firm about drafting all who are able," said Kavi quietly. "Pat—Someone told me it's their way of making a new-conquered land truly a part of the empire. That serving in the army makes the men feel like citizens, in their hearts."

"I don't care what's in his heart," said Nadi. "I'm trying to keep his body safe. The Hrum are saying a lot in your presence, aren't they?" Her gaze was shrewd and curious. Kavi felt as if the needles that had tattooed his shoulder, marking him as a Hrum agent, still pricked. But Nadi hadn't seen that mark, and only Hrum officers knew what it signified, anyway.

"I went to Desafon after it fell," Kavi told her. "I wanted to see what kind of conquerors the Hrum were likely to be." To see if Patrius' word held good—which it had, for the most part. "For the most part, I think they'd be better than the deghans, if it wasn't for the draft."

He remembered the shocked dismay on the faces of Desafon's folk. The way the women had clutched their husbands, fathers their sons. Five years of service. Citizens of the Hrum empire grew up with the notion, planned their lives around it. For the Farsalan peasants, it was almost as great a shock as it had been for Kavi. Because peasants didn't fight. That was a deghan's . . .

"Deghans," Nadi hissed. "At least they'll be small loss. I used to think you were too harsh, talking about them, but they surely failed their end of the bargain."

The ancient bargain: Peasants farm; deghans fight and rule. Still . . .

"They tried," Kavi told her. "They died almost to a man in the trying. You have to give them credit for that."

Nadi's brows lifted. "You almost sound sorry for them!"

"Why not. They died. I'd think you'd be sorry for them, tenderhearted like you are."

"And I wouldn't expect you to be sorry for them, hating them like you do. Or is it 'did'?" Her voice had gone very soft.

"Do," said Kavi firmly. "But . . . I went to that battlefield afterward. Not right after. The bodies were all buried and gone. But so much blood had been spilled, you could still see the stains in the grass."

"Why did you go then?" Nadi asked reasonably.

"I wanted to get a close look at one of the Hrum swords," Kavi admitted. "I told you about that other piece of watersteel I saw?" A stolen dagger that a stranger had brought to show off to Kavi's master. It had to be stolen, for the Hrum never let their steel out of the hands of their own people. "The Hrum's watersteel broke our Farsalan blades like green sticks, but I figured there had to be a few broken Hrum swords on that field as well."

He'd groped for marks through the churned grass, and gotten sick when he realized that the dark flecks clinging to his fingers were dried blood. But after he'd emptied his stomach, he'd gone right on searching. It wasn't just curiosity, either. He wasn't quite sure of his plan yet, but if the weapon-smiths of Mazad could make a steel that could stand up to the Hrum's, it would certainly help.

He'd found a piece eventually—small, which was probably why the Hrum hadn't picked it up along with the bodies. Just a large chip, really, snapped out of a blade that had struck something hard at a bad angle. A razor-edged half circle, about a quarter the size of his palm. But in its thick edge Kavi could see the layers that created the rippling pattern on the surface, hundreds upon hundreds of layers, dark steel and light. And what was that dark steel, and how in creation had the Hrum smiths made the layers so thin, and welded them so tightly that they made a solid piece of steel with no flaw? Perhaps Tebin would know—this was master smiths' work for a certainty. But it might be some time before Kavi could show it to his old master, for there were other things he had sworn to do. And he knew the folk of Mazad well enough to be sure they would hold out for a good long time, even without outside help.

Nadi had been watching his face. "Seeing where so many died finally made you stop hating them?"

"No," said Kavi. "It was seeing their families and survivors in the slave pens did that."

Nadi's mouth tightened. "I'd heard that the Hrum kept slaves. I'd been hoping it wasn't true."

"It's not our folk they'll take," said Kavi. "Only those who fight against them. And you said yourself that the deghans were no loss."

"No loss as rulers. But no one deserves to be a slave."

"The Hrum aren't like the Kadeshi," Kavi protested. "They treat their slaves better—better than the Kadeshi treat their peasants."

"They're still not free," said Nadi.

Kavi couldn't meet her eyes. She was right. And he only hoped that the Wheel would never turn in such a way that she would learn that *he'd* had a hand in putting them there. At least, not till he'd had a chance to make it right.

"And at least the deghans weren't taking our sons off and getting them killed," Nadi finished. "Kavi, if anyone will know this, you will—is it true the Hrum can't be bribed?"

"I don't know about can't," he said slowly. "They're human, after all, and in any group of humans there'll be some as can be tempted. But it's not common with them, like it was with the guard. And their commanders won't be looking the other way. So first you'd have to find a man that could be bribed, and then you'd have to pay him enough he'd risk . . . well, losing his job for certain, and likely a flogging too. And any honest man you approached would turn you in just for trying. Bribes aren't the way, not with them."

"I feared that," Nadi admitted. "So what can

we do? I thought of having Sim fake some injury, but—"

"But you'd be needing Sim's cooperation for that."

"And I'm not going to get it." Nadi sighed. "They know how to handle boys, those Hrum. I swear I'm almost desperate enough to rig some accident and injure him in truth!"

Kavi started to laugh, but stopped at the sight of her grim expression. "Don't even think about that!" He laid a hand over hers, gripped together on the table. "We've got years to work on this, you know. Things might change."

"What things? Change how? The Hrum are here to stay, and this has been their law for who knows how long? They're not going to leave, and they're not going to change it." Nadi sighed again. "Though why I think you can do something about it, I don't know. I'm sorry, lad. I might as well have asked you to stop the dawn from coming, mightn't I?" She tried to smile, but it didn't come off very well. Kavi patted her hand.

"You asked me because I have a more devious mind than anyone you'll ever meet. And I don't think it's impossible. In fact, I'm working on an idea right now. Mind you, it's going to take a while, but we've got six years. If I can't figure out how to accomplish anything in six whole years, then call me . . . call me an honest man!"

Nadi laughed. "You are an honest man, scamp. Almost entirely."

"Oh, now it's insults, is it?" But her face had already turned sober again. "Please, Nadi, give me a year or two before you start worrying."

"You do have something in mind." Her brows drew together in a puzzled frown. "What could you possibly do, to stop the Hrum from drafting my boys?"

"Any number of things," said Kavi airily. "Passing them off as imperial heirs in disguise is the first to leap to mind, but—"

"No, you're thinking of something real." She had always been able to read him. "What is it?"

"Sorry." Kavi patted her hands again. "I'd tell you, but you'd think me mad. And we can't be having that."

Her frown deepened. "I won't have you put yourself in danger. Not even for Sim and Pesh."

Kavi snorted. "I'm not that mad! Or maybe I am, but it's a cautious, peasant madness, with a working brain behind it. I'd tell you not to worry, but I know that worry is your natural state."

This time his teasing didn't even make her smile.

"Promise me you won't go running yourself into danger." She turned her hands to clasp his, her dark, direct gaze intent on his face. "Promise."

"I promise you," said Kavi with the ease of an almost honest man, "my plan for the next year is simply to go on making my rounds through the countryside."

It was true, as far as it went, for he'd realized weeks ago that any resistance would have to come from the countryside. Farsalan towns were too big and soft a target. Except for Mazad, of course. Mazad was the key to everything.

But even Mazad couldn't hold out for a year unless it had help from the countryside, so the countryside was the key to saving Mazad. And Kavi, known in every village north and south of the Trade Road, was just the man to turn that key—turn it till it set Time's Wheel itself to turning, and dumped the Hrum down into the Flame of Destruction.

Peasants would succeed where the deghans

had failed—with just a little help from a wandering peddler, to get them all pulling in the same direction. Yes, Kavi's folk could do it. They had to. They were the only ones left.

UNTIL NOW, NO ONE *has known of the origin of the young man who appeared after the Hrum army first entered Farsala. But newly discovered sources have made many things clear. The youth, who in the time to come called himself Sorahb, was in fact a young deyhan. Perhaps he was a third or fourth son, or a poor cousin in some great lord's train. Even the documents to which I, and I alone, have gained access do not record his name.*

But this unnamed youth took part in the Battle of the Sendar Wall. He was felled by the Hrum, and injured, but not slain. So the line of battle passed over him, leaving him alive on the field where so many had died. By the time he recovered himself enough to stand, the Hrum had gone, and only the bodies of the slain surrounded him.

Clouds covered Azura's sun, and Azura's tears fell as rain, washing the noble deghans' bodies as the youth walked among them, seeking kin and friends, and finding them far too often.

After a time he stopped and stood, with the rain pelting his face. He knew he was but one man—and so young many would not have called him man at all. He had seen for himself the might of the Hrum, their weapons, their power.

But he didn't care. Raising clenched fists to Azura's sky, the youth swore a mighty oath. He would free Farsala. He would hold the land for one full year. He would humble the Hrum's mighty army, return those taken prisoner, and restore the honor of the slain. The deghans had fallen, but Farsala would stand!

As he swore, lightning split the sky asunder; the thunder crashed so powerfully that the earth trembled and the dead seemed to stir, as if in answer to some distant summons. And if, in that moment, the spirit of a long dead champion was reborn into the body of an unknown deghan youth, only Azura himself could say for certain.

CHAPTER FOUR

JIAAN

RIDING RAKESH OVER THE LAST of the low hills to the north of Mazad, Jiaan could tell from a league's distance that word of the Hrum's coming had already reached the towns-folk. The cliff that separated the high, grassy plains from the fertile lowlands had been worn down by the meanderings of the great Sistan River. Mazad lay just beyond the hills' border, on a low rise within the river's slow curve. The city's suburbs, sprawling down the slopes and clustering densely around the river, were comprised of wooden buildings, only one or two stories tall. The great stone walls of the inner city—at least five stories high—towered above them, looking as solid as the bones of the earth. Reassuringly solid. The line of people on the road that led to the great main gates in the city's south wall emerged from the suburbs' outskirts, their feet raising a thin haze of dust now that the dry months of summer were beginning. That line must be almost a quarter league long, and Jiaan knew it would seem even longer as he and his companions waited their turn to enter.

"They look like ants, fleeing into their mound to escape a flood," said Kaluud.

Jiaan had brought all three deghans to Mazad with him, in part because he didn't want to leave them behind to make mischief with the army in his absence, and in part because he entertained a sneaking hope that he could convince them to remain in the city. Surely defending Mazad against the Hrum siege was a better task for warriors than skulking in the hills with a bunch of peasant-born archers. And if withstanding a siege consisted of mostly sitting on your butt being bored, well, he doubted the deghans knew that. If only he could get the governor to accept their services before they opened their mouths and revealed themselves for the idiots they were.

"They're trying to save their businesses, and their families," he told Kaluud wearily. "What would you have them do? Stay outside to watch, while the Hrum burn their shops and take their wives and daughters into slavery?"

Though that wasn't quite fair to the Hrum, who so far seemed to have burned very little, and had taken only those who resisted them as slaves. And if they took wives and daughters they also took husbands and sons, and Jiaan had been told that the women weren't mistreated — or no more than the men were, which seemed unbelievable. Perhaps the fact that they had women among their own soldiers, which seemed even more unbelievable, accounted for it.

"So they're saving their families," said Markhan. "I suppose that means you expect us to wait on this road all day, while peasants push goats through the gates?"

"Yes, I do," said Jiaan. He was learning to be firm with Markhan. Sometimes it even worked. "Do you really think getting in to see the governor half a mark sooner is more important than these people's livelihood?"

Markhan opened his mouth, probably to say

yes, or something even more foolish, but Fasal spoke up first. "They'll need goats in the city during a siege. And probably all the other supplies these people can carry in."

There were moments when Fasal showed a glimmer of sense, though he didn't look much happier than the other two when Jiaan guided Rakesh to the end of the line.

In fact the line, which soon carried them in between the buildings, moved fairly quickly. It was only the presence of the sulking deghans that made the time seem eternal. Though judging by the comments of the crowd, Jiaan wasn't the only one who felt that way.

Among the small shops and houses, people crammed together, packing the dirt road. Everyone, even small children, carried the largest bundle they could manage, and a few men had pushcarts. Looking at the bright colors and detailed embroidery on the women's skirts and men's vests, Jiaan realized that they were rescuing their best clothes by wearing them. He hoped they had more workaday clothes in their bundles, but if they didn't, it was probably better to wear their best to rags than to give it to the Hrum to steal or destroy. The bright clothes might have lent the street a festival atmosphere, except for the grim faces, and the terse fear in women's voices as they called their children to them.

Despite Fasal's comment, Jiaan saw little livestock—just a few caged chickens, and far down the line, a huge pig. These were the people who lived and worked in the suburbs. Jiaan noticed a saw slung over one man's shoulder, and several people carrying spinning wheels. The two men just in front of him carried a bundle of long, carved planks that Jiaan guessed was a disassembled loom. Weavers, along with their workers and dependants. Had the country folk already brought their livestock in? Or were they planning on taking their chances outside the walls? Surely they knew that a besieging army would strip the countryside for leagues around. But if they all came in, was there enough food stockpiled in Mazad to feed everyone for a year? Jiaan knew there was supposed to be, but still . . .

As they neared the wall the line slowed further, but eventually they moved into an open square with a fountain in the center, and the great gates on the opposite side. Even in the open space, the folk in line kept order. Good, lawful citizens, who would keep order in a siege as well, or so Jiaan hoped. He didn't know if the square had been left open because it made the final approach to the city more impressive, or to give men in the towers that flanked the gate a clear shot at anyone bringing up a battering ram, but he approved. In fact, the houses and shops that approached the wall on either side of the square—some built right up against the stone—would have to be cleared. If they made careful use of the buildings, an army could come right up to the wall before the defenders were aware of their presence. And shouldn't the governor have done something about that before now? Why—

The crack of a bull whip distracted Jiaan's attention in time for him to see the first of four ox-drawn carts coming into the square from one of the side roads. Laden with cured hides, they moved as fast as oxen are willing to move, with almost a score of men and women walking behind them. The carters cracked their whips again, pushing them faster. Those oxen would help feed the city, but why were they heading straight for the gates when the line . . .

The tanner had no intention of respecting the order of the line. The first ox pushed its way into the crowd in front of the gates and then jerked back, bawling.

"What did you do to him?" the tanner yelled. "We got good, cured hides here. Leather the city will need. Not like your useless dyes!"

"I got a right to be carrying whatever I want," a man's voice snarled. "You go to the end of the line, like everybody else."

The crowd around Jiaan muttered angry agreement. Jiaan frowned. "Come with me," he told the others quietly, pulling Rakesh out of line to ride forward. But many men seemed to have the same idea. The orderly line was dissolving, and Jiaan watched the crowd warily as Rakesh threaded his way through.

He was too far off to see exactly how the fight began, but he heard the thud of the first blow, and saw the crowd by the gate shift like windblown grass as some surged toward the brawl and others tried to move away. The crowd in front of him solidified, and Rakesh was forced to shoulder men aside. Jiaan heard Fasal curse behind him. The smack of a quirt striking flesh was followed by a shriek. At least they weren't using their swords. But would the peasants see it that way?

A shout arose behind him. The fight was spreading, but Jiaan didn't turn back. He knew where he had to go. Rakesh, confronted with a solid knot of struggling men, was forced to stop, and several hands reached for his bridle. A burly man, his face red with anger and fear, reached for Jiaan.

He threw himself out of the saddle, leaving Rakesh's solid body between him and his attacker, and darted into the mob. Most of the men were involved with each other, and Jiaan, not interested in fighting, was usually able to weave through them. Even so, a boot heel tramped down on his toes, and someone's swinging elbow connected painfully with his eye. He slipped nimbly around a punching match, only to be knocked to the ground and trampled by two grappling, grunting men. He was breathless and disheveled when he finally reached the gate, where a line of guardsmen stood. Their tabards were the black and green of Mazad's guards, they held their swords and shields at ready—and they did nothing but watch.

"Close the gates!" Jiaan demanded.

The nearest guard looked at him and grinned. "Why should we?"

Jiaan stared at him, astonished. "There's going to be a riot out here! If you close the gates, I can stop it."

"Can you? I don't think they're going to stop till they've fought it out. And anyway, what goes on outside the wall isn't the guards' problem."

Anger replaced astonishment. "Your duty is to keep order, no matter where the trouble is."

The guard scowled, but his gaze had found the steel rings sewn onto the padded silk of Jiaan's armor. His posture began to straighten, but his voice was still sullen. "Maybe. But our *orders* are to keep the gates open until the Hrum army shows up. Besides, no one could stop that." The guardsman gestured to the escalating brawl. "Who do you think you are? Sorahb reborn?"

Jiaan took a deep breath and settled his hands on his belt, like his father used to stand, centered and firm.

"I am the son of Commander Merahb, high commander of the gahn's army," said Jiaan distinctly. And if it wasn't completely clear whether he or his father was the army's commander, that mattered far less than the guard's recognition of the pure, deghan's accent his father had insisted he learn. "And you're going to close the gates, because I told you to close the gates."

The guard looked closely at Jiaan's face—and he must have seen Commander Merahb at some time or other, because his face paled. "Drop portcullis," he shouted. "Close the gates."

The iron grating began to rattle down—slowly, Jiaan was relieved to see, for he knew they could drop it in an instant. He'd have felt triumphant, but he knew it was his father's reputation, not his own order, that had brought the gate down.

"Will you come in, sir?" the guard asked swiftly.

"No," said Jiaan, stepping back. "Once the gates are closed, I can settle this. But I want a squadron here, ready to answer to my command if I need them."

The portcullis rolled down between them as he spoke.

"Yes, sir," said the guard. "Baz, send for a squad and tell the governor that the army has sent a representative. Though we heard the army was all being killed, sir," he added, turning back to Jiaan.

"Not all of it," said Jiaan coolly. The fighting in the immediate vicinity of the gate was beginning to die, and someone shouted in protest.

"Close the inner gates now, so everyone can see," Jiaan added.

"Inner gates!" the guard called, but he was looking at the padded silk beneath the steel rings, at the stains that cold water without soap hadn't even begun to remove. "Did you fight at the battle of the Sendar Wall, sir?"

"It was leagues from the wall," said Jiaan. "But yes, I was there."

The guard straightened to attention and bowed, just before the heavy, wooden gates swung forward, forcing him to step aside. Jiaan's lips twitched bitterly. Most of the blood had come from Rakesh's shoulder when he'd pulled the lance splinter from it, but if it gave Jiaan command authority—well, he needed all the authority he could get.

He turned to face the crowd, waiting as even the distant sounds of fighting began to fade.

"Here! What's going on? Open up," a man

shouted. Blood trickled from his rapidly purpling nose.

"They won't," said Jiaan. "Not until I tell them to."

"And who the Flame are you?" another man snarled, shouldering his way through the crowd. He had lost his whip, but Jiaan recognized him as the tanner who'd started the trouble.

"I'm the son of High Commander Merahb," said Jiaan. He was beginning to feel as if his father's name was a magical incantation, to ward off any who questioned his authority. "I've come to offer the governor the assistance of the gahn's army against the Hrum. And you would be? . . ."

"Oh, nothing so fancy as that," said the tanner, folding his own arms. "Just an honest workman, trying to get goods inside the walls that'll help us withstand this siege!"

"We have a right to carry whatever we want," a man yelled.

"You got no right to jump the line!" another man chimed in.

An ominous rumble rose from the bystanders.

"Feel free to fight about it," Jiaan told them. "But the gates don't open till I say so."

"And you think you've more to offer this city, from a scattered, beaten army whose commander is dead, than four carts of good hides?" The tanner was trying to sneer, but his eyes were fixed on the stains on Jiaan's ring-studded armor.

"It doesn't matter what I think," said Jiaan. "It doesn't matter what you think. What matters is what the governor's guards, who control the gates, think. And you'll notice, the gates are closed."

And why did a common tanner know more about what had happened to the army than the guard did?

"The gates will remain closed," said Jiaan, raising his voice to carry throughout the square, "until order is restored to the line. And no carts will be allowed through the gates till all the foot traffic has passed through. People before goods."

"What? But he can carry his stinking dyes on his back." The tanner gestured to the dyer, who smirked. "Hides are heavy. Bulky. It takes a cart to haul them!"

"Too bad," said Jiaan. "People first, then goods. Carts can line up along the wall"—he pointed north—"and then on down that road. As soon as all the foot traffic's in, the carts can start.

And if you go now," he added, "you can be first in that line."

The tanner searched his face, then turned away, cursing, to line up his carts beside the wall. Jiaan wiped his palms on his thighs and tried to look calm. A few moments of shuffling followed, as people argued about precisely what place they'd held in relation to whom, but within an amazingly short time Jiaan was able to call up to the men on top of the wall the order to open the gates.

A squadron of guards stood at attention inside, trying not to pant from their rush to get there swiftly.

"We're prepared to escort you to Governor Nehar, sir," their commander said smartly. "If you'd care to enter?"

"I'd be happy to," said Jiaan. "In my turn."

He could feel their astonishment behind him as he walked back to the place, at the far side of the square, where the deghans waited for him. Kaluud had the beginnings of a black eye, and Markhan held Rakesh's reins. All of them looked happier than they had in weeks—Azura help him. So Jiaan probably wouldn't get too much grief for not taking them in immediately.

But it wasn't that, or the approving smiles and murmurs of the crowd as he walked back down the line, that made him so certain he'd done right. He knew it was what his father would have done.

"I MUST APOLOGIZE for that . . . unfortunate incident at the gate," the governor fussed. "You handled it well. Surprisingly well, considering . . . um . . . considering. But the guard should have kept the situation more tightly in hand."

The guards hadn't had the situation in hand at all, but Jiaan knew better than to point that out.

"No harm done," he murmured, reaching for the nearly priceless glass goblet that held his wine.

Governor Nehar's dinner table was set with gold and silver dishes. Aside from his fear of breaking a goblet that cost more money than Jiaan had ever seen in one place, this didn't bother him. All high-ranking deghans had such things—and used them too. It was for show, like the subtle-toned silk overrobe the governor wore, and the almost equally expensive overrobes he'd lent to his guests.

But as honey-glazed suckling pig was followed by saffron pheasant on a bed of rice with figs, which was followed by fish with wine sauce, Jiaan began to worry. Didn't Nehar *know* there was a siege approaching? Or was there really enough food stockpiled in the city to feed everyone for a year? There wasn't enough food in the land to feed them, if they ate like this. Oh, none of it would go to waste—Jiaan knew that whatever the governor and his guests failed to consume would go to the servants, their families, and even their neighbors. But if Nehar ate like this and the common folk went short, there would be resentment. How could he ask about the food supply without questioning the governor's competence?

"I'm curious, sir, about conditions in the city," said Jiaan. "Your troops seem well armed for the siege, but I know that's not everything."

"Indeed it's not," said the governor. "There are many, many things to consider. Internal security, for instance. Just a few days ago, my guard commander discovered half a dozen Hrum spies inside the city. Most had come in recently, but one—a woman, can you believe it?—had been here for almost three years! She was running some sort of importing business: spices, or silk, or something of the sort. And a wom—"

"Remarkable," Fasal broke in politely. "But if their spies are so well hidden, how can you be certain you've found them all?"

"Ah, well, that's my guard commander's doing. His job, of course, but he's a solid man, Siddas. Though he still needs direction from time to time."

Which meant that the peasant-born guard commander did all the work, but was smart enough to make it look like Nehar was in control. Not a bad juggling act—though Jiaan's father had given short shrift to anyone who tried it with him. With him, it hadn't been necessary.

"Amazing, sir," said Fasal, with a show of sincerity Jiaan could never have managed. "How did he find them out?"

"Well, that's the amazing thing." Nehar leaned forward confidentially. "It seems the Hrum mark everyone in their army with tattoos—including their spies! Five diamonds, touching, across their shoulder—just like part of a bracelet. They say it's so a spy can prove his identity to any officer of their army, and of course, the nature of the mark is a great secret, but can you imagine anyone marking their own spies? If this is an example of Hrum tactics, we'll surely have no trouble beating them!"

He laughed heartily, and Jiaan smiled politely as the others joined in.

"But we won't be trying to beat them, sir," he pointed out as the laughter died. "Our purpose is simply to hold Mazad for a year; then their own laws will force them to retreat."

"Yes, of course," said the governor. "And I assure you Mazad will have no problem doing that."

Jiaan would have found that more reassuring if the governor had met his eyes when he spoke. He found himself wondering if the expensive tableware had been unpacked from a traveling case to serve this dinner. But surely that was ridiculous.

"Just ten months, sir," he said bracingly. "The first battle was fought on the fifth day of Stag. If Mazad can hold out till then, it's all over except the negotiating."

"Ah, yes, we shall have to negotiate when the time comes." Nehar grabbed his goblet and took a sip, but he looked as if he wanted to gulp it. "Certainly."

The back of Jiaan's neck prickled. He sat up straighter. "But we don't negotiate until their year is up. We will never surrender. Never."

"Oh, of course! There will be no negotiations, until the proper time comes, of course." The room was warm, but no one else was sweating.

Jiaan met the eyes of the three young deghans and saw his own dismay reflected there. He had hoped to leave them here just to get rid of them, but leaving someone to keep the governor in hand was beginning to seem like an even more urgent necessity.

"It's an honor," said Markhan, "to be here tonight with the deghan who will be responsible for the defeat of the Hrum. This will be a historic siege!"

"That it will!" Nehar sat up a bit, looking more cheerful. The deghan who would defeat the Hrum. This leaking bag of suet, to succeed where his father had failed. The room was suddenly too warm, the scented candle smoke thick in Jiaan's lungs.

"If you'll excuse me?" He pushed back his chair and rose, bowing thanks for the meal. "I have duties I must attend to."

It was a squire's excuse, and he saw Kaluud's lip curl in a sneer, but it got Jiaan out of the fear-filled chamber and onto the gallery, where he could take deep breaths of the fresh, night air. Some thoughtful servant had laid their padded tunics over the gallery railing.

Inside the courtyard of the governor's manor the noises of the city were muted, and Jiaan wasn't familiar with Mazad's normal night sounds. But the lowing of cattle, uneasy in their strange surroundings, the clatter of carts over the cobbles, even after dark, gave the city an air of tension. The Hrum were coming, soon, and the governor wasn't the only one who was frightened. Fear could open gates no ram could penetrate. It was the Hrum's best weapon, stronger than their superior swords, with a longer reach than any lance.

Jiaan pulled off his silken overrobe and put on his tunic—then he went in search of Commander Siddas.

HE FINALLY FOUND THE MAN at his own desk, studying a scroll by the light of a few dim lamps. The sight was oddly reassuring. How often had Jiaan found the commander poring over his papers, long after the rest of the army was abed and snoring?

This man was older than Jiaan's father, perhaps

in his fifties, wearing only a rough tunic. He'd obviously shaved that morning, but at this late hour the lamplight picked out pricks of silver in the stubble on his cheeks and chin. Though the cramped, stone-walled chamber in the base of the wall tower was less luxurious than even his father's field pavilion, this was clearly where command lay. Jiaan sighed, and Commander Siddas looked up and smiled.

"I was wondering if you'd pay me a call. If you give me a moment, young sir, I'll be at your service."

"You don't have to 'sir' me," said Jiaan, sinking onto one of the plain wooden stools that faced the desk. "Take all the time you need."

One gray-threaded brow rose. The commander put down the scroll he'd been studying, pinning it flat with his inkwell, and what looked like a common river stone. The eyes that studied Jiaan were peasant brown and peasant shrewd. They lingered on his blood-stained armor.

"A bit of lemon-oil soap will help with that," he said. "But I think I'll be calling you 'sir,' nonetheless."

Jiaan blushed. "It's my horse's blood. I had to pull a splinter out of his shoulder after the battle."

"And the way you're holding your arm, you got that from pulling out a splinter?" Jiaan let go of his elbow and sat up. He had abandoned the sling a week ago, but his shoulder still ached by the end of the day. "You should keep it in a sling, if it pains you," the commander went on. "No point in pain that I ever saw. But how can I be helping you, Commander Jiaan?"

"I thought there might be some way I could help you," Jiaan told him. Somehow, he wasn't surprised that this man had learned his name. "There's not much left of the army, though men are beginning to come to us now. Is there anything we can do to help Mazad hold out for ten months?"

He had no doubt that this man knew all about the Hrum's strange laws.

"Hmm." Siddas tipped back in his chair. "I've got one problem you might be helping me with, though I'm not sure how."

"Food?" Jiaan guessed. "We've stockpiled a bit, but we can get more. It'd take at least two weeks to get it here, though, and I don't think we could arrive before the Hrum."

"Oh, the Hrum will be here tomorrow morning," said Siddas. "That's not—"

"Tomorrow!" Jiaan jerked upright. "Then I've got to leave. I can't afford to be trapped here."

"Don't be worrying about that," said Siddas. "I can get you out of the city. I'll have to blindfold you, mind, for that route is a secret I won't be revealing to anyone. You'll have to do a bit of bending and climb a ladder, but if you can do that blindfolded, we can get you away."

"That's not a—wait—what about my horse? Rakesh can't—"

Commander Siddas grinned. "I've made arrangements to have all your horses taken outside the city later tonight—as soon as the civilians clear the road. They're too fine to eat in a siege."

"Thank you," said Jiaan. "But that brings us to food. Do you have enough for ten months?"

"No," said Siddas calmly. "Not with all the civilians we've brought inside the walls. But we've enough for four or five months, and right now I'm less worried about food than about Governor Nehar."

"I know." Jiaan rubbed the place between his brows that was beginning to ache. "He's terrified."

"Considering how the Hrum executed the gahn, he's maybe got reason. But Mazad's guard is under his command. Oh," he raised a hand to stop Jiaan's protest, "there's nearly two-thirds would follow me no matter what Nehar said, but the other third are his men. And division in the ranks is the last thing we'll be needing."

Well, that accounted for the guards Jiaan had met at the gate. He was glad they weren't all like that.

"So you see," Siddas continued, "the governor has to stand fast. And I think . . . you really can't blame the man for panicking. All he knew, all he relied on, has been destroyed by the Hrum. I think if he had other deghans about, it would give him something to hold on to."

"I was planning to leave the others here," Jiaan assured him. "And they're true deghans, not like—" He stopped abruptly, and the commander smiled.

"You think I don't know that High Commander Merahb's heir is a toddler? Though he's not going to be inheriting much now. The Wheel's turning with a vengeance these days. Nehar's not the only one to fear where it might stop."

"It will stop here," said Jiaan. "Because we're going to stop it."

"Ah, but the Wheel never stops," said the old commander. "It may turn fast, it may turn slow, but it's always in motion."

Jiaan knew his peasant mother, had she survived the fever that had taken her when he was a child, would have said the same. Deghans blamed the workings of the djinn for all that went wrong, and struggled to defeat them, but peasants saw both good and ill as part of a natural cycle, to which man must adapt as best he could.

"All right, maybe we can't stop Time," said Jiaan. "But at least I can leave you some deghans to prop up the governor."

"If he stands firm for just a few months, I'll have the townsfolk behind me," said Siddas. "Once I have that, we'll be able to hold out even if a third of the guard folds."

"The townsfolk?" Jiaan remembered the grim, fearful faces in the crowd that morning. How they'd fought one another, just to get through the gates a bit sooner. "What have they to do with it?"

"In a siege, it's the townsfolk who count for most, in the end." The commander's lined face was suddenly sad. "They're the ones who'll put out the fires on the roofs and pull survivors out of smashed buildings when the Hrum bring up the catapults. They'll cook for the soldiers and give them shelter that's warm and dry. They'll tighten their belts and take to the walls themselves, with clubs, if it comes down to that. They may not be warriors, but anyone can wrap a bandage, or push a ladder off the wall with a forked stick. Walls like Mazad's can hold for years, if we can get supplies and the people have the heart for it. And I have plans for getting supplies."

"Umm," said Jiaan.

Siddas laughed. "Don't look so dubious, Commander. Mazad's walls are thick enough to last out the Flame for a few turns."

"Well, when I've got an army assembled, I'll find a way to support you," Jiaan promised. "Though if I'm not to know the route in, how can we communicate?"

It was evidently the last question he'd needed to ask, for Commander Siddas smiled and rose, holding out his hand to grip Jiaan's wrist. "I'll have the man who takes you out show you a place where you can leave a written message. And don't go lingering nearby once you've left it—it won't be picked up till after you leave. Just mention where you can be found in your note, and I'll send someone."

Jiaan frowned. "I'm not asking for details, but if you can come and go so freely, how can you be sure that the Hrum can't come in the same way?"

"We'll be guarding it, for one thing. But it's a secret long forgotten, even by most of the townsfolk. If the Hrum spies had learned of it they'd have used it themselves, and there's been no sign of that."

Probably an escape tunnel, built by some long-past governor—or even by the gahn who'd ordered the walls' construction. Jiaan had heard of such things, in ballads, at least.

"All right." He'd turned to go when another question occurred to him. "What did you do with the Hrum spies, anyway?"

"Kicked them out the gate and told them not to come back." Siddas smiled at Jiaan's sagging jaw. "Why not? Now that we know how they're marked, they're easy to spot. Or are you thinking like Nehar, that I should have hanged them off the battlements? Or worse? They're just men doing their jobs, when all's said. Well, and one woman. Doing it bravely, too."

"But they'll go straight back to the army and report! They'll tell them everything!"

"You think they haven't told them everything about our defenses months ago? That cursed, clever bitch sent out reports in every shipment of goods."

"But . . . but they're *spies*!"

"So they are," said Siddas. "And by most folks' laws of war, I'd be entitled to kill them. But I've a hope that if I'm sparing them, then maybe the Hrum will show a bit of mercy to my spies if they catch them." He laughed again at Jiaan's expression. "Oh, come, lad. How do you think I found out how their spies are marked, except with spies of my own? Do you think your father never used spies?"

"I know he did," said Jiaan. "Though he didn't talk about them much. But he told me once that they were the bravest men he knew."

"And so were the Hrum I turned loose," Commander Siddas agreed. "At least, I hope you aren't fool enough to think that our spies are brave heroes and theirs are all scum."

"No," said Jiaan, rapidly changing the comment he'd been about to make. "I don't think that." After all, a loyal Hrum spy wasn't the same as a Farsalan traitor.

But the conversation lingered in Jiaan's mind as he bid the commander farewell and returned to the governor's house.

He found the young deghans drinking a final cup of wine in Fasal's room, and the talk stopped so abruptly when Jiaan entered that he knew they'd been talking about him. It made his tone more curt than it might have been when he told them they were to remain in the city.

"You think we need *you* to tell us our duty?" Markhan asked.

Kaluud snorted and reached for the wine without even bothering to speak. Fasal was scowling.

Jiaan clung grimly to his temper. "I think it would be best if we all understand clearly what must be done. If the governor doesn't stand fast—"

"We understand," said Markhan with exaggerated patience. The tone was rude, but his expression was serious, and Fasal nodded.

It was probably the best Jiaan could expect, and all that he needed, so he nodded in turn and left them. But it was a long time before he slept.

HE WAS AWAKENED BEFORE DAWN by a hand shaking his shoulder. "Forgive me, sir, but

Commander Siddas thought you'd be wanting to see. The Hrum are coming."

The speaker was a kitchen boy, judging by his rough tunic—thin, grubby, and no older than twelve. His voice shook with the same combination of excitement and terror that flooded Jiaan's veins.

Jiaan summoned a reassuring smile. "I certainly do want to see. And so should you, lad! Mazad's defeat of the Hrum will become history— you'll be telling your grandchildren about it."

The boy's expression brightened. Jiaan sent him off, and hurried into his clothes and his padded silk armor without stopping to wash.

The sun hadn't risen when he emerged from the governor's house into the street, but the sky was gray with its approach.

Word of the Hrum's arrival was spreading. People poured out of their homes. Some wore only a nightshirt and cloak over their shoes, but all were hastening in the same direction. Jiaan followed.

He wouldn't have seen the stair that spiraled up to the top of the great wall without them, tucked as it was beneath the walkway's shadow. Up on the wall, the cold wind tugging at his loose britches, he struggled through the press for almost a dozen yards before he could elbow through the gawking crowd to look out over the plains.

It was lighter now, light enough to see a distant cloud of dust rising from the road.

"Well, it's not a cart train," a man muttered. "Not traveling at this hour."

"Not even a huge shipment would raise that much dust," another man agreed. "It's an army, all right. It's them." His voice held the same excited fear as the boy's, but there was a note of proud determination in it as well. His father would have tried to work with that pride.

"Take a good look," Jiaan told them clearly. "That's what Mazad is going to beat!"

There were grins on the faces around him when he left to search for Commander Siddas.

Jiaan found the commander on the wall, not far from the gates. Several men in the tabards of the town guard, with the lean alert look of message runners, lingered nearby, but at the moment the commander stood alone, watching the rising sun strike sparks on the Hrum's helmets.

"Where's the governor?" Jiaan asked softly, coming up beside him.

"Probably still dressing. I sent for him just before I sent for you."

"He's *dressing*?"

"Well, it wouldn't do for him to show up all rumpled and unkempt-like, now would it?" His expression was sober, but his eyes, taking in Jiaan's appearance, were alive with amusement. Jiaan wished he'd taken the time to comb his hair.

"How many of them?" he asked, turning back to the approaching army. They were marching five abreast, and the dust obscured the end of their line. Dust . . . or distance? A chill brushed Jiaan's heart.

"Only two tacti," said Siddas. "Two thousand men, and assorted officers."

"How do you . . . oh."

"Yes, spies again."

"*Only* two thousand? How many men do you have here, sir?"

"Almost eight hundred guardsmen," said the commander. "Within walls like this that's plenty, but you'll be understanding why I don't want to deal with a split command."

"Yes," said Jiaan. "But I know the three I'm leaving you. You can count on them to fight to the end." You couldn't count on them for brains, or

94

even simple common sense, but for courage and honor they could be relied on. It wasn't such a bad thing. Especially since Jiaan no longer had to deal with them.

"At all events, it's time you were going," said Siddas, almost as if he was reading Jiaan's mind. He gestured to one of the messengers.

THE STREETS THROUGH WHICH the guardsman led Jiaan were so empty they echoed. He brought Jiaan to a wheelwright's shop, in the north side of the city. The shop appeared to be empty, but the gate from the alley into the work yard opened when the guardsman pulled the latch string. The yard was full of workbenches, sawdust, and the clean scent of fresh-cut wood.

"I'll leave you here," he said, pulling a large cotton square from his belt purse and flipping it expertly into a roll. It looked like the kind of cloth peasant women tied over their hair, but old and ragged. "I hope you don't mind waiting blind-folded?"

"Not at all," said Jiaan, though he wasn't sure it was true. "I see you've done this before."

The guard looked flattered. "Only once," he

admitted. "And I never take anyone past this point. I don't know where the entrance is, but most of the guards don't even know there's a . . . way."

Which was sensible if Siddas wasn't certain of their steadfastness.

Jiaan turned his back and allowed the guard to tie the cloth over his eyes. He'd never been blindfolded before, except for childhood games. Now he realized that the indulgent adults who'd tied those blindfolds had deliberately left them loose enough for a child to see the ground at his feet. The tight-tied cloth pressed on his eyelids. When Jiaan opened them a crack—as wide as he could, without the cloth getting into his eyes—he saw nothing but darkness.

"All right?" the guard asked.

"I . . . Yes, it's fine," said Jiaan firmly.

"Then I'll leave you. You shouldn't have to wait long," he added kindly.

Jiaan heard the yard gate open and close. He hadn't noticed that it creaked when they came in.

It was unexpectedly disconcerting, being sightless in a strange place. Even though Jiaan was certain Siddas would send only men who would help him, he found himself thinking about how vulnerable he was. Anyone could take him out with a single blow from a club, and Jiaan wouldn't even know it was coming. No doubt that was why he'd been left in this enclosed space, so no ill-intentioned bypasser could take advantage of him.

He thought about taking the blindfold off—or loosening it—but he knew that if he was caught doing so, the guides would take him no farther. So he kept his hands down, as the moments dragged by. He wondered what the Hrum were doing now. Had they reached the city yet?

He was almost ready to start groping for a bench to sit on—why hadn't he noted their location before the guard blindfolded him?—when he heard the gate creak again. He stiffened in alarm, even as a man's voice said softly, "Ready to go, sir?"

"Yes." Jiaan knew he sounded curt, but it felt strange to talk to someone whose face he couldn't see.

The man tucked Jiaan's hand through his elbow, as though he was blind in truth. The cloth of his sleeve was warm, and had been coarse, but it was now soft with wear and washing. He led Jiaan out through the gate, but instead of turning back toward the street, they headed farther down the alley. Jiaan tried to keep up with the man's walking pace, but the stones were rougher than on the main streets. The man seemed to be leading him carefully, but Jiaan still stumbled several times.

Carefully, but confusingly. After a score of turns, Jiaan became certain the man was walking him in circles—yet another precaution Jiaan approved of, though he couldn't help but try to remember their route, to attempt to determine their direction in the rare moments when he could feel the sun on his face and hands.

They walked for what felt like a very long time, but Jiaan guessed they were no more than a handful of streets from where they started when his guide came to a stop. "A moment, sir."

Metal clashed softly, and stone grated on stone. The sound echoed, and Jiaan frowned. They hadn't entered a building—he could feel the breeze—but he also sensed some sort of enclosure. How was that—

"Here's the ladder, sir. Hold on here, and feel down with your foot."

Both the uprights and rungs of the ladder were made of iron, cold and rough. The draft that blew up past him was filled with the sound and scent of water. Not an escape passage, an aqueduct like they had in Setesafon, doubtless bringing water from the Sistan River. But how could such a thing be kept secret from anyone? The townsfolk must know where the water came from. Setesafon had bragged of its sewer system, but Jiaan had heard only of Mazad's deep wells.

He counted sixty steps down before his groping toe found a flat surface beneath it. He stepped onto the floor and moved to one side to let his guide descend, though he kept a good grip on the upright pole. He didn't think this was just a ledge, surrounded by an even greater drop, but if he was wrong he didn't want to find out the hard way. The sound of water wasn't loud, but Jiaan had a feeling that a lot of it was running very near.

"Right then," said his guide. "You can be letting go, sir; we're down. But keep your right hand to the wall. It's a bit narrow."

A walkway, then, following the watercourse. At least here the guide couldn't lead him in circles. They walked straight ahead, the slight uphill slope yet another confirmation of Jiaan's surmise. What was the point of the blindfold, when all this could be deduced so easily? Jiaan hoped the entrance was well hidden.

They traveled for what felt like a long distance before the guide stopped. "Last ladder. You're almost there." Was there a note of approval in his voice? Jiaan had almost become accustomed to not seeing his face.

The trip up the ladder was shorter, only forty-three rungs. This time the guide went first, telling Jiaan to wait when they reached the top. Jiaan heard the mechanism grate and squeal—louder than the first. The warm air that wafted down smelled of dust, and of the small, leafy trees that dotted the hills around Mazad.

Jiaan heard the guide start to climb again and needed no urging to follow him out, half crawling over a stone lip and onto the rocky, grassy soil. The sun was warm on his hair and shoulders, but when he reached for the blindfold, a hard hand gripped his wrist. "Not yet! Sir."

"All right." Jiaan took the guide's arm again, but he wanted to be done with this—to see, djinn take them!

Perhaps it was only his impatience, but it seemed as if the guide led him in circles even longer this time, and the rocky, root-strewn ground was rough going. He heard no sounds of battle, not even in the distance, though the Hrum must have reached the city by now. Was that smoke he smelled? Finally the guide came to a halt.

"You've done well, sir. Put out your hands."

The rustling leaves had already told Jiaan he faced a tree. He reached out and touched rough bark.

"Good. About two feet above your hands is a hollow. That's where you can leave a message, if you're wanting to contact Commander Siddas. Don't—"

"Don't wait to see who picks it up, I know." Jiaan was beginning to be impatient with Siddas' security precautions. On the other hand, he couldn't have found his way back to the aqueduct hatch he'd just emerged from, nor could he have described the entrance to it in the city, except for a guess that it was somewhere near the north or west wall. Perhaps Siddas' precautions weren't as inadequate as they'd seemed.

"Right then." Definite amusement in the man's voice now. "I'll ask you to wait for a slow count of thirty before you take off the blindfold. Then find the hollow, and make sure that you can find this place again. Once you've done that, go south. Your horses aren't far."

"Thank you," said Jiaan.

"Thank you for behaving yourself. I'd have hated to . . . Well, never mind that now."

Listening to the retreating footsteps, the back of Jiaan's neck prickled. Siddas had let Hrum spies go unharmed; surely he wouldn't have ordered Jiaan's execution, even if he had seen too much. No, not his execution, but Jiaan would probably have been dragged back to the city, and held until the siege ended.

Jiaan abandoned the notion of cheating on the count, and even went to thirty-five before he yanked off the blindfold.

The sun was too bright; it made his eyes water. The tree before him was larger than most, but other than that it was perfectly ordinary. The leaves were a bit dusty. It looked wonderful.

Blinking, Jiaan gazed around and discovered that he was standing on a road, though the surface was so rutted and rocky it was hardly smoother than the rough ground. To the left of the tree was a pile of rocks that looked like a crouching dog, from the right angle. From any other angle it looked like a pile of rocks, but Jiaan took the time to memorize them, and the tree, and the shape of the hills that cupped the road. He would need to be able to find this place again.

The hollow, when he finally stepped onto a gnarled root to climb up and look for it, was just a cavity formed where a branch had fallen away and the wood behind it rotted. Nothing to distinguish it.

Jiaan walked down the road to the south, making note of its twists and turns. After only a few hundred yards he found the horses, tied neatly to a tree that looked very like the message tree. Hadn't Siddas said someone would be holding the horses?

Wait, there was someone—but he wasn't holding the horses, he was lying on top of the low rise, looking south. He wore a subtly colored shirt that blended with the grass, but his straight, black hair contrasted sharply with the pale sky. Even before he turned, revealing his face, Jiaan's heart had started to sink toward his boots. It was Fasal.

Jiaan set his teeth and began scrambling up the

slope. "What in the name of all djinn are you doing here? I told you to stay in the city!"

Fasal's dark brows rose. "Markhan and Kaluud will be enough to keep an eye on the governor." *And I don't acknowledge your right to give me orders.* He didn't say it aloud; he didn't have to.

"I went to check on the horses last night," Fasal went on. "When I found out that the Hrum would arrive today, I realized that if I stayed I'd be caught in the siege, so I left with the horses. One of the guardsmen told me I could meet you here. I've been watching the Hrum all morning."

Jiaan reached the top of the slope and sank down beside him, acrimony forgotten. "What are they doing?"

But he could see that for himself. They were burning the suburbs.

"I don't think they intended to do it, when they first arrived," said Fasal.

Looking down, Jiaan realized he was in the hills north of the city, just where he'd expected to be. The view, looking over Mazad's rooftops and the walls, to the flaming buildings in the south, was magnificent and terrible. The Hrum had clearly started the fire on the outskirts of the main road, where Jiaan had ridden in . . . only yesterday? But the wind was blowing it west toward the river. The first few blocks of the southern suburbs were already a charred wasteland, with thin wisps of smoke rising from them. Looking down on the city from the other side, Jiaan could see the bright-clad townsfolk crowding the parapet, watching their homes and businesses burn.

"The first thing the Hrum did was to begin setting up camp," Fasal went on. "In those fields by the river. But soon they sent a few score of men marching on up the road. When they came into arrow range, they stopped, all but one unarmed officer who went on, almost up to the gate—probably demanding surrender."

"Evidently the governor didn't oblige," said Jiaan.

"He won't surrender," said Fasal. "Especially once the first few attacks have been beaten off, and he sees that it can be done."

"What makes you certain he'll hold on long enough to figure that out?" Jiaan demanded. "You should have stayed to help prop him up."

"Kaluud and Markhan will do that. After all, the army they want to fight is here, not—"

"Skulking in the hills, like rabbits," Jiaan finished. "You really think they can keep the governor's nerve steady?"

"Without difficulty," said Fasal. "After you left the dinner table, Markhan reminded the governor that all the high houses are gone. If Mazad holds for a year, there won't be anyone for the Hrum to negotiate with, except Governor Nehar."

The fire was already thrusting greedy fingers into the thick suburbs that surrounded the river. It might not cross the water, but the buildings between the river and the wall were clearly doomed.

"Markhan didn't come right out and say it," Fasal continued. "But Nehar could easily end up gahn—by Hrum decree, Arzhang take him."

The djinn of treacherous ambition would have no trouble claiming that one. "You're right," said Jiaan. "If anything could put steel into Nehar's soul, the hope of becoming gahn would do it." And trust another deghan to figure that out. He really might become gahn, with Markhan and Kaluud as his right and left hands. It was a prospect so dismaying that Jiaan began to laugh—it was that, or cry. But Fasal was looking at him oddly. "Sorry.

Anyway, the governor refused to surrender—then what?"

"Well, I don't know what he said," Fasal went on, "but it was evidently . . . firm. The officer marched back to his men, all stiff spined, and a few moments later they sent a flight of arrows at the walls. I think it was mostly meant as a gesture, but the wind was with them and a few of the arrows made it. So our people fired back, and even with the wind against them the extra height told in their favor, so some of their arrows reached the Hrum as well. Those people can raise their shields into formation unbelievably fast."

Jiaan laughed, with real humor this time.

"Aren't you upset about this?" Fasal gestured to the burning town. "They set the fires as soon as their own people marched out. Weren't you the one who was so concerned about saving peasants' livelihoods?"

"The suburbs couldn't have survived," said Jiaan. "And it's not like there's anyone left there. So, far from being upset, I'm delighted. This is the first stupid thing I've seen the Hrum do."

"I don't think it's stupid," said Fasal. "I think seeing their homes burn will make these people frightened, and hopeless, and they'll be more likely to yield."

"And I think it will make them angry," said Jiaan, "and more likely to fight to the death. But what really matters is that once the fires have died, the ground around the walls will be clear of all but rubble. Any approaching force will be visible. If the Hrum hadn't burned those buildings, Commander Siddas would have had to, but that wouldn't have been a popular move, so he maneuvered the Hrum into making it for him. And if the Hrum commander is that foolish . . . Well, let's just say that I'm feeling very good about Mazad. Especially if we can give them some support. But we'd better go. Eventually, even that commander is going to stop watching the bonfires and send out some patrols."

Fasal followed him down the hill and mounted in thoughtful silence. He even took Markhan's horse's lead before Jiaan asked him to.

"Why didn't you stay behind?" Jiaan inquired. Markhan and Kaluud stood a good chance of becoming the new gahn's right and left hands; Fasal could have been the new gahn's brain.

"I want to fight for Farsala," said Fasal, "not Governor Nehar. Not even if he's the only one left to become gahn."

"That's a horrible thought, isn't it?"

Fasal stiffened. "The gahn is the gahn."

Jiaan suppressed a sigh. "So why didn't you stay? The fight for Farsala *is* the fight for Mazad."

"I know," said Fasal. "But they don't need me, and you . . . the army does."

And you need all the help you can get. At least he hadn't said it aloud. Jiaan sighed.

CHAPTER FIVE

SORAYA

PLEASE, SIR, I'M NEEDING work."
Soraya had never tried to speak
with a peasant accent before—
Sudaba would have skinned her
alive if she had—but she'd been practicing on the
road for several weeks. She feared she was over-
doing it, but hopefully the Hrum wouldn't be able
to tell. And she prayed there would be no real
Farsalan peasants in the Hrum camp to give her
away.

In the months she had dwelled with the Suud,
Soraya had learned that despite their primitive
technology they had a strong code of personal
honor—stronger than that of many deghans.
Farsalan peasants were another matter. Soraya

had no idea whether she could trust them, but she wasn't about to bet on it.

It had taken weeks for Soraya to catch up with the Hrum's main army, and if they hadn't stopped to make a permanent camp outside Setesafon, she might not have reached them still. She'd been surprised that they hadn't occupied the gahn's palace. The Hrum commander— "Governor" Garren, he called himself, as if all Farsala was no more than a city!—claimed that he wouldn't take possession of "his" palace till his right to do so was established beyond all doubt.

The country folk, from whom Soraya had heard the story, said it was more likely that the palace had been so damaged in the fighting that tents made a better lodging—that Garren would be moving himself in the moment there was enough of a roof to keep him dry, right or no right.

When she approached the sentries at the perimeter of the Hrum encampment, Soraya had feared she would have to meet with the new governor, but instead a young soldier had taken her to the camp's ordnancer.

"What work have you had before . . . Sani, is it?"

"Yes, sir." She bobbed her head awkwardly, swinging her hair even farther over her face. The ordnancer was in his forties, a balding man, with a face she'd have thought kind if he hadn't been a Hrum officer—and if his gaze, taking in the ragged, too-large skirt and blouse she'd bought from a used-clothing barrel, hadn't been so shrewd.

"I've mostly worked as a kitchen girl," said Soraya. "I can peel and chop, and fetch and carry." In truth she had very little idea what went on in kitchens, but surely they peeled and chopped things.

"Why did you leave your old job?"

Soraya blinked. Why should he care? Wasn't it enough that she needed a new job now? But she sensed no suspicion in the emotions that reached her—just a hint of patience. "The family I worked for, they were . . ." She was about to say "burned out," when she remembered that the Hrum had burned very little. "They weren't a high house, you understand, not one of the twelve, but they had money. Some city property. They feared they'd be losing it all when the army came, so they sold up and fled to Kadesh. But they only took the upper servants with them. They said they could hire Kadeshi, probably cheaper than us."

If Sudaba had had the sense to flee, that was what she would have done, so it should ring true. Soraya herself would never have given a thought to the plight of undergrooms and kitchen girls. She ran her hands down the shabby skirt. There were patches where her knees hit the fabric, and the over-large garments made her look as if she'd lost even more weight than the weeks on the road had actually cost her.

"I see," said the ordnancer thoughtfully. "You're not afraid of the army?"

"I need work, sir. And I heard . . . I heard that the army's been leaving our women alone." It was true, and Soraya thanked Azura for it—had she heard otherwise her resolve might have failed. This was frightening enough as it was.

"Very well." The ordnancer sounded like a man who has just made up his mind. "As it happens, we're short of kitchen help. As the army spreads out, we usually hire from the local populace, but very few Farsalans have approached us for work."

Good. Soraya managed not to say it aloud.

"So I've . . . I'm being hired?" Curse this ridiculous accent! Where was Ahriman, the djinn of lies, when you needed him?

"We'll try you for a month," the ordnancer corrected her. "If you've worked well during that period, then we'll hire you."

"I'm to work a month without pay?" Soraya asked in confusion. Surely that couldn't be right.

"No, no, we'll pay you, and provide food and shelter, but you won't receive a ranking till you've earned it."

"Ranking? But I just want kitchen work!" And that didn't sound at all humble. "Sir," she added quickly.

The ordnancer laughed. "You've got a great deal to learn about us, Sani, but for a start, I'm Ordnancer Reevus. I know it's a mouthful, but we're fussy about rank here, and 'sir' is for regular officers."

"Yes, si—Ordnancer Reevus." Her tongue stumbled on the unfamiliar word. She had already noted that the sentries had spoken good Faran; the ordnancer barely had an accent.

Hopefully she could learn what she needed and depart before the fact that she didn't sound like a Farsalan peasant became obvious. Should she have claimed to come from some distant village, with a different accent? Too late now. Soraya bit her lip.

"Don't worry, girl," said Ordnancer Reevus, mistaking the cause of her concern. "We'll teach you. For now, all you need to do is work hard and obey the cooks. You'll be paid three of your Farsalan iron coins—mares, is it?—a week."

Only three mares? But Reevus was smiling, as if he'd offered a very good wage.

"That'll be . . . being fine, sir, um, Ordnancer Reevus."

"Come with me, then, and I'll introduce you to the kitchen master."

Reevus talked about the Hrum army camp as they walked through it, explaining that each unit was organized by tens, hundreds, and then into a tacti, a thousand men, which was the largest unit of the army. Soraya cared nothing about the Hrum, but she was surprised by the camp, then reluctantly impressed, and finally amazed. It was so big! She'd known the Hrum army was large, but just walking from the perimeter to the central square where the kitchen tents were located seemed to take forever. It was bigger than most Farsalan towns, though no town she'd ever seen was laid out in such neat squares, with wide, flat roads between them. Even some of the soldier's tents had wooden walls built halfway up their sides, and the entire square, when they finally reached it, was surrounded by buildings, bright with the glow of new timber. Accustomed to seeing even peasant homes built of stone, the wooden walls looked somehow unfinished. Impermanent. But still, they were buildings, and the Hrum army had been here less than two months!

Soraya was walking backward, gawking at a man who was driving a flock of ducks across the square, when Reevus reached out and yanked her out of the way of a lumbering oxcart.

The driver was speaking Hrum, so Soraya couldn't tell exactly what he said, but she thought the gist was, "Keep your half-witted servant girls off the road." Reevus replied in the same language, defending her, to judge by the carter's scowl.

"I'm sorry," Soraya mumbled, looking down so her hair hid her face.

"It's no matter," said Reevus calmly, taking her arm to steer her onward. "It's natural you should be curious—our camp is new to you. But keep an eye on where you're going. This is a busy place."

He kept hold of her arm to assure that she would. Given her recent behavior, Soraya could hardly blame him—and if keeping hold of her like that was intolerably rude by deghan standards, well, he didn't know she was a deghass. And the square was surprisingly busy.

"Is . . . is this a market day?" she asked. Sounding like a credulous country girl came easily now.

Reevus laughed. "No, we don't hold markets. But we're doing a bit of building, so it's busier than usual."

A bit of building. By the summer's end they'd have a town. But they would need a town, Soraya realized. They were here to stay. Tears stung her eyes, but she blinked them back. There was nothing she could do about the Hrum. She was here to learn where Merdas and Sudaba had been sent, so she could follow and free them, and then take them to live safely with the Suud. If it took time, then she'd have patience. And courage, and endurance, and anything else it took.

The kitchens, and the meal tent where the

soldiers ate, took up the whole south side of the square. And if the square had been chaos, the largest kitchen was bedlam. Men and women raced back and forth with baskets and trays, cleavers thudded into cutting boards and everyone seemed to be shouting—in Hrum, of course.

Reevus wove through the mob, still gripping her arm, until he came to a stop before a short man with curly dark hair, who was inspecting a barrel of cabbages. At the sight of Reevus, he burst into furious speech—in Hrum.

Reevus had let go of her elbow, and Soraya fought down a shameful impulse to burrow against his side.

"I've brought you some help," he said cheerfully, in Faran. "Unless you frighten her to death. Stop ranting, man. This is Sani. She's worked as a kitchen girl—midsized household, from the sound of it. I've taken her on for a month's probation. Sani, this is Kitchen Master Hennic."

"Ha!" The short man looked her up and down. Soraya felt her cheeks grow warm and looked away. "She is . . . What is the word? Scrawny. She is scrawny. You sorry for her."

Soraya glared.

Reevus laughed and said something in Hrum. The cook snorted and eyed her sharply. "So, kitchen girl. Can you cook? Or is it just rough work?"

Rough work? "I can't cook," Soraya admitted.

"Humph. Hands are hands. If no other choice, I take what is given. Here, girl, you will start with pots."

He grabbed her elbow and led her off. She looked over her shoulder at Reevus, who smiled and made shooing gestures.

Pots? The kitchen master led her through an open doorway in the back of the building, and into a dirty-looking, fenced yard, turning toward one corner. She'd already admitted she couldn't cook, so what could she be doing with . . . Pots. A pile, a mountain, of huge iron kettles, filthy with the remains of various porridges, stews, and shit, for all Soraya knew. She flinched.

"Scrape into the midden troughs first," said Hennic briskly. "Then get hot water from the *fur*—the big tanks. Over there." He gestured to the west. "The man there will give you soap. Scrub with that brush, rinse, and rinse again—with *hot* water—and pour into that trench." He pointed to a small ditch with a trickle of water running along the bottom. From five yards away she could smell it. And she didn't even want to touch those pots.

"I do *not* . . ." *No. Merdas, just three years old.* Soraya took a deep breath. She had seen Golnar wash dishes. She had curried horses. How bad could it be? "I don't know what to scrape them with."

"This." Hennic handed her a flat wooden disk with a thick edge designed for a grip. "I will *hubar*—will look close at the pots when you finish."

He turned and stamped off, leaving Soraya staring at the pile. She stepped closer, and peered gingerly into the nearest kettle. Bean paste of some sort. At least, she hoped it was bean paste. And if Sudaba would have fainted to see her doing this, well, so much the better. Soraya gritted her teeth, picked up the kettle, and hauled it over to the midden trough. The trough was half full of leaves and peelings and bits of bone and gristle, and already smelled rotten. Would she have to eat the food that produced this mess?

She would eat it, and smile, and pretend to be grateful for it if she had to. A deghass didn't let anything stop her.

Scraping the pots took a long time, and when she was finished, her hands and arms were covered with things Soraya preferred not to think about.

The hot-water tanks, set up in an open yard to the west, were quite ingenious. Eight bronze tanks, each one larger than a big horse's body, perched on stone walls about three feet high. They each had a funnel at one end where water could be added, and a tap on the end of a long pipe emerged from the other. Beneath them, beds of embers glowed, and logs burned in the center of several fire pits.

"Delfi emma quan, amas?" The man who came around the side of one of the tanks was even shorter than the cook, only a bit taller than Soraya herself. His hair was graying, but his face wasn't too lined, and his smile was open and easy.

Soraya found herself smiling back, despite her aching arms. "I'm sorry, I don't speak Hrum."

The man's brows rose. "Farsalan? You're the first they've hired. At least . . ." Doubt shadowed his expressive face.

"Yes, I was hired," Soraya assured him. "But if I'm the only one, where did you learn such good Faran? Everyone seems to speak it."

"Well, it's required," said the man. "Put your kettle under the tap there. Out a bit more, that's it. Whenever the army goes into a new country, everyone is required to learn the language — so the soldiers can understand what the people around them are saying."

He took a cloth, folded it several times, and used it to protect his hand as he turned the tap. Steaming water gushed out, and Soraya made a mental note not to touch any part of the tanks with her bare hands.

"Of course, slaves aren't required to learn," the man went on, "but I like languages. Since I'm fluent, they send me to do the marketing, and I like that, too. Lets me see a bit of life outside the camp."

Soraya gasped, and stared at his rough tunic. It didn't look like a Hrum army tabard, but neither had the cook's clothes. She'd taken him for a servant. "You're a slave?" she blurted out. "I'm sorry. That is . . ." Her voice trailed off as the man laughed.

"Yes, I am a slave, but you needn't be sorry. At least, you haven't done anything to be sorry for yet. My name's Calfaer." He turned off the water tap as he spoke.

"I'm So—Sani," said Soraya hastily. She

couldn't lower her guard, not with anyone. She looked down. "I don't know why I was so stupid. I know the Hrum keep slaves. I mean, they've taken enough of our people." She reached for the kettle handle, intending to retreat.

"Wait," Calfaer told her. "I'll get you some soap." When he returned with a small mound of greasy-looking soap in a wooden bowl, he grasped the other side of the kettle's handle. "Let me help you with this—it's heavy. Trust Hennic to set you to scrubbing pots on your first day."

"Are pots a particularly hard job?" Soraya asked hopefully. The kettle was heavy, and water slopped onto her skirt.

"Not particularly," said Calfaer. "But usually two people do them together. I'd help you, but I'm supposed to be tending the *furniculum* today."

"That's all right. I don't want to get you in trouble," said Soraya.

"I'd get in no more trouble than you," he assured her, setting the kettle down carefully. "The Hrum aren't bad masters. They've even got laws about it. And since my master willed me to the army as a whole when he died, well, I hardly have a master anymore."

Soraya reached for the scrub brush, stalling for a moment to think. She didn't want to make her interest in Farsalan slaves too noticeable, but surely it wouldn't seem odd to ask a few questions. "So the Farsalan slaves aren't likely to be—being treated too bad?" She'd all but forgotten her accent—and he spoke even better Faran than Reevus had. She bent over the pot and began to scrub, hiding her face.

"No, they won't be treated badly." Calfaer's voice was gentle. "Though they're grieving, and angry, and afraid. I spoke with some of them, trying to help. And I noticed that an unusual number of them have hair like this." His fingers brushed her face, tucking the long black strands behind one ear. But that was a question Soraya had prepared for. She looked up, meeting his gaze casually.

"My mam was the first of our family born with it. And the master of her household found my greatmam a husband before Mam was born, so she wasn't shamed."

Calfaer's brows rose. "Wasn't shamed? I'd think . . . Or do you mean she wasn't forced?"

Soraya stared at him in astonishment. "You

mean raped? No!" She had based her story on the birth of her father's bastard son—and he certainly hadn't raped anyone! But was she so certain that the mothers of all the black-haired children she'd seen chasing birds out of the new-planted fields had been willing? Soraya's gaze fell, this time in genuine shame. "My grandmother wasn't raped," she said. "But that's not always the case, with ser—us servants."

She wondered fleetingly if her father's bastard had survived the battle. He probably hadn't, and in truth Soraya didn't much care. She'd seen less of her father's page, and cared less about him, than she did about the grooms who had cared for her horses. Not like Merdas . . .

She plunged the scrub brush into the pot, hoping that if Calfaer saw her working he'd let the subject go. But the water was too hot, almost scalding. Soraya drew a breath, letting go of embarrassment and tension. Once she was centered, she reached out and touched the water's shilshadu—it rolled in the kettle, mindlessly rejoicing in even that simple motion. The water liked being hot, but when Soraya reminded it of melting snow, and deep, cold ponds it liked that, too—the only difficulty was to stop it from cooling so quickly that it became frigid. No, she'd gotten it right; warm, but no longer hot. Water was too cursed agreeable. Soraya scrubbed industriously. Small waves slopped over the kettle's brim.

"Here," said Calfaer. "Let me pour most of that into the next kettle. That way it can soak while you're cleaning this one. Just put a bit of soap on the brush. And if you find a bit that's hard going, pour some water back in and let it soak a while longer."

"Thank you."

His words were casual, but Soraya sensed some emotion behind them that he wasn't revealing. She had learned, over the past few weeks, that touching another person's shilshadu was still beyond her, but there were other ways. She found her own shilshadu again and . . . opened it. Not reaching greedily, but waiting, receptive to whatever chose to come. *Yes.* She could sense his spirit more strongly now. Curiosity and . . . suspicion? But why? Surely he hadn't guessed she was working magic, or his emotions would be far stronger. Her accent? But whatever had caused that prickly suspicion, it was accompanied by sympathy and a desire to help. This was someone she could trust—at least a little bit. That knowledge felt like shackles falling away from her heart.

"Thank you," said Soraya again, smiling up at him. "I can manage from here."

Why did he look so astonished now? Still, he smiled in return. "I'm glad. But I'd advise you to stick with your first plan, girl, and hide that face behind your hair." This time when he reached out, he pulled the strands forward. "The Hrum aren't bad men, for the most part, and they treat rape as the crime it is. But a girl who looks like you, in an army camp, is trouble on two feet."

"Oh." Soraya closed her sagging jaw. She'd been thinking of those who might recognize the high commander's daughter who had been displayed to the whole city last fall because of the political machinations of her father's enemies. She hadn't thought . . . "You're right. I'll be careful, with everyone but you."

"Good girl. I've got to get back to the *furniculum* now, but come to me if you need . . . more hot water."

Anything, he meant. He turned and walked out of the yard, and Soraya returned to her scrubbing,

127

with a brush full of soap and a lighter heart. She had made a friend.

SORAYA NEEDED FRIENDSHIP, in the next few days. Her pots passed Kitchen Master Hennic's inspection, but her hopes that that would earn her a reprieve were instantly banished. One onerous task succeeded the next. Soraya hadn't dreamed how much work went on in a great kitchen. She fetched wood, fetched water, hot and cold, fetched vegetables, and flour, and blood-dripping meat from the butcher's shed. After one glance at the peelings that fell from her clumsy knife, Hennic had proclaimed that Farsalan kitchens were run by wasteful, dirty pigs, and sent her out to scrub off the big tables in the meal tent instead. At least the soldiers who lingered there, playing a noisy, complex game they called battle dice, barely glanced at the grubby girl who scrubbed around them. But it wasn't Soraya's fault—she'd never had to peel a turnip in her life! She simply didn't have the skill that created the long, thin curls of turnip skin that fell from the others' blades. Not all of them were girls, either—there were boys among the kitchen workers, just as there were women among the soldiers.

Ordinarily, that would have interested Soraya, but now she barely had the strength to wonder at it before falling exhausted onto her pallet to catch a few marks of sodden, dreamless sleep. And then rising before dawn, to work to exhaustion again.

Only two things made that first rigorous week tolerable. One was Suud magic. Soraya had learned to make magic while meditating in the warm peace of Maok's hutch. Now she learned to apply those lessons in the midst of work, at a moment's notice. Suud magic kept the water she washed with at the right temperature. Her fires lit swiftly and burned well. And at night, when she unrolled her straw pallet beside one of the kitchen fires, all lice, fleas, and spiders were suddenly seized with the notion that her bedroll and person were bad places to be. Reaching the shilshadu of animals, even insects, was easier than touching the spirit of inanimate things, for animals had minds that could be changed. Of course, shilshadu to shilshadu there could be no lies, but Soraya's determination to squash any multilegged creature that took up residence near her was a truth so deep it sent them all scrambling.

And magic helped in another way—not so practical, but perhaps more important, for even the smallest bit of magic working kept a core of peaceful memory alive in her heart.

The other thing that allowed her to survive those first weeks was Calfaer's friendship. He didn't help her any more than the others, for that would have been noticeable. But whenever she tackled a new task he was there, with hints on how to do it faster or more easily.

He had his own work as well—in fact, he seemed to be the one who filled in whenever anything needed to be done. Soraya had seen him polishing armor, herding livestock, and even helping the cobbler cut leather for an urgently needed pair of boots. So how did he always manage to be working nearby when she needed him?

She'd also seen him helping the clerks inventory new supplies. A casual question had given her the information that the clerks kept records of everything that went into or out of the army camp, including slaves.

After that, Soraya regarded the wood-sided tent where the records were stored with the most covetous desire she'd ever experienced. But the scroll boxes were locked, and because the tent that held them also held pay records and seals, there was a guard posted outside at all times. Even that might not have stopped her from doing something foolish, but there was one other problem—the records were written in Hrum.

Patience. She had already begun to learn the language, from both Calfaer's lessons and Hennic's curses. She was a deghass; she wouldn't despair. Besides, despair took energy, and if the kitchen staff hadn't been required to wash themselves each night before bed, Soraya would have been filthier than the meanest beggar. In fact, begging was beginning to look like a better career choice than kitchen work. At least you wouldn't have to scrub floors.

But if kitchen work seemed to encompass an incredible number of backbreaking tasks, a surprising number of them took her outside the kitchen. When she had the energy to notice things, Soraya learned a lot about the Hrum camp. For instance, she was stoking the ravenous bake ovens that lay behind the meal tent, when she saw the peddler walking toward the square. Surely he couldn't be the same young man her father had hired to bring news and goods to the croft where she'd been hidden? It was too great a coincidence, too . . . But it *was* him. What in the name of all djinn was he doing in the Hrum camp? Was he a trai—

A hard yank on her hair made her yelp, and the stack of wood she carried scattered as she spun to face her tormentor. But her protest died at the sight of Kitchen Master Hennic, who reached out and calmly slapped her face.

"You're not paid to gawk at handsome officers," he snapped. Soraya's hands itched with the need to strike back, but . . . all the last week's work for nothing? It would be, if she was fired. She knelt instead, to gather up the wood she'd dropped and hide her expression, ignoring Hennic's snarling voice. She could take revenge later—there were things she could do. And the hair that fell over her face also let her sneak another look at the peddler.

She hardly noticed when Hennic finished his lecture and stamped away.

Yes, it was the same man. An officer had joined him, and they were chatting casually, ignoring the clumsy kitchen girl being scolded by the cook. The officer didn't look handsome to Soraya, in his thirties, she guessed, with a narrow, stern face. By the way they talked, the peddler knew him well, and by the amount of bronze decorating his breastplate he held high rank. Soraya cursed herself for not having learned what the swirling insignia meant. Her first thought was that the peddler had come to betray her to the Hrum, but that was absurd, for he couldn't know she was here. And he hadn't told anyone about the hidden croft — at least, not while it mattered — or someone would have come for her, and no one had. So if he wasn't here about her, then what was he doing?

The officer shook his head ruefully and led the peddler toward the other side of the square where the officer's quarters were located. Soraya's next thought was that the peddler was selling Farsalan secrets to the Hrum, but what secrets could he know, besides hers? Perhaps he was simply selling his wares. He was a peddler, after all. No Farsalans had approached the camp for work, but Soraya knew that merchants were selling their goods to the Hrum. The young man she remembered would be perfectly willing to sell to the enemy, Borz take him. The djinn of greed owned all merchants anyway.

Just a coincidence, after all—and she'd acted the fool, staring so openly. It was a good thing Hennic had come by when he did, or she might have been recognized. She should probably be grateful to him. Soraya's mouth twisted; her cheek still stung from his slap. She wasn't grateful, and Hennic was the spawn of Gorahz, so there!

But her hidden smile died at a sudden memory, and both her cheeks were burning as she picked up the last piece of kindling and began stoking the fire. Had her own maids cursed her for the spawn of Gorahz, when she slapped them?

CHAPTER SIX

KAVI

PATRIUS MET HIM BEFORE he even reached the square, which probably meant that Kavi's services were still held to be worth something. Either that, or they didn't trust him to walk around the Hrum camp unwatched. Though now it was beginning to look more like a town than a camp. Kavi eyed the elaborate bronze patterning on Patrius' breast plate—it hadn't changed. "Tactimian still? I thought everyone was getting themselves promoted, now that Garren's a governor and all."

"Not everyone, just the ones that don't arg—why do I say things like that around you?" Patrius demanded.

"Because you know I don't like Garren any better than you do," said Kavi. *Because you trust me.*

The thought didn't show in his expression. Kavi had been betting his life on lies for almost a year now. He could control his face. But something in his heart still ached at the thought. He liked Patrius. Betraying him hurt—far more than betraying the deghans had.

Patrius turned, leading the way toward the officer's quarters, and Kavi followed.

Betraying Patrius hurt, because Patrius had been honest and dealt fairly with Kavi, and the deghans hadn't. No, he felt few regrets for his part in casting the deghans out of power—but they hadn't deserved to be taken into slavery, either. At least, not all of them. Kavi remembered the hatred in the eyes of the deghass—he'd never learned her name, for a deghass didn't offer her name to a wandering peddler—who'd accompanied that lady-bitch Soraya when he first met her. Almost as plain as the other was beautiful, she'd been as decent as her class allowed her to be. His last sight of her had been in the slave pens, about to be shipped off to a strange land and sold. As if a girl—any girl!—was of no more worth than a goat.

No, he had to get the slaves back. And to stop this madness of drafting peasant boys for soldiers as well. If that meant betraying Patrius in turn, then so be it. Kavi had long since decided that consistency was an overrated virtue, but by the time this was over, he'd be having everyone on both sides out for his hide. And as so many people had told him, a peddler with a crippled hand wasn't hard to find. Kavi flexed the weakened hand that had cost him his true trade, and might betray him in yet another way if his part in any of this ever came out.

So I'd better lie well.

He'd already started, speaking quietly to the angry, adventurous young men. The same young men the Hrum were about to start drafting, though they'd only given their three-month notification in the cities so far. Just a few small suggestions that when the army came this way, it might be slowed a bit if this bridge was gone, those fields flooded . . . And of course, you couldn't draft a man you'd never seen a sign of, now could you? Or tax grain that was no longer in the storage bins?

They all knew him, of course, so there was no

way to keep his name out of it—and Kavi knew that if he kept on with this to the point it started to cause the Hrum real problems, sooner or later, they'd come looking for the source. So when the peasants asked him who was behind all this— couldn't be him, after all; a peasant just turned twenty?—he'd given them a name.

At first they laughed, then their faces turned thoughtful, and finally glowed with relief. Surely only a deghan would dare to claim *that* name. Kavi thought them insane, to actually want a deghan in command of this insanity. But if it made them feel better—and made him a bit safer!—let them think what they would. The cursed deghans had to be good for something.

The square to which Patrius led him was surrounded by wooden buildings now, though the common soldiers were still living in tents. Kavi was amused to see they'd laid out their new town in the same formation they'd laid out their camps.

"You people are being fond of squares, aren't you?"

Patrius shrugged. "It works. Everyone knows where everything is. A messenger coming from another camp—from another army—even in the middle of the night, he doesn't have to go wandering around looking for the strategus' tent."

He led the way into his quarters—floored, roofed, and walled in planks so new that beads of sap pooled on them. There was no door yet, nor shutters on the windows, but it was the same size and shape as the tent that had preceded it.

Kavi snorted. "What did you do, just build the walls up around the canvas? No, I know. It's practical, and the furniture all fits. Why bother to build, if you don't build better?"

Patrius smiled. "It is better; it's cooler now that the sun's getting hot, and will be warmer and drier in the winter. There's always a substantial force gathered near an imperial capital, so buildings will be needed. Did you have any trouble getting in?"

The slight shift in his voice, from friend to officer, was subtle but clear. It always was.

"No trouble." Kavi touched his shoulder. "This always gets me in. I came to tell you, I just paid a visit to Mazad. I thought you'd like to—"

"Mazad?" Patrius' gaze sharpened. "Did anyone there see your tattoo?"

"No," said Kavi. "How could they? I'm not

exactly showing it off, you know. Someday, word of what those marks mean is going to get out."

"It already has," said Patrius. "In Mazad. They expelled our spies just a few weeks ago, and they found them all. Even a woman who'd spent years building her new identity. They examined everyone in town for that tattoo."

Cold flooded Kavi's veins. "That must have been just after I left." Just after he'd brought them word that the Hrum army was only a four-day march down the road. If they'd seen the tattoo, known him for a Hrum spy, would they have believed him? Not likely. A vision touched him — the Hrum marching up the familiar road from the south, the only warning of their approach the dust cloud raised by their boots. The farm folk scurrying down the road before them; the suburban shopkeepers snatching up goods at random and streaming toward the gate, the only gate, where only a few could enter at a time. Screaming children pulled from their mother's grip in the struggle, bodies going down amid the trampling feet. It could happen, if panic took a town.

But it hadn't happened in Mazad. The warning, the summons to gather their possessions and come in, had gone out before he left. Kavi drew a deep breath. "How could they have learned what that mark means? You assured me it was a big, dark secret that no one could be getting at!"

If he went back to Mazad now, what would he face? He couldn't return to his home . . .

"It is a secret," said Patrius, "but it isn't wholly unknown in imperial lands, and we aren't the only ones with spies. I was hoping you could tell me how they found out."

"If I knew that, I'd likely not be standing here now. Farsalan deghans hang spies. After they've told all they know." Would even the villages, where they'd known Kavi for years, trust him when this news spread? Or . . . "In the villages, they'll likely be stoning me," he added. Unless he could talk to them, make them understand first.

"Well, our spies in Mazad weren't hanged. Only expelled, as I said."

"Expelled? They weren't killed?"

"No. Not even harmed, most of them."

"Hmm." That had to be the guard commander. Tebin had said he was a sound man—peasant-born, and sensible with it. Tebin hadn't said anything of the kind about Governor Nehar.

"We've had no indications that anyone has learned of it outside Mazad," Patrius went on. "And with the city under siege, they won't be able to spread the word. You should be all right. For a time."

"And when that time ends, then what?"

"By then, if you're lucky, this will be a settled imperial province," said Patrius. "And those marks will be a badge of honor. Of service to the empire, just like our rank tattoos." He touched his own arm, where the elaborate marks of a tactimian were hidden by the cloth of his sleeve. "If you're discovered before things settle . . . You knew the risks when you took this on. But once Mazad falls, they'll have other things to think about. You should be wary, of course, but I don't think it will be a problem."

"You're sounding very certain. 'Once Mazad falls.' What I came to tell you is that Mazad is prepared for a siege. Stockpiled food, and the town guard armed and trained. Even the townsfolk have been instructed in their duties, formed up into fire brigades, and rescue squads, and whatnot. Mazad won't be taken easily."

How simple it was to sound helpful, reporting something that you knew they knew.

"We've already discovered that," said Patrius.

"Already? You've attacked Mazad already?" His tone was a masterpiece—startled, but not too startled.

"Yes. I'm surprised you didn't pass our army on the road."

Was there a trace of suspicion in Patrius' voice? "I went north after I left the city," Kavi told him. "Visiting a couple of mining camps on my route. I hadn't realized you'd be going in so fast."

He had paid those camps a flying visit to warn them of the army's approach and try to talk them into . . . Not *refusing* to sell to the Hrum—no, that would be a big mistake. But if the ore in this part of the mountains was of the poorest quality, well, that explained why there was so little to tax, now didn't it?

"Ah. Well, we've sent two tacti to besiege Mazad, and they've fought off several attacks— and suffered some casualties, if I'm reading the substrategus' . . . equivocations correctly. So I'm afraid your warning comes too late. I'll see you're paid something for it, though."

You had to keep your spies motivated, after all.

"The Wheel always turns swifter than you think it will." Kavi shook his head ruefully. "I thought sure I had time. But did you say two tacti? That'd be . . . a fifth of your army, right?"

"Yes. Why?"

"I don't think that's enough. Not with Mazad's walls."

"Ah, but Substrategus Arus swore on the iron crown that he could do it with just one tacti." Patrius' voice was rich with irony. "Who were we to say otherwise? Especially since . . . Never mind."

"Since 'we' are already arguing with Strategus Garren in the first place?" Kavi guessed.

"Governor Garren," said Patrius. "But they've cut off the city's supplies and settled in to wait them out—which is just what they should have done three hundred-plus casualties ago."

"Well, I've seen Mazad's stockpiles," said Kavi. "And they're in for a long wait. I thought Garren—oh, all right, Governor Garren—wanted Mazad to fall fast, to please his father back in the senate."

Patrius sighed. "Yes, but if he requests another five tacti, which is what . . . Well, it would be more impressive to the senate if he succeeded with the ten tacti he currently commands. And his father isn't the only one he needs to impress. Not if he wants to be governor."

"I thought if you conquered the country, you got to be governor automatically," said Kavi.

"You become governor automatically," said Patrius. "To remain governor you have to govern reasonably well. Of course, only a handful of governors have ever been dismissed. On the other hand, many of the senators were . . . dubious when Substrategus Garren was given this command. So I understand why he wants to succeed swiftly, using minimal resources."

"Conquer a country swiftly, and with minimal resources," Kavi repeated. "I'm not being any kind of soldier, but isn't that the equivalent of demanding the best possible blade, and wanting it tomorrow?"

"I'm not a weapon-smith," said Patrius. "But I've heard that it takes weeks to make a really good blade."

"And one made fast is almost certain to be flawed," Kavi confirmed. "So . . . he's spreading his troops thin, is he?"

Patrius' lips tightened. He wasn't supposed to criticize his superiors, after all. But Kavi had already noticed that, for all the business in the square, there weren't many troops here. It might not be obvious to the folk of Setesafon, but Kavi had seen the Hrum army camp before—a man hadn't been able to move without tripping over soldiers: drilling, practicing with weapons, polishing things, guarding things . . .

Had Garren kept his most disaffected officers under his eye and sent the ones who agreed with him—the incompetent ones—off to conquer the towns and subdue the countryside? Kavi suppressed a grin. He couldn't have planned it better himself. And if Garren was skimping on Setesafon's garrison, what else was he skimping on?

But the silence was stretching too long. "All right, whatever we do, let's not be criticizing the governor. Although speaking of things you haven't said, I still wish you'd told me that you'd be drafting peasants into this army of yours."

Honest anger roughened his voice even now, and Patrius sighed.

"I told you about the draft several times. That

all men fit to serve between the ages of eighteen and twenty-three must—"

"And I told you that peasants aren't fit to fight!"

"Why not?" Patrius' gaze was honestly puzzled. "I know it wasn't your custom, but all a man needs to make himself a soldier is a healthy body, and the will for it."

"Well, there you go—we haven't the will."

"You've been taught that you haven't the will," said Patrius. "But what I've seen in the early training, especially among the younger recruits, tells me otherwise."

"But . . ." Kavi remembered Sim's bright face. What could he say? *But their mothers object?*

"I know it seems strange," said Patrius. "And harsh, perhaps, but—"

"It seems like another form of slavery," said Kavi bitterly. "Your folk are being fond of that notion, aren't they?"

Patrius' brows rose, but his voice was mild. "A slave, even one of ours, would disagree with you. But slavery, and the draft, support the first and fourth principles of empire. They're not going to change. And once you become accustomed to the idea, the draft has many advantages."

"The principles of empire?" Kavi repeated curiously.

"Emperor Scandius' five principles," said Patrius. "He was—do you know anything about Hrum history?"

"No," said Kavi. The words *Why should I?* hovered on his tongue, but he bit them back. Anything he could learn about the Hrum was to the good.

"Well, originally the empire wasn't an empire, but five warring city-states. Though, sometimes one would conquer another for a time, or there would be some internal division and one state would become two. But mostly they fought each other—for centuries—until Strategus Agravius figured out that men who fight together, as a unit, are far more effective than people crashing about on their own."

Like your deghans did. The unvoiced words filled the room for a moment, then Patrius went on. "Anyway, he created the basis for our army as it is today, and promptly conquered, and unified, all the original city-states. That's why there are five points on the emperor's crown." He gestured at Kavi's shoulder, at the tattoo that echoed that crown. "And because the city he originally served was Hrumana, he called the new kingdom Hrum.

"This may surprise you"—Patrius smiled— "but they enjoyed several generations of peace, under Agravius and his heirs, and came to value it highly. With peaceful trade, and the peaceful exchange of knowledge, the Hrum cities became very rich. Until one day a neighboring kingdom, the Sca, decided to do a bit of raiding, and promptly found themselves conquered, since Agravius' heirs hadn't forgotten how to fight. That kind of thing happened several times, until finally Emperor Scandius realized that every people we conquered added to our wealth and knowledge— and that the knowledge, which can only be gained from willing people, was the real source of the wealth. So he created five principles for trans-forming a motley conglomerate of conquered peo-ples into an empire."

"And those would be?" Kavi tried to sound nonchalant, but it was hard. The empire Scandius' principles had fostered had conquered half the known world—and it showed no sign of stopping.

"The first principle is to get rid of the old rulers entirely," said Patrius. "That's where slavery comes in. I know it seems barbaric, especially when we're talking about children, but if you think of how other countries dispose of the governments they cast down . . . Well, I think you'll agree that there are worse ways."

Kavi's eyes fell. The Farsalans had never conquered anyone, unless you counted the demons who were said to have dwelled in Farsala in the time of legends, but he'd listened to traders who had traveled in Kadesh, and in the savage lands beyond. There were indeed worse ways.

"The second principle is to levy taxes, but never so heavily that people will rebel. And even more important is that no part of the empire is ever forced to pay a higher percentage than the others. The third principle is to give people fair value in exchange for their taxes: just laws, roads, aqueducts, sewers, public baths . . . When people see what their taxes buy, the impulse to rebel usually dies. Though not the grumbling, I'm afraid."

Patrius' usually sober eyes danced, and Kavi laughed. "No, I expect folks will always grumble about taxes. I can guess at the next part—these roads, and baths, and whatnot are built by your army."

"Which brings us to the fourth principle," said Patrius. "The army comes first, always. All fit men give five years of their lives to it. It defends our borders, enforces law, builds public works—"

"And conquers the next nation down the road," Kavi finished dryly.

"Yes, but that's less important than the fifth principle," said Patrius. "That there will be peace within the empire. And it's army service, imposed on all the empire's populations, that creates peace. Not enforces it—creates it. Your men will put on our tabards and march into other lands, and in their hearts, they'll still be Farsalan peasants. But when they return five years later, they'll be Hrum soldiers. And in just a few decades, in your people's hearts as well as by force of arms, Farsala will be a part of the Iron Empire."

"And when it happens in folks' hearts," said Kavi softly, "that's what makes it real."

He could see it clearly, in his imagination. Eager, bright-eyed boys like Sim, marched off into Kadesh, or even farther lands, where folks would look at their scarlet cloaks and see Hrum soldiers. Soon they would begin to think of themselves that way. Kavi had never before considered the unified might of a twenty-eight-nation empire, but now he did, and he shivered.

They could crush Mazad like a walnut, if they brought in enough troops. And there was nothing to stop them, except for Garren's prideful foolishness.

On the other hand, as a peddler Kavi had found that foolishness and pride were two of the most powerful forces known to man. His job would be to stoke that pride, use the foolishness, and never make a move so bold it might pressure Garren into forgetting those things and bringing in a large army, as sensible men like Patrius were no doubt urging him to.

That shouldn't be impossible. His folk might not be warriors, but that didn't mean they weren't effective. Kavi already had a few ideas.

THE YOUNG DEGHAN WENT FIRST *to the mighty fortress of Mazad, for it was the only place in Farsala that might withstand the Hrum's army.*

Mazad's governor had learned of the deghans' fate, and he trembled with fear.

"Stand firm," the youth told him. "Be strong. Mazad must hold while I build a new army."

"Build an army from what?" the governor demanded. "From bones and dust? Our warriors are slain, and the wealth of Farsala taken. What is there left for us to do, except die?"

"Hold Mazad," the young deghan repeated. "And I will build an army. Not of deghans—as you say, not enough survive—but of farmers, craftsmen, and merchants. I will

take any man, regardless of rank or trade, who is strong of arm, stout of heart, and willing to fight for Farsala."

"An army of peasants? Against the Hrum? Only Sorahb," the governor scoffed, "could do such a thing."

"Then call me Sorahb," said the youth. "For I am going to do it."

THUS IT WAS THAT SORAHB gathered a great army of farmers and carpenters, miners and merchants. He taught them to fight as he had been taught, with horse, sword, and lance. It was hard for those peasants, for they were not raised to fight, and were reluctant to abandon the old ways. But for Sorahb's sake they did try, for they wished to defend Farsala, and they loved their young commander well.

CHAPTER SEVEN

JIAAN

H E CALLED HIMSELF *WHAT*?"
"Sorahb, sir." A grin lifted
the miner's scruffy mustache.
"By Azura's hand, I swear that's
what he said. Oh, not that he was Sorahb; he was
just passing on his commander's instructions. But
that's the name his commander's using. Someone's
got a pretty fair nerve, if you ask me. But aren't
you working for him too? When you showed up, I
thought—"

"We are," said Fasal swiftly. "We just hadn't
realized that someone else had reached this camp.
I . . . ah, I take it he delivered the message?"

Jiaan glared at him, though he could see Fasal's
point. To tell these men that the so-called Farsalan

resistance was so scattered and disorganized that the army didn't even know who else was involving themselves . . . Well, it wouldn't generate much confidence.

Lamplight glowed on the face of the mining camp's headman—which seemed very odd in mid-morning. But when Jiaan had mentioned that it might be better if few people saw their faces, the headman had led them to a small room carved into the rock off the main mine shaft. It obviously served as a place for the miners to eat, and perhaps even sleep when the winter cold set in. But now it was empty except for themselves and the headman, seated at the dusty table.

Jiaan and Fasal had spent the last hot, dusty month training their new army, and trying to visit enough towns and villages to get the word out that the army was gathering and needed more men— and offhand, Jiaan couldn't decide which task was going worse. At least the archers and foot soldiers who had survived could teach what they knew to the totally ignorant men who trickled into the hidden croft. But trying to recruit more men, without getting caught by the Hrum themselves or revealing their secret to anyone who might pass it on to the Hrum, was like trying to balance on the edge of a sword. And juggle.

The good news was that few Farsalans were inclined to help the Hrum. The draft, which had now been formally announced in all the towns, if not yet in the smaller villages, was bitterly resented. No one was thrilled about the new taxes, either, though as far as Jiaan could tell they weren't much different than those the deghans had collected—lower in some places, higher in others, but averaging out about the same. And the Hrum taxes would go for good roads, and straight, well-drained canals, where most of the money the deghans collected had paid for the gold plates and fine furnishings the Hrum had looted from the deghans' houses.

When he'd mentioned that to Fasal—once the young deghan finished sputtering with outrage— Fasal had pointed out to Jiaan that telling that to men they hoped to recruit to fight against the Hrum was a really bad idea.

Jiaan knew that—it was why he'd only offered his thoughts to Fasal. Concealing how very disorganized they were was just more of the same, but lying to men he hoped to lead felt . . . awkward. Jiaan sighed.

But the miner was answering Fasal without a shadow of suspicion in his voice. "Yes, he asked us to show the Hrum only our worst ore, and advised us to hide our young men so they couldn't be drafted—not that we hadn't figured that one out ourselves. As for the ore," amusement lit his eyes, "well, that seems to be taking care of itself."

"What do you mean?" Jiaan asked. This "Sorahb" had advised the miners to hide their best ore from the Hrum? How clever! And why hadn't he thought of it?

"Word spreads among the camps, you know," the miner replied. "We passed Sorahb's message on to the west, but the Hrum who are occupying Desafon had already visited several of their camps before they could receive it."

"So they'll know that our ore is good," said Jiaan wearily. Too bad. It had been an excellent idea.

"Well, they saw our ore right enough," said the miner. "But according to what we heard, they sneered at its quality, and offered far too low a price. Seems our steel's not good enough to serve the 'Iron Empire.' Though having seen that bit of blade the . . . Sorahb's messenger brought, I can understand that."

"He had a Hrum sword?" Jiaan's voice was sharp with excitement. That had been the other thing he intended to ask the miners about, but without a sample . . .

"Not a whole sword, just a piece of one. Though that was actually better, since you could see the layers inside. If you looked close, in a good light, that is. I never imagined you could make steel that thin."

"Layers?" Fasal asked.

"The whole piece was a series of layers, dark metal and light," the miner confirmed. "That's what's making the pattern on the surface, where they break through each other. But they're unbelievably thin, and I've no idea how the Hrum do that. Ask a sword smith—that's what I told the other one. I've a guess as to what the layers are, but that's all."

"What are they?" Jiaan asked.

"Well, different kinds of iron ore make different colors of steel," said the miner. "You likely haven't noticed, for it's subtle. But the lighter steel is softer and more flexible, and the dark is better, at least for weapons. It's harder, and will take a sharper edge. Of course, if it's too dark it gets brittle, so swords are made with a mid-to-hard mixture. But that Hrum sword was made of hard and soft layers, not a mixture—and the dark layers were darker than any steel I've ever seen. So maybe they'd a right to be sneering at our ore, though djinn take me if I understand why putting the steel in layers makes the sword both sharp and flexible. When we mix the metals, we just get steel that's medium flexible and medium sharp."

A cart rattled past in the main shaft outside, but the miner didn't even look up.

"The ore that makes dark steel isn't common, not even in the mountains," he continued. "I've heard men say they've seen signs of it in the badlands, and rumor has it that their ore works better than our dark. In fact, rumor has it that their ore is better than any ore ever found, more valuable than gold, and when you dig it up, it's already been shaped into swords by the hand of Azura himself. But that's rumor—the only thing I know for truth is that folk who go into the Suud's desert aren't coming back." He shrugged, leaning back in his chair, but his gaze was intent.

"We're going—," Fasal began, but Jiaan elbowed him sharply in the ribs.

"I'm glad you got the message," he said. "And

our commander will be glad as well. Could you tell us who passed it on so promptly? We'll see he gets proper credit for it."

The miner scratched his chin. "Well, he asked me not to be giving out his name, just as you did. And since you're both working for the same luna—ah, person, you can find out from him if you need to."

"Sorahb isn't a lunatic," said Fasal firmly. "We will free Farsala from the Hrum! And your refusal to sell them your ore will help our cause."

It sounded pretty crazy to Jiaan, listening to Fasal say it, but the miner just smiled and nodded. Though all he'd really agreed to do was to sell the Hrum substandard ore for a high price, so he could afford to smile. Nonetheless . . .

"We thank you for your assistance," said Jiaan, rising to end the interview. "If any of your men chose to join the Farsalan army instead of yielding to the Hrum's draft, have them go to the place where the Khaquan River flows out of the foothills and wait there. A guide will appear to take them to the army camp within a few days."

Fasal was frowning. "But why don't we—"

"No," said Jiaan. "Forgive us for leaving so abruptly, but we have far to go."

Emerging from the mine's dimness, the summer sunlight was blinding.

"All right," Fasal muttered, shielding his eyes with one hand. "Why didn't you want to tell him that we're going to the desert next? You said that miners looking for better ore have been sending expeditions into the badlands for centuries. They might have offered us a guide."

"And we'd have had to refuse," said Jiaan. "Which would be embarrassing at best, and insulting at worst. I told you, the commander thought the Suud killed the miners he was sent to find—and would have killed him and his troops, except that he offered them no harm. If the Suud and the miners are at war, the last thing we want is to show up with a miner as our guide."

Jiaan's vision had cleared enough to find his way to the post where Rakesh was tethered. Jiaan untied his reins and mounted, knowing that the well-trained horse would find the way, even if his rider was still squinting.

Fasal, fumbling with his horse's tether, snorted. "Peasants squabbling with barbarians hardly constitutes a war. If you want to create a secure base camp in the desert, then take some men and build it! We've got over a thousand men now—I can't imagine why you think you need the Suud's permission."

"You'll see," said Jiaan grimly. "Soon enough, you'll see."

BUT FIVE DAYS LATER . . . "We haven't even set eyes on the Suud!" Fasal complained. "If they're afraid to show themselves to just two men, what makes you think they could do anything to an army?"

"They haven't shown themselves," Jiaan admitted. "But that doesn't mean they're afraid. I wonder what they're going to do, now that we've stopped letting them lead us in circles."

The moon was just past full, so there was plenty of light for the horses to find their way through the maze of rock spires. But the still, moonlit landscape was so eerie that a distant jackal's howl was enough to make Jiaan jump. And the light clearly displayed Fasal's grin when he did so.

They had descended to the desert three evenings ago. Even Fasal had been impressed by the trail that snaked down the great cliff, though Jiaan was annoyed to see it hadn't left him damp-palmed with fear. On the other hand, if Fasal hadn't been present to remind Jiaan of his dignity, he might have succumbed to his own impulse and crawled down the trail—a fine picture that would have presented to the watching Suud.

After several nights in the desert, Jiaan was certain that their every move was being watched, even during the day, when the Suud had to wear robes to protect their white skin from the blazing sun.

Jiaan had insisted that he and Fasal sleep during the day and search for the Suud at night, as a matter of courtesy. To show up at a Suud camp in midday would be as rude as waking anyone else up in the middle of the night. That was why he'd timed his visit to coincide with the full moon.

But after his first day in the desert, Jiaan had realized another advantage to the Suud's habits— he wasn't certain either he and Fasal, or the horses, would survive the heat of the desert on a midsummer day. Jiaan had never encountered anything like it; the dry air seemed to suck moisture from his mouth and body. Even sleeping in the shade, he woke at dusk with an aching head and a ravenous thirst.

The first two nights, he and Fasal had followed the Suud's small, clear footprints wherever they led. Fasal, because he believed they were about to come upon the camp at any moment, Jiaan, because he hoped that eventually the Suud would get tired of leading them in circles and make contact. And the fact that the tracks had crossed streams often enough to allow them to fill their water skins and let the horses drink, assured him that at least the Suud weren't trying to kill them. If they hadn't been led to those streams, and the stream they now followed, they'd have been forced to leave the desert on the second night. But if the Suud weren't trying to drive them off, why didn't they reveal themselves? The last time he'd been in the desert, his Suud guides had made him feel welcome.

Of course, Jiaan reflected grimly, the last time he'd been invited.

"I still don't know why you let them lead us around like that," Fasal grumbled. When Fasal had finally realized they were traveling in circles, the rocks had rung with his outrage. Jiaan hoped none of the watchers spoke Faran. "There's hardly any water in this Azura-forsaken pit. If we keep following this stream we're bound to come to one of their encampments, sooner or later."

"That's what I'm afraid of," said Jiaan. "If we start heading straight for one of their camps, what do you think the Suud are going to do?" Though he had to admit, he too was tired of simply going where the Suud led them. That was why he'd agreed to the change of plan.

"Don't be such a . . ." *Peasant coward.* ". . . so silly," Fasal corrected himself. "What could a bunch of barbarians possibly —"

Fasal's mare began to buck. Fasal wrapped his legs around her barrel and swore. Jiaan eyed the ground at her feet, looking for a serpent or a scorpion — anything that could have caused her reaction, but there was nothing there.

Then Rakesh snorted, shied like a gazelle, and began to kick as if surrounded by a swarm of hornets. Jiaan's legs could get no grip on his slippery hide. If he was to be bucked off, he'd best do it with as much control as possible. Rakesh bucked and Jiaan, feeling his rump leave the saddle, released his death grip on reins and mane and let himself fly free.

By some miracle he managed to land on his feet, off balance, staggering. But he might have remained upright if not for the spear butt that struck his ankles, sweeping his feet from under him. He hit the ground hard and lay still, blinking up at the cloud of spear points that hovered over him. It was several moments before he could tear his eyes from the glittering steel to look at the grim, white faces beyond them.

The sound of thudding hooves drew his attention. Fasal was a true deghan, and he rode like one. It took a carefully timed blow from a spear butt to knock him off the gyrating mare, who promptly stopped bucking and stood, snorting and shivering. Rakesh had also quieted, and Jiaan's gaze returned to his captors.

At least they were using the spear butts to subdue them, not the points. That was a good sign, right?

"I hope you speak Faran," he said.

If they did, they weren't admitting it. Only the bouncing babble of Suud sounded as a man approached the group around Jiaan. He was even shorter than most of the small, fine-boned Suud, his hair a cloud of white curls around his stern face. He said something and the spears withdrew—but not very far. He held out a leather cord and motioned for Jiaan to sit up. The Suud was small, but his arms were banded with muscles. Jiaan still might have tried something stupid, if it weren't for those hovering spear points. Besides . . .

"I didn't come here to fight with you," said Jiaan. He sat up slowly, and at a gesture from the man, turned and knelt with his hands behind him. "I came to ask for your help."

Firm hands bound his wrists together. The cord was tight, but it wasn't uncomfortable. "Not fight," Jiaan repeated. "Help. I need your help."

If they understood, they showed no sign of it, and Jiaan cursed himself for his lack of forethought. The Suud he'd dealt with before had spoken Faran, rough and fractured, but enough that Jiaan could communicate. But those Suud were traders the high commander had found in the marketplace at Setesafon—of course they spoke Faran. He had been foolish to assume that all the Suud did.

But since the Hrum had invaded, no Suud had come to the Farsalan markets, so he couldn't have brought a translator even if he'd thought of it. Their absence was one of the things that had made him hope they might be willing to help. Now that hope seemed naive.

Four of the spear carriers remained to guard him, while the rest went to surround Fasal, who seemed to have been stunned by the fall. It was the first time Jiaan had ever seen a large group of the tribesmen; in the markets there were never more than three or four of them, and the tight-woven robes they wore to protect their milk white skin also obscured their strangeness. Here, in their moonlit desert, they wore only a cloth wrapped around their hips—even the women. Did they allow women to hunt, perhaps even to fight, as the Hrum did?

Jiaan looked away from their naked breasts. Ordinarily he would have found the sight . . . interesting, at least. But the Suud women, moving over the sand like ghosts, with their white hair drifting around their shoulders, were just too strange. Jiaan would as soon have bedded a corpse.

Last autumn, dealing with the Suud who had helped him escort the lady Soraya to the hidden croft, Jiaan had dismissed the rumor that the Suud were some sort of lesser djinn, or related to them.

Many deghans believed in the djinn, or at least claimed to, when it was to their advantage, but his father hadn't, and his peasant mother had called them deghan nonsense. Watching now, as several spear butts prodded a dazed-looking Fasal to his feet, Jiaan's mind still knew the Suud were human, but his prickling nerves were no longer quite so certain.

A spear butt connected with his rump, bringing him to his feet. The Suud talked among themselves as they marched Jiaan and Fasal through the rock maze. They still followed the stream, Jiaan noticed, so Fasal had probably been right that their camp was beside it. Jiaan was concerned for Fasal, who staggered along in silence. His hair was dark, so Jiaan hadn't seen the blood till it ran down the back of his neck and stained his shirt. But when he tried to speak to Fasal, a white-skinned hand rose and cuffed his head. The blow was more warning than punishment, but it still made him stumble, and Fasal looked over and met his eyes, shaking his head slightly.

Jiaan subsided, aware of the Suud's sharp gazes. He had met peasants whose eyes were pale, but none who had eyes with that unnatural, crystalline iris. In the moonlight you could barely see the irises at all, just black pupils lost in a sea of white. Like djinn. But the Suud traders he'd dealt with just a few months ago had eyes like that, and though Jiaan had found their appearance strange, he had laughed and joked with them. He had liked them.

Being invited made a difference, it seemed.

But if he had led himself and Fasal to their deaths, why hadn't they been killed already? No. Jiaan took a shuddering breath. The only reason for taking prisoners was because you wanted them alive. They hadn't even been harmed, except for the damage they'd sustained being bucked off their horses.

Those same horses were now being led by the last of the Suud, as quietly as if nothing had happened. How had the Suud made Rakesh buck like that? Throwing small rocks? Jiaan wouldn't have thought Rakesh would react that violently, but horses feared what they didn't understand, and if several had struck him at once . . . Jiaan pushed the thought of djinn magic from his mind. The commander had lived among the Suud for a time, and he said they were just people—good people

171

for the most part. And the commander was never wrong. Right?

Their arrival at the camp distracted Jiaan from his whirling, half-panicked thoughts. There were more Suud here, more women, and tiny, shrill-voiced children. He had never seen tents like these, round, and arching over bent poles. Their tops were made of stitched hides, but their sides seemed to be made of Farsalan silk. They were scattered like bubbles across a flat crescent, nestled in a wide bend of the stream. Fires glowed in front of most of them, and a huge firepit, with an iron cauldron hanging above it, marked the rough center of the camp.

Jiaan had no time to see more. He and Fasal were thrust into one of the tents—the door was so low he had to shuffle through on his knees, bending his head. Two guards followed them inside, making the small, hutlike tent very crowded, even after they pitched out several baskets and bedrolls to make room. Firelight flickered through the silk walls, but the light was dim. The guards pushed Jiaan down, and then rolled him over to untie his wrists. The ache in his shoulders intensified as he moved his arms. Jiaan murmured, "Thank you," and was cuffed for his pains.

And he'd spoken too soon, for the guards pulled his wrists in front of him and bound them to one of the sturdy poles that supported the tent. It would be more comfortable, but Jiaan feared that only meant he was going to be there for some time.

"I need to talk to some—" Another cuff, harder this time. Fasal hadn't even tried to speak. In another man, Jiaan would have taken that for common sense; with Fasal, it made Jiaan fear that his head injury was worse than he was letting on.

Jiaan lay on his side, gazing at the tent pole to which his wrists were tied. After a time, he tried to loosen it. He took care to move slowly, but a spear butt nudged him immediately and he subsided. The pole hadn't shifted at all, as far as he could tell—it must be driven deep into the sand. More time passed. An old man entered the tent, carrying a bowl. Jiaan had to twist his neck, but his eyes had adapted enough for him to watch as the man bathed Fasal's head.

"What's in that water?" Fasal demanded suddenly. "My headache's better."

The cuff was aimed at his head, but the old man intercepted it and said something sharp in

Suud. The guard shrugged and rapped Fasal's hip with his spear butt instead.

As his fear of being slaughtered wore off, captivity proved to be a cursed bore. Just before dawn the guards took them to relieve themselves, and drink from the stream, but then they were returned to the tent.

Jiaan hoped their guards would leave them, and sleep during the day, but of course the Suud weren't that foolish. They came and went in three shifts, carefully robed to protect them from the blazing sun.

At least Jiaan discovered why the tents were built as they were, for the leather roof made a solid patch of shade, and the silk sides could be rolled up, to admit the breezes that blew off the creek, or rolled down to block the sunlight. If he'd been lying on a bedroll instead of the gravelly sand, and if his hands had been unbound, Jiaan would have been as comfortable as it was possible to be in the heat of the desert day.

As it was, he dozed fitfully, waking when the guards' shift changed, or when Fasal, who was making up for his earlier silence, was cuffed for talking.

Jiaan was never so grateful to see the sun set. Since his side of the tent had been raised, he was free to watch the tribespeople emerge from their tents, yawning and stretching in the gathering dusk.

He and Fasal were taken, one at a time, to wash in the stream and eat several pieces of flat bread spread with some sort of vegetable paste. It was sweetish, and oddly seasoned, but by now Jiaan was hungry enough to eat anything.

He hoped to be allowed some freedom—or at least that they would keep the tent side rolled up so he could watch the camp, but after he ate, he was returned to the same place and bound there, and the silk was rolled down again. He considered protesting but Fasal beat him to it, and Jiaan winced at the thud of wood on flesh. The guards seemed to be getting tired of Fasal.

More time passed. Jiaan alternated between dozing and wondering if it would be worth being beaten to get some attention.

He was on the point of deciding that it might be, when he heard a disturbance in the camp. As the night passed, he had become accustomed to the rise and fall of Suud voices. Now there were many voices, all babbling at once, and though the discussion started in the distance, it seemed to be moving closer. They didn't sound frightened or angry, so the Farsalan army hadn't miraculously come to the rescue. The Suud sounded . . . welcoming? Excited?

The crowd stopped not far from the tent, and Jiaan heard a woman's voice, both sharp and amused. Then a series of rapid steps, and the tent flaps few open.

Jiaan twisted his neck and saw the wrinkled face of an old Suud woman peering within.

"I'm sorry," she said in accented Faran. "You will be uncomfortable. It takes time to bring me here. Things will be better soon."

Jiaan turned his face back to the tent wall, hiding the tears of relief until he could blink them back. But true deghans were evidently made of sterner stuff.

"Release us this instant!" Fasal demanded.

"Ah. Maybe. But not the instant." The old woman began speaking in Suud and the guards untied Jiaan's wrists, allowing him to crawl from the tent. He hoped never to enter it again. The moonlit night was gloriously cool, and he'd have felt free if he hadn't been surrounded by a fence of spear points.

The old woman followed Fasal out. "Better?"

"Much better," said Jiaan, smiling at her. "But there's no need for this." He gestured at the spears, taking care to move slowly. It wouldn't do to get himself skewered when the translator had finally arrived.

"Maybe," said the woman. "Maybe not. If you did not wear your father's face, you would not be here now."

"My fath—These people knew my father?"

"This was the . . . group? clan? where he stayed," said the woman. "But the ones who speak Faran are gone now."

Gone as in absent, or gone as in dead? Jiaan couldn't think of a tactful way to ask, but Fasal had no such qualms.

"If the high commander was treated as rudely as we've been, it's a wonder you're not all 'gone,'" he said stiffly. "Bring us to the person in charge—we require the Suud to assist the Farsalan army."

Jiaan winced, but the woman grinned. "Always need 'assistance,' you people." Why did that make her face soften? But the gentle expression soon vanished. "So, you come to ask for help. What help?"

"We're forming an army to fight the Hrum," said Jiaan hastily, before Fasal could say something even worse. "They have . . . How much do you know about the Hrum?"

"Not much." The woman's gaze seemed casual, but Jiaan could feel the intensity beneath it. "Hard to know a people who do not teach their language."

"They don't . . . teach their language?" asked Jiaan, puzzled.

"Do not allow army people to teach it to Farsalans," the woman confirmed. "They think it is safer, to speak and Farsalans not understand. But all learn Farsalan themselves. Not stupid."

"No," said Jiaan slowly. "Not stupid at all. That's why we need your help. Our army is small, and hidden, but soon it will grow, and we'll start using it against the Hrum. When that happens, I fear they will discover where we're hidden—and we will still have a smaller force than theirs." The Farsalan army would always be smaller than the Hrum's, he feared. "So we need another place to hide. A secure base where the Hrum can't reach us, where they couldn't even find us . . . unless you guided them."

Even the old woman's formidable composure was shaken. "You want to bring your army here? Your father promised never to come back with anyone, though he could not stop others."

"I didn't know that," said Jiaan. Why had his father promised such a thing? "My father is dead, but even if I'd known of his promise, I would have come. We need to build a base in the desert. But we came to ask your permission, not to act without it."

Fasal snorted. "We can build—"

Jiaan hastily stepped on his foot, despite the shifting spears.

The woman frowned. "I must speak with others." She turned away, and the spear points prevented Jiaan from following.

"Maybe we'll finally get to talk to someone with authority," said Fasal. "Why did you stop me? We can build a base here, with or without their permission. If they knew that, maybe they'd leave us alone."

Jiaan looked at their guards' wary, white faces. A moment ago he would have sworn that none of them spoke Faran—now he wasn't so sure.

"You're an idiot," he murmured, smiling at the guards. If they understood, their expressions didn't show it. "We came to ask these people's help. And we *can't* do it without them. Suppose we don't return to the croft, then what?"

Half a dozen older men and women had gathered around the translator. They spoke with animation, using their hands for emphasis. It seemed to Jiaan that they were arguing, though he couldn't tell who disagreed with whom about what.

"Then the army sends a squad to find us," said Fasal impatiently. "They knew where we were going, and the miners will tell them when we left their camp."

Several of the people arguing with the woman were looking in their direction now. It made Jiaan nervous. Had Fasal somehow missed the fact that the Suud had captured the two of them with no trouble at all?

"And suppose the squad doesn't come back, then what? Miners have been sending expeditions—squadrons of men—into this desert for centuries, and they never return. Do you really think they all got lost and died of starvation?"

Fasal scowled. "But the Suud don't kill people — they're supposed to be timid!"

The argument seemed to be over; several Suud were grinning now, and one was coming toward them.

"Of course they don't kill people when they come to trade baskets in the market," said Jiaan. "But careful isn't the same as timid. And even if it was, it doesn't matter — all they'd have to do to get rid of us is provide the Hrum with a few guides."

Fasal's mouth snapped shut, but Jiaan took little satisfaction in winning the debate. Something in the expression of the man who approached them made him brace himself, though he didn't know why. A flurry of orders were issued to the guards, and he and Fasal were taken over to the main firepit, where four men were driving a pair of tall, sharpened stakes into the ground. Their purpose became clear when Jiaan and Fasal were pushed down to sit with their backs to the stakes, their wrists bound together on the other side.

Jiaan sighed. Freedom had been good while it lasted, and leaning against the stake wasn't too uncomfortable. Yet.

A man came up, humming under his breath, and laid an iron fire rod down, with its tip in the coals. He looked at them, grinned, and walked away. Jiaan's stomach knotted. *Surely not!* They didn't have any information the Suud might want!

At least Fasal had finally fallen silent.

After a few moments the old woman approached. Touching the handle carefully, she lifted the rod and examined the blackened tip. "Not for a time," she announced.

"What . . ." Jiaan's throat was dry. "What have you decided?"

"We do not know you well enough to decide," said the woman. "So we must know. You will take our warrior's test, for courage, and"—her hands groped for a missing word—"for good, strong spirit. Then we will know better if we can trust you."

Looking at the rod, now nestled back in the coals, Jiaan found his voice was quite gone.

"We will take your test." Fasal spoke proudly, but his voice held a hint of a tremor.

Jiaan swallowed.

The old woman smiled. "Your father passed

the warrior's test, and he asked for less than you."

Jiaan tried frantically to remember any burn scars on his father's body—but his father had been fighting the Kadeshi since he was younger than Jiaan. He'd had dozens of scars.

"We ask a great deal, I know," he said. "But what will it prove if we pass your test, or if we fail for that matter? Surely you don't . . . Do all your warriors have to do this?"

And if they did, how bad could it be?

"Not all," said the woman. "Hardly any."

Very bad.

"But the last . . . warrior who approached us brought a gift, and she asked very little." The woman settled herself cross-legged, a careful distance from the fire. "And she asked politely—a wondrous thing, that was." She laughed softly, curse her.

"We could bring a gift," said Jiaan. "A big gift."

"Don't sound so craven," hissed Fasal. "It's a *warrior's* test."

The woman laughed again. "Not a gift to buy what you want. And it is not a matter of price, though that question comes. Why should we help you? These Hrum do not trouble us."

"They will," said Fasal. "They are evil—djinn in human form! Once they've defeated us, they will burn your camps, kill your men, and rape your women. And those they don't kill, they take as slaves."

Was the rod's tip beginning to glow? "That's not true," said Jiaan absently. "They don't rape, and they only burn and take slaves when people resist them. But their nature is to conquer. And they will draft your young men into their army for five years."

"That's a problem," the woman admitted. "We need our young men. But we have always kept alone, and the desert is ours. It will be hard to get anyone to change that."

The iron tip was definitely beginning to glow, but something in her voice drew Jiaan's gaze. "You'll have to change," he said. "Whether you help us or not. The world has changed."

"So it has," the woman sighed. "The omm shilshadu, the creation spirit, must be very bored, to have kicked the world so hard this time."

Jiaan found he would rather watch her wrinkled face than the glowing iron. "Kicked it?"

"Yes. This is why the world changes." She leaned forward, as if she was sharing a secret. "The spirit of creation walked through the darkness, making small lights, but when it had made many and many, it grew bored with them. So here, in the middle of things, it sat down and made the world and all the life and people in it. And it liked the world, and went off to make others. But after long and long, it grew bored with making worlds, so it came back to see if the first one it made had done anything interesting while it was gone.

"But when it reached here the world was just the same. The omm shilshadu was angry, so it kicked the world, and water went over the land, and grass places became swamps, and . . . well, many things happened. That was the first time the world changed. It has changed two more times since, and I am afraid this is time four. It's hard to live with a great spirit who gets bored."

Her ancient eyes danced. Despite the sinking dread in his heart, Jiaan smiled. "Yes, it is. May I ask your name? I'm Jiaan, and my friend is Fasal."

"Better than the last one," the woman said. "I had to tell her to ask. My name is Maok."

She rose and picked up the iron rod—the tip glowed cherry red. But before Jiaan had time to do anything more embarrassing than flinch, she thrust the glowing point into the sand.

"What are . . . I don't understand."

"You passed the test," said Maok. "As your father did. You told the truth, even afraid, even not thinking about it. As your father did."

What had his father told the truth about? Jiaan's thoughts tumbled like a stone in a flooding stream, but it seemed he wasn't going to be burned with hot iron. He drew a deep breath and tried to stop shaking. "Does that mean you'll let us bring our army here? And hide us from the Hrum?"

"That I cannot say," said Maok. "I must speak with many people before we answer that. It is hard to know what to do."

"You can change a little for us," said Jiaan. "Or you can change a lot for the Hrum. I'm sorry, but those are your only choices."

"Few choices? Maybe. But not few questions. A big question: Will you win over the Hrum, or will the Hrum win over you?"

"We will win," said Fasal instantly. He sounded more confident himself, now that the rod's glowing point was cooling in the sand. "By Azura's hand, I swear it."

As if the people who knew that the Hrum refused to teach conquered people their language wouldn't know that the Hrum had beaten the Farsalans in every battle to date.

"We're going to try," said Jiaan. "I think we have a chance. A better one with your help."

Her shrewd gaze searched his face. "They said you are his son," said Maok. She looked at Fasal, and then at the rod buried in the sand and sighed. "I will meet you at the top of the canyon where you come from the desert, at the night of moon bright. Full moon, you would say. I will answer then. But I cannot say what it will be. When the world is kicked, it is hard to trust. Hard to remember old debts, even shilshadu debts. Even big ones."

What did my father do for these people?

"I'm not my father," said Jiaan. "You owe nothing to me."

"We know that," said Maok. "We will soon learn what you are."

CHAPTER EIGHT

KAVI

THE CART LURCHED DOWN the road in the golden light of sunset. The barrels lurched on the cart, and inside the barrel, Kavi banged the back of his head against the unyielding wood and suppressed a curse. He knew that the creaks of cart and ox yoke, and the rattle of the barrels against the sides of the cart and one another, would hide an occasional soft thump—but it might not cover a furious diatribe about the reality of the Hrum's much vaunted roads.

Of course, the Hrum had constructed the track that led from Desafon to their huge, new supply depot in a bit of a hurry.

Kavi had spent many nerve-wracking weeks

preparing for this night. The tattoo on his shoulder might get him into Hrum camps without question, but finding out when essential supplies were going to be shipped, and doing that without showing so much interest that he might be remembered later, was far harder. At least finding men in and around Desafon to aid him hadn't proved as difficult as he'd feared. Their sons were already in training with the army, and the first group was due to march out in little more than a month.

Given the amount of anger that had stirred up in the town, it had been absurdly arrogant of the Hrum to hire local people to build their big warehouse. Despite his discomfort, a slow grin spread over Kavi's face. In fairness to the local Hrum commander, he hadn't had much choice. Substrategus Arus' ever-mounting demands for more troops to assault Mazad, and the need to take and garrison the smaller Farsalan towns, had stripped the garrison left in "quiet" Desafon to the bone.

The barrels lurched again, knocking against one another. It was like being inside a drum, and Kavi flung up his hands to cover his ears and then

winced as his elbow banged into the wood. Then
the barrel jostled to a stop. Kavi's heartbeat quickened as he realized that the cart had stopped. They
had arrived. He tried to brace himself inside the
barrel. At least he needn't worry that the difference in weight would be detected—the Hrum
guarded the carts going in, and there were two soldiers patrolling outside the warehouse, but local
people drove the carts and did the heavy work of
loading and unloading.

The hardest part had been to set this up in such
a way that no local carter or merchant would be
implicated, but with Kavi's connections in the
countryside, it had proved possible—easy in the
end. No reason for anyone to suspect a bargeload
of wine barrels floating up the big, slow
Hamaveran River. The grower claimed he had a
good crop coming on, and needed ready coin to
pay the cooper.

The Hrum ordnancer had tasted the wine and
approved it—Farsalan wine was good, and this
was the best Kavi had been able to coax out of the
farmer, who had big grape fields and three half-
grown sons. Of course, the grower's mark on the
barrels in no way resembled the farmer's own. The

farmer himself, an unaccustomed mustache obscuring his face and his hair stained dark with walnut dye, had consented to come and act as the seller. Kavi had wanted to do that himself, but a twenty-year-old farmer with a scarred hand would be too easily connected to a certain young peddler whom all too many of the Hrum were coming to know.

The farmer had done well, even bargaining up the price when he offered his bargemen as loaders. After all, if the Hrum used local men they'd have to pay them, and the Hrum paid fair. Just as they would be too fair to blame the local carters when the load of wine they carried turned out to be something quite different. For two other men rode in barrels alongside Kavi's, and while most of the barrels were filled with wine, several were filled with lamp oil, to act as an accelerant.

And one was filled with water, to give the men who would set the fire time for rescue to arrive.

Kavi's barrel tipped to one side, and rolled on its bottom rim. Kavi's forehead slammed into the wood, and his stomach rolled at the motion. *Please, Azura, don't let me get sick in here.* Within moments the barrel was lifted and fell off the cart into the waiting grip of the loaders, two of them for each barrel. Kavi's barrel rocked and bounced as it was carried into the warehouse and banged down on the floor, but at least they hadn't dumped him on his head.

Kavi listened while the rest of the barrels were unloaded. A few bumped against his, but for the most part he was able to relax—as much as he could in such a cramped space. Eventually the muffled sounds of trampling feet and moving barrels ceased. A few more moments passed. Kavi guessed they were now locking the supply depot's big double doors. The carts would soon be on their way back to town, but they still had a long time to wait. Time for the carts to reach their destination, for the loaders to rejoin the barge, which would set off down the river as soon as darkness fell. Time for the Hrum in the nearby encampment—which was a town now, all built in wood—to settle into sleep, leaving only the sentries patrolling. The reason the Hrum felt safe with just two men marching around the warehouse was that a single shout would alert the camp's watch, and the troops could arrive as soon as they put on boots and grabbed a sword and shield. That, too, was a part of Kavi's plan. In fact, his life would depend on it.

The padded mallet, thumping on the lid, made the barrel ring. Kavi crouched with his arms over his head as the lid thumped twice more, then it tipped down and was lifted out.

"Why so early?" he whispered. He could barely make out Dalad's face.

"I thought you'd be more comfortable out here with us." Dalad's voice was low, but not a whisper. "You'll be getting cramps if you stay in there much longer."

"I've already got cramps," Kavi grumbled, struggling to stand. "And it's still light out. What if someone from the camp comes in for something? Are the doors locked?"

"If someone comes we'll hear when they unlock the doors, and hide behind the crates. Don't be such an old woman."

Dalad was a year older than Kavi, a woodworker, like so many of Desafon's townsfolk. But he already owned his own shop, which he would lose when the Hrum drafted him. When Kavi had started looking for recruits for this part of his scheme, Dalad had seemed sober and responsible—not at all the reckless lunatic he'd turned out to be. Of course, this part of the plan needed a lunatic. And his younger brother, Tur, who was mute though not deaf, and who worked as Dalad's apprentice, was a reliable lad. In fact, when his frowning gaze met Kavi's, he seemed like the older of the pair. The oldest of the three of them? Kavi grinned.

He reached into the barrel and extracted the scarlet cloak he'd been sitting on. It wasn't an exact match to the Hrum soldiers' cloaks, the worried dyer had told him, but in the dark, in the firelight, it was close enough to pass.

Kavi walked up and down the cleared aisles, stretching his stiff legs. "Have you found all the other barrels? I mean, do you know which is which?"

Tur nodded, but it was Dalad who answered. "Yes, grandma. The lids on the water and the lamp oil are already loose—just a push will open them, and then we can get started. I left the wine kegs sealed. It's not water, but it doesn't burn well. Not much better than beer."

"All right," said Kavi. In Desafon, the city of wood, they knew more about fire than any other town in Farsala. "What's in the rest of these crates?"

"How should I know? Army stuff. Do you want to be trying to open them? Without making any noise?"

"No." Kavi grimaced. "I just hope it's something that will burn. If they get the fire out in time—"

"Don't worry about that," said Dalad confidently. "We built this place to burn. Those vents under the eaves, we were telling the Hrum they'd let out the summer heat. And so they do, but they'll also act as chimneys and pull the fire up the walls. And all the planks are just dry enough to burn, but not so old the pitch has seeped out of them."

Dalad grinned. "A couple of folk, they warned the Hrum that putting all their stuff in one big building like this was just asking for the Flame, but they said their safety techniques were 'far superior' to ours. Then they accused us of trying to create more work for ourselves. Of course"—Dalad's grin widened—"it turns out they don't know good wood from tinder. But that's not being our problem, is it?"

Tur shook his head sadly, but Kavi had to stifle a laugh. He had given the country folk of

Farsala dozens of suggestions for quietly hinder-ing the Hrum in the last few months, but when it came to local matters they were always at least a step ahead of him, and often two or three.

Trust the locals always. They know their own busi-ness best.

If the Hrum had had the sense to practice that, they might have saved themselves a lot of trouble. Patrius had talked a good game about the Hrum seeking to learn from their conquered peoples, but the reality encountered by Farsalan peasants was an arrogant assumption that the way the Hrum did it was always best.

Yes, the Hrum were arrogant, and they had their draft. And they kept slaves. But they prac-ticed evenhanded justice and paid fair. Kavi flexed his crippled hand, which wouldn't be crippled if the deghans had paid fair—or even if the bastard who'd walked out of his master's shop with a stolen sword, leaving a maimed apprentice behind him, hadn't known that he could get away with it.

So were the Hrum better than the deghans, who hadn't kept slaves? Or worse? The Hrum were both, Kavi decided with a sigh. Good and bad, all mixed. It was enough to make you believe in the deghan notion that the djinn and Azura fought for control of the world through the hearts and minds of its people.

Then a thought came to him, so startling that he stumbled on the smooth plank floor, and Tur cast him a worried frown.

Had the deghans also been both good and bad?

It was hard to think of much about them that was good. There were some evils, like slavery, that they hadn't practiced. And they'd kept the old pact and fought, so Kavi's folk didn't have to. Fought with courage, give them credit for that at least.

Aside from that, there wasn't much, even when he tried to be fair. They'd mostly sustained order in the land they governed, but their idea of justice was a joke—a bad joke, when it came to Kavi's people. And for arrogance they put the Hrum to shame. They had some foolish form of honor, but as far as Kavi could tell it had only served to aggrandize them, not to help anyone else. Even their code of hospitality, feeding anyone who came to their door, was really just a subtle way of saying, "Look how rich I am."

No, on balance the Hrum were better rulers.

He'd been right about that—right, when he passed the Hrum the Farsalan army's battle plans.

So what was he doing here, risking torture, perhaps his life, in order to get rid of them?

But he knew the answer to that. There were no deghans left now, or at least, not enough to burden his folk, even when the Hrum sent their slaves back. So if the Hrum were gone, there might be a chance for something truly right to grow, once Time's Wheel rolled away from the Flame. Kavi's job was to see that those who didn't deserve it weren't destroyed, as the Flame of Destruction burned down the old to make way for the new.

Memory of the lady-bitch, Soraya, flickered through his mind. Her father, with typical deghan indifference, had blackmailed Kavi into his service, taking goods to the croft where she was hidden— though, again in fairness, the man had promised payment and might even have made good on it if he'd survived. When Kavi had remembered her at all, he'd assumed that she'd stayed with the family her father had hired to look after her. But he'd seen them working for a farmer near the vineyard where he bought the wine, and the woman told him the girl had fled.

Probably got herself taken by the Hrum, but Kavi wasn't worried about her—she was too cursed nasty to die. She would come back when the rest of the slaves returned, and doubtless cause more trouble in the world.

The sun had set. Only the fact that Kavi's eyes were adapted to the darkness let him find his way to the crates where the two brothers had seated themselves. Even close up, their faces were just pale blurs.

"How long should we wait?" he asked softly. "Any idea?"

"There'll be a bit of moon rising in a few marks," Dalad replied. "I'm thinking when we can see it through the vents, that'll be the time. The barge long gone; all the soldiers asleep in their beds."

"We don't want them too sleepy," said Kavi. "They're the ones who have to get us out of this."

Tur's hands flashed through a series of gestures. It was too dark for Kavi to see them clearly, but Dalad grinned. "He says, 'Tell me again why we have to be on the inside to light this fire?'"

"Because the sentries are on the outside," said Kavi. "They might be getting suspicious if they saw us painting lamp oil on the walls, don't you think?"

Tur's swift, white grin was his only answer. Madmen, both of them. *And what's that making me?* Kavi sighed.

The candlemarks dragged on, until moonrise cast a line of silver rectangles on the wall opposite the eastern vents. After the total darkness of the last few marks, it seemed very bright. Kavi could make out his companions' expressions now, and see when Tur's hands began to move. A clenched fist over the heart in approximation of a Hrum salute, a hand to the lips, and several gestures Kavi didn't understand.

"He says the Hrum are going to be asking about this," said Dalad. "He wants to know what the townsfolk should say." He smiled at his brother. "I'm for telling them that a djinn did it, like the deghans would've."

Kavi's breath puffed in a soft laugh. "No, tell them it's Sorahb who did it. Restored to life, now that the land needs a champion and all."

With Dalad and Tur, he'd made no pretense that this plan wasn't his own—he'd scarce had a choice, since he'd made up most of it on the spot.

Dalad snorted. "That's even less convincing than a djinn."

"It serves a purpose," said Kavi. "Most folk I talk to think some deghan is in charge of all this and is using that name to hide his identity. If we can get the Hrum to waste their time chasing after 'Sorahb,' then the rest of us are that much safer."

"Hmm. Sorahb it is, then." Tur snorted, and Dalad ruffled his brother's hair, grinning when he ducked. "Never thought you'd be part of a legend, did you?"

Tur scowled and pointed to the moonlight, which was creeping down the walls.

"He's right," said Kavi. "It's time."

Kavi's first thought had been to pour the lamp oil on the floor, but Dalad had advised painting it on the walls instead.

"Like varnish," he repeated now, "only it will burn even better." He didn't lower his voice till Tur glared at him. In all the time they'd waited they hadn't heard a sound from the sentries patrolling outside, and they were getting careless. Kavi was beginning to wonder if the sentries were even out there. They'd better be! No, they would be. With deghans he wouldn't have been certain, but the Hrum were as reliable as good steel.

They painted the walls as high as they could reach, using the short-handled brooms that Tur had brought in his barrel for brushes. Oil dripped onto their hands, and over the floor, but when they finished they still had half a barrel of lamp oil left.

"Pour it out?" Dalad asked softly. "It could make one corner of the room go up real quick."

"No," said Kavi grimly. "If it goes too cursed quick, we'll be regretting it. Leave it here, where it won't catch for a while."

Dalad nodded. Even his expression was somber for once.

They had discussed the timing over and over. How fast would the building burn? How fast would the Hrum arrive? Dalad swore it would take time for the fire to take good hold, that painting the walls as they had was the only way to make certain it couldn't be put out.

Kavi had sworn that the Hrum would respond quickly, arriving to fight the fire within moments. But in the end they were both guessing. Educated guesses, but guesses nonetheless.

"Get the striker," he told Tur.

Before they set anything alight, they wiped the oil off their hands and soaked themselves in the water barrel, sitting in it to saturate every scrap of clothing, dunking their heads to soak their hair, tying wet scarves over mouth and nose. It was harder to breathe through the wet cloth, but Kavi knew he'd be glad of it soon enough.

The scarlet cloaks were the last to go in—they held water like sponges and seemed to weigh forty pounds, but no one wrung them out.

It was Dalad who took the striker and lit the torches, good Desafon torches, made by men who understood wood and pitch. The flames boiled up, revealing serious eyes over the scarves that concealed his companions' faces.

"You two take the sides," said Kavi. "I'll get the back wall."

They hadn't painted oil on the wall with the big double doors in it, by unanimous consent. This whole scheme was crazy enough—they had to set some limits.

To Kavi's relief, the lamp oil didn't instantly burst into sheets of flame, but wherever his torch touched the wall, flowers of fire opened and began to spread. There were lots of crates, bales, and canvas bags stacked against the back wall. Kavi had to detour around them in several places.

A startled shout from outside was echoed by more distant shouts. Kavi grinned, for he knew the Hrum word for fire. *Right on time.* So why was his heart beating like pigeon wings?

By the time he reached the far corner, where Dalad had started toward the front, flames were pouring up the side wall and reaching around the corner to ignite the back. The heat was fierce. Clothing that had been cold and clammy when Kavi started was now warm and clammy, and he drew the scarlet cloak's hood up over his head, grateful for the thick, sodden fabric.

Even over the noisy rush of the flames, he could hear the voices of the approaching Hrum — not just cries of alarm, but firm, shouted orders.

One of the Hamaveran's tributaries ran only a few hundred yards away. The Hrum would have a bucket line set up in moments. Then they would open the doors.

Kavi started walking toward the other end of the warehouse, where Dalad and Tur waited by the barrels. The cloth over his mouth was still damp, but smoke stung his eyes and was beginning to sear his throat, even though most of it was pouring out the roof vents, just as Dalad had promised. They should wet their scarves again.

But it wasn't just the smoke that dried Kavi's throat, he admitted wryly. Vines of flame were climbing up the walls now, and despite the certain knowledge that the Hrum would open the doors in a moment, Kavi was beginning to seriously doubt the wisdom of setting fire to a building when he was locked inside.

He began to run, eyes fixed on the brothers who were standing near the barrels, so he saw it happen.

Flames sprang suddenly down a pile of neatly stacked bags. Kavi didn't know what was in them, grain perhaps, but the rough sacks ignited far too quickly. Tur, watching the doors, surrounded by flames, didn't see it till his sleeve caught fire. His mouth opened in a silent cry. He leaped toward the water barrel, knocking into several others on the way, and thrust his arm inside. One of the barrels he'd run into was the one still half filled with lamp oil. To Kavi's horrified gaze, it seemed to tip in slow motion, farther, farther, and then it fell and rolled, dispersing its contents in a shimmering stream of oil. It became a stream of flame before the barrel hit the crates and stopped rolling, cutting Kavi off from the rest of the warehouse, off from the doors.

Dalad's eyes, above the cloth that covered his mouth, were wide with shock. He looked from one side to the other, seeking a way around the flames, but the crates the barrel had rolled up against were too close to the burning walls.

Kavi looked at the fiery track that danced across the floor. It was expanding slowly, but not yet so wide that a determined man couldn't jump over it, at least if he got a running—

An ax crashed through the warehouse door.

If he didn't jump now, he might not have a chance later—but if they were seen inside the locked warehouse where the fire had started, scarlet cloaks or no, they would all die.

Kavi darted sideways, between two stacks of crates, and watched Dalad drag his brother into another narrow isle. The crates gave him some welcome protection from the heat, since even his thick cloak was beginning to steam.

The big doors flew open with a rush of wind, which was greeted by a rumble from the fire. The sudden burst of flames forced Kavi down to the floor, seeking cooler air. He crawled to the corner and peered out.

If the Hrum who entered shouted, their voices were lost in the fire's waterfall roar. Trying to fight this was useless—and with a sinking heart, Kavi knew that the Hrum would soon realize it.

The band of fire on the floor was growing.

The first soldiers through the door cast the contents of their buckets on the flames and ran out as others came in—in through the left door and out through the right, with perfect Hrum efficiency.

In the flame-lit, smoke-filled chaos, no one but Kavi saw that two more scarlet-cloaked figures had joined the exiting men. Exactly as planned, Kavi reflected bitterly, except for the blazing section of floor, which was now so wide that even in the chaos a man who tried to jump over it was bound to be noticed.

He would have to wait, wait till the Hrum gave up trying to put out a volcano by pissing on it, and follow the very last of them out. At least by then Dalad and Tur would have shed their cloaks and vanished into the brush-shrouded fishermen's trails that lined the riverbank.

But while the Hrum were fighting their futile fight, and Dalad and Tur were escaping, the river of fire on the floor grew wider and wider. It was too wide now for any sane man to jump, but Kavi was ready to try. *Feel free to give up any time now.*

Being Hrum, they continued to dash in and out like suicidal ants. Kavi dug his fingernails into his palms. Soon he would have to choose between death by fire, or death by Hrum torture, and he wasn't at all certain which would be worse. *Quit, you stubborn bastards!*

Finally the stream of men coming through the left door slowed. The last of them cast their water onto the flames, barely glancing at the fire anymore, and ran out, arms raised to shield their faces.

Kavi was already sprinting from his hiding place when two more Hrum rushed into the inferno.

Flame take them! It seemed to be a literally likely fate, and Kavi could wait no longer, no matter who saw him.

But where the last dozen men had cast their buckets at the fire near the doors and exited as fast as possible, these men ran to the center of the warehouse and threw the contents of their buckets onto the burning floor.

One of them was smaller than the other.

As a patch of blackness swept through the shimmering flames, Kavi began to run. His folk might not be fighters, like the deghans had been, but they were the bravest and best of comrades. The thought lightened his heart, lightened his heels, so when he leaped he sailed through the flame-striped space, lit firmly on the charred patch the soldiers' buckets had created, and made for the door without breaking stride.

He barely had time to whisper a prayer that no one would notice that three had come out where two had gone in, then he was through the door, running away from the fire, into the cool dark.

The first breath of fresh air raked into his lungs, and he fell to his knees and began to cough. His throat felt as if he'd tried to swallow a pinecone, and it had gotten stuck halfway down. He knew he should rise, and casually wander off before some helpful Hrum surgeon approached, but his lungs had a will of their own and took over the rest of his body. All he could do was try to drag in air between the spasms.

Then Kavi felt strong, woodworker's hands grip his arms and lift him away from the fire, away from prying eyes. They all but carried him, for he could offer little help.

He was just beginning to get his feet under him when they dragged him into the river's shallows and dropped him. Cool water flowed over scorched skin, easing, steadying. Small sips soothed his roughened throat—and if the water wasn't clean, Kavi didn't care.

In a few moments he was able to wipe his streaming eyes and sit up, looking back at the fire.

He needn't have worried about anyone counting who went in and out the doors, for the scene was a fire-lit bedlam of running men. They were trying to clear the brush around the building, and wetting the ground where it would fall. Soon now, for the flames were eating through the walls and beginning to seep through cracks in the roof planks. Nothing could survive in there now, Kavi realized. He shuddered.

"Thank you." His voice was a husky rasp. He'd best not be talking to any Hrum for a few days.

"What, were you thinking we'd leave you to

burn?" Dalad's voice sounded almost normal, which was good, since the Hrum would be questioning the townsfolk.

Tur, who had no voice to betray him, nodded emphatically.

"Is your arm bad?" Kavi croaked. "Will they—" He broke off, coughing again, though not as convulsively now.

"Barely scorched," said Dalad, and Tur nodded again. "His sleeve will hide it—it won't even be showing in two days."

"No one saw your faces?"

"You are a proper old woman, aren't you?" But Dalad's hands, as he released the clasp on Kavi's cloak, were gentle. "Everyone in that crowd had scarves tied over their faces. No one looked twice at us. Just like no one's looking now. Time to go, grandma."

He was right, Kavi saw. Even the men lifting buckets out of the water paid no attention to two soldiers helping another who'd been overcome by the smoke.

Kavi kept alert as they eased into the bushes, but no one was looking their way. No shouts rang out. They were almost a quarter league away when he heard the distant crash as the warehouse finally collapsed, but unlike Tur, he didn't look back.

The Hrum were a careful folk, for all their arrogance. They'd be standing well back when it went down. Kavi's second venture into sabotage hadn't taken a single life—unlike the first. He greatly preferred this peasant way of fighting.

Despite the lack of bloodshed, it was effective. They had just destroyed the largest Hrum supply depot in Farsala, and all the goods within. It was Sorahb's first open move against the enemy, and a worthy one. Kavi couldn't help but wonder how the Hrum would react to it.

CHAPTER NINE

SORAYA

ORAYA'S DAY USUALLY STARTED when someone tripped over her bedroll, beginning the incessant round of wood, water, and wash. But as time passed, muscles already strong from hunting and riding grew stronger and ceased to ache, and her sore hands grew callused and tough.

As she became more accustomed to the constant round of work, Soraya learned even more about the Hrum—the more she learned, the sooner she'd be able to find out where her mother and Merdas had been taken. She paid particular attention to the security that surrounded the locked record chests, and the small shack—which had originally been a tent—where they were stored. She discovered which clerks had keys, and how the sentries' shifts changed. But none of that would matter until she learned to read Hrum, so she asked Calfaer to teach her to read it, as well as speak it, "for no one ever taught me reading afore."

He cast her an amused glance, though she was better at maintaining her accent these days. And since the time one of the kitchen boys got a good look at her and instantly professed himself smitten—she'd been forced to box his ears to disabuse him of the notion—she'd been careful about hiding her face behind her hair. The servants she could deal with, but if one of the soldiers reacted that way . . .

But they hadn't. In fact some of the soldiers, and many of the officers, seemed to think that servants had neither ears nor brains. Soraya would have found it insulting, if it hadn't been so convenient. She wondered what she had said in front of her maids—what had gone on in the minds behind those timid exteriors?

"I'll be glad to teach you," Calfaer told her. "If I'd ever been given a choice, I might have become a teacher. And if you're literate in Hrum, as well as fluent, you can rise in their service—or perhaps be hired by an officer when he leaves the army. But don't let the Hrum know you're learning. They don't begin teaching their language to conquered folk till they're certain the country is subdued, and that goes double for writing."

Soraya had blinked in surprise. Farsala wasn't sufficiently subdued? More and more merchants were selling freely to the Hrum. They'd even made a deal with the local farmers to haul off the kitchen midden and waste from the latrines and the stock pens and use it to fertilize the local fields—just like any peasant village.

Calfaer's gaze was ironic, and Soraya sensed that he suspected her motives, but he asked no questions, then or ever. At first Soraya supposed that ignorance was safer for a slave, that he would seek it instinctively. But as she spoke with Calfaer, in Farsalan when others were nearby, and in Hrum when no one listened, she learned he hadn't been born a slave. He'd been the son of a family of wealth and power before his country, a place called Brasnia, had been conquered. He was twelve at the time, he told her, and his father, along with the rest of Brasnia's nobility, had fought the Hrum.

"We might have won too," said Calfaer, "if our own serfs hadn't joined with them, fighting against us." It was the first time Soraya had heard bitterness in his voice.

"Serfs? I don't know that word."

"Like your peasants, only obliged to till the land, or perform other tasks their masters assign to them."

"So serf is another word for slave?"

"No, no! We never kept slaves." Though as he proceeded to talk about serfdom, the only difference Soraya could see was that to buy a serf you had to purchase the land they farmed as well, and that serfs were—usually—allowed to keep a small portion of the fruits of their labor. But Calfaer's father had owned serfs, and Calfaer had been a slave most of his life, so he doubtless knew more about it than Soraya did.

And there was another important difference: A serf couldn't be separated from his family. Calfaer had a wife and children, back on his old master's estate. But that master had chosen Calfaer to accompany his son into the army, and the son had willed Calfaer to the army when he died. He would probably never see his family again, though he wrote to them all the time, and sometimes received their letters in return. He hadn't seen them for over twelve years.

The reminder that families could be sold apart chilled Soraya to the bone, though by this time she knew that by Hrum law no child under thirteen could be separated from its mother. Merdas was only three, she reminded herself. Ten years would be far longer than she needed to find and free them, no matter where in the vast Hrum Empire they'd been sent. But as Calfaer spoke to her of land after land, she began to realize just how vast the empire was, and she had to admit that it might take years.

Merdas had loved her as much as a two-year-old could love anyone. Would he even remember her by the time she found him? No matter—her love for him was motivation enough. Whatever it took she would do it, one step at a time. And the first step was to learn to speak and read Hrum. Under Calfaer's competent tutoring, she was making good progress in reading, and excellent progress in understanding the language. She couldn't speak it well, but she already understood most of what was said. It was as if that strange sense she'd developed for people's emotions lent her an edge in guessing the meaning of words she didn't know.

Soraya also learned the history of other servants in the camp besides Calfaer. There was big Ludo, who was supposed to have been dropped on his head as an infant, though Soraya thought he'd probably been born simple. But he could lift a huge kettle of boiling soup without spilling a drop, carry two flour bags on his shoulders at the same time, and he always smiled. He was the only one to whom Soraya dared to show her face.

Another servant she liked was Casia, a strong, middle-aged woman, who had married young, raised her children, and lived all her life in the same small village. When her husband was trampled by an ox and died, she'd scandalized her whole family by taking up with the army for the adventure of it.

Most of the servants, Soraya had been surprised to learn, had freely chosen to work for the army. The pay was good, they told her, and they got to travel and see other lands. And if the people there were a bit hostile at first, well, they usually got over it quick enough.

Soraya, seeing the small signs of acceptance

among the people of Setesafon, feared they were right. But that didn't matter anymore. Farsala was taken, and she couldn't change that no matter how much it hurt. Merdas and Sudaba were what mattered. The only difference those treacherous peasants' acceptance made was that sooner or later one of them would approach the army for work, and that would increase her risk.

It was the risk she thought about when Casia, who usually served in the governor's quarters, slipped on a piece of fallen peach and twisted her ankle, and Hennic looked around the kitchen and picked up the big tray filled with small cups and handed it to Soraya.

"You will go serve. Farsalan girls know how to carry a tray, don't you?"

"Of course I can carry a tray," said Soraya tartly. For all his quick temper, Hennic didn't care who talked back to him, as long as they worked quickly and well. Soraya hadn't suddenly made his tea scalding hot for several weeks now. And she'd never done it too often—only when he really deserved it.

"But I've never served the officers before," she went on. "How do I know who'll want what?"

The tray was heavy. Soraya braced it against her stomach to keep it from tipping.

"You know because you ask them." Hennic spoke with exaggerated patience, as if he was talking to Ludo. Except Hennic was genuinely patient with Ludo. "Beer, sir, or mint tea? You know how to say that?"

"Yes, but . . ." *But what if some officer has seen enough deghans to recognize one? What if one of them sees my face and wants me to bring something to his quarters late one night and stay till dawn? What if one of these men is responsible for my father's death?*

But she knew that one of the Hrum officers had killed her father.

Whatever it takes.

"Yes, Kitchen Master Hennic," said Soraya.

She shifted the tray and walked toward the door. Casia had been helped onto a bench, where she sat clutching her ankle and waiting for the surgeon. The lines on her face had deepened with pain, but when Soraya passed she summoned a smile and winked.

"Nothing to it, girl. It's just like serving a table in the meal tent, and you've done that dozens of times."

In fact, having spent years watching her mother direct their maids in the art of gracious and invisible service, table service was one of the few things Soraya did well. She knew the small tricks, like always standing so the person served could take what you offered with their right hand. Her father had taught her to move silently for the hunt, and making herself invisible in plain sight was a skill she'd perfected over the last few weeks. She sometimes wondered if she was using the strange sense she'd developed for people to make them overlook her. Could she possibly be using shilshadu magic without knowing it? Surely not.

At least she had nothing to fear in serving in the governor's quarters, Soraya reassured herself as she threaded the busy traffic of the central square. After all these weeks, proper service was something she could do without even thinking about it. But in Garren's quarters she'd have to keep her wits about her. If she did that, she'd have no trouble at . . .

Soraya came to a stop, staring at the governor's quarters closed door. She had no hand free to open it and if she kicked it, to approximate a knock, she'd interrupt whatever was going on inside. She could have set the tray on the ground and opened the door, but one of Hennic's rules was that nothing that held uncovered food was to be placed on the ground. And it was no use thinking he wouldn't know—Hennic always found out about things like that.

Three officers came up the path where she was standing, and Soraya stepped aside. Since the summer's heat had set in, the Hrum had started wearing sleeveless tunics that showed off their rank tattoos. The markings these men bore indicated two substrategi and a tactimian—high officers. They paid Soraya no attention as they passed, but as they went through the door one of the substrategi, a huge man with a bushy red beard, held the door open and looked back at her inquiringly.

"Thank you, sir." Soraya scuttled through, like a beetle darting into a crack.

Governor Garren was the only officer who'd had his quarters built bigger than his old tent had been, but the front room, where business was conducted, was still crowded. The governor and a handful of substrategi sat around the table, and everyone else stood.

Soraya went to serve the governor first. She had seen Garren often enough, in the meal tent, which they still called a tent, though it was now completely framed in wood. Like most of the high officers, the governor ate in his quarters, but he sometimes came to the meal tent to address the troops. He wasn't a bad-looking man, she supposed, though his face was too sharp for her taste—when she first saw him, she thought he looked like a shopkeeper. It wasn't until he spoke that his total lack of warmth, humor, and compassion made itself felt.

"Beer or mint tea, sir?" she murmured, presenting the tray by his right hand.

His gaze flicked over her, and he chose tea without another glance in her direction.

The rest of the substrategi had the same oddly mixed appearance as the rest of the Hrum army. There was even a woman among them, hard muscled, and battle scarred. The red-bearded substrategus was the only one who chose beer, and he nodded an absent thanks as he took the cup.

The woman, seated next to him, cast him an envious glance. *But if she wanted beer, why did she choose tea?* The answer dawned, and Soraya suppressed a grin. Her father had been powerful enough to attract sycophants, and he'd had small patience with them. "I need people who'll argue when I'm wrong, Razm take them!" But Soraya had seen plenty of men, and women too, who ate what the powerful ate, drank what they drank, and laughed when they laughed.

Was Garren the kind of commander, of ruler now, who was flattered by such attentions? If so, it probably wasn't a disaster. Most of Farsala's gahns had been the same . . . and Farsala had fallen.

Soraya moved on to serve the lesser officers, and noted that most of them chose whatever they preferred without looking to see what the governor was drinking. She recognized the tactimian who'd been talking to the peddler, but he paid her no more attention than the others. The door opened and shut several times, and the crowd became denser still, dense enough that it was hard to move through it with a large tray, but Soraya did her best imitation of her own mouse-mannered maids, and no one seemed to notice her.

As soon as a harried-looking man filled the last empty chair at the governor's table, Garren rapped on the wood and the room fell silent.

"I have called you all here to report an incident in Desafon. Our supply depot there was set afire and burned to the ground."

Soraya served her last two drinks and stepped back to stand against the wall, ready to go for more refreshments if the need arose. In the consternation rippling through the room, it was easy to remain unnoticed.

One deep voice, that of the red-bearded man, rose above the disturbed murmurs. "*Set* afire, sir? Deliberately?"

"Yes, Barmael. The ordnancer had just purchased eight barrels of wine from some downriver farm and stored them in the warehouse. The men who fought the fire didn't have time to investigate, but they noticed that several of the barrels were open and one had been knocked over. Since the sentries observed nothing until the fire was well started, Tactimian Nellus concluded that the arsonists were carried into the warehouse inside the barrels."

"Then the freight handlers must have been in on it," said a centrimaster. "There would have been a big difference in the barrels' weights."

"There doubtless was," said Garren coolly.

"But the men who crewed the barge also acted as freight handlers. They even got paid extra for it."

There was a moment of chagrined silence.

"Someone's got a nerve," said the red-bearded officer, Barmael. His voice was mild. "Did we lose anything of importance in the fire? Any casualties?"

"No deaths," Garren replied. "And no supplies that can't be replaced—at least Nellus had the sense to keep the pay chests in camp! Though the surveyors you requested had sent their supplies on ahead of them, and those went up with everything else."

Color rose in Barmael's face till it almost matched his hair. "We need better maps. And I'm afraid we're going to need them even sooner than I thought."

"The surveyors themselves will arrive as scheduled," said another officer soothingly. "They can make a start—"

"What good is a surveyor without a sextant and line?" Barmael rumbled. "We need to order more equipment as soon as possible, Governor."

"It will come with the rest of the supplies," said Garren. "And long before it arrives,

Tactimian Nellus should have the men responsible in custody, where they will name their accomplices and die. So it won't happen again. I merely wished to make this incident known to all of you, so you could tighten security procedures in the areas under your command."

"Hard to tighten anything, when you've only got a thousand men to patrol a city the size of Desafon," one of the officers near Soraya murmured to the man beside him. "I'm surprised the whole place hasn't gone up in flames."

"Shh," his companion hissed.

"I've been telling you, the countryside's restive," said Barmael. "That's why we need better maps. We're going to see a lot more of this kind of thing." His voice was still mild, but several men near Soraya stiffened, and even she was surprised. Saying "I told you so" to Governor Garren struck her as a truly stupid thing to do. And yet . . . *I need men who'll argue with me.*

Garren's gaze, resting on Substrategus Barmael, was very cold. "Do you really think a handful of disorganized farmers can threaten the army of the Iron Empire?" His voice was even softer than Barmael's, but Soraya shivered.

"They just burned down a warehouse in Desafon," Barmael pointed out. "And what if they get themselves organized?"

"Then we shall crush them, just as we crushed the last force that came against us," said Garren. "But I believe that a bit more heed to security on the part of *competent* officers will solve the problem. Once the cities are taken, the countryside will settle."

Had Tactimian Nellus been judged incompetent? Evidently! Soraya looked down to hide her face. A fierce elation filled her at the thought of any Farsalans resisting the Hrum, but she feared Garren's estimate of their chances was accurate. She had learned something of how vast, how powerful, the empire truly was. No, peasants could never succeed where deghans had failed. But she liked the fact that they were trying. She hoped they escaped to the last man, and struck again and again!

"Now let us proceed to a more important matter," Garren continued, in a voice that made it clear the previous topic was closed. "Tactimian Rodden has taken the port city, Dugaz."

This time the rumble that filled the room was one of surprised pleasure, and Soraya sighed.

"Well, perhaps taken is an exaggeration." Garren was smiling himself, though Soraya thought it a small, wintry smile. "When the tactimian approached the city he found the streets undefended, and he soon learned that the Farsalan city governor had fled some weeks before. He reports that the populace seems . . . unconcerned about the matter of governance, so I will replace him with a centrimaster, with three centris under his command. If you have any centrimasters under you who you think would do well governing a quiet city, please bring them to my attention."

"Three hundred men?" The tactimian she'd seen with the peddler spoke up for the first time. "Sir, isn't that a bit light to hold any city, even if it seems quiet?"

"I won't send troops to garrison a peaceful city when they can be put to better use elsewhere," said Garren in his argument-ending tone. "From Rodden's report, a few deci could hold that town. The clerks will distribute lists of the lost supplies, with notes on how it may affect your own commands. If you uncover any problems you can't solve, bring them to my attention. That will be all."

Soraya gathered up the empty cups as the officers departed, and then slipped out of the room. She doubted any officer would be presenting Garren with problems, no matter how insoluble they proved. The judgment "incompetent" had been yoked to that sentence like a cart to an ox.

It was disappointing that Dugaz had yielded so easily. Not surprising, perhaps. Her father had once said that Dugaz was the sewer of the realm, with no redeeming feature except the toughness of its rats, but still . . .

Soraya returned to the kitchen. Casia was seated beside a tub of carrots, with a knife in her hand and neat strapping wrapped around her ankle. She grinned at Soraya. "See, I told you. Nothing to it."

"You were right," Soraya admitted. "How's your ankle?"

"Oh, it'll mend. In another month or two." Casia grimaced. "So you'll be serving in the governor's quarters for some time."

"I don't mind," said Soraya. "Though Governor Garren seemed . . . um . . ."

"He's a right cold bastard," said Casia cheerfully. "But he doesn't even notice you if all goes well, and if anything goes wrong, all you get is a freezing look as you go for a cleaning rag. He doesn't even complain to Hennic, if it's an ordinary accident. Beneath his high notice, people like us."

Calfaer, who was carving a new handle for one of the big pans, snorted. "You say that as if it's a bad thing. The less interest we get from officers the better, whatever the reason. I prefer the stupid ones, myself."

The rest of the staff chuckled, and Soraya frowned. She was still surprised, almost shocked, at how irreverently the servants discussed their superiors—at least among themselves. She wondered what her mouse-timid maids had said behind her back, and winced.

"Here, girl, if you're afrai—nervous about it, Hennic can find someone else to serve," said Casia kindly.

"No, I don't mind," Soraya repeated. "Some of the officers seem decent enough. That Substrategus Barmael, he's being a kind man, isn't he?"

Casia opened her mouth to answer, but Calfaer beat her to it. "Of course he's kind to servants— he's no better than a servant himself!"

Soraya's jaw dropped—she'd never felt Calfaer radiate such curt dislike.

"He's an officer now," said Casia gently. "And you'd best remember it, at least to his face."

Calfaer's scowl deepened. "He's barely fit to keep my father's pigs!" He stood and stalked out, leaving Soraya staring after him in astonishment.

"What in the world?"

Casia sighed. "It's a long story, but the short of it is that both Barmael and Calfaer are from the same land. Brasnia, it's called."

Soraya frowned, comparing the burly, red-haired man to Calfaer's small, slim frame. They were much the same age, but . . . "They don't even speak with the same accent."

"That's because our Calfaer was from a family of high lords, and Barmael was a lowly peasant type. A serf, I think they called them. But what Calfaer really holds against him is that Barmael fought against the rulers of his own land, to help the Hrum conquer it. Young he was then, scarce more than a lad, but he's been rising in the Hrum army ever since. And Calfaer . . ."

She sighed, and Soraya nodded understanding. People were altogether too complicated.

THE COMMON PEOPLE OF FARSALA *rallied behind Sorahb's banner. Though they did their best to learn to fight as the deghans had, they were still far from skilled, and the Hrum took town after town.*

So Sorahb called his army to him. "The Hrum are too strong," he told them. "And we are still unready. We must weaken them before we can hope for victory."

Then Sorahb called for the best night-hunters among them to come forth. He led this small band to the conquered city of Desafon, where the Hrum had built a great storehouse to hold their supplies. Sure and silent as the night itself, they crept past the Hrum sentries and set the storehouse alight.

All who witnessed this fire say it spread and grew far

faster than any normal fire could, and the Hrum's efforts to contain it proved in vain. This is when the rumor that Sorahb was a sorcerer was born. But if that fire spread faster than any set by mortal hand, there is still one other hand that might have been involved in it.

CHAPTER TEN

KAVI

THE SWAMP MUD STANK, and it seemed to Kavi that he slipped in it with every other step. But as long as he followed Duckie's round hind quarters, the water splashing around his soaked boots was never more than ankle deep.

The sun had set half a candlemark ago, but a waxing moon sailed serenely through the summer stars—a clear night, Azura be thanked.

Ducks being day creatures, most of the flock that had surrounded Duckie earlier had vanished with the sun. But two stubborn drakes still swam and waddled beside the mule, quacking companionably and getting under Kavi's feet. He'd have been more exasperated, if he hadn't occasionally seen the mule cock a long ear in the direction of one of her feathered confederates, and then abruptly change direction. But that had to be nonsense. Mules and horses were known to have better instincts for finding good footing than men had, even without the mystical guidance of ducks.

After a tuft of grass that looked as solid as any in this forsaken bog had sunk underfoot, pitching Kavi hip deep into muddy water, he had been content to let Duckie take the lead. Especially after the sun had set.

In some ways Kavi was glad to see it go. The sunlight turned the brush-choked marsh into a steam bath, and biting, stinging insects had swarmed over his damp clothes and sweating skin whenever he stopped moving. Sometimes the moths that fed on the mull bushes came to join them, stifling in their numbers, though they didn't bite or sting. But with the coming of night the insects, like the ducks, retired. The air, though still as warm and soft as water on his skin, was cool enough for him to walk without sweating. And if Kavi could see little of the cluttered ground beneath his feet, well, he was seeing Duckie's rump just fine, and she was a better guide than his eyes in this treacherous muck.

Duckie herself, carrying only a light pack that held food and dry clothes, and surrounded by water and a pair of her favorite feathered companions, was perfectly content. Of course, she didn't know that mules could get swamp fever too, Kavi reflected sourly.

His feet slipped again, and he swore and clutched a mull bush to keep his balance. A cloud of moths fluttered up and slowly settled.

The fever was more virulent in the summer too, but Kavi had heard it seldom afflicted those who only stayed in the swamp for a short time. He had no intention of lingering any longer than it would take to deliver his warning, and his plea, and get out. But when he'd heard that the Hrum were sending a new governor to Dugaz, with only a small escort, the opportunity had seemed too good to pass up.

It seemed like half the night had gone by, but the moon had only covered a small arc of starry sky when Duckie stopped, ears pricked and nostrils flaring. Kavi, coming up beside her, saw campfires crowning a small rise some distance away.

He neither saw nor heard any sign of a sentry, and if Duckie did, she wasn't letting on, but Kavi knew they had to be there. Still, no one stopped him as he clambered onto the lower slopes of the rise, leading Duckie, now that they were on higher, firmer ground. He should have found their willingness to admit him reassuring, but it made him nervous instead. *Sure, getting in is easy. Getting out may be a different matter entirely.*

"Hello the camp," he called. The standard travelers greeting.

"Camp?" The mischievous voice behind him made Kavi jump. *"Camp?* This is the palace of the swamp lords! And if you doubt me, well, we're being richer men here than any dwelling in some manor in Setesafon. That I promise you."

The man who leaned against the trunk of one of the low trees stepped forward into the moonlight, and perhaps his claim to wealth wasn't without foundation. The silk vest, bright with embroidery, Kavi had half expected. After all, the famous Farsalan silk, gossamer light, yet strong enough for armor and tents, was produced in these swamps, and spinning and weaving it was Dugaz' only industry. Well, aside from fleecing the sailors who came into their port, and of course, smuggling. It wasn't that there was any prohibition against selling Farsalan silk to anyone who wished to buy, but it was supposed to be taxed first.

No, Kavi had expected silk. But he hadn't expected the wide gold bracelets that adorned— and protected—the man's wrists, or the glass inlay on the hilt of his dagger. At least . . . no, surely it was only glass. Glass was expensive enough!

"Palace of the swamp lords," Kavi repeated. "Would you be their king, then?" He kept his voice very mild.

The man grinned. "For the moment, my friend, for the moment. King is a title that comes and goes with distressing speed around here. I'm called Shir. And you would be? . . ."

"Rudib, of Dilam," said Kavi. "But I'm here as a messenger, for someone else."

"Messenger." Shir's brows climbed. He was dark for a peasant, but he didn't have a deghan look to him. Fathered by a foreign sailor perhaps. There were many such men in Dugaz. "Folk don't often send us messengers."

He sounded as if a "messenger" was an unusually tasty tidbit, and Kavi sighed. "I've a warning you'll want to hear, but it comes with a favor being asked as well. Which won't surprise you. Do you want me to say my piece here, or shall we go up to the fire where we can see each other's faces?"

Shir threw back his head and laughed. "Oh, we'll offer you our hospitality, be sure. But first come to the stream and wash a bit—you stink of the swamp."

He turned and led the way, and Kavi followed. To his nose everything stank of the swamp, but he wouldn't mind a chance to be rid of the sticky mud.

The stream was only about a foot across, splashing down one side of the rise, but the water was clear instead of brackish. Kavi ignored Shir's critical gaze as he shed his dirty clothes and rinsed them as clean as he could. He knew that at least part of the reason Shir had offered him a chance to wash was to see if he carried any weapons. But as he unpacked a dry shirt, the swamp king reached out and grasped Kavi's left arm, turning it to the moonlight.

"What would this be?" His voice, as he gazed at Kavi's tattoo, was only casually curious—so why was the back of Kavi's neck prickling?

"Just a bit of decoration." Kavi made his own voice casual and commanded his muscles not to tense in Shir's grip. "It's common in the lands east of Kadesh, or so I'm told. A merchant talked me into trying it. Swindled me into it I should say, for he got a good knife out of the deal and all I got was this."

"I see." Shir's gaze rose higher, finding the scar where an arrow had grazed Kavi's shoulder when a bunch of Farsalan deghans had interrupted a secret meeting with Patrius. But that didn't matter, for the deghans were dead, and all men had scars. Shir probably had dozens of them.

After he put on clean clothes, he contemplated his muddy boots and shrugged. He could clean them, but they'd just get muddy again when he left. The night was warm enough he scarce needed them, and Shir himself was barefoot, so there couldn't be too many thorns about.

Shir saw Kavi look at his feet, and grinned again. "You're right, you don't need boots here. Tie your mule to the post and come. I'm curious to hear this message of yours, and we seldom have a chance to offer our hospitality to strangers."

Sensible strangers. He sounded friendly, but Kavi

thought he'd probably never been in the presence of a deadlier man. He tied Duckie's tether to the hitching post reluctantly; it was hard to go into enemy territory without any allies at all.

The firelight camp to which Shir led him didn't look like enemy territory. In fact it didn't look like anything Kavi had ever seen. The shelters were scattered about with no order to them. No streets. They appeared to be a cross between a house and a tent; they were built on wooden platforms, which meant wooden floors, and had proper, wood-shingled roofs. But the walls were made of bright-patterned silk, and a few of the dwellings had their "walls" tied to the rafters, revealing beds, tables, chests, and chairs inside. It felt odd to see the inner workings of a building so exposed, but Kavi had little time to study them, for most of his attention was on the people.

The first thing he noticed was how scruffy the men looked. Almost all Farsalan men, peasant and deghan alike, were clean shaven except for the occasional mustache. Even Shir appeared to have shaved fairly recently, but his followers sported the most ragged collection of beards Kavi had ever seen.

However, he doubted anyone mentioned it to them, for despite the silks, and jewelry a deghass would envy, they were also the toughest-looking men he'd ever seen. There were a few women among them, he noticed, but they looked as tough as the men—hard muscled, hard faced, and even better armed.

No one was surprised by his arrival. There had indeed been sentries.

"We've company, my friends." Shir clapped his hands. "Cushions, refreshments! Let's show some hospitality!"

They didn't exactly leap to obey him, Kavi noted, but eventually a couple of men dragged over a wooden pallet and set it on the damp ground by one of the fires. Another brought out a big cushion, and a woman fetched a carved and padded chair for Shir.

Kavi sank down on the pillow—silk, of course—as another man approached, eyeing him. "Been fishing, Shir? You should've thrown it back, so it could grow fatter."

A few men laughed, but most didn't, and the stranger glowered at them. Did Shir have a challenger for his title? It didn't look like the man had much popular support. He was shorter than Shir, and wore a woman's earring half buried in the thick curls of his hair and beard—gold, with a red glass bead that gleamed like an ember when the firelight found it.

"Now, now, Nazahd. He's a messenger, with an important message, just for us." Shir turned his mocking gaze on Kavi. "What would you like, Messenger Rudib? Wine, beer, tea? Something stronger?"

All he really wanted was to leave, as quickly as possible. "Tea," said Kavi. "Thank you."

He had chosen tea because it was the least intoxicating option, but when they hauled out the bag to brew it, his eyes widened at the sigil painted on the side. Sek soochii tea came from the lands east of Kadesh, and in the very best taverns it sold for three copper stallions a *cup*.

"So will you be enjoying our hospitality for long, messenger?" Shir asked.

"I'm afraid not." It was hard to sound politely regretful, but Kavi managed. "I have other messages to deliver after this. I'm working for a man who is trying to organize resistance against the Hrum."

"Against the Hrum?" Shir's dark brows rose again. "Brave soul! What does he want with simple folk like us? The Hrum have already taken Dugaz, for all the good it will do them."

"First, he wants to warn you," said Kavi. "The Hrum are sending a governor for the city. He'll be imposing new taxes, and drafting all men between eighteen and twenty-three into the Hrum army."

Shir snorted. "We're tax exempt here, my friend. And as for the army . . . What's it like?"

Kavi blinked. Tied to their farms and businesses, that was a question no Farsalan peasant had bothered to ask. But Kavi described the Hrum soldiers' tasks and duties as well as he knew them. The tea arrived as he spoke, and he almost choked when he saw the gold-footed, glass cup it was served in. He had never held anything so expensive in his life. The tea itself had a delicate, flowery taste. Nice, but not worth three copper stallions. Certainly not worth dying of fever for.

He finished his account of the life of a Hrum soldier, and Shir, who had also chosen tea, eyed him thoughtfully over his own expensive cup. "So what you're saying is that it's hard work, under rough conditions, and every now and then killing some poor, desperate bastard before he can kill you. Sounds like a typical week. How much do these Hrum pay? Do you get to keep the loot?"

Even Nazahd laughed, and Kavi gritted his teeth. "You don't keep the loot. It all goes to the empire. Just like a tax. And they pay one gold centirus—that's a bit smaller than one of our eagles—per quarter." It was more than most city journeymen made, and room and board was included. And that was just the Hrum's starting salary, but Kavi saw no need to mention that.

"One eagle a *quarter*. Only *one* eagle a quarter? The cheap bastards," said Shir. "Well, that settles it. We'll miss out on the draft."

"You won't have a choice," said Kavi, "once the governor is installed here. That's what Sorahb wanted to—"

"Sorahb?" Shir's voice rose. "The reborn champion himself, no less! You work for the high and mighty, my friend."

"He just uses that name," said Kavi impatiently. "But he wanted to let the fighters of Dugaz know that this Hrum governor will arrive soon, and he'll only have a few hundred men with him. If you organized the townsfolk, you could probably take the city."

"We don't want the city," said Shir. His voice was almost gentle. "Neither will the Hrum governor when he gets to know the place, but that's being his problem."

Kavi had figured that for the answer as soon as he met Shir, but he had to give it one more try. "It's only for a year," he said. "Less than that, just eight and a half months now. Surely you could hold off the Hrum that long."

"I'd heard that," said Shir curiously. "That the Hrum would retreat if they couldn't complete their conquest in a year, but I've never believed it. Why would they quit, instead of fighting on until they won?"

"It's because of something that happened far back in their history," said Kavi, remembering the tale Patrius had told him. "They set out to conquer some country—I've forgotten its name. They succeeded in the end, but by the time they finished fighting there was nothing left worth conquering. The empire was decades in recovering too. That old emperor decreed that the Hrum would never again fight a war where the cost of winning outweighed the gain. They always count cost, the Hrum."

Unlike the deghans, who had never counted cost, since they so seldom paid.

"If you make the cost of taking this swamp too high, for just eight months, they'll never trouble you again."

Shir smiled lazily. "They don't trouble us now."

His voice was soft, but Kavi knew a final answer when he heard it. "Very well, then." He finished his tea and set the cup carefully on the wooden pallet. "I'll carry your regards to my master and be going now. Thank you for the—"

"Thanks?" It was Nazahd who spoke, stepping forward to look down at Kavi. "You drink our tea, and share our fire, and 'thanks' is all we're getting?"

Kavi rose to his feet too, but slowly. If he tried to run they'd bring him down like jackals. He looked at Shir, who smiled, shrugged, and leaned back in his chair, clearly ready to be entertained. What was one more murder to him? Kavi was on his own.

"I have nothing else to offer, except a purse

too thin to interest you," he said. "Though you can surely have it. If I had a snug house and plenty of coin, I wouldn't be out running errands for a lunatic, now would I?" His heart was hammering.

"You may not be having money," said Nazahd. "But if this Sorahb is hoping to finance a rebellion, he must have a tidy bit put by. If he was getting a package with one of your ears, or a finger or two in it, how much would he pay to get the rest of you back?"

"Not much," said Kavi. He had planned for this, but he was still sweating as if he struggled through the swamp, under the midday sun. "He has plenty of messengers. He can afford to lose one. But . . . He did give me something. I'm supposed to use it to buy supplies for Mazad. I shouldn't . . ." He looked around, as if searching desperately for some other way out.

Shir was leaning forward now, interest in his lean face. "If you've the means to pay for our hospitality, messenger, let's see it. Or we might be getting impatient."

Nazahd drew his knife. Kavi took a step back, reached into his purse, and drew out a cloth-wrapped bundle.

"Here it is!" It was all too easy to sound pan-icked. He untied the cloth and held it out, so the firelight gleamed on the big, gold buckle. Designed to hold a deghan's sword belt, it was as large as Kavi's fist, and the workmanship was fine. He felt a genuine pang at parting with it—it was one of the finest forged pieces he had left. But he knew that, unlike the high commander, these men would never cut it open to find the lead-filled bronze inside. No, his work would be properly appreciated here.

He smiled ingratiatingly and held the glitter-ing thing out to Nazahd, who snatched it from his hand. If Kavi had read the signs aright, Shir couldn't afford to let Nazahd keep it, even if he wanted to. And if Kavi had read the signs wrong, he would probably die.

"Thank you, messenger. That'll do nicely." Nazahd was grinning, and so were the men who'd laughed at his jokes.

"It will indeed." Shir sounded relaxed. Even his eyelids seemed to droop, sleepily. Kavi didn't think anyone was fooled. "Bring it here, Nazahd."

Nazahd tucked the glittering buckle under his belt. "You come get it, ki—"

Shir leaped like a panther, his dagger already

in his fist. But Nazahd wasn't surprised, and he sprang back to give himself room. The crowd eddied around them.

Kavi watched with the others as Shir and Nazahd circled—feinting, striking, springing back. Though he faced the same direction as the rest of them, Kavi let the jostling movement as they followed the fight push him slowly from the front of the crowd to the back. When there was no one behind him, he turned and walked away.

If there was anything certain in this world, it was that both Nazahd and Shir were skilled knife fighters, so the battle should last for some time. Still, his fingers shook with haste as he pulled on his boots and untied Duckie's tether.

He sent Duckie splashing into the swamp, in a different direction than the one from which he'd come. He hoped to confuse pursuit, assuming anyone bothered to pursue him, but they had to know he didn't have any more pieces like that—his purse wasn't big enough.

Several more ducks, or perhaps the same two with a friend along, rejoined Duckie, and with their assistance the mule steered Kavi safely around the sinkholes.

If there were sentries, they evidently had no orders to stop him. Or perhaps the knife Kavi had pulled from Duckie's pack was enough to discourage them. After all, what was one less murder to them?

He'd been mad to try to recruit such men. Fighters they might be, but . . . Azura help the Hrum, if they ever tried to control Dugaz in anything but name!

Though if the Hrum did hold Dugaz, life for the townsfolk might improve. Unlike the swamp bandits, the Hrum took responsibility for their actions, for the people they governed. Or would the wealth, the feverish allure of fortune and death, rot even the Hrum's iron discipline after a time?

The moon was low, but they'd have a few marks before it set, and Kavi trusted Duckie to get him back to the road. The silver light glowed on silver moth wings, coating the mull bushes like ghostly leaves as the insects recruited their strength to eat, spin their cocoons, and die. Trapping the men who dwelled in this fever-ridden pit as surely as men trapped the moths. No amount of money was worth this!

And did someone who'd made money plating lead-filled bronze with gold have any right to be complaining about the morals of others? But it wasn't the same. Kavi's forgeries had killed no one. Even those who'd discovered the sham had taken no harm beyond a pinch in the purse and a bruise to their pride. No, it might have been wrong, but Kavi had killed no one . . . until he started meddling in politics. And he was taking responsibility for that, as best he knew how, even when it led him into risks like this. Where might it be taking him next? Kavi shivered.

—◆◆◆—

CHAPTER ELEVEN

JIAAN

JIAAN WAS WORKING WITH the intermediate swordsmen when the message arrived. It made him self-conscious to work with these men, for he was only a few steps above intermediate himself. He'd been trained to fight as an archer—his father had taught him a bit of swordsmanship and lance work only because Jiaan was his son, and because he loved to teach.

These men had moved beyond the simple exercises that Aram was running at the bottom of the meadow, where the formal rhythmic clacks of the beginners' wooden practice swords echoed through the hills. They were still in the mountains, even though the Suud had agreed to let them build a camp in the desert. The Suud had located a desert canyon for the Farsalan army that was so well hidden that Jiaan knew he wouldn't be able to find it again without a guide, and he'd been there twice. The first time that he'd gone with Fasal to see the site and approve it, it had been night. When he returned a few days later, with the veterans he'd promoted to squadron leaders and the army's building experts, it had been midday, and the blazing sun turned every rock in the desert into a scorching anvil. The site was perfect, all had agreed—but they would return and take up residence in Eagle, when it would be cooler, or perhaps even Bear, when the winter rains would have begun. And if the Hrum found out about their mountain encampment before then, Jiaan thought, they could relocate ahead of plan and copy the Suud, sleeping in tents during the day.

Meanwhile, Jiaan could enjoy the cool breeze flowing over green meadow grass—it was the only pleasure to be found in his current job. The intermediate swordsmen had progressed beyond drill and were fighting each other—or trying to fight each other. Jiaan winced as one man overreached a lunge, slipped, and fell flat on his butt, where his opponent gleefully skewered him. He was swearing as he climbed to his feet, but at least he knew what he'd done wrong. Jiaan sighed and moved down the line, correcting one man's grip, another's stance.

Almost all the survivors of the Battle of the Sendar Wall had been archers. Only two foot soldiers, who'd actually been trained to fight with swords, had survived the battlefield. And that was only because they'd been so badly wounded they could no longer fight, and the Hrum had ignored them, giving them a chance to escape. It made Jiaan realize how lucky he'd been, to get off with no worse than a broken collarbone and a knock on the head.

These survivors had only recently recovered enough to find their way to the army. One of them still limped badly, though the elderly healer-priest, who'd joined the army shortly after the high priest swore to support the Hrum, said he'd continue to heal over time. The other had lost his right hand. But he told Jiaan he wanted revenge against the men who'd maimed him, and if he could no longer swing a sword, he could still load a cart, he said, or groom a horse, or scrub a floor, or—

Jiaan banished pity from his face and voice, and told the man that any idiot could load a cart or scrub a floor—it took a soldier to teach a man to use a sword!

The sudden, proud lift of the man's head had warmed his heart—and it had been true, too. Aram was a surprisingly good teacher and he had a thorough grounding in the basics of fighting with a sword . . . on foot.

A practice sword hurtled out of its owner's grip and flew past Jiaan's ear, making him duck. He picked it up and returned it to its shamefaced owner, corrected the man's grip, and moved on.

The army had metal swords, smuggled out of Mazad through the useful aqueduct, but they hadn't let anyone outside the advanced class even touch them yet. And the advanced class . . . Jiaan sighed.

Aside from Fasal, Jiaan was the only man in camp who'd even tried to use a sword or a lance from horseback. But with so many chargers available in the horse markets—at absurdly low prices—Fasal was determined that they would have at least a squadron of cavalry. He was working with the advanced class now, trying to teach them the simple maneuver of striking a post with their wooden practice swords as they cantered past. It wasn't too difficult, if you'd been riding from the time you were small, and if your father started teaching you swordsmanship when you were ten. Jiaan was capable of that much. But for infantrymen, who'd rarely ridden horseback before, and archers who'd never so much as touched a sword . . . The men were placing bets on when they'd be allowed to work with real swords, but if the practice blades had been sharpened steel instead of blunt wood, they'd have chopped off their own legs and killed all their horses in the first week.

Jiaan sometimes wondered if he'd been right to let Fasal go on with this—they only had eight months before the Hrum would either be gone, or hold Farsala for good. But he knew Fasal was right that even a small group of cavalry would provide a mobile strike force, which could greatly aid any group of footmen who found themselves in trouble. At least it kept Fasal too busy to come up with anything worse. The advanced class was improving too, just as having Fasal beat him black and blue in their demonstrations was beginning to improve

Jiaan's skills. And Rakesh's skill kept him from looking too foolish. But whacking a post with a stick was a far cry from fighting an opponent who could fight back, and . . .

The sound of pounding hooves caught Jiaan's attention, for the advanced class were using all the horses and they had dismounted and were gathered around Fasal, who was explaining something with vivid hand gestures. This was only a single horse, and it came from the direction of the camp, so it had to be someone the sentries had allowed in—in fact they must have told the rider where he could find Jiaan. So it had to be . . .

A man in the black-and-green tabard of the Mazad town guard cantered out of the trees. Jiaan wondered if he'd donned the betraying garment the moment he was out of range of the Hrum's patrols, or more sensibly, just before arriving at the army camp. Either way, Jiaan was grateful to Commander Siddas for the consistent respect his men showed for the Farsalan army.

Of course, they've never seen us practice.

The practice was drawing to a close, as men lowered their swords to watch the messenger trot up to Jiaan and hold out a sealed scroll.

Jiaan eyed the sweating horse quizzically as he broke the wax. "You couldn't have left this in the message tree? Your horse would have been grateful for it, and my people check there every few days."

He wondered if the other Sorahb had struck again. Siddas had told him about the burning of the Hrum's supply depot in Desafon. As far as Siddas could tell, the Hrum still didn't know who'd done it, but the name "Sorahb" was being whispered in taverns from one end of Farsala to the other. Siddas thought it was probably local men, but Jiaan wondered. He knew that there was more than one man calling himself Sorahb these days. Several of his new recruits had committed some minor act of sabotage under that name, before coming to join the army. But the destruction of the supply depot had the same feel about it as the suggestion that the miners sell the Hrum inferior goods. Bloodless, efficient, and untraceable. Jiaan had come to believe that there was only one "Sorahb" behind most of the really effective sabotage. He'd have liked to meet the man, if he'd had any idea how to find him.

"We couldn't wait for you to pick up the message this time, High Commander," the messenger replied, sounding for all the world as if he spoke to Jiaan's father instead of a youth not yet twenty. "Commander Siddas says it's urgent."

Jiaan's heart stilled, and then began to pound. Siddas had sent him messages before, both through the tree and by courier; weapons delivery, news of the siege, the need for healer-priests to fight disease in the town before it spread. No message had ever been "urgent" before.

He began to read. Then he read it again, and was starting on a third time when Fasal shook his elbow. "What does it say?"

"He's received intelligence from his spies," said Jiaan. "Commander Siddas, that is. He—"

"I know who sent it. What intelligence?"

"The Hrum are sending reinforcements to Mazad. Governor Garren decided that Substrategus Arus' claim that he could take the city with just one tacti is ridiculous—or at least too slow—and he's sending another. Siddas says that two tacti, or rather a tacti and the seven hundred men Arus has left could put real pressure on the city, so he wants to destroy as many of Arus' forces as he can before the others arrive. He says this is the best opportunity he'll . . . we'll have, to try something like this with any chance of success."

Jiaan's stomach felt cold, but Fasal's eyes were shining.

"Does he have a plan?"

"A good one," said Jiaan slowly. "He and his men will open the gates and attack the Hrum camp. They've never tried to attack before—he says the Hrum will be totally unprepared. As soon as he and his men have them fully engaged, we're to attack from the rear." The chill in Jiaan's stomach was spreading. "He's not proposing that we fight to the death, just a quick strike, to force the Hrum to turn and fight on two fronts. To give the guardsmen the advantage of a few moments' chaos. When the Hrum begin to rally, his clarioneers will sound retreat, and we'll all disengage at once. That will force the Hrum to either choose one target and let the other go, or to split their forces, giving each of us a better chance of escape."

Jiaan had never told Siddas, in so many words, how inexperienced his men were, but the old commander clearly understood. It was a plan designed to use Jiaan's army as lightly as possible—a diversion, instead of a real fight. It should work, but . . .

Jiaan's gaze swept the meadow. Almost a thousand men looked back at him, gripping their wooden practice swords firmly. Wooden practice swords. "We're not ready."

"When do the reinforcements arrive?" Fasal asked.

"In three weeks. Just enough time for us to get there, set this up, and plan our escape."

Escape for whoever survived. The Hrum wouldn't be using practice swords.

"Then we're as ready as we're going to be, aren't we?" Fasal was trying to sound calm, but excitement shivered in his voice.

Jiaan stared at him. "You've been training them." The others were too far off to hear. Even the messenger had withdrawn to give them privacy, but Jiaan lowered his voice anyway. "Look me in the eyes, and tell me you think these men are ready to fight the Hrum."

Fasal met his gaze. "They're not. They never will be. Certainly not in the year—less now—that we have. These are peasants. They'll never be good enough to fight the Hrum, and you knew that when you started this. But they might be good enough to create a distraction, so trained soldiers can fight the Hrum. And right now, that's the best use of this army I can see. Is this an army, or isn't it?"

His voice was rising and Jiaan glared at him. Fasal grimaced, but when he spoke again, his voice was very soft. "A deghan would do it."

Jiaan snorted. He knew a deghan would do it. A deghan would do it in an instant and never count the cost. And he cared nothing for the growing contempt in Fasal's eyes, either. Still . . .

Is this an army, or isn't it?

What had he gathered these men for, what was he training them for, except to fight the Hrum? The plan Commander Siddas proposed, a plan that took their inexperience into account, that didn't demand a sustained battle, was surely the best way to fight without getting too many of them killed. But men would die. Jiaan had no doubt of that. He had fought the Hrum before. However badly led, however unprepared for attack, the Hrum would never be easy opponents.

Is this an army, or isn't it?

Jiaan looked again at the watching men.

Wooden practice swords or no, their eyes were steady on his.

"All right." He took a deep, sustaining breath. "We'll do it."

He turned and walked away from Fasal's whoop of joy, away from the grins spreading across the faces of the men who were close enough to guess what was going on. He would have to delay the messenger for a day or so, to discuss tactics and how best to coordinate their movements with those of the city guard. The sinking in Jiaan's stomach didn't seem to be going away now that he'd made his decision, which was probably a bad sign, but he'd stick with that decision. And not because of Fasal. He could have stood up to Fasal. But he knew that this was what his father would have done.

IT WAS GOING TOO WELL. Everything had gone smooth as new cream, from the conference where Jiaan and his veterans gathered with the messenger to plan their tactics, through the journey to this dark grove on the other side of the Hrum camp. They'd avoided the two patrols they'd seen with ease, and Fasal hadn't even argued very long about attacking them. They still had a week before the Hrum reinforcements could arrive, and the moon was so full and the weather so clear, that even Jiaan's small, new-minted army could handle a night attack. They would be able to see the gates open, and could probably even judge for themselves the right moment to charge the Hrum's backs—and they had agreed on a clarion signal, if for some reason Siddas wanted them to charge early.

No one had even so much as nicked himself with his new, metal sword. It was all going perfectly, and Jiaan was half insane with the tension of wondering what was going to go wrong.

Jiaan sensed, more than heard it, when Fasal stiffened in the bushes beside him. He looked at the gates.

In the moonlight the high stone walls appeared to be a single piece of stone, unbreakable as the mountains. The great wooden gates were of a piece with them, unyielding as stone. But they moved now, swinging wide, as the portcullis lifted and men raced out running to where their units would form, all in a silence so eerie that Jiaan blinked, doubting his eyes.

Then the Hrum sentries shouted, and a drum rattled a frenzied tattoo. The camp erupted into activity as men hurtled from their tents, clothed only in their tunics, carrying breastplates, shields, helmets, some with boots in their hands, buckling on their swords as they ran.

They were still assembling their armor and pulling on their boots as they formed up into ten-man squads, and then, as the drumbeat changed, into a line three men thick. Even Jiaan, who had seen it before, shook his head in disbelief at how fast they could find formation.

But the town guardsmen had emerged from the gates and formed their own units, blocks of about twenty men each. They looked sloppier than the Hrum, but they had almost as many men, Jiaan noted with a leap of hope, and they'd had plenty of time to arm and prepare. When Jiaan's army joined them they would outnumber the Hrum by almost three to one—and if that was dishonorable, Jiaan didn't care. It was Farsala's turn!

When the clarion sounded, the thunder of the Farsalan battle cry almost drowned the higher notes of the horn as Siddas' guardsmen charged.

The drumbeat altered again, and the Hrum marched out to meet them. Some of them were still trying to fasten the buckles on their breastplates. And they had no long lances this time, no knowledge of the enemy's plans—this time the Hrum would be surprised!

There were about two thousand yards between the Hrum camp and the city walls, and months of siege had removed all the brush and rubble, so Jiaan had a clear view of the meeting of the two armies. Mazad's guardsmen were running, shouting, and they crashed into the Hrum's line like a storm wave hitting a wall.

The Hrum line swayed and bent under the impact. Metal clanged on metal, thudded on wooden shields, and screams and shrieks added themselves to the din. Jiaan's mind had expected those sounds, but his body remembered the last time he'd heard them and his blood ran cold and thin, too thin to sustain his racing heart. He shuddered, trying to control his breathing. He had to watch, to be aware, to get his men ready . . .

Jiaan never knew quite what it was—the battle looked the same, as swords rose and fell, and men struggled to break the Hrum's tight formation. Perhaps something in the sound changed, though men still shouted and cried out in pain. The sound was . . . different.

Jiaan had already stood, breaking cover, and lifted his hand to signal his men when the clarion sounded. His hand swept down.

The men charged without shouting, as Jiaan and his squad commanders had drilled into them over and over on the week of the march — *No reason to warn them we're coming, lads.* But they couldn't cross the Hrum camp in total silence.

Jiaan, trotting Rakesh behind the running mob and trying to watch over everything at once, saw a woman in a servant's drab gown emerge from a tent with an armload of cloth, probably intended for bandages. She screamed when she saw the men racing toward her, then threw her bundle in their direction and leaped back into the tent again. One of his men tripped on the cloth, Jiaan noted with resignation, but he staggered back to his feet and ran on.

Crashing between the tents Jiaan couldn't see everything, but he heard a man shouting warning, and what sounded like someone running into a stack of cooking pots. Still, among the shouts, screams, and clangor of the battle, any noise from the camp would be lost.

They got past the tents and Jiaan saw that the Hrum had pushed the town guard back several yards, and they were about to gain more ground . . . except for Jiaan's army.

The muscles of his cheeks ached, and Jiaan realized he was grinning, a frozen, teeth-gritting grin. His own men were only a few dozen yards from the Hrum's backs, and would reach them in seconds. Jiaan raised his arm again, and waved to signal the archers.

The Hrum's first warning of the Farsalan army's presence was the arrival of their arrows. Given the fact that their allies stood just beyond their intended targets, Jiaan had refused to allow any but the best and steadiest of his archers to use their bows—and that at a range where a skilled archer couldn't possibly miss.

The arrows' hiss-and-thud was so soft compared to the clamor around them that only the Hrum whose neighbors fell, with feathered shafts protruding from their backs, were warned at all. A handful of Hrum were starting to turn when Jiaan's men reached them.

The cavalry consisted of Jiaan, Fasal, and five other men from the advanced class who Fasal thought might be more useful on horseback than on foot. Like the archers, they were supposed to keep to the rear and only go in if the foot soldiers found themselves in trouble.

But as the third rank of the Hrum line spun, raised their shields, and began to fight, Jiaan realized that his whole army was in trouble.

He saw one man go down, not wounded, merely knocked aside by a blow from a Hrum's shield, while his partner engaged the Hrum desperately with his sword. Jiaan pulled out a javelin and clapped his heels to Rakesh's flanks.

A roar rose from the front line, as the second line of Hrum turned to face the threat at their backs, and the town guard fell on the first line with renewed ferocity.

The Hrum Jiaan was watching smashed the sword from the peasant soldier's hand, and lifted his own blade to cut the man down. Jiaan's javelin, cast overhand in the clean, swift sweep his father had taught him, caught the man in the side of his neck, not the center as Jiaan had intended, but at least it had missed his armor and hit flesh.

Blood poured blackly over the Hrum's shoulder and breastplate as he fell to his knees, dropping his sword.

Jiaan's peasant soldier darted to pick it up, and Rakesh wheeled away before Jiaan's heels even touched his sides.

Jiaan drew his sword. He watched another of his soldiers cut into the back of a Hrum soldier's knee, and as the man fell, half turning, helpless, the soldier lifted his sword and froze, staring at the man he could kill.

The Hrum soldiers in front of the fallen man were engaged with the guardsmen, but the Hrum soldier beside the fallen man had no such difficulties. Jiaan swung at the arm he raised, and the Hrum's sword fell as the man's wrist spurted blood, broken and half severed. Jiaan struck at the next man's throat, but hit his face instead. The Hrum's helmet deflected part of the blow, but Jiaan felt his sword grate over bone. The man cried out, swinging his own sword, and only Rakesh's nimble leap kept the blade from severing Jiaan's thigh.

Jiaan swung again. The Hrum's shield blocked the blow, the force of it numbing his wrist. Then the counterblow came and Jiaan parried desperately, and parried again.

In the shadow of the helmet, the Hrum's blood-covered face showed no expression, but Jiaan sensed his grim satisfaction as Jiaan backed up a few feet, then a few more . . .

The Hrum's mouth opened in a soundless scream as the peasant Jiaan had rescued hacked into his neck like a butcher felling an ox. The peasant nodded at Jiaan and turned back to the line, seeking more targets.

But the Hrum were moving again. Somehow, even in the press of battle, they were reforming their lines. Where there had been three ranks now there were four, two facing in each direction, and their formation was growing more solid before Jiaan's eyes. It was time—

Siddas' clarioneer blew the retreat, the signal for Jiaan and his men to disengage, turn and run, after which the guardsmen themselves would turn and flee. But disengaging wasn't as easy as it had sounded when they planned this. Several men could and did run, but men who were exchanging frantic blows and parries couldn't simply turn their backs and walk away.

Jiaan cantered down the line, disrupting fights, using Rakesh's big body more than his sword. He saw a Farsalan sword shatter under a Hrum blade, and hurtled Rakesh forward to slice his own sword into the Hrum's exposed neck. It cut half through and wedged, wedged in the man's spine, Jiaan realized. The Hrum dropped his sword, looking up at Jiaan even as life drained from his eyes. His body began to fall, pulling the sword with it, and Jiaan gritted his teeth and shoved his boot against the man's face, pulling his sword free in a splatter of blood. His stomach heaved, but he fought it down.

"Run, you bastards!" It was his own voice, screaming, and he realized he'd been screaming similar words for some time, hardly aware of it.

He charged Rakesh at another skirmish, riding between two peasants and a Hrum soldier who appeared to be pressing both of them, striking at the Hrum almost blindly, counting on Rakesh to save him. When the town guard fled, any of his men who were left here would die. "Run!"

Then he realized that the town guard was retreating, not running, but backing off, and the Hrum followed them. Several of them looked as if they wanted to stay and fight Jiaan's force, but they were too well disciplined to break their formation. All down the line Jiaan's men were withdrawing, turning, running back through the Hrum camp.

A quick glance up and down the line showed Jiaan no more he could do. But he noticed—for the first time, he had a chance to notice—the bodies lying on the trampled earth. Some wore Hrum armor, but more, far more wore the thick leather that was all Farsalan peasants-turned-soldier could afford.

"Get out of here, you idiot!" It was Fasal's voice, screaming almost in Jiaan's ear, and it was Fasal's heel thudding into Rakesh's hindquarters that sent Jiaan galloping away, through the Hrum tents and into the quiet darkness of the trees.

THE SMALL RAVINE WHERE they had planned to gather after the battle was about a quarter league from the Hrum camp—far enough to remain unheard if they were quiet, and invisible from the road.

The Hrum had pursued the town guard all the way back to their gates, capturing almost a dozen men who couldn't make it in before the gates closed. Now they would be binding their wounds, restoring order, but soon they would come looking for Jiaan's people—which meant they had to get moving. Though Siddas had had a plan to help them escape, as well.

It had seemed to Jiaan that the entire population of Herat had met them where they crossed the road. As soon as his troops passed, Herat's citizens had emerged from the brush, hurrying down the road to their village, leaving a mass of fresh tracks for the Hrum to follow. Jiaan had his doubts as to whether the Hrum would mistake the tracks of this mob of peasants, fully half of them women, for his army. But if they did, when the Hrum arrived at Herat, the army would appear to have vanished into thin air. When they searched the houses of the local peasants they would find nothing but farmers and their families, none with so much as a scratch on them, and not half enough men in the whole village to make up the force that had attacked them. Siddas said the villagers would be safe, even if the diversion worked. Jiaan prayed it would, for it would be hard for his army to move fast . . . what was left of it.

A third of the remaining men had minor wounds, and a handful were seriously injured, though the healer said he thought they'd live. Jiaan himself had a cut just below his knee, still seeping blood—but he knew it wasn't serious, and there wasn't time to attend to minor cuts now. It stung and throbbed, but it could have been much worse. His father used to swear that he'd never have survived a battle without Rakesh. Jiaan was beginning to understand why.

The ones who hadn't been wounded weren't much better off—what seemed like another third of his men were hiding in the bushes, vomiting. Jiaan would have joined them, except that a commander shouldn't show that kind of weakness. Especially a young commander who had just led men in battle for the first time . . . who was too green to even be certain if they had won or lost.

Jiaan shook himself and urged Rakesh over to where Aram, who had stayed behind with the healer, was organizing the retreat. He waited until the older man finished instructing a handful of soldiers on how to make a litter for carrying the worst wounded. Aram had to repeat himself, for even these men seemed a bit dazed, but at least they weren't vomiting, and they nodded when he finished and moved off with a purposeful air.

Aram looked up and met Jiaan's eyes — his face was calm, but Jiaan could see the tension in it.

"I know you ordered the count," Jiaan said. He dreaded the answer, but he couldn't put off asking any longer. "How many did we lose?"

"There are a hundred and seventy-four men currently missing," said Aram. "But a few more may be trickling in. Things happen in a battle, in the dark. You get separated."

"A hundred and seventy-four?" Jiaan closed his eyes, as if he could block out the knowledge along with the moonlight. He'd known it was bad, but . . . "A fifth," he whispered. "A full fifth of my men dead."

"Or enslaved," said Aram calmly. "Not all of them will be dead, and the Hrum take prisoners. They'll be coming home again if you succeed. And you struck a blow for that tonight, young sir, no doubt about it. It was mostly the town guard did the killing, but I'm guessing we left almost three hundred Hrum dead or severely wounded. That's a third of their forces. The guardsmen couldn't have done it without us. And they only lost a score or so, most of them captured at the gate."

"So we won." It was Fasal's voice, rough, because he'd just returned from vomiting in the bushes. He evaded Jiaan's gaze. Heaving up your guts after a battle was a very undeghan-like thing to do. It made Jiaan think better of him. But still . . .

"You think that's winning? That we killed more of them than they did of us?"

"Yes," said Fasal, and this time he met Jiaan's eyes. "In a war, that's what winning is. You hurt them worse than they hurt you, and then you do it again, and again, and again, until they give up and go home."

That was how the deghans did it. How they had always done it, and they had won far more often than they lost, and kept Farsala safe for a millennium. But after the battle by the Sendar border, Jiaan had vowed to be done with fighting by deghan rules.

So what are we doing here?

"We need to leave," said Jiaan. "How soon can the wounded be moved?"

"As soon as the litters are made," said Aram. "Healer's finishing up, and most of the men are back with their squads. Though I've put a few squads together, to make up the proper numbers. Some were hit harder than others."

"Then the cavalry will start scouting ahead," said Jiaan, which sounded impressive, though in fact he and Fasal were the only cavalry left. Only one of the others had died, but they'd all lost their horses. At least the horses could be replaced.

"We'll come back when we're certain the first stretch is clear. Be ready to move out." He turned Rakesh, and walked him out of the makeshift camp. He wanted to wheel and gallop off, away from pain, from responsibility for the pain and the deaths he had caused. But that would have been noisy, and silence was important now. And Rakesh was too tired for galloping around in the dark, which was a stupid thing to do in the best of times.

Not that the battle would have gone any better in the daylight. Away from camp, the moonlit hills were quiet. Even Fasal, riding after him, was silent for once, though Jiaan knew that wouldn't last.

We tried to pit our weakness against their strength. Of course we died.

Fasal cleared his throat. "I know . . . I know how it feels now, but we destroyed a third of a tacti. That's almost as many as the real army killed in that first battle. And we lost less than two hundred men."

"Yes," said Jiaan. "That's true."

They had surprised the Hrum out of a sound sleep, attacked them on two fronts, one of those attacks a successful ambush, and they'd outnumbered them almost three to one—and the Hrum's casualties were only fifty percent higher than theirs. And the Hrum could send for more men, and more, and more, from every corner of their vast empire.

"We need to find another way. A way to pit our strength against their weakness."

"That sounds like an excellent plan," said Fasal politely. "Any idea how to do it? No? Then while you're thinking about it, I think we should bash them just like we did tonight, as often as we can get away with it. I'm not proposing we charge into their teeth. But well-laid battle plans, where we have the advantage, can work! We've proved it! We *won*."

But even Fasal, Jiaan noted, didn't sound happy about it.

"I don't know how to do it," Jiaan admitted. "But there has to be a better way. That other Sorahb doesn't get a fifth of his men killed every time he strikes."

"It wasn't a fifth," said Fasal. "And more men will come in. And that 'other Sorahb' hasn't done anything except burn down a warehouse. We crippled the force besieging Mazad."

"Until their reinforcements arrive," said Jiaan. "Once that happens, it won't mean anything."

"Except that they won't have enough men to take the city," said Fasal, "which is exactly what we set out to accomplish. You did a good job tonight."

Coming from Fasal, that statement was so startling that Jiaan pulled Rakesh to a halt and stared at him.

Fasal sighed. "It's the truth. You think like the commander used to. You plan ahead, and you can convince men to follow you, even though you aren't true blood. Look at the battle tonight."

"It was Commander Siddas' plan," said Jiaan.

"Maybe, but you were the one who made it work."

If Fasal thought losing a fifth of his force was

doing a good job, then it was just as well that Jiaan had taken command. Still . . .

"I bet the other Sorahb would have found a better way."

"Forget the other Sorahb," said Fasal. "He thinks like a peasant."

So he did. Jiaan frowned. Could that other man actually be a peasant? Surely not. But . . . "Whoever he is, I need to find him," said Jiaan firmly. "That's the first thing. And we need to get swords as strong as the Hrum's. The only reason ours didn't break, like they did in the first battle, is that our soldiers' grips were so bad that the Hrum knocked the swords out of their hands. That has to change too."

"Of course we need more training," Fasal admitted. "But where are you going to get better swords? The Hrum guard their smith's secrets tighter than they guard their gold, and none of our smiths have a clue how they do it."

"I know," said Jiaan. "But we have to get them. And finally, we need allies. Real soldiers, who will fight on our side. No matter how many men we kill, the Hrum can just send for more. We need to be able to do that too."

"Magnificent: unknown tactics and impossible-to-obtain swords," said Fasal. "I think you need to let Siddas continue planning the strategy. Where are you going to find this mythical army of allies? Tucked in your pocket?"

"No." Jiaan drew a deep breath. Fasal was going to hate this idea, and his men wouldn't like it much better. He didn't like it. He just didn't see a choice. "No, they're not tucked in my pocket. But I know where to find them."

CHAPTER TWELVE

SORAYA

HIGH SUMMER MADE THE kitchen's heat intolerable. Soraya was grateful for any task that took her outside, especially serving in the governor's quarters. It had turned out to be far safer than she'd feared; the men meeting with Garren were too preoccupied with business to notice the timid girl who served them. But even wiping down the tables in the meal tent was better than working anywhere near the hearths—or still worse, tending the bake ovens in the yard.

Especially when, like today, Calfaer had stopped by to help her, and give her another language lesson.

"Summer is a good time in Brasnia, where I

come from," he said in clear Hrum. He wrapped a corner of his damp rag around one finger and wrote the Hrum word for "summer" on the dry table.

"It is good here, too," said Soraya. Her Hrum had a marked accent. "Cooler in the high plains than in the lower lands." She took her own rag and wrote "summer good here" in Hrum.

Calfaer smiled and wiped the table clean. "In my land we worship the sun, with a festival called Sunhigh." He wrote "festival" and "sun" on the table and Soraya copied the words.

"Our winter festival is biggest," said Soraya. "In summer the only thing that happens is the priests carry Azura's statue through the town to drive out the djinn. And there are horse races, but the priests don't like that. They say it distracts men's attention from the god."

Last year she had stayed with her cousin Pari during the celebration. She hoped, for the dozenth time, that Pari had found a safe place to weather the invasion. She probably had—her mother was a sensible woman, and neither of them were likely to have resisted the Hrum. This year Setesafon's high priest had declined to carry the statue through the town. He did it hoping to please the governor, though Soraya didn't think Garren cared one way or the other.

At least the high priest's hypocrisy had settled her fear that her father's refusal to allow her sacrifice had caused his defeat. If the high priest himself had no fear of the djinn, then they were only a deghan superstition, just as the peasants claimed. Though Soraya considered the peasants' superstition that Time was an unstoppable cycle of good and ill fortune just as foolish.

"Our summer festival is the best," said Calfaer. He had stopped writing and simply cleaned. His voice held only a trace of wistfulness, but Soraya sensed a surge of homesickness that woke an answering longing in her own heart, and her eyes stung.

"We offer thanks to the sun for the bounty it bestows. And it's not bad for the serfs to have a day of feast and a day of rest afterward—though that's mostly to recover from their hangovers," Calfaer added wryly. "Sunhigh is in the midst of their hardest working season. There's music, and dancing, and contests of strength. Family members and friends give each other gifts. And the lord of the land provides a great feast, free to all, with beer for the serfs and wine for the noble folk." He was still speaking Hrum, but at a natural pace, not the carefully correct words of the language lesson. "Then, just as the sun sets, our priests honor the sun with sacrifice—or they used to, before the Hrum put a stop to it. Then bonfires are lit and the serious drinking begins. It can get pretty wild after that," he added, with a reminiscent grin.

"Sacrifice?" Soraya wasn't certain she'd heard aright, though Calfaer had taught her the word not long ago, in a discussion of the various religions practiced in the empire. "You don't mean . . . What sort of sacrifice?"

"Well, now it's only a pig," said Calfaer. "Though before the Hrum came, it used to be a human. That shocks you?" His expression was rueful and mild. "But it was an offering of honor to the sun itself—how could it be a lesser creature? We drugged them, so they felt nothing. And it was usually a child who was crippled or simple, or sometimes an adult, ill or in pain, who asked for the honor. Small loss for anyone. And they were serfs, of course."

"Not criminals?" Soraya asked. In the ancient times before Rostam cast down the djinn king, when priests who truly believed had sacrificed many lives to the djinn, it was usually criminals they had chosen. And that was hundreds, maybe thousands of years ago. Soraya's stomach felt hollow. Calfaer had become such a good friend; it startled her when he said or did something to remind her that he was from a very different place, that his heart belonged to a different people.

"How could offering a criminal honor anyone, much less a god?" asked Calfaer reasonably. "A sound pig is probably better than that!"

But with that reasoning, wouldn't a healthy child be better than a cripple? Or a noble better than a serf? And as for the simple . . . Soraya thought of Ludo's strong arms and happy face, and shivered. It seemed that everyone was blind to logic when it came to their superstitions. She wondered how they'd been killed—the knife, burning, drowning? The ancient priests of her own land had exposed sacrifices to the elements, and according to the legends they hadn't all been criminals either. So who was she to start throwing out words like "barbaric." Still . . .

"I have shocked you," said Calfaer apologetically. "If it's any consolation, it doesn't happen anymore. The Hrum put a stop to it."

"It's not that," said Soraya slowly, although it was. "I was just wondering if maybe Substrategus Barmael might have had a crippled brother or sister."

Calfaer stiffened at the name of the hated traitor, and after a few moments the language lesson resumed, on a topic far removed from festivals. But he was quiet and thoughtful for several days after that.

Soraya wasn't surprised when, in the feverish glow of the late-setting sun, she saw him approach the door of Substrategus Barmael's quarters and call for admittance. The door opened and he went in. The door closed. Calfaer hadn't come out by the time Soraya went to bed.

SHE WONDERED WHAT HAD PASSED between them, but that question was driven from her mind by the news, the wonderful news, that "Sorahb" had struck again. It had taken time for that name to reach the ears of the servants in the Hrum camp—and possibly even longer for it to reach the Hrum command. Soraya had already heard it connected to the warehouse fire. Connected to a cartload of supplies that had included several months' pay for a local garrison, and which had rolled into the Hamaveran and sunk. Connected with a dispatch that disappeared, and even a batch of "bad soap" that turned several tubs of scarlet cloaks a muddy orange-brown.

It seemed to Soraya that the peasants were telling the Hrum that every natural mischance was an act of Sorahb. Though she'd also heard a rumor that the djinn were awakening to fight the Hrum—as if the djinn ever did anything that useful, even in the ancient times when they might have existed. Soraya had begun to believe that the warehouse fire might have been an accident after all. Certainly the Hrum hadn't found the men who were responsible for it.

But this, this could be nothing but the work of Farsalan rebels!

She didn't hear of it firsthand; Governor Garren barred all servants from the meeting where he discussed this with his staff. But listening to the gossip of the soldiers, in the breathless heat of the meal tent, she pieced it together.

It seemed that the Mazad town guard, after months of staying safe behind their high walls, had launched a surprise attack on the Hrum camp. Even that paled into insignificance, compared to the news that another force had ridden out of the hills and attacked the Hrum from the rear—at just the right tactical moment!

Reports of how many there were varied from rumor to rumor. Some said there had been several thousand, and they would have overwhelmed the garrison if they hadn't fought so poorly. Some said there were only a few centris, but that they fought with a ferocity and skill that the desperate garrison had been unable to match. But even the most conservative reports confirmed that Arus' tacti had been badly mauled, and the less conservative claimed that only a handful survived.

Soraya knew better than to put much credence into any of the rumors, especially the one that claimed that the rebel army vanished into thin air after the attack. Still, someone out there was fighting against the Hrum! Helping Mazad to resist. She wished she could help them, whoever they were. If she could find them, perhaps she could pass on some of the information she overheard. In reality, she had no idea who these men might be, much less how to contact them—and between fetching water, scrubbing pots, serving tables, cleaning tables, and scrubbing more pots, she didn't have the time or energy to try. But it made a wonderful fantasy to beguile the boring marks. All the more boring, since Calfaer seemed to be avoiding her these days.

It wasn't that they didn't meet, or that he was angry with her, which had been her first thought. But he didn't seek her out to offer lessons, and when she did see him, she sensed some sort of tension, almost fear, underlying his usual calm.

So she wasn't completely surprised that morning, when he failed to appear at his usual chores. Hennic was missing as well, and when he finally arrived—looking to be in an even worse temper than usual—Ordnancer Reevus was with him. The ordnancer was unshaven and rumpled, which was most unlike him.

"After breakfast has been served, you will all gather in the yard beyond the ovens," Reevus told them grimly.

A ripple of consternation passed through the staff. Soldiers were punished in the main square, where all the troops could gather to witness the consequences of breaking army rules. And even though it hadn't happened in the months Soraya had been here, she knew that servants were punished in the yard beyond the ovens—smaller, for the servants who were required to watch were a far smaller population, and there was no need to disrupt the lives of the troops and officers with their discipline. And Calfaer was the only one missing!

What could he have done? She had thought Calfaer was resigned to his lot, if not content with it. He had no quarrel with anyone Soraya knew of, except Barmael, who seemed like a decent man. But did she really know the substrategus?

Hennic slammed a pot onto the hearth with a crash that made everyone jump. "Back to work! Breakfast won't make itself, and if three thousand troops go hungry you'll all feel the lash!"

The lash? Soraya shivered, and went back to fetching vegetables for the cook who was starting the midmeal stew. What had Calfaer done? Was there some way she could help him? Without giving herself away? No. She had to put Merdas and Sudaba first. She had to! But if there was anything she could do for Calfaer . . . He was her friend. How could she fail to help him, whatever the cost? But even if she was willing to abandon her family—and she couldn't do that—what could she do?

At least torture was against Hrum law—they considered it uncivilized. But their military discipline was almost as harsh. Calfaer had told her the difference was that the law prescribed both the types of penalty that were acceptable, and when such penalties could be applied, while a torturer could do anything. Soraya didn't consider that much of a difference.

All too soon, breakfast passed. Even before the last of the soldiers had left the meal tent, Hennic was herding the servants out of the kitchen, striking those who lingered with a big, wooden spoon. Soraya, feeling the dread and regret that underlay his anger, hardly blamed him.

Three deci surrounded the small, grave group that gathered by the big ovens—as if it took thirty armed soldiers to stop the kitchen staff from trying anything. Ordnancer Reevus was there, grim and sorrowful, but he wasn't the highest-ranking officer present. Barmael's blunt, bearded face was even more expressionless than usual. Calfaer, standing with his hands bound in front of him, glared at the substrategus with angry defiance.

Had her comments on sacrifice led to this? Soraya's heart ached. But what could she do?

"You have been called here to witness the punishment of the slave Calfaer," Ordnancer Reevus said firmly. "As you know, respect for officers, in word and deed, is required from all members of this army. This is the rule Calfaer has broken."

Lack of respect didn't sound bad, but Soraya knew that the Hrum regarded it as part of their military discipline and took it seriously. And if she knew that, Calfaer had to have known it too. What could he have said or done—

"The slave Calfaer has attempted to 'ill-wish' Substrategus Barmael, by means of a charm thought to be of great power in the Brasnian culture," Reevus went on.

A charm? Calfaer had said nothing to indicate the Brasnians believed in any kind of magic. And she knew he thought the tales she told him of Farsalan djinn were silly, though he'd been too polite to say so.

"He did this by making this charm, imbuing it with ill will, and placing it under Substrategus Barmael's bed," Reevus went on. He pulled a small cluster of leaves from his pocket and held it out for all to see. For just a moment, contempt for Barmael, for his vindictive superstition, flickered across the ordnancer's face, then he banished it. He handed the bundle of leaves to the nearest servant, who happened to be Casia. "In their culture, this constitutes a personal attack."

Soraya's gasp was lost among the others. Attacking an officer, even plotting to do so, could be punished by death.

"But Substrategus Barmael has been persuaded to content himself with a charge of disrespect, though he insists on punishment for that."

Soraya's throat was tight. The substrategus, with his unshaven face and his strange accent, had seemed a kind man. She reached out and took the small bundle of leaves from Casia, closing her eyes, reaching for the leaves' shilshadu. Using the ability in her work—to heat water, to coax fire to life—had made her far quicker at it. Dried basil, with prickling thistles mixed in. A shadowy memory of life, of long sunlight and quenching rain. Nothing but leaves.

She opened her mouth to say so, to tell them there was no magic here . . . but how could she explain her knowledge? Her palms stung, and she realized she had clenched her hands on the thistles and let the bundle drop.

"Wait," said Hennic. "How do you know it was Calfaer that did it? It could have been someone else, couldn't it? I mean, Substrategus Barmael's not . . . um . . ."

He meant that Barmael's criticism of the governor's policies was earning him enemies among the officers. But they would hardly show their enmity by putting leaves under his bed, and besides —

"This form of . . . attack is particular to the Brasnian countryside," Reevus explained. "And Calfaer is the only Brasnian besides the substrategus currently in camp. When we asked him about it, he confessed. Although . . ." He turned to Calfaer, a bit of hope creeping into his expression. "If there is anything you want to say, any explanation you want to give, you may speak now. Ten lashes is the minimum disciplinary penalty, but it may be lessened if there are exculpatory circumstances."

All eyes turned to Calfaer, who lifted his head. He turned to Barmael and spoke directly to him. "You are not fit to keep my father's pigs." Then he spat on the ground at Barmael's feet.

Barmael's expression didn't change, but Reevus' face hardened. "Twelve lashes. Guard."

Two husky soldiers stepped forward to pull the slight, middle-aged slave over to the fence rail. Calfaer meant to go without resistance, Soraya saw. To walk with dignity. But as he approached the fence his steps began to slow. The soldiers had to drag him the last few yards, stumbling and slipping as he tried to brace his feet. They looped his wrists over the top of one fence post and tied them there, so that Calfaer stood with his back to the crowd.

Soraya couldn't stop it, but perhaps there was another way she could help. Maok had spoken of healers sharing the shilshadu of pain, but Soraya hadn't paid much attention, since that kind of advanced Speaking was far beyond her ability.

Now she closed her eyes and steadied her breathing, reaching deep—deeper than she had in months—into the still darkness where her own spirit dwelled. She tried to ignore the sounds of people moving around her. The arms master who was to execute the sentence tested his whip on the air, and the sound made the fine hairs on Soraya's neck prickle. *No, it's not relevant. Deeper.*

Her grasp on her shilshadu was shakier than it should be, but it would soon be too late to try anything. She summoned up her memory of the warm, wry brightness that was the core of Calfaer's spirit and opened herself to it—careful not to reach, for she knew that would fail.

There he was, full of fear, but also . . . satisfaction? Soraya opened her eyes in confusion. No one had rescued him. Calfaer was still tied to the fence. The arms master who trained the soldiers to use a whip was stepping up behind him, cutting open the back of his shirt, pulling it off his shoulders.

Calfaer was about to be flogged, and he knew it, but shilshadu to shilshadu there were no lies. Under the hammering fear was an intense sense of achievement—almost joy.

What in Azura's name was going on here? Soraya opened her sensing further. She had more experience with Calfaer, and she'd always found his shilshadu easy to touch, as if their spirits were well matched. But she also knew the others around her. There was Hennic, his pain already turning into anger. Ludo and Casia's distress. But they weren't the ones she was looking for.

Reevus and Barmael stood watching as the arms master picked up his whip—there was no more time. Soraya closed her eyes again and tried to concentrate, to ignore what was about to happen. It was hard to open herself, instead of trying to grasp at Calfaer's shilshadu, especially when the need was so urgent. But she'd become more adept at her summoning in the last few months. She was almost—

The whip whistled down and snapped on flesh, and Soraya jumped, her thoughts scattering. Calfaer made a choked sound of pain.

She put her hands over her ears, scuttling deeper into her spirit, like an animal seeking shelter in its burrow. *Calfaer, Calfaer's spirit.* She opened to it as fully as she knew how, feeling the jagged spike of pain as the whip hit again. She could feel it but she didn't know how to share it, to ease it, as the Suud healers did.

But even as the pain increased, as his will shattered and he began to scream, that strange sense of victory grew. His body might wince but his spirit was content, almost welcoming the blows.

It was *another* spirit, grave and soft, but also

sharing some part of that odd satisfaction, that flinched at every cut.

Soraya opened her eyes. For the first time in the months since she'd left the Suud, she had reached the full shilshadu trance. Ordinary objects—the rough-woven cloth of Casia's tunic, the drab clay of the hot ovens—were distinct in Soraya's vision, as if illuminated by some inner light. The splattering drops of Calfaer's blood glowed with color, with life, like sun-drenched, crimson glass. Soraya looked at the faces around her: horrified, avid, sickened, smug. It was easy to read them, to sense the emotions behind the masks of flesh.

She looked for the other spirit she had touched, searching only with her eyes, her spirit held carefully quiescent.

There. Him. Barmael. His face was expressionless, but his spirit leaked pain and regret more freely than Calfaer's back was bleeding. And the same satisfaction that cradled Calfaer's spirit was there too—softer and less urgent in Barmael, but still the same feeling that everything was going according to plan.

What plan? It was almost as if—

"Are you all right, Sani? Come on, it's all . . . It's over."

A firm hand, Casia's hand, shook Soraya's shoulder, pulling her up through the warm layers of the trance. Objects lost their strange luster. The faces around her became ordinary, the emotions behind them decently hidden.

Soraya gasped and shook herself free of the last of the trance. A surgeon was cutting down Calfaer's limp body, easing him onto the waiting litter.

The beating had ended, and she hadn't even noticed.

"Are you all right?" The sharp concern in Casia's voice wasn't only for Calfaer. Soraya summoned up a smile.

"Don't worry, I'm just . . . I'm fine."

Soraya took another breath and approached the surgeon. He had Calfaer on the litter now, almost ready to go.

"Sir," said Soraya humbly. "May I be tending to him? Calfaer's a friend of mine." She meant it too, though the sight of the ragged cuts, still oozing blood, made her stomach turn. But she couldn't let Calfaer lie unattended.

"Don't worry, girl." The surgeon's voice was cool, but not unkind. "We'll take good care of him."

"Yes, but after he's been bandaged he'll still need—"

"We're to nurse him," said the surgeon. "Substrategus Barmael's orders. He'll have to have nursing, if he's to travel in just three days."

"Travel? Travel where?" It came out more sharply than humble servant girls were supposed to speak, and Soraya bit her lip. The surgeon didn't seem to notice.

"That's right. Bar—the substrategus doesn't want to share camp with someone who can ill-wish him."

The surgeon's neutral voice held the same contempt for barbarian superstition that Soraya had sensed from Reevus. But surely . . .

"Travel where?" she demanded, no longer caring how she sounded.

"Back to his old master," said the surgeon. "I told them it was a long trip for a man who's just been flogged. But his master left him to this unit of the army for as long as they needed his services, and if we didn't want him he was to be returned to the man's family, along with the rest of his personal belongings. We evidently needed him at the time, but if he's being kicked out . . ." The surgeon shrugged.

Two soldiers stepped forward to lift the litter. Calfaer moaned softly. The surgeon shrugged again and strode off after them, clearly having no more time to waste on servant girls. No time for slaves, when they weren't injured. No time to know that "back to his old master" meant back to his wife and children.

Calfaer was going home.

SORAYA DIDN'T GO to see him during the days Calfaer lay in the surgeon's building. She didn't need to, and she knew he didn't need her, or anyone here any longer.

Had they planned it together, he and Barmael, that first night Calfaer approached him? How convenient it was, that there were no other Brasnians in the camp to say that there was no such thing as 'ill-wishing' in their culture. Still, Calfaer had paid a high price for his homecoming. Soraya was happy for him, though she knew she would miss his company.

On the morning when the cart train in which Calfaer would travel was ready to set off, Soraya went to bid him farewell.

It was already a breathlessly hot day, with a brassy taste in the air that Soraya knew meant clouds were gathering over the sea. The first of the summer thunderstorms would arrive late today. Soraya hoped the cart train would have reached shelter by then, for Calfaer was in no condition for a drenching.

He hobbled out of the surgeon's building, walking on his own, though he moved as slowly and stiffly as an old man, and the carter had to help him into the cart.

Soraya waited till his breathing eased before she approached. "I came to wish you well," she said. "Though I know you'll be well, where you're going."

"I will indeed," said Calfaer. His face was tight and pale with pain, but the satisfaction had changed to an incandescent joy, as clear to Soraya's senses as a shout of triumph. "Though I'll miss you, my girl. Be . . . Take care."

Be careful. How much of Soraya's story had he guessed? It didn't matter, for she knew he would never tell anyone.

A clerk hauled a chest of documents up to the cart. "Io, it's hot already! What's it going to be like this afternoon, if it's this hot now?"

It might well be raining, at least by evening.

The carter snorted. "It'd be less hot if you just brought the scrolls I need, instead of lugging the whole chest around."

"Think I don't know that? But it's even hotter in the record room. The candles are melting! Well, they're getting squishy. And the windows there are so cursed small you can barely see to read, even in broad daylight. Besides, most of these are yours anyway. I hope you've got a document box."

The carter had to move several bundles to extract the document box from under his seat, but eventually he got it out and the clerk unlocked the chest and started sorting scrolls—dispatches, supply requests, accounts. Soraya would have spoken with Calfaer, but he was watching the clerk with a curious intensity.

"And travel orders for the slave," the clerk finished. "He's going all the way to L'dron, so you'll have to pass him off to another cart train in the capital, but it's all here, with proper authorization." He handed over a final scroll, and some of the tension eased out of Calfaer's shoulders.

"Did you doubt?" a soft voice behind Soraya rumbled. She jumped, then stepped aside. How could a man as big as Barmael move so quietly?

Calfaer, perched on the cart, looked down at the man he considered a traitor. "No. I didn't doubt."

"Then good Sunhigh to you," said Barmael. His voice was placid, his face expressionless as usual. The carter, knowing nothing of the story that lay between them, paid no attention—and the clerk, who did, probably took it for irony, or some barbarian insult. But Soraya, remembering that Sunhigh was a time of gift giving as well as sacrifice, held her breath. Barmael had sacrificed the respect of men like Reevus and the surgeon, to give this gift.

"A good Sunhigh to you too . . . sir." Calfaer's voice was soft, and ironic. It might be taken for either a final defiance, or an admission of defeat. Soraya knew that he had called a man not fit to keep his father's pigs "sir," and he had meant it. Her eyes were wet.

The carter, caring less about good-byes than his schedule, goaded the ox into motion. The cart lurched away, making Calfaer wince. It would be a long journey, Soraya thought, and painful at first, but he would make it. She stood and waved until buildings hid the cart from sight. When she looked around, Barmael had gone, and the clerk was reloading his chest.

"Can I be helping carry that, sir?" Soraya asked, as a humble kitchen girl should. Especially a kitchen girl who never passed up a chance to peek into the small building where the records were stored.

She had never been allowed inside—no one was, except for authorized personnel, which didn't include curious servants. But it seemed that the heat melted rules as well as tallow candles. When she and the clerk puffed up to the small, covered porch that sheltered the door, each carrying one end of the heavy chest, the guard simply unlocked the door to let them pass.

"Over here." The clerk steered them into a corner where they laid the chest on top of several others. "Io, this place is hotter than an oven."

"That's maybe because the windows are small," said Soraya in her best ignorant-country-girl accent. "There's lots of records in here, aren't there?" She scanned the boxes as closely as she dared. Her fingers itched to pry into them.

"And Marcellus will skin me if I get them out of order," said the clerk. He took a small box from a cabinet, opened it, and dropped in the key. It clanked as if there were other keys there, and Soraya's eyes widened. She looked down hastily, peering through her hair as the clerk replaced the box and closed the cabinet. "Thank you, lass. Let's get out where it's cooler."

He didn't seem to expect a reply, as he guided her out of the record room—which was good, for Soraya wasn't sure she could have controlled her voice. She knew where the keys to the chests were kept! All she had to do was to get into the building—the locked, guarded building—and find and translate the right records. Soraya had been watching this building for months; the door was always guarded, but the windows weren't.

Of course, they'd deliberately made the windows small, too small for a grown man to climb through them. But a slender girl might manage it, if there was something going on to distract the guard from any small noises she made. Something like the first summer thunderstorm, which would probably arrive tonight. Soraya shivered. She had seen a man flogged for disrespect, just a few days ago. She didn't dare imagine what the Hrum might do if they caught her. But now she knew where the keys were. This was her first chance to get her hands on those records. Her best chance. She would try it tonight.

MONTHS WENT BY, *and Mazad's walls held fast, so the Hrum became impatient and decided to send more troops. Then the governor of Mazad, once more grown fearful, sent a message to Sorahb. "The Hrum are sending a great force to overwhelm us. It is time for you to fulfill your promise, and come to our aid."*

Sorahb was sorely torn, for he knew his soldiers were not as skilled as the Hrum, but he had given his oath to assist the governor in time of need. The honor of the Farsalan army was at stake, so Sorahb led them to Mazad.

"Fear nothing," he told his men, as Azura's sun illuminated the trampled plain and the Hrum's mighty host. "The Hrum are skilled, but they fight only for pay, at the

command of their officers—their true hearts are not here. But we are fighting for our families and our homes, and mere mercenaries can never defeat such men."

Sorahb's soldiers cheered, and Sorahb's sword flashed in the new sun as he raised it. Then Sorahb himself led the first charge against the Hrum camp.

All that day the battle raged. At first the Hrum were surprised, so advantage fell to Sorahb's peasant army. But soon the Hrum's superior experience asserted itself, and they were able to hold their ground. Yet Sorahb's army outnumbered them, and as Sorahb had told them, they fought for their homes, so they fought strongly if not well, and refused to be defeated.

The charge Sorahb led against the Hrum camp was the first of many. Time and again he led his forces against the Hrum's formation, felling the soldiers who guarded the Hrum commander like a scythe, almost killing the Hrum commander himself on more than one occasion. His soldiers, watching, marveled at his skill, and were further heartened by their young commander's courage.

But in the end the Hrum were too skilled, too experienced to be defeated. Sunset drenched the battlefield in light the color of blood, and Sorahb saw that for all they had accomplished, his army could not win. He signaled for retreat, and the Hrum were glad to see them go and did not pursue them.

But later, when the count of the wounded and the slain had been tallied, Sorahb found he had lost a full third of his men to death or capture, and many more were wounded and would not be able to fight again for a long time, if ever. Though he knew they had hurt the Hrum most sorely, it was not enough to break the siege. And he realized that more Hrum troops would be sent out, and then more, and more, until sooner or later, Mazad would fall.

"So I am forsworn perforce," Sorahb whispered. "And these men I have trained and led to their deaths, have died for nothing. How could I be so mad, so vain, as to think I could lead peasants to defeat this army when they had defeated deghans already? The fault is mine."

Unable to bear the sight of the misery he had caused, Sorahb abandoned his army, and fled into the darkness.

CHAPTER THIRTEEN

SORAYA

THE STORM'S FIRST FURY had eased, but rain still pounded on the kitchen's roof, noisy enough to drown far louder sounds than Soraya made as she slipped a few things into a sack and made a quiet exit. Not that she feared waking the other servants, who slept on the floor beside her—if anyone woke, she would say she was going to visit the privy. If anyone noticed the amount of time she was gone, she would say that after so much heat, the rain had tempted her into going for a walk. It should ring true—if she hadn't had other plans for the night, Soraya might have done just that, for she had always loved storms. Until tonight.

Unrolling her pallet on the floor, trying to behave normally, Soraya had sensed the storm hovering out at sea, the dark clouds boiling over the stars, the rising wind that sang in her blood. The humming tension that preceded lightning.

Hours had passed, and the storm stubbornly refused to approach land. It happened sometimes, especially with the first storms of the season. They spent all their power at sea, trapping the fisherfolk in their docks, cursing the landsmen with heat and bad tempers, without the cooling relief of rain. But Soraya needed it to arrive tonight!

Storms resonated with her shilshadu as nothing else did, not even fire, but the last time she had opened herself to a storm the lightning had come seeking her, and only her sudden panic had pushed it away to strike elsewhere. When you opened your shilshadu to fire it wouldn't harm you—Soraya wasn't at all sure the same was true of lightning.

Lying in the warm darkness of the kitchen, surrounded by the servants' peaceful snores, Soraya had opened her shilshadu to the storm. It rushed to fill her, vast and careless, dancing with delight at its own power. For a time Soraya's spirit danced with it—it was all she could do to remember that she was a human thing, to summon human will and try to persuade the storm to come toward her. For all its might the storm's shilshadu was thin, eluding her will as if she was trying to catch mist in her hands. A headache grew behind her eyes, and sweat rolled down her still body. When the storm, ever so slowly, started toward land, Soraya wasn't certain if her own will was moving it, or if it had finally decided to come on its own. Once she was sure it would continue in the direction she had chosen, she sighed with relief and released it.

But the storm wouldn't let her shilshadu go. Soraya's heart began to pound. She had pulled her spirit back into herself, well contained in flesh and bone, but she still sensed the storm's shilshadu, fixed on her, seeking its dance partner.

Soraya sat up in bed, no longer caring if she woke the others. She pinched herself, hoping pain would center her spirit in her flesh sufficiently that the storm would lose its hold. She banned all thought of magic from her mind, anchoring herself in her body alone.

Perhaps it had worked—perhaps it was only

her awareness of the link that had dimmed. All she knew for certain was that the leading edge of the storm had crashed over the Hrum camp like the wrath of Kanarang. Soraya wasn't the only one who cowered in her bed in terror of the lightning.

Eventually the violence of the storm front passed on. The other servants, grumbling, had resettled themselves for sleep. Now the thunder only rumbled in the distance, and the lightning was an even more distant frisson at the edge of her sensing as she crept out of the kitchen. Only the rain remained, pelting through her hair in thick, wet drops, turning the dusty streets to mud, and keeping everyone but the night watch snug in their quarters.

She would never have a better chance.

Soraya had been scouting the positions where the sentries were posted for months now. It took a little extra time, especially in the rainy darkness, to make her way to the back of the record room without encountering anyone, but it was far from impossible.

Barrels had been placed at the corners of many buildings to catch the clean rainwater, and Soraya crouched beside one, listening for any sound that could make itself heard over the soft rush of rain. For a long time she heard nothing. She weighed the stupidity of going close enough for the guard to see her against her need to know that he was where she thought he was. Before impatience lured her into foolishness, she heard the small clanks of metal on metal that accompanied the movement of armed-and-armored men.

From the sounds, she guessed the guard had started pacing back and forth on the covered porch—perhaps for warmth, perhaps to keep himself awake, but it didn't matter. What mattered was that, like any sane man, he stayed under the shelter of the small roof instead of moving out into the rain. Feeling the drops crawling under her saturated hair and down her neck, Soraya grinned and moved to the narrow window at the back of the building. It was placed too high beneath the eaves for the rain to enter, so they hadn't bothered with shutters, but it was also too high for her to climb in without help. No matter.

Soraya went back to the rain barrel and dragged it to the window. It was already half full, and might have been too heavy for her to move if the mud hadn't lubricated its passage.

Clinging to the edge of the window for balance, she pulled herself up till she knelt, then stood on the barrel's rim. First she lowered her supply sack through, then she carefully reached down and swished one muddy foot, and then the other in the clean water. Not knowing where she might have to go next, it would be best if she could leave the Hrum camp without arousing suspicion. She'd already prepared her lie for Ordnancer Reevus—an ailing aunt in a distant village, who might be moved to make a helpful niece her heir.

The window was a tighter fit than Soraya expected, long and narrow, and it was very dark inside. A quick wiggle took her head and shoulders through, but then she had to squirm forward, dragging her ribs painfully over the hard wood. Even her slim hips almost wedged, but she rocked back and forth and her bones passed the frame, her buttocks squashing through behind them.

Fortunately no one had moved the stack of document boxes she'd noticed beneath this window—though the room was so crowded, it would have been hard to find any wall space that didn't have boxes stacked almost to the rafters.

Careful as she was to move silently, knees and elbows hitting wood made a few soft thumps as Soraya groped her way to the floor. But the rain on this roof was as loud as it was in the kitchen, and Soraya didn't think the guard would hear.

Still, once her feet found the floor, she closed her eyes and waited, listening again, till her pounding heartbeat slowed and her breathing quieted. If the guard was out there she couldn't hear him, so hopefully he couldn't hear her, either. Good enough.

Soraya opened her eyes and considered her first problem: Inside the record room it was pitch dark. The windows made squares of slightly lighter blackness, and she thought she could make out the corners of a few of the higher boxes, but even the Suud, with their wide-dilating pupils, couldn't have read anything.

She'd come prepared for this, though she'd hoped it wouldn't be necessary. Half a dozen drying cloths from her sack covered the windows, secured with nails from the blacksmith's reject pile, pushed into the cracks between window frame and wall. She rolled another pair of cloths together and laid them quietly along the bottom of the door, for light seeping through that crack would certainly alert the guard.

Making any kind of light was still insanely risky, but Soraya had no choice. Surely working magic now wouldn't attract the distant storm. Suppressing the apprehension that quickened her pulse, Soraya pulled flint, steel, and a candle from her sack, and summoned up a light shilshadu trance. The clicks of flint on steel sounded very loud. Without magic, no one could ignite a candle with a single spark. With her mind touching its shilshadu, Soraya was able to convince the tiny flake of fire's birth that here were air and fuel aplenty. It responded to her persuasion with a brighter glow, a wisp of smoke, and then flame bloomed.

Candlelight illuminated the small room, bright after the near total darkness that preceded it, and Soraya watched the door, holding her breath. No exclamation. No startled, running footsteps. No key rattling in the lock. Soraya took a deep breath and began to read the labels on the crates.

Calfaer had taught her the written Hrum words for money, pay, and supplies, and she thought she could ignore those boxes. The first unfamiliar words sent her for the box of keys, still in the cabinet where she had seen the clerk put it this morning, though many men must have used them since. Such methodical people, the Hrum.

To her delight, the keys were numbered to match the chests.

Opening box fourteen enabled her to deduce the Hrum word for "map," another to guess at "building plans." Yet another phrase she didn't recognize led to a box filled with closely written documents that might have been letters or reports—whatever they were, they didn't look like records of slaves, so she relocked that box and went on. Between excitement at being so near her goal, fear, and the need for haste, her fingers began to shake. The lid of the next box slipped, and it closed with a thud. Listening through the pounding of rain on the roof, she still heard nothing from the guard, and the same rain pounded on the roof over his head as well. She was safe. Soraya took a deep breath and forced herself to relax. This was going to take time—she would simply have to resign herself to that.

But only three boxes later she came across a box of neatly rolled scrolls, each labeled, not with some Hrum word, but with the name of a Farsalan town or village. Her heart beginning to pound, Soraya took the top scroll and opened it. The first item was a rough map, showing where in Farsala this village lay. There followed a list of names, and each name was followed by several paragraphs of writing. Dates, written in the Hrum manner, began each paragraph, but Calfaer had taught her to read them.

On 23 Hyrum, 204, Duram, butcher, adrias *to sell* murous *meat to the garrison, in order to . . .*

Soraya's eyes moved past the details of this Duram's crime and capture, though not without a flicker of curiosity about how he'd poisoned the meat, and what he'd been trying to accomplish by doing so. At the end of the paragraph she found what she was looking for.

After his capture, Duram was varsele *and sent to the* sele *market in K'navan, in the imperial province of Drhur.*

Sele. Slave. She'd have felt better if she had any idea where Drhur was, but if Sudaba and Merdas had been sent there too, then she'd find out.

Soraya rerolled the scroll and put it back.

Sudaba and Merdas had been taken on the estate of High Commander Merahb. She spent some time looking for her father's name before she came across that of the small village that served the manor.

Her lips compressed. To say that Merdas and Sudaba had been captured in Paldan, amid the grooms and laundry maids, was an insult. But the Hrum would hardly care for that, and it was the nearest village to the manor. When she told her mother this story, she could leave that detail out. *When she told her mother . . .* Soraya's hands were shaking again as she pulled out the scroll. She would have to edit a lot of details about this adventure. Her mother would be aghast at the very idea of her working as a servant—especially in an army camp. On the other hand Sudaba had been a slave for several months now. What work might she be doing? Would it change her? It was hard to imagine the haughty Lady Sudaba doing menial work, or changing in any—

A key rattled in the lock.

Soraya dropped the scroll, then snatched it back before it had time to touch the box, and leaped for the pile of crates below the far window. Scrambling like a squirrel, she had her head and shoulder through and was wiggling her hips past the frame when a firm hand closed around her ankle and dragged her back into the room.

She skidded over the crates, knocking her chin on the edge, and crashed to the floor with a violence that stunned her.

Half dazed, still clutching the precious scroll, she rolled over and stared up at two soldiers, and the astonished, affronted face of Master Clerk Marcellus.

"Wait, I've seen you before!" Marcellus exclaimed. "You're one of Hennic's assistants, aren't you? What under three moons are you doing here?"

Three moons? Where in the Hrum's vast empire did this man come from? But Soraya had heard many odd exclamations from the soldiers. She struggled to gather her wits. Her chin hurt. "I'm that sorry, sir, truly I am. There's a woman in town, she's being a friend of mine. She has a nephew, a dye trader, who went to Desafon a few months back and they haven't heard from him since. Rumor has it he was getting himself caught up in something, and shipped off as a slave. She was asking, begging me, to find out if it was true."

There, not bad for such short notice, and the tremor in her voice at the end was particularly good. As long as no one asked for the nephew's name.

"Hmm." Marcellus rubbed a bristly chin. He wore nothing but a light tunic and boots, with a cloak over the top, as a man will when suddenly wakened to investigate a suspicious disturbance. Soraya wished he looked sleepier. "If that's the case, why didn't this woman come and ask about her nephew?"

Soraya felt her eyes widen in genuine surprise. Could someone simply ask the Hrum about the contents of these scrolls? Well, perhaps some could, but not Commander Merahb's daughter.

"She was afraid, sir. I told her that you weren't being such hard folks, but she didn't believe me. And I like this job, truly I do. I'd hate to jeopardize it."

"But the scroll you're looking at isn't for Desafon," said Marcellus slowly.

How could even a clerk see that, at this distance, in this light?

"I had this one in my hand when I started to run," Soraya lied. "I don't even know what town it's for."

Every instinct screamed in protest as she held it out to him, praying for belief, for forgiveness. And if he was willing to tell the Farsalans who had been captured, and where they were sent, could she get a list of names from Setesafon's townsfolk, and slip Sudaba's and Merdas' names in among them? After all, the scroll would say that they were taken in the village.

Marcellus took the scroll, but he was staring at her face . . . no, at her hair. The long, straight, black hair that was the mark of pure deghan blood.

"'. . . *jeopardize* your job,'" he said slowly, and his accent on the word was the same as hers had been—a deghan's accent. This was a man who had dealt with many Farsalans: merchants, peasants, deghan captives, slaves. Soraya closed her eyes in sudden despair.

"'. . . rumor has it . . .' You don't sound much like a kitchen girl . . . Lady?"

"I'm not being a lady," Soraya protested, trying to sound frightened instead of betraying her sudden fury. She'd been so close! "My grandmam worked in a deghan's household. That's where Mam and I got the hair."

"And the accent? Did you get that from your 'grandmam'? Oh, don't bother. We'll find out, one way or the other. Take her to the holding pen. We'll send for someone who may be able to identify her."

"The holding pen? Where the slaves are being kept?" It wasn't hard to sound appalled at that. "Please, sir, won't you just send for Master Hennic? He'll be punishing me proper. I promise—"

"Don't bother," Marcellus repeated. "I wouldn't dream of letting this pass without investigation. But I will give you a word of advice . . . Lady. It's not that your deghan's accent shows, it's that your peasant accent's so exaggerated. The lowest hick from the smallest village doesn't talk that broadly."

Soraya gazed at his calm, shrewd eyes. He knew, and he wouldn't let it go. If nothing else, catching her would look good on his record. "Arzhang take you then," she said, dropping into her own, clear, deghan's speech. It felt strange on her tongue after so many months, but good. Like walking into a familiar room after a journey.

THEY TOOK HER TO THE holding pen. There was no real building there, just a shed filled with straw, open on one wall so the watch could see in.

329

The soldiers seized her wrists and searched her clothing for weapons before they thrust her through the gate in the high fence. Their touch had been utterly impersonal, but it was still an insult, and Soraya gritted her teeth. The open ground had turned to mud, but at least the rain was finally lessening, and by heaping the straw around her, Soraya was able to keep warm. Despite her fear, and the furious frustration of her shattered hopes, she had actually fallen asleep when rough hands pulled her out of the straw and swept her tumbled hair away from her face.

Blinking in the torchlight, Soraya could see nothing beyond the fence that surrounded the pen, for the Hrum had threaded boards through the iron ribs that curved inward at the top. But she heard voices, one Hrum and one with a Farsalan accent—the clearer speech of the city, she thought, though she couldn't make out most of the words. On the other hand, the clink of coin changing hands was unmistakable.

She'd been identified. All Setesafon had seen her last year, and of course the Hrum had paid informants in the city—men who wouldn't want to come to this camp in the daylight.

Fine then! She was glad to be rid of that humble, pathetic Sani. Of scrubbing, and fetching, and avoiding Hennic's slaps. She'd had to pay attention to the temper of a cook! No more. For better or worse, she was the lady Soraya. And the lady Soraya would never dream of missing the warm bulk of Casia's body between her and the hearth, or the comforting drone of Ludo's snores. Or the wry laughter of a slave . . . a slave, for Azura's sake! The lady Soraya needed no one.

The lady Soraya cried herself to sleep.

IT WAS AFTERNOON WHEN they took her to the governor's quarters. No breakfast, no midmeal. Soraya had done her best, combing straw from her hair with her fingers and braiding it back — so good to have it off her face, instead of hiding behind it — but she still felt grubby, unkempt, and very tired. The kitchen girls were allowed to wash . . but evidently not the prisoners.

She stepped through the door, head lifted proudly, and every officer gathered in the big room turned to stare at her. She knew a moment's longing for the time, only yesterday, when men's eyes had passed over her as if she wasn't even there. But that time was gone, so she stiffened her neck and stared back, not even flinching from Ordnancer Reevus' angry astonishment.

The guards pushed her forward to the cleared space before the governor's chair. Garren rose and walked around her, studying her with appraising eyes, like a man considering the purchase of a pig.

"Remarkable," he said. "From what I've heard of deghasses, I wouldn't have believed one would lower herself to pass as a servant, not for any cause. You must be very devoted to this 'Sorahb,' Lady Soraya."

She'd expected him to use her name, to throw her off balance. "I already knew you'd iden . . . Devoted to *who*? There is no Sorahb. That's a legend." Surely Garren's spies had told him that.

"I refer, of course, to the man who calls himself Sorahb. Though it might be a woman, I suppose." He watched her face closely, as if he expected her expression to give something away. But if it accurately reflected her feelings, Soraya's face would show nothing but confusion.

"I know someone's using the name," she said.

"The whole camp was talking about it when he attacked Mazad. But what does that have to do with me?" It felt good to speak firmly, after so long in Sani's humble skin.

"Ah." Garren shook his head in mock sorrow. "I feared you wouldn't admit it."

Soraya began to be afraid. "Admit what?"

"That you've been spying for Sorahb, of course. I knew he had a large organization, but I must say, it surprised me that he was able enough, and bold enough, to slip a spy into my own camp."

"I'm not a spy!" Soraya protested. She gazed around the room in search of support. Reevus' face was tight with fury, and the others showed nothing but varying degrees of anger or interest. Barmael's face, as usual, had little expression at all.

"Really?" Garren's quiet voice drew her gaze back to him. "Then perhaps you'd care to explain where you learned to speak Hrum? Since we've only just begun teaching it to our new recruits."

He was speaking in Hrum, she realized, and had been since she entered the room — she had replied in the same language without even thinking. Soraya closed her eyes in despair. A few marks' sleep in a pile of cold straw, and a day without meals, was poor preparation for matching wits with a snake like Garren. But she'd had no reason to expect traps, much less this absurd accusation.

"I'm not spying for Sorahb," she said, opening her eyes to face Garren squarely. "I'm not here to spy for anyone."

"Yet you haven't told me where you learned our language—and so swiftly too, though your accent leaves a bit to be desired."

She'd learned it from a slave, who'd departed just yesterday morning, and who could easily be returned for questioning . . . and be detained, perhaps on a permanent basis. She didn't dare to so much as whisper Calfaer's name. So what could she say?

"My father had me taught," said Soraya. They knew who she was, so it might seem plausible . . . barely. "He thought you should learn all you can about your enemies, including their language."

There! At least they couldn't disprove it. She glared at Garren defiantly.

"Hmm. But to teach it to you means he must

have realized his army would fail to stop us, or at least he knew it might, and he had already planned a second line of defense. Is this Sorahb carrying out some plan of your father's?"

I wish he was! "I don't know," said Soraya honestly. "I know nothing about Sorahb, whoever he is."

"Yet your father taught you Hrum, so you could spy for him."

"Not to spy—for anyone! It was because . . ." Now what? There was no plausible reason for her father to have taught her Hrum. "I was curious," she finished lamely.

Several of the officers snickered, but Garren simply watched. "You know, Lady Soraya, once we knew who you were, it wasn't hard to figure out why you wanted this." He picked up a scroll from the clutter on the table, and turned it so she could see the name of the village written on the outside.

Soraya suppressed a gasp, but she couldn't keep her hands from twitching toward the scroll. She had wanted it so badly, for so long. She still did. She clasped her hands behind her back and said nothing.

Garren smiled. "Your mother evidently wasn't

privy to her husband's plans. She put up quite a fight. Pity she was hurt so badly."

Soraya's heart lurched. But no, that peasant, Marlis' husband, had assured her that Sudaba and Merdas were both well and whole.

"Ah, so you already know she survived her folly unharmed. But you don't know what happened after she left Farsala. Probably not even where she and your brother were sent."

He was clever—too clever for her, as weary as she was. "Please." Begging this man for information would cost her any scrap of pride she had left, but Soraya cared more about Merdas than her pride. "Please, Governor Garren, I implore you—tell me where my mother and brother were sent." The effect might have been somewhat marred by her grinding teeth.

"Why?" Garren asked mildly. "So you can follow? Buy them? Free them? You're a slave now yourself, Lady. You'll go nowhere but where you're sent."

"But I haven't resisted anything!"

"You've spied for the resistance," said Garren. "And you're resisting now, refusing to reveal this Sorahb's identity."

"I don't know who he is!" Soraya wailed. "Truly!"

Garren smiled again—Soraya thought she'd never seen a smile so cold. "This gets us nowhere. Let's change the tenor of the discussion. If you tell me who Sorahb is—or if you truly don't know, tell me how you're contacting his people— then I will not only tell you where your mother and brother were sent, I'll have you sent to the same city, the same slave market! Your odds of finding them would be very good, and under our laws slaves who work hard enough can buy themselves free, though they're not allowed to return to their own land."

Soraya's breath caught. Sent to the same city! She wouldn't have to travel, alone, across the strange and hostile lands of the empire. In the same city surely she could find them—arrange some escape. But . . .

"I'm not a spy." She meant to say it firmly, but her voice came out in a whisper. "I can't tell you anything, because I don't know. But surely this Sorahb can't cause you too much trouble. The soldiers say that all you have to do to take Mazad is send for enough troops."

She hated herself for saying it, but if the common troopers knew it, then every man in this room must know it too. Mazad was strong, yes, but not invincible.

"I'm not concerned with Mazad," said Garren. "I'm concerned with Sorahb. And telling me at least the identity of your contact is your only chance of finding out where your family was sent. Certainly your only chance of getting there. Slave."

The word chilled her, as it was meant to, but why wasn't he concerned with Mazad? He had to take all the cities, or the Hrum's own laws would set Farsala free. And all the slaves they'd taken would be returned. Could she run some bluff of her own? Give him the name of some hapless resident of Setesafon? But she didn't know anyone in Setesafon, and even if she did, or if she simply gave them a description . . . Her father would never have forgiven her. She would never be able to forgive herself.

"I don't know who this Sorahb is," said Soraya, making up her mind. "But even if I knew, I wouldn't tell you. No deghass would, not even to save her family. Besides, if he wins, the slaves will be returned anyway—I'd rather bet on him than on you!"

Garren actually laughed. "No deghan would? Tell that to the gov—never mind. You're making a mistake, girl. There's nothing in the way of our conquest but this sorry fool Sorahb, and we'll certainly catch him sooner or later. The only reason I'm offering you this opportunity is that we might find him sooner with your help. I admit that. And in exchange for your help I'm offering you a chance, the only chance you'll get, to see your family again. What's left of your family, that is."

Soraya flinched. This was the man who'd led the army that killed her father. But she'd been watching him for weeks now, and cold as he was, he wasn't gratuitously cruel. He was trying to rattle her, to throw her off balance, to distract her from . . . From what? *Tell it to the gov—*

"You've suborned the governor of Mazad," Soraya whispered. "He's going to betray—"

Garren moved as fast as the snake she'd called him—Soraya barely had time to see the blow coming, before it knocked her off her feet.

She lay on the carpet looking up at him, trying

to hear through the ringing in her ears—to think through the pain that radiated from the left side of her face.

"Pick her up and take her back to the holding pen," said Garren. "No, to that other slave's quarters. She may as well begin her new duties tomorrow. The rest of you may go, all but Tactimian Brathat."

The guards hauled Soraya to her feet and dragged her, stumbling, from the room. Brathat was in charge of the camp's security. No doubt Garren would put a guard on her. No, not a guard, a subtle watcher, so her supposed allies would be tempted to make contact. If there was anyone Soraya really hated, she could wait a week or two and then try to get in touch with them. But she hated no one . . . except the Hrum!

She should have been grateful they were civilized enough to make torture illegal, or this might have been a very different interview—but she wasn't. Garren had suborned the governor of Mazad. What was his name . . . Nazahb? She tried to remember what her father had said of him, but she remembered nothing except that he was the gahn's cousin. It hardly mattered. She hadn't been working for Sorahb before, but she was now! She had to get word to him, to the city of Mazad, that their governor planned to betray them. Mazad's resistance through the Hrum's time limit was her only chance of seeing her family—what was left of it—again. It was a good thing she was working for Sorahb now. Spies didn't cry.

CHAPTER FOURTEEN

KAVI

AVI WADED THROUGH the aqueduct into Mazad, water soaking his stockings, expecting an ambush at any moment.

He'd been surprised to find the tunnel's entrance unguarded, but a moment's thought made him realize that a crowd of men in the bushes along the riverbank were more likely to attract the Hrum's attention than anything else. There were certainly enough patrols around to notice them. Kavi had lost over an hour eluding them before he reached the entrance. So it made sense to him that only the scrub oak's thick dusty leaves guarded the unobtrusive cut where the great hatch was located. Apparently that was enough, for if the Hrum had found these tunnels they'd surely have tried them. Even as Kavi turned the wheel that opened the door the old masons had used to cart in their supplies, he was listing the sudden turns in the corridor, the sheltered niches, the high ledges, all connected by hidden passages behind the aqueduct walls, designed to let Mazad's defenders turn their aqueduct into a death trap.

No, they were right to set their guards in the tunnel, instead of outside. Kavi, born, raised, and taught a craft in this town, knew the tunnels well. He remembered half a dozen good places for an ambush—and they'd already passed two of them. But aside from a creeping sense of anticipation, he wasn't afraid. Two dozen mules followed him up the passage, laden with grain, dried vegetables, and salt meat. They would be sufficient proof of his good intentions, even without the local farmers who now accompanied him.

It was the mules that forced them to wade, or rather, the fat bundles they carried, for the mules themselves were thin enough to manage the walkways that lined both sides of the tunnel. But if the aqueduct's floor was covered in sand and gravel carried in by the river, it was also level enough that he needn't fear tripping, and Duckie carried his dry boots. At least this was the inflow, bringing water from the Sistan River into the city, for washing and industry, instead of the outflow that carried the city's sewage back—

Half a dozen lances whispered into the water in front of his feet, and Kavi leaped back, swearing. "Hey, watch that! I'm barefoot."

He waited, letting the torches the farmers carried show that he had no weapons. A few moments later a man popped out of one of the nearly invisible niches and came down the walkway toward them. He carried another lance in his hands, but the tip was politely lowered.

"What goes on here?" He looked to be in his late twenties, his face tight with nervousness. Despite the passage of almost five years, Kavi recognized him as a journeyman carpenter—at least, he'd been a journeyman when Kavi left.

"So, are you a master carpenter now? Or do they still have you cutting kindling? Though your master claimed that was all your work was good for, as I recall." He wished he could remember the man's name, but he'd been almost ten years older than Kavi, training in a different craft. It probably didn't matter, for the man's face lit with sudden recognition.

"Kavi! I thought you were still palming off failed ironmongery."

"Not failed," Kavi protested. "Maybe not city-fancy, but still sound goods. And you know those farmers—nothing to pay in but food. So I thought I'd dump some of it on you."

The carpenter's gaze, taking in the line of laden mules stretching out behind Kavi, brightened even further. "The supplies? Commander Siddas said he'd arranged for them, but he didn't know when the folks outside would be able to get the shipment together."

Four other men appeared on the walkway as he spoke, but Kavi knew that several others would be lingering behind the tunnel walls to keep watch, or if it proved necessary, raise an alarm.

"We've three more loads this size waiting in the bushes outside the entrance," Kavi told them proudly. "We're hoping to get it all in, and the mules away tonight. The longer we're at this the more risk for everyone. But speaking of risk, why's a journeyman carpenter playing tunnel guard? Aren't we paying the town guard for that?"

"It's master carpenter now, you young lout, and the guardsmen are all needed on the walls. If I weren't posted here tonight, I'd probably be up there with them. This new group of Hrum isn't as foolish as the first. They've been pushing us. Last time they set fire to the main gate, and we had a hard time driving them off and putting it out. We lost several men."

Grief showed in his face, even in the wavering torchlight, and Kavi saw the same expression on the faces of the men beside him. In Kavi's day, the townsmen hadn't cared much for the guard—and vice-versa. The siege was changing things.

"How are you holding up?" Kavi asked quietly.

"Oh, we're doing fair. We smuggled out most of the children—all the babes—and their mothers with them, so it's just adults left. Which is good when the Hrum shoot fire arrows. We've too much thatch here. But we were running low on food. This"—the carpenter gestured to the mule train—"will help a lot. In fact you'll be getting a hero's welcome, so we'd best be—ah, almost forgot. I need all of you to take off your shirts."

Kavi's heart sank. Surely he couldn't know . . .

"Our shirts?" asked one of the farmers. "Why do you want our shirts off?" But he was removing his as he spoke, the last words muffled by folds of cloth.

"Turn so I can see your shoulder, please," said the carpenter. "All right, you can put it back on. It's not important," he added reassuringly. "Just something we're supposed to be checking for. On everyone."

His eyes were on Kavi now. Not yet suspicious, but his hand tightened a bit on the lance.

"Ah . . . There's something I need to explain to you," said Kavi. "You see —"

It was another man who leaped from the walkway, tackling Kavi into the water. He didn't resist, keeping his muscles limp in the other man's iron grip. After a moment the man stopped trying to wrestle with him, and hauled him to the surface. Kavi reached up to wipe his face, but hard hands seized his wrists, pulling his arms behind him. Three were in the water now, including the carpenter, but two more men had appeared on the walkway, lances ready.

"Take it easy, all of you. I said I'd explain."

The carpenter's knife ripped through the cloth of his sleeve, exposing the tattoo and the arrow scar above it. The hands gripping Kavi's arms tightened, bruising, and one man spat.

"What's going on here?" an older farmer demanded. "What is that?"

"I really can explain," said Kavi, but the carpenter's voice overrode his. "This is how the Hrum mark their spies."

"Their spies? But that's ridiculous. He's been helping us. Besides, why would anyone mark their own spy?"

"It's so I can convince any officer, even one who doesn't know me, that I'm working for them," said Kavi wearily. "But I'm not—"

A fist exploded into his stomach and he bent over, wheezing. Rough hands pulled his wrists together, binding them behind his back.

"No." The farmer's voice was firm now, and determined. "I don't care how he's marked, he's been helping us—for months! He organized these supplies! They come from villages all through this part of the country, and he's the one who set up all the deliveries. And other things too. He works for Sorahb! He can't be a Hrum spy."

"You're probably working for them too," one of the townsmen growled. "And the food is probably poisoned."

A number of lances were pointed at the farmers now. The siege had frightened the townsfolk, Kavi realized. Hardened them. He wondered frantically what he could say that would make matters better instead of worse.

"Don't be an idiot, Damad," said another farmer impatiently. "You've known me for years. How often have you picked fruit in my orchard? You can't possibly think I'm a Hrum spy."

"Then why is he marked as one?" another townsman demanded.

"I don't know," said the old farmer. "But he says he can explain, so I suggest you listen. Unless you plan to slit his throat here and now—"

The townsmen rumbled agreement, and Kavi winced. Of all the fool suggestions!

"But if you do, we're taking this food right back down the tunnel. And if you kill us and take it—and you'll have to kill us, if you kill him!—then you'll never see another shipment. How long can you survive without food from outside? You slit his throat, then sooner or later you'll be wearing

Hrum tattoos yourselves—slave tattoos! So you'd better listen to him, because he's been helping us against the Hrum for months. He really is working for Sorahb," the farmer insisted. A rumble of agreement from his own men backed him up.

Slowly they all turned to where Kavi stood, blinking water out of his eyes. "I can explain. But it's being a long story, and I'd rather not tell it twice. If you'll take me to the Craft Council, or Commander Siddas, I can tell everyone at once."

"We ought to take him to the governor," one of the townsmen grumbled. "He's for hanging Hrum spies from the battlements, and no questions asked."

"He was for doing that," said the carpenter slowly. His face, in the flickering light, seemed to have aged more than five years could account for. "If you'll remember, the commander stopped him. And the council agreed. All right. Bring him with us. But send men ahead, and not just to the commander and the council. I want an escort of real guards waiting when we get out of the tunnels."

THEY DRAGGED KAVI THROUGH the water— harder to keep his balance in the shifting gravel with his hands tied behind him. When he stumbled, they hauled him up and set him in motion again with cuffs and kicks.

At least they weren't taking him straight to the governor to be hanged, but how much difference would that make in the end? Kavi knew they had released the Hrum spies they'd caught earlier, but that was before the siege, before hatred had had a chance to grow. And they might be seeing a difference between an honest Hrum spy, and a Mazad man who had spied for the besiegers. Kavi shivered.

The farmers, seeing that he wasn't really being damaged despite the townsmen's anger, kept their peace. But Kavi felt battered as well as bedraggled when they finally emerged from the aqueduct into one of the warehouses that abutted the walls.

A guard unit was waiting for them, but they didn't look like the easygoing street patrols that had sometimes caught Kavi in childish pranks. For all their scruffy tabards, these men looked like soldiers, professional and dangerous.

The guard squadron's commander questioned both the farmers who'd accompanied Kavi and his captors. After some discussion, it was decided that he wasn't important enough to get the commander and the council out of bed in the middle of the night.

The cobbles were hard under his bare feet, but Kavi made no complaint—no one had expressed any hesitation about getting the governor out of bed.

The quiet, dark streets woke memories of dozens of childhood pranks, some as innocent as slipping out to try night fishing in the Sistan River, and some . . . Well, given who he was going to face tomorrow, Kavi was glad no one had ever found out who had managed to coat the Craft Hall steps with grease on the night before the parade of crafts, when each craftmaster emerged from the hall in his best finery . . . and most slippery shoes.

In the daylight the streets would be even more familiar, echoing with the clamor of a busy town, brimming with familiar faces. Kavi knew every twisting street within the walls, and most of the suburbs as well. The suburbs were gone now, burned in the Hrum's first fury, but the people had survived to fight.

His town.

Had the guard allowed him, he could have led

them to the lockup in the basement of the Craft Hall, even in the dark.

It wasn't a cell, just a storeroom with a stout door and bolts on the outside, and Kavi had slept there before. He hadn't gotten away with all his pranks. But in the morning he would face, not just the master metalworkers but the whole council, for this was no childish prank, to be taken care of by a small fine from his master and a few weeks confined to the yard. He could hang for this.

Despite the semifamiliar surroundings and the reasonable comfort of straw tick and blankets, Kavi slept badly.

THEY GAVE HIM BREAKFAST but no chance to wash or shave, though Kavi asked—no use appearing before the council looking more of a ruffian than he had to.

In fact it wasn't long after breakfast when the guards came, binding his wrists once more, leading him up the winding stone stairs to the great hall.

Despite the open windows, high in the walls, and the colorful weavings displaying the labor of each trade, the dark, gray stone made the huge room into a dim cavern. Only in full festival, with tables laid, full of brightly clad masters and their wives, and apprentices hurrying back and forth to serve them, was the great Craft Hall really alive.

Now, with only the craftmasters seated at the high, curving table at the end of the room, it felt as empty and imposing as a djinn's cave. Meant, no doubt, to intimidate hapless miscreants such as himself. Kavi set his teeth, lifted his head, and walked toward the open space before the raised dais without the guards' prodding. As if he had a townsman's right to the fair judgment of his friends and neighbors. He'd been away from the city, wandering the roads as a peddler, for half a decade. Would they still see him as one of them?

The guard commander, Siddas, sat in a chair to the right of the table, Kavi saw—not part of the council, but placed level with them. That too was a change. In his time, the guard captured people for the council, as well as for the governor, but they'd nothing to do with judgment.

His old master, Tebin, sat in a chair to the left of the metalworkers' craftmaster, but that wasn't unusual—a man's master would always be called to bear witness, for or against him. With Tebin it had been about fifty-fifty, at least where Kavi was concerned.

He came to a stop and gazed up at them, old men's faces, lined with years of work and responsibility. Even their disapproval was familiar. These were his people, and this his town. No wonder he had never betrayed Mazad.

"You first, Tebin." It was Golbas, the leatherworkers' craftmaster who sat in the central chair this year, for leadership of the council rotated among the trades, each in turn. "Is this man your journeyman Kavi?"

Ex-journeyman, the bitter thought flashed through Kavi's mind.

"He is," Tebin replied calmly.

Golbas sighed. "Well, his identity is established. Guard, turn him so we can see—"

"There's no need," said Kavi, trying to sound calm and assured, despite the pounding of his heart. "The Hrum marked me as one of their spies some six months ago."

"And why would they be doing that?" Golbas sounded as if he was honestly curious.

Kavi took a deep breath. "Likely because I agreed to spy for them."

The faces of the men on the dais showed surprise at this damning statement. Kavi had spent most of the night weaving tales, each more fantastical, more exculpatory, than the last. He wasn't sure when he'd decided to tell the truth, but Mazad deserved truth from him. He knew it was the right choice. He hoped it was. He was staking his life on it.

"I can explain," he said, for the final time. "But I don't know if you'll understand. When the Hrum first captured me, they were spying themselves, scouting inside our borders. They were all for slitting my throat once they knew I'd identified them. I was promising to say anything, do anything, to keep them from killing me right that moment. I was thinking I could promise now, and escape later."

Heads nodded around the table. These were practical men, who knew a practical choice when they heard it.

"Ah, so that's how you came to be marked. And you didn't, in fact, spy for them." It was the metalworkers' craftmaster, glad to see the matter so easily resolved.

"Not at first," said Kavi. Where had this

strange compulsion to speak true to these men, to cast himself upon their judgment, come from? After months of siege, he was taking the Flame's own risk!

"At first I just wanted to escape. But then I got to talking with them. One man in particular, a tactimian, Patrius. He told me a bit about the Hrum. A lot, actually. And they . . . They're better than the deghans, you know. They really are. Or so I thought. I still think so, in most ways, though I didn't know about the draft."

Not very clear, that, and not persuasive, but his quaking nerves were clouding his wits. *Calm.* He had to stay calm.

Golbas was considering his muddled explanation. "So Tactimian Patrius recruited you? And he lied about the Hrum? Emphasized their good points and ignored the bad?"

It would have been so easy to say "yes."

"If you knew Patrius, you'd know better than that," said Kavi. "He's one of those honorable, earnest types. He was scrupulously honest. That's what made it so effective. That I didn't know about the draft, that was just . . . a cultural misunderstanding."

The guard commander, Siddas, was listening intently, but he showed no desire to intervene. Kavi had known him by sight in the old days, and had heard he was a fair man. He wished he'd known the man better, for Kavi wasn't fooled by that modest chair, set off to the side. If this man chose to take the matter to the governor, Kavi was dead, no matter what the Craft Council decided. At least, that was the custom under the old law. The deghans' law.

"I hated the deghans," he said aloud. "I hated them so much, the Flame itself looked better to me than they did."

It had burned within him, that hate, stifled for years, since he'd known he'd never have a chance to avenge himself on the deghan who had maimed his hand when Kavi tried to stop him from stealing a sword from Tebin's shop. Or at least, he'd known that if he avenged himself he wouldn't survive it. Then the Hrum had offered him a chance. . . .

The craftmasters' expressions were changing, some growing softer, some harder, as they remembered his story. This was his town—he didn't have to explain his history to these men. Even

Commander Siddas' face bore the mark of sudden understanding.

"So you agreed to spy for the Hrum?" Golbas asked. "Of your own free will?"

"Yes," Kavi admitted, praying he wasn't signing his own death warrant with the words. "I found out about the deghans' troop movements, their battle plans. It helped the Hrum defeat them."

Tebin rubbed the bridge of his nose, concealing his face. Kavi wished he wouldn't. Even through his fear, it mattered to him what this man thought. Then again, perhaps he should be glad his master's face was hidden.

"If you wanted revenge, you seem to have achieved it." It was the millers' craftmaster, dry as the flour he ground.

"I did, and I did," Kavi confirmed. To his own surprise, his voice was steady. "But after that . . ."

How to explain what had happened after that. The night that had followed the battle, as the Hrum celebrated their victory. Kavi had left a bag of gold coin in his tent, uncounted, and wandered through the camp. He'd seen a girl he'd liked, for all she was a deghass, about to be hauled off to a life of drudgery as some Hrum merchant's kitchen slave. How to explain . . .

"Well, the matter seems clear to me," said the craftmaster of the weavers and dyers. "He admits to having spied for the Hrum, and with some success—by his own account! So we must—"

"But the farmers with him swore he's been helping them resist the Hrum," said the millers' craftmaster. "With equal success, by their account. Without the shipment of food he organized and brought in to us—almost all his doing, according to the farmers—we wouldn't have lasted more than another month. Don't you want to ask him why he did that?"

It was also the Hrum gold Kavi had earned that had paid for most of the food—but now probably wasn't the best time to bring that up.

The master weaver snorted. "All right. Why?"

All eyes turned to Kavi, awaiting his answer.

"I changed my mind." How lame that sounded. The watching faces were stiff and cold. Truth, it seemed, had some serious drawbacks. His heart beat as if he'd been running.

"It was the slaves," said Kavi. "I knew they kept slaves—Patrius told the truth of that, like everything else—but when I actually saw them—"

"All your hatred for the deghans vanished, and you were filled with repentance?" The master weaver was sneering now.

"No," said Kavi slowly. "No, I still hated them. I still hate them. But at their worst they never kept slaves. I realized that if I allowed—helped—to enslave these people, then I'd have become one of them. And I didn't want that."

The silence should have been weighty, but it felt strangely light. As if, having spoken the ultimate truth, their judgment mattered less. Which was absurd, for their judgment could have him hanging from the battlements of the city he loved.

"I knew if the Hrum were defeated, then the slaves they'd taken would be returned," he went on. "And I found out about the draft, how folks hated it. And it seemed to me that with the deghans gone, if we could get rid of the Hrum, we could be ruling ourselves for a change."

It felt odd to say it aloud, his most secret hope.

"I see," said the master weaver coldly. "So you say that you worked for the Hrum once, but not any longer. You say that now you're fighting against them. And if we ask, you'll no doubt say that we can trust you, and you'd never betray us to your Hrum friends . . . again. But we've nothing except your word for any of that, and all we can see is the Hrum's mark on your shoulder."

So much for telling the truth. Tebin's eyes met his for a moment, then turned away, and Kavi felt a flash of pure despair.

"That's not entirely true," said the master miller. "If you go down to the warehouse, you can also see a large enough shipment of food to keep this city fed—and fighting—for two months. And if you'll open your stubborn ears and listen, which you seem not to have done so far, you'll hear the farmers who helped him bring it in tell you that this young man organized the whole thing. That he was likely the only one who could have done so, because he's the only one the people in all the scattered villages around Mazad know well enough to trust. If a stranger rides into one of those villages and says, 'I need you to contribute food to help Mazad resist the Hrum,' what do you think they're going to say?"

The weaver attempted to answer, but the miller rolled over his voice. "They'll say they'd never dream of resisting the Hrum. Loyal citizens of the empire, that's what they are. They'll say it because they won't trust a stranger not to get them all hauled off as slaves. But they do trust their peddler, and I think they're right to do so. Because something else I saw is that none of the growers' marks on those grain sacks is familiar to me—not one. And I've been grinding grain from all the farms in this area, man and boy, for most of my life. I don't think the farmers would have thought to use false marks themselves. Not all of them."

Inquiring gazes turned to Kavi, who shrugged. He hardly dared to hope. "It's a simple precaution. If they're stopped on the road, there's got to be a mark on the sack, or the Hrum patrollers will get suspicious. But unlike the craftmaster, they don't know the local marks. And if the Wheel should dump us down, then nothing can be traced back."

"Hmm," said Golbas. "To my mind, the evidence speaks in your favor. On the other hand, that mark tells against you. And for your intentions at that time, and for the future, we have only your word. So what it comes to is: Do we believe you? Do we decide to trust you?"

"I will offer bond for him." It was the first time Tebin had spoken since he'd identified Kavi. His voice, rueful and resigned, was just as Kavi remembered it in times past when his master had retrieved him from the authorities. But this . . .

"Master, you can't. If you offer bond and I let you down, you could be asked to pay any penalty short of hanging. If I'm lying, you could be ruined!"

Tebin shook his head. "You never did know when to stop talking. But if you're lying, we'll probably all end up Hrum slaves—can't get much more ruined than that."

Several of the men had been grinning, but that sobered them.

Golbas sighed. "True enough. Masters, if there are no objections, I'm inclined to take Tebin's word for this man." He looked around the table. The weaver glared, but even he nodded consent. "Very well then, he's yours, Tebin. Try to keep him out of trouble."

This time several laughed, but not Kavi. Hope thundered through him, but still . . . "You can't just write this off like . . . like an apprentice prank!" His gaze went from the craftmasters, who were rising from their chairs, stretching, beginning to chat, to Commander Siddas.

The commander jumped down from the dais and came toward him. "Hold out your hands," he said. "And stop talking for a moment."

Kavi complied, and the commander began pulling at the knot that tied his wrists. "It's not so much that they treat it lightly," Siddas said. "It's that they want those food shipments to continue. We've had several people offer us aid, but when it came down to actually helping, only one of them came through—and he's having enough trouble feeding his own people. You're the first to deliver food in any quantity, you did it before we were starving, and you say you can do it again." The commander's voice dropped lower still. "If there's a crime you could commit that they wouldn't ignore right now, I can't think what it is. So consider your confession well timed, and come see me before you leave. I'll tell you our exact supply situation, and you can tell me what you can bring in and when. I've hesitated to impose rationing if I don't have to, for hungry people lose heart. But if it proves necessary, I can do it. And there may be other things you can supply. I could use a man who can move freely in the Hrum's camp."

"But how can you trust me?" Although Siddas' cynical explanation for the council's leniency was reassuring, Kavi still found it hard to believe that they would let him off so easily. "How can you just let it go?" He nodded to Siddas' uniform tabard. Not that of a man in the deghans' army, but still . . .

Siddas snorted. "What, you think I'm more eager to become a Hrum slave than they are? I'm no more a deghan than you, boy. I don't hate them as you did, but I don't have your reasons, either. So I'm inclined to let it go. Especially since the alternative is starving myself into slavery." His expression was full of rueful self-knowledge, and that kind of honesty was something Kavi seldom encountered in any man.

"Most would be lying to themselves about something like that," he said. "Making up excuses for me—for themselves, for letting me off."

"I'm defending a city, under siege by the mightiest empire in the world," said Siddas. "I can't afford to lie to myself. Well, just one lie."

Kavi's wrists came free. He stuffed his hands into his pockets to conceal their trembling.

One lie. Kavi thought he knew what it was, but

there was little use and less kindness in speaking it aloud.

He turned to Tebin, who had descended from the dais and was waiting for him, the familiar resignation in his eyes. "Honestly, lad, you sound like you're trying to get yourself hanged."

"If I was, then you've no business throwing yourself in the way. I'm not your journeyman anymore." The words were harsh—Kavi meant them to sound harsh, but his voice softened on him. When Tebin held out his arms, Kavi walked into his embrace as if this man was the father who had died of fever when Kavi was a boy.

"I didn't mean to cause trouble," he muttered into Tebin's muscular shoulder.

"You never did," said his master. "But that never stopped you from doing it." He pulled back and gave Kavi's shoulder a bracing slap. "Come on home, and we'll get some food. They got me out before breakfast for this!"

FOR YEARS KAVI HAD THOUGHT he had no home, except perhaps for Nadi's house. He had returned before, of course. Most of the goods he sold came from this very shop. But since he first left to take up his new trade, he never felt—had never let himself feel—the old sense of belonging here. Now, settling onto a bench in the yard in back of the smithy, with a tankard of ale and a thick, salt-beef sandwich, he realized that this place, with the clamor of men and boys working iron, and the acrid scent of hot metal coating the back of his throat, this was home too, and always would be. At least, as long as Tebin was here.

"You're making nails?" It had been too hot to linger in the forge, but taking note of the apprentices' work as he passed by came as effortlessly as breathing.

"The boys are making nails," said Tebin, sitting down beside Kavi with his own sandwich. "I'm working on hinges today, and some of the journeymen are making cart braces."

Unlike his master, Kavi had been given breakfast, but he suddenly found he was hungry. "Not swords?" He took a bite of his sandwich. "I'd 'a thought—"

"Just because we're under siege, it doesn't mean life stops," said Tebin. "I'm actually preferring hinges these days. Though we've made swords enough. Especially after a fight, for ours break like sticks on that cursed watersteel. Fortunately, there aren't many sword fights in a siege." Tebin's voice held all the bitterness Kavi had felt when he realized how inferior Farsalan swords were, and the same combination of hatred and longing when he talked about their watersteel. A bitterness that was personal.

"You sound like you've seen our swords break yourself," said Kavi curiously.

"Near enough," said Tebin. "I saw the wounded when they brought them in. You've heard about the guardsmen's raid on the Hrum camp?"

"A bit," said Kavi. "I didn't know how much to believe. Especially since rumor had Sorahb himself leading an army to support them."

Tebin laughed, and Kavi's brows rose.

"Oh, I'm not laughing at the men who came to our support," said Tebin. "They fought with courage and paid a high price, from what I hear. It's this Sorahb foolishness. The lad who leads them is called Jiaan. He's the son of—what?"

Kavi tried to get control of his expression. "It's just that I've met this Jiaan. At least, if he's the son of Commander Merahb."

Commander Merahb's bastard son. Kavi

wondered again what had happened to the daughter, but the thought was fleeting. "Yes, I met him. He'd make a fine Sorahb, reckless, honorable fool that he is."

"Maybe it's fools we need," said Tebin gently, "to be taking on the Hrum with swords that break."

"Umm!" Kavi chewed and swallowed, suppressing a surge of guilt. "I've got something to show you!"

He fished the chip of Hrum steel out of his pocket. He'd showed it to a number of village smiths over the last months—usually he had to start by explaining what it was. Tebin knew instantly. He dropped his sandwich to the table and wiped his hands on his britches before reaching out to take the gleaming metal crescent.

"Time's Wheel, lad, where did you come by this?"

"Off the battlefield," said Kavi shortly. "But I can't figure out how they get the layers so thin. I asked a miner about it, and he said the dark—"

"Dark steel's hard, takes a great edge, but it's brittle," said Tebin absently, turning the fragment in his fingers. "Brittle steel's even worse for hinges

and plowshares than it is for swords, which is why
miners smelt it into a mix, but I've seen it. Worked
with it a bit. But when you blend it with softer
steel, you just get—"

"A blend," said Kavi. "But the Hrum swords
aren't a blend—they're as sharp as the hard steel,
and as flexible as the soft at the same time. And
this isn't blended; it's in layers as thin as frost on
stone. So how do they do it?"

"You say you worked with the Hrum for a
time," said Tebin. His voice held nothing but professional curiosity now. "Couldn't you get in to
watch their smiths work?"

"No," said Kavi. "They kicked me out, even
when they were only making horseshoes. And
threatened me with worse if I came back. When
they're making swords, they actually put guards
around the smithy."

It had frustrated him so much at the time, but
somehow sharing his frustration with Tebin eased
it. "Can't really blame them, I suppose."

"I can't say for certain," said Tebin slowly.
"But there's only one way I can think of to do this.
They're folding it."

"What?"

"They're folding the metal. You start with two or three bars—three, say, since the pale layers look bigger. Light, dark, light. Like a sandwich. Heat them till they're pliable and beat them together. I'm not sure if they're going wider or longer, but I'd go longer. Beat your bar out till it's twice a sword's length, and fold it over on top of itself—now you've got six layers."

Kavi shook his head. "I see what you're saying, but you'd have to work forever—there are hundreds of layers in this blade, maybe thousands."

Tebin laughed. "And you a peddler! Do the math, lad. One fold gets you six, two, twelve . . ."

Kavi counted folds on his fingers as he added them up, eyes beginning to widen at the fifth fold. "By the Tree! Just eight folds gets you seven hundred and sixty-eight layers. And nine gets you . . . a thousand five hundred and thirty-six."

"Exactly," said Tebin. "Looking at this, I think they're stopping at eight. Eight's work enough! But if it got you watersteel . . . You say you talked to the miners. Could you bring in some bars of dark steel? I've got to try this!"

"I can," said Kavi. "Some. The miners don't find much of the ore that makes it. I've heard rumors that the ore from the Suud's desert is better, though there's no way to be knowing the truth of that. But, Master . . . even if we learn to make watersteel, we still won't be able to beat the Hrum. Not forever. Not even for eight more months. They've got ten thousand more men, just over the border in Sendar. All Garren has to do is send for some of them, and they'll overwhelm Mazad."

That was the one lie Siddas was allowing himself: that it was possible for them to win.

"I know they've got the men," said Tebin. "But one thing you'll realize when you've lived a bit longer is that you can't ever tell what direction Time's Wheel will turn. Why, look at this morning."

Kavi snorted. "You mean when I got off for a crime they should have hanged me for?"

Tebin set the chip of watersteel on the table. "Do you think you should have been hanged? Really?"

"No," Kavi admitted. "But then I wouldn't, would I? There are a lot of people who wouldn't agree with me."

"Maybe, but the council did. For all of Siddas' talk of how much we need that food—and we do!—they wouldn't have let you off that lightly if they didn't accept . . . extenuating circumstances. But that wasn't what I meant, anyway."

Kavi struggled to track the conversation back, and Tebin grinned. "Don't bother. What I meant was that this morning, Time's Wheel turned to bring my best—and worst—journeyman back to me. And if that can happen, lad, then anything is possible. Anything."

CHAPTER FIFTEEN

JIAAN

PEOPLE SCAMPERED OUT of the streets of the Kadeshi village as Rakesh carried Jiaan closer, and he sighed. It was more than a month after the battle before Jiaan felt he could leave his troops and go in search of allies. But now, as summer dragged itself to a close in a spate of afternoon rains, the wounded were all well on their way to healing—except for one man the healer-priest couldn't save, and he had finally died.

It happened after a battle, Jiaan told himself firmly. He had visited the man when he could, and tried to forget him as he went about his business the rest of the time. It was Fasal who had made a habit of speaking to the man daily, who had sat out the death watch in the healer's cabin until, in the dark time before sunrise, the man had died.

Fasal had asked for permission to take the man's body home to his village, but Jiaan had refused—he needed Fasal for training.

Jiaan wasn't certain if Fasal had changed, or if he was seeing something he had missed before. But the army had definitely changed. They were angry now. Angry at the Hrum for killing their comrades, but even more angry at themselves for the lack of skill that had made it possible for the Hrum to slaughter them so easily. Jiaan was surprised they weren't angry with him for leading them into battle so ill trained, but they didn't seem to be. Instead they tackled their training with a fierce determination, driving themselves harder than Jiaan and Fasal had ever thought to drive them. And they were learning fast. The beginning swordsmen had almost outstripped Jiaan's tutoring—he could leave them to Fasal's training now, and turn his attention elsewhere.

It had taken almost a month for him to get a Kadeshi warlord's permission to enter his land for a parlay, anyway.

That was the second reason he was leaving

Fasal behind. Someone had to supervise the training, and he now felt it was safe to leave the army in Fasal's charge. But the real reason he was leaving him behind was that Fasal had been so outraged at the very thought of asking the Kadeshi for aid. *They're our enemies! We've been fighting them for thousands of years. And they may not be as strong, but they're* worse *than the Hrum!*

At this point, two days' ride past the ambiguous, shifting border between Farsala and Kadesh, Jiaan was beginning to think Fasal might be right.

At the time Jiaan had pointed out that better or worse, they were the only ones who could bring an army to Farsala's assistance. Since they were the next conquest in the Hrum's path, they might be motivated to fight that battle in someone else's country instead of their own.

It wasn't the patrols that troubled Jiaan—though when the first ragged band galloped up and surrounded him, Jiaan had taken them for bandits instead of warriors, and he still wasn't certain he'd been wrong. But whatever they were, the intricately embroidered strip of silk that Warlord Siatt had sent to Jiaan as a pledge of safe conduct had stopped them, snapping and snarling like dogs restrained by a master's hand on the leash. It had also protected Jiaan from the next two groups he'd encountered, so they probably weren't bandits — though Jiaan hated to think what might have happened if he hadn't had that strip of silk. No, it was the villages that bothered him.

He told himself that he was accustomed to seeing doors and shutters bright with peasant paint — that it was the absence of color that made Kadeshi villages look so bleak and dark. And that might have been true. But he'd never seen any Farsalan village where the women and children ran and hid when a man wearing a sword rode in. At first Jiaan hadn't noticed that all those he spoke to were men. He'd ascribed their wary, guarded gazes to the fact that mounted on Rakesh rather than one of the Kadeshi's tough, shaggy horses, with his ring-studded, silk armor, he was clearly Farsalan — an enemy solider to them.

It wasn't until a young girl who'd been uprooting weeds in a field hiked up her muddy skirts and darted into a grove of trees at the sight of him, that he realized the truth. And she, and the others who hid from him, might have been doing so just because Jiaan was Farsalan . . . but somehow, he doubted it.

Rakesh was currently plodding between the first decrepit houses on the muddy street of a village that looked even more ramshackle than the others Jiaan had passed through—he was glad he would be spending the night at the warlord's manor. He tried to convince himself that it was just the effect of the gathering clouds, but the growing overcast hadn't caused the sagging thatch, or the door that listed off its hinges. And while the Kadeshi were a slender people, these men's bones were far too prominent.

The man he was looking at shrank from his frown, and Jiaan hastily softened his expression. The man's robe was even more ragged than the buildings.

"You, man. I need to find the house of Warlord Siatt. Can you tell me where?" His Kadeshi was rough, but all Farsalan soldiers spoke a bit of it—especially any who had worked for High Commander Merahb. And he understood it better than he spoke it, which might be useful.

The man was still backing away, and Jiaan didn't think it was his accent. He pulled out his purse and the jingle of coin froze the man in his tracks.

"It's not far," he said, his voice barely loud enough for Jiaan to hear him. "Just take that road around the side of the hill, and you'll see it."

Jiaan smiled and tossed him a coin. Ordinarily such a small service would only call for a brass foal, but he'd offered a copper stallion instead. For a moment, seeing the man's eyes widen, he wished he'd given him a silver falcon, or even a gold eagle. But Jiaan had a whole army to feed, clothe, and shelter. There were no eagles in his purse, and very few falcons.

Kicking Rakesh into motion he hoped, wryly, that Warlord Siatt wasn't expecting to be bribed.

As Rakesh carried him around the broad slope of the hill, Jiaan wondered what a warlord's manor would look like in this land of shoddy buildings. But the reality, perched on another hill directly in front of him, left him breathless.

It wasn't the high walls surrounding it. Jiaan knew that, unlike Farsalan deghans, the warlords fought among themselves as often as they fought outsiders. He had expected something defensible, but defensible was an understatement; storming this towering fortress struck Jiaan as pure suicide.

But what amazed him was the manor, whose

towers he glimpsed beyond the walls, glowing even in the dim light. It seemed to be made of polished marble in dozens of different colors, and the builders had laid patterns into the tower walls. One was layered dark and light, like the goal post in a flags-and-lances match. Another had a pattern of diamonds spiraling up the side, and on another, light stone fountained up the darker background like leaping water. Each tower flew its own banner of bright, streaming silk, but the tallest tower seemed to be roofed in . . . No, it had to be polished brass, despite the way even the diffuse sunlight made it gleam.

Jiaan set Rakesh trotting up the twisting road that led up the hill to the . . . palace was the only word. This was no simple manor house, like the high commander's. At every bend he realized how vulnerable an army on this road would be—all the defenders would have to do was roll down a few rocks. Archery fire from those walls would be pure murder.

As he drew near, the walls and the thick, iron-plated gate looked even more defensible than they had from below. Evidently the sentries were alert too, for the gate was already opening as Jiaan approached. He rode down the echoing tunnel through the wall, very aware of the gratings overhead.

Siatt's offer of safe conduct was evidently sincere, for he came out into the courtyard unscathed. A man waited to greet him, clad in the good but sober robe of a Kadeshi upper servant. One servant, and a dozen armed warriors.

"Lord Deghan Jiaan," said the servant in good Farsalan. "Warlord Siatt is pleased that your journey has come to a safe end."

Not all deghans were lords, and Jiaan wasn't even a deghan, but saying any of that wasn't a proper reply to the traditional Kadeshi greeting. "All journeys end safe, in Warlord Siatt's house," said Jiaan formally. He couldn't help adding, "Please, call me Commander Jiaan." He wasn't really comfortable with that either, though he'd begun to get used to "young commander," which was the title the army had settled on. But if he wanted the warlord to pay any attention to him he had to have some rank, and it was better than "Lord Deghan."

"Commander Jiaan," the older man repeated, accepting the correction with polished grace.

"Will you care to refresh yourself before your audience with Warlord Siatt?"

Given no other alternative, Jiaan took that as an order despite the courteous tone. In truth the chance to wash, to change into the good clothes he'd purchased in a town near the border, was welcome—though Jiaan wasn't accustomed to either the presence of a servant who the older man had summoned to assist him, or washing in rose-scented water. But after seeing the silk draperies—expensive, Farsalan silk—and the carved, inlaid wood, the porcelain vase, so brilliantly glazed and so delicate, Jiaan knew that even his new tunic wasn't up to the surroundings. He was a little surprised that the wash basin was made of plain bronze—but if that was intended as some kind of subtle insult, Jiaan didn't care.

When he was dressed, he told the servant he was ready to see the warlord, and the man nodded and departed in the same silence he'd practiced so far. Mute? Or too discreet to gossip with strangers?

Jiaan's father believed that you should learn everything you could about an enemy. Jiaan had thought he knew a lot about the Kadeshi, but now he realized he hadn't learned nearly enough.

The superior servant returned—and if Jiaan's tunic wasn't up to his standards, his face was too well disciplined to show it.

He led Jiaan toward the warlord's rooms. Jiaan could tell when they grew near, for the furnishings grew richer and the carpets grew deeper with each corridor. The thunder of the approaching storm rumbled distantly, softened by the thick walls. The door the servant finally stopped outside was plated with gold. He opened the door, stepped inside and intoned, "Most glorious warlord, savior of your people, vision of the god's grace, supreme warrior, mighty leader in battle—Commander Jiaan comes to beseech your aid."

Because Jiaan was struggling not to laugh, the magnificent tapestries, the thick carpets, even the enormous, gold-plated throne failed to have the effect they were probably intended to.

The plump figure, at least three inches shorter than he was, who descended from the low dais to grip Jiaan's shoulders didn't intimidate him either, for all the wealth the rustling silk robe implied.

"Welcome, welcome! It is a great honor to greet the mighty warrior who resists the Hrum— and with so little!"

The fact that the words were fluent Farsalan was a relief, but the eyes in the plump face sparkled with malice. And the hands that gripped Jiaan's shoulders weren't the least bit soft. Kadeshi warlords had to fight their neighbors on a regular basis, and had fought Farsala's deghans to a bloody draw. Underestimating this man would be a bad idea.

"It's true we have few resources," said Jiaan. "For few survived the Hrum's first assault. But those who survive are determined. And if we should fail, despite our determination, I can promise that the Hrum will leave you with no more than they did us."

"Straight to the matter!" Siatt released him, to Jiaan's relief, though the man's smile was almost more cloying. "A warrior's approach. But surely you have time to dine before we speak of such grim subjects."

It was the Kadeshi tradition to do so, Jiaan reminded himself, summoning up a smile. When he'd first learned of it, he'd thought it sounded hospitable—civilized. But as one course yielded to another, the attentive servant filling and refilling his goblet with wine as strong as the vintage was good, Jiaan began to wonder if Kadeshi custom was about hospitality, or about softening up the enemy. He'd been hungry when he sat down on the cushions by the low table, but by the end of the meal he was only nibbling from each dish—and taking very small sips of wine.

The thunder of the summer storm was barely audible in this civilized chamber. Jiaan remembered the villagers' tattered houses. How well would they stand up to the lashing wind and driving rain that he couldn't even hear?

Finally the servants carried out the last of the dishes. Jiaan praised the meal and thanked his host. He felt overstuffed and sleepy, but at least his head wasn't spinning. Unfortunately, Siatt didn't appear to be drunk either.

He noticed Jiaan's scrutiny and smiled. "Ah, the impetuosity of youth! You wish to speak of the matter that brought you."

"If I may," said Jiaan, trying to sound old and sophisticated, instead of young and impatient. "My first officer is in charge in my absence, but I don't wish to leave my command too long."

"Your command." Siatt's voice seemed to caress the words. "You seem young to command an army. However, that is no doubt the custom in your land, and probably superior to our own."

You know it's not, you toad. But perhaps there were things he didn't know. Jiaan lowered his eyes modestly. "I inherited command from my father." It was more true than not, when he thought about it. "And I have subordinates who are more experienced than I, and who advise me. And of course, Sorahb is in charge of the resistance as a whole."

He watched through lowered lashes as Siatt sat up straighter. "I have heard rumors of this Sorahb. I thought he was a myth."

"That's what he wants the Hrum to think."

Jiaan could almost see the thoughts racing behind Siatt's eyes. If there was an adult in charge, a deghan, then he'd have to consider the offer seriously, no matter who presented it. *By all means, warlord. Underestimate me. Please.*

"I see," said Siatt slowly. "A clever ploy. But Sorahb hasn't the might to drive the Hrum from your country himself?"

"No," Jiaan admitted, since there was no way around that part of it. "The army is growing, and they've already fought one successful battle against the Hrum, but they still aren't sufficiently experienced. We need a real—an experienced army to assist us."

Siatt's eyes gleamed at the slip. "So if we give you a 'real army,' my fellow warlords and I, what favor might we expect in return?"

Jiaan took a deep breath. "The favor of our assistance when the Hrum attack you."

Siatt blinked in honest surprise. "That's all? From a land as rich as Farsala, Lord Deghan, that seems a very . . . stingy offer."

"From a land as rich as Farsala was, perhaps," said Jiaan. "But all our wealth has vanished into the coffers of the empire. They've captured the deghans' manors, the gahn's palace, the treasury. Do you think they didn't take the money? If we defeat them, my understanding is that they return their loot, along with the slaves. But even if that happens, very little"—none—"of that wealth would be mine. You would doubtless have the gratitude of the child gahn, but I can't make promises in his name, or his advisors'. And anyway . . ." *How do you phrase "pay in advance" politely?* "The Kadeshi are well known for their wisdom in not risking their warriors' lives on promises which might, after all, prove empty."

"True, that is our custom. So why, I ask once more, should we come to the aid of those who were our enemies—and may be again? And please, don't speak to me of a possible Hrum invasion, sometime in the future. As you've said, we don't fight for promises—or threats."

Jiaan's head began to ache. "But you have to know that the Hrum will attack you next. You're not stu—you're wise enough to know that they won't just look at your border and abandon a policy of conquest that has lasted—and succeeded—for centuries."

"Perhaps not. But let me ask you a question, Commander Jiaan. Do you think the Hrum could take this fortress?"

"By assault? Probably not. Certainly not easily or quickly. But unless your wells are deeper than any I've ever heard of, they'll simply surround you and wait till your cisterns run dry. And even if your cisterns are deeper than I think, eventually they'll be able to starve you out. No one's stockpile lasts forever."

Consternation flickered across Siatt's face. He had expected Jiaan to look at his impregnable fortress and see no further. And Jiaan might have done just that, if it hadn't been for his father's teaching.

"Even if you could hold out for over a year," Jiaan pressed on, "one or two fortresses aren't enough to keep the Hrum from making their conquest official. Unless one of your major towns is as well fortified as this palace"—which according to his father they weren't, since the warlords didn't build walls to protect anyone's wealth except their own—"then no matter how many years you resist, when you finally give up, the Hrum will be waiting to take you. It's the land itself they want, not the palaces."

For a moment he saw real fear in Siatt's face. That was something the warlords found incomprehensible, that anyone would find their filthy cities and miserable villages of value, and feel that their mighty fortresses . . . didn't count.

Jiaan smiled grimly. "When you come down to it, you're in a worse position to resist the Hrum than we were."

"Then it's a good thing wealth is portable, isn't it?" said Siatt with a pleasant smile.

"As long as your fellow warlords, or the bandits, or the government of the land you flee to doesn't take it from you," Jiaan countered.

"Either way, you're taking a big risk. You'd . . ."

You'd be better off, have the better chance, fighting with us. It was true, and he'd driven Siatt into a corner where he could probably force the man to see it if he continued to push, but suddenly Jiaan couldn't say the words. He didn't want this man as an ally.

"Since the risk is so great," said Siatt, "I think I must wait and study the matter until the wisest choice becomes clear. Perhaps if your army has some further success, we would be willing to join you—even for a promise."

Jiaan gazed at the plump, smiling face, and a chill ran down his spine. He meant that if the Farsalans were already winning, the Kadeshi would send troops. And after they'd won? After the Hrum were gone, leaving the Farsalan army exhausted, the Kadeshi would be fresh, almost unblooded, and already within their borders.

"You do understand," said Jiaan, "that since you offer no commitment now, you wouldn't be allowed to enter Farsala without Sorahb's full and formal consent. Any Kadeshi force that crossed our borders without invitation would, I fear, be regarded just as they always have been."

"Of course, of course. You could hardly do

otherwise! And may I say, your Commander Sorahb chose his ambassador for this mission more wisely than I had first thought."

He sounded almost sincere, and with another man, Jiaan might have been flattered. But Siatt didn't look like a man who'd been outmaneuvered. And why should he? If the Farsalans defeated the Hrum, their exhausted, battered troops would probably find themselves at war with the Kadeshi on their eastern border before the last Hrum troops had marched out in the west.

Jiaan rubbed his aching forehead again. *Worry about that tomorrow. We haven't even figured out how to beat the Hrum yet.*

"It seems we understand each other," he told his host. "And there is no more—wait, I do have one thing to ask. Do your weapon-smiths know anything about how the Hrum's watersteel is made?"

He knew they didn't have the secret—if they did, the Kadeshi would have those superior swords themselves. But they might know something, and at this point Jiaan would welcome the smallest hint.

"Not how they make it, of course," said Siatt. "But I believe my smith has made some study of the subject. I'll give him instructions to speak to you before you leave."

THE WEAPON-SMITH LIVED in the village, which surprised Jiaan. It looked better in the morning sunlight than it had under cloudy skies, but not much.

The smith, lean for all the muscle in his arms, studied the scrap of paper on which Siatt had written his request. His expressionless face had a bad burn scar on the left side, it looked as if it had barely missed his eye. Most smiths carried burn scars—it was a hazard of the trade—but Jiaan had seldom seen one that severe.

"I don't know how much I can tell you," said the smith. "If I knew the secret of watersteel, I wouldn't be here. Sorry."

He handed the paper back to Jiaan politely, but something in his movements told Jiaan that he wanted to cast it to the ground and stamp on it instead. Jiaan's hand twitched toward his purse, but then he hesitated. Most Kadeshi weapon-smiths lived in their warlords' palaces. This man had chosen to live in a village, and make hoes and pot hangers in the time he could spare from making swords. He wouldn't be open to bribery.

"Please," said Jiaan in his stumbling Kadeshi. "I know that you don't know the secret, but my people fight these men, who wield these swords—they die on them. I truly need all the knowledge you can give."

The scarred face remained inscrutable a moment longer, then the smith sighed. "Come inside."

Jiaan followed him into the small house behind the smithy—just two rooms, but made of stone, not flammable wood. Though the furnishings were worn, the place was scrupulously clean. Jiaan sat at a bench by the table, and watched the smith make tea. He suspected he'd find more ease in this poor man's tea than in the great feast Siatt had offered him.

The man set a thick pewter mug in front of Jiaan, and seated himself before he spoke again. "Like I said, I don't know the secret. But I saw a bit of watersteel once—just a hilt, with the blade snapped off. The carter who owned it, he charged smiths money just to examine it for a short time. I mended some tack for him."

"Only a hilt?" Jiaan's disappointment must have showed, for the man smiled.

"It was better than a whole blade, young sir, for broken like it was, I could see it was made of hundreds of layers of dark and light steel. Very thin. It took some time, but eventually I realized that they must have beaten several bars together, and then folded them. I got all excited about it."

Jiaan was beginning to feel excited himself. "Folded them?" he repeated, hoping he had the Kadeshi word right. "I know that the dark steel is better—"

"It's not better," said the smith, "just harder. And that makes it brittle. Don't look so hopeful—I got some dark steel and tried folding it with the lighter steel myself. The blade took a fine edge but it was too brittle—it chipped and broke. You couldn't use it to butcher a big-boned animal, much less fight a man in armor who also has a sword. So I'm sorry for your soldiers, but I can't help you."

Jiaan sighed. "I know more than before, and I thank you for this. And for the tea. Can I . . . I don't want to ill-speak you, but . . ."

The smith smiled bitterly. "This is a poor village. We'll take what coin you offer and be grateful for it."

We. Whatever coin Jiaan could spare would feed the hungry children he'd never seen, because they ran in fear when an armed man approached.

He had pulled out his purse and was sorting out coins when the thought struck him: "You would not tell me if you knew, would you?"

"What?"

"Even if you knew the secrets of watersteel, you would not tell me. You want the Hrum to come here."

"In Farsala, I don't care one way or the other," the smith admitted. "I don't think winning or losing in your land would stop the Hrum from coming here. In fact, if you beat them quickly they might come here faster, so the only thing that stops me from telling you the secret is that I don't know it. But if it would make a difference, I'd do nothing that might stop the Hrum from taking this land as fast as they can. A Hrum invasion is the best thing that could happen for our people. Even at worst . . . it couldn't be worse."

JIAAN RODE OUT WITH a lighter purse, and a heavier heart. Being stopped in Farsala might make the Hrum hesitate, at least for a few years, before pressing on. But deeply as he pitied these people, he couldn't sacrifice his own land for them.

Fasal had been right, for once; the Kadeshi

were worse than the Hrum. The thought of having them as an ally made Jiaan's flesh creep—and he knew they wouldn't remain allies for long.

Jiaan was glad that Siatt had refused him. Though now, there was only one place he could turn.

SORAHB WANDERED THE *war-torn land alone. When it rained, he paid farmers to let him shelter in some barn or shed, but on the dry nights, he made his camp in the wilderness to spare his purse even the loss of those few meager coins, for equipping an army had left him with little.*

On one such night, a ragged old man with a peasant's accent approached and asked to share his fire. Sorahb would have preferred to be alone, but the deghan code of hospitality prevailed, and he agreed.

Sorahb had only a pot of thin soup and a bit of coarse bread for his own supper, but the stranger ate the share Sorahb offered as eagerly as if he were starving. Seeing this, Sorahb ate lightly so the other could have more.

Later they fell to talking, as men will by a fire.

Sorahb learned that the man had been a prosperous farmer, whose wife was some years dead, and whose daughters had married and gone. A Hrum squadron had demanded that the old man sell them his grain store, and offered a price far lower than the seed was worth. When the farmer refused, they accused him of resisting the empire; his farm was taken, and he himself barely escaped. So now he wandered a conquered Farsala, where few dared shelter him for long.

When he came to the end of his tragic tale, Sorahb sighed. "I can do nothing to stop the Hrum," he said. "But I can ease your way in the world, at least for a time." And Sorahb gave the peasant his purse, which held all the scant funds he had left.

He expected the peasant to make some objection and was prepared to argue, for the old man clearly needed the money more than he.

But the old peasant took the purse without protest.

"You offer me a great gift," he said. "And though you don't know it, I have given you a greater one in return, for only a man who has nothing left to lose is truly free."

With that, he rolled himself into his tattered vest and went to sleep beside the fire. When Sorahb awakened in the morning, he was gone.

CHAPTER SIXTEEN

~m~

JIAAN

THEY SEEMED TO COME OUT of nowhere, out of the muddy hummocks of swamp grass, the rustling leaves of the mull bushes, the shimmering glare of light on water. Only Rakesh's frantic leap saved Jiaan from the club that whistled past his shoulder.

Unfortunately Rakesh's sudden movement also cost him his balance. Jiaan, slipping on the smooth leather of the saddle, gripping Rakesh's mane with both hands and his body with both legs, had all he could do to stay on the horse's back. He couldn't draw his sword.

Rakesh must have known his rider was in trouble, but he had no time to let Jiaan regain his seat. The gelding spun in place, forcing the man who was trying to catch his bridle to jump back. Then he planted his front feet and kicked.

Jiaan heard the cry of pain and grinned, even as Rakesh's violent movement broke his grip and he slid off into the mud.

Rakesh had been trained to go on fighting if his rider was thrown, but Jiaan wanted to talk to these men, not to kill them—and he didn't want Rakesh to be hurt.

As he floundered out of the mud, rough hands seizing him, he saw Rakesh sink his teeth into a man's arm. The man shouted, dropped the short cudgel he held, and reached for his knife instead.

"Go!" Jiaan yelled. "Get out of here!"

Rakesh stopped, snorting in confusion. He knew that command, but he usually heard it after he'd been unsaddled, groomed, and given a handful of grain—and it was accompanied by a friendly slap on the shoulder or rump.

The bandit drew his knife, swore, and transferred it to his left hand. Panic sharpened Jiaan's voice. "Rakesh, go!"

The gelding snorted again and wheeled around, knocking the knife wielder into a bush.

Then he galloped off, splashing in and out of sink-holes with little grace, but with a speed no human could match in this muck—though the man with the knife tried. Within moments the man saw it was useless and came stamping back to the others, rubbing the scratches on his face and swearing.

With Rakesh safe away, Jiaan took stock of his own situation—it wasn't good. There were six assailants, bearded and dirty—now that he had time to count them. Though at this point Jiaan wasn't exactly clean. They'd all carried cudgels at the start, and had knives at their belts, though two had dropped the short clubs to hold his arms, pressing him down to his knees. The swearing man had lost his cudgel when Rakesh bit him, and yet another stood clutching his shoulder, his face pale and tight with pain.

"Broken," he said. "That Flame-begotten monster broke my collarbone."

Jiaan had recently broken a collarbone him-self. Remembering how much it hurt, he was glad Rakesh was well away.

"Flame-begotten?" One of the men who still had his club, taller than the others, gazed after the departing horse admiringly. "That was Kanarang with hooves!" He looked down at Jiaan. "I hope you're carrying enough to recompense us for his loss, or we're likely to get . . . disappointed. You'll be real sorry if you disappoint us."

Jiaan fought down a chill of fear. This was what he'd come to accomplish—even if he hadn't intended to accomplish it in quite this way. "The offer I carry is worth more than anything in my purse." He tried to sound bold and calm at the same time. "I need to speak with your leader."

"If all you want is to talk to him, then you won't mind if we take this," said the other man who'd kept his cudgel. He pulled Jiaan's purse off his belt and poured out the coins to count them. All but the two who held Jiaan gathered around him, and even they were watching.

"Humph. Not much," one of them snorted. Jiaan bit his lip. It was all the money he had, for he'd left most of the funds he'd been offered for the army with Fasal. Crossing half the width of Farsala, from Kadesh to the swamps of Dugaz, had taken much of it, and he still had to cross the land lengthwise to get back to the army. It had been over a month since he left, but he hadn't wanted to return until he accomplished something.

"Not nearly enough to compensate us for the loss of a warhorse as fine as that," said one of the men who held Jiaan's shoulder. His grip tightened enough to make Jiaan wince.

"I have a message, an offer, that your leader will want to hear," Jiaan told them firmly. Showing fear might prove fatal—and not just for his plans. "He'll be angry if you keep him from hearing it."

"He'll be angry we lost the horse," said the tall man. "And he won't know about the offer, if you're not there to tell him."

"He won't know about the horse unless we tell him either," the man Rakesh had bitten pointed out. "And I'm glad we're not trying to drag that djinn-beast back to camp. We might not be surviving it. If this 'offer' he's talking about is profitable, we might get a share."

The other man who held Jiaan snorted. "Not much of a share, once Shir takes his cut."

"Better than a thin purse," said Bitten. "Which is all we've got now."

"My shoulder's broke," moaned the man Rakesh had kicked. "I need a sling. I need someone to strap it up for me."

"What exactly is this offer you're talking about?" asked one of the men holding Jiaan.

Somehow Jiaan didn't think an offer to help them fight the Hrum would interest these men. "That's for your leader's ears—not for yours."

Bitten drew his knife. "I bet I can change that."

Jiaan was grateful he was already on his knees—otherwise, the way his legs were wobbling might have been visible. "You might," he admitted. "But Shir won't be pleased if you do."

And if this Shir wasn't their leader, he was probably dead. He hoped Rakesh would end up in good hands.

Bitten stopped. "How do you know Shir's name?"

Jiaan shrugged. "My offer is for him."

"He's lying," said the taller man. "We mentioned Shir's name. Didn't we?"

It took them a short eternity of terrifying debate, but eventually they decided they had more to gain from taking Jiaan to see Shir than from a corpse left floating in the swamp.

Jiaan prayed this Shir wasn't cut from the same cloth. He might be gambling his life on it.

*

IT WAS SOME TIME AFTER he arrived at the bandits'
village before Shir came to see him. At least, Jiaan
supposed it was a village. The strange houses,
perched on wooden stilts, with their silk walls, were
unlike anything he'd ever seen. If it wasn't for the
smears of mud that coated everything in sight, they
might have been pretty. As it was, they were almost
as drab as the scrubby trees that surrounded them.
Jiaan had plenty of time to form impressions, for
they tied his wrists to a tree at one side of an open
space between the houses—Jiaan hesitated to call
it a square—and left him there.

The sun was past the top of its arc, his wrists
and back hurt, and he was certain he'd been bitten
by every bug in the swamp by the time he saw a
slender man, smooth shaven and cleaner than
most, approaching with three other men.

He probably wasn't much older than thirty,
and at first Jiaan thought he was one of Shir's
aides, come to fetch Jiaan to see the leader. But as
he came nearer Jiaan noticed the wide, gold
bracelets on his wrists, and the woman's earring—
a ruby, he thought—that glinted in the man's ear.

"Are you Shir?" he asked, as the man reached

him. "If so, I've an offer for you." Jiaan hesitated, but he had to say it sooner or later. "An offer of alliance, against the Hrum."

The slim man laughed. "Why do people keep thinking we want to fight the Hrum? Do we look like soldiers? Or idiots?"

The men with him grinned—Jiaan had never seen such wolflike smiles on human faces. "I heard you killed the Hrum's new governor of Dugaz, within a week of his arrival. I hear they're sending another man," Jiaan said.

"They already did," said the man he assumed to be Shir. "We sent him back. Well, pieces of him. Meddlesome men, these Hrum governors."

He drew his knife. Glass glowed on the hilt, but the blade was plain steel, honed to a razor's edge. Jiaan swallowed, struggling desperately to think of something more persuasive to say, but the bandit simply reached down and slit the sleeves of Jiaan's shirt from cuff to shoulder, baring his arms.

"Why are you doing that?" Jiaan asked, hoping that the fear that made his heart hammer couldn't be heard in his voice.

"I was wondering if you were working for 'Sorahb,' like the last one was."

"In a way, I suppose I am," said Jiaan. "These days everyone who commits an act of resistance uses that name."

"Ah, but some of you are more Sorahb than others."

What did that mean? Had the other Sorahb, the one he wanted to meet, already been here? He thought about asking, but too many questions might make his hosts nervous . . . and that was the last thing Jiaan wanted.

"If you've killed two of their governors, then you're already at war with the Hrum," he said. "They won't rest until they've captured or killed you. You need allies. And you need to help the people who are trying to hold out for a year, because you can't fight them alone. Not forever."

Shir gazed down at him for a moment, a smile lingering on his lips. "It's too hot to talk here. Cut him loose, Hassa. He's not foolish enough to be trying anything without his weapons."

Jiaan knew he was right. "Thank you," he said, and then cursed himself for sounding so pathetically sincere.

"I'm not doing it for you," said Shir, turning away.

Still, it was cooler in the open-walled shade of the house they took him to, and a woman brought Jiaan a flagon of mint tea that was almost cool. And if he was forced to sit on the floor at Shir's feet, well, it was better than sitting on the ground at his feet, tied to a tree. And much better than having his throat slit, which was looking more like a possibility all the time.

"You've told me what you think is going to happen," said Shir. "And you sound like you believe it. But let me give you my . . . vision of the future. The Hrum will send us a few more meddlesome governors and we'll send them back—just like we have in the past, when some foolish gahn tried the same thing. But sooner or later the Hrum will pick a man who's not as suicidal as the rest, and he'll come live in the manor, and collect a few taxes, and not interfere with . . . well, me, not to put too fine a point on it. I'll return the favor by not killing him. And the Hrum will figure out that a live governor and some taxes are better than a stream of dead governors and no taxes, and they'll stop sending governors who interfere. And life will go on, and we'll all keep getting richer and richer. That's my vision of the future. What do you think?"

"I think the Hrum care more about their laws, and their taxes, than you think they do. I think — you know about their time limit, don't you?"

The bandit chieftain nodded. All Farsalans knew about the time limit now. Jiaan couldn't believe the news had spread that rapidly without someone behind it. The other Sorahb? It felt like his methods: quick, subtle, and above all, untraceable. The men who were now coming to join his army, from every corner of the land, had all heard it from different sources — a neighbor, a peddler, a river bargeman. It was as if the wind itself carried the rumor.

"Well," Jiaan went on, "I think that they'll keep sending governors until about two months before their year is up — or maybe a month after Mazad has fallen, and that army is rested. Then they'll send about five tacti to search the marshes and kill or capture every man here. And when they're finished with you, they'll leave a few tacti with the new, strong governor, and then rule all the land, including Dugaz and its marshes, till the end of time. But as a slave, or a corpse, that part won't bother you."

"Not bad," said Shir. "Mind, these swamps

will swallow five thousand men without even belching, but it's a good prediction and well argued. Might even come true. But consider this version instead. You take my offer—not to trouble any governor who doesn't trouble us—back to your masters. Then the Hrum can claim the land is subdued without killing thousands of their own men in the marshes. For whoever we don't get, the fever probably will. Outlanders are particularly susceptible to it, especially if they come from a cold land, which I'm told the empire is."

Jiaan frowned. "My masters? Do you mean Sorahb? But—"

"I'm assuming that the Hrum have finally had the sense to stop marking their own spies," said Shir calmly. "At least, I hope you're a Hrum spy, because if you can't carry my message back to them, I've very little use for you."

This was probably the point where he ought to say that he was whatever Shir wanted him to be, and get out while he could, but Jiaan's head was spinning. "I heard about the Hrum marking their spies, but how do you know about it? I thought it was a secret."

Shir grinned. "Dugaz is a seaport, boy. Sailors

talk about the places they've been, and the things they've seen. Especially to women. I started learning everything I could about the Hrum, oh, eight years ago I think. I knew they'd get to us eventually, and I wanted to be prepared. And one of the things I learned is that most Hrum governors are too practical to go to war when there's no need. Particularly when their year is still running. So you take my message back to Governor Garren like a good spy, and we can all go about our business."

"But I'm . . ." Deny it or not? If he denied it, he might not leave their camp alive, but if he didn't, he'd lose his only chance to convince this ruffian to continue to resist the Hrum. Five tacti floundering around the swamp, trying to catch these tough bastards, struck Jiaan as a really promising way to end the Hrum's year with Farsala still unconquered. "I'm . . ."

Shir's expression changed. "You're not a Hrum spy." It wasn't a question. Jiaan had waited too long.

"What made you think I was?" Jiaan asked. "You know the Hrum mark their spies, and I'm not marked." He tugged one of his ruined sleeves.

"I thought that because the last 'Sorahb' who came here, trying to convince me to resist the Hrum, was one of their spies." Shir settled back in his chair with a thoughtful scowl. "I figured he was here to scout out our camp, but he . . . departed before I thought to have him carry my counteroffer back to Governor Garren."

A chill swept over Jiaan, despite the sweaty heat. "Departed. You mean you—"

"No, I mean he departed." Shir fingered the ruby hanging from his ear. "He created a diversion and slipped off—neat as I've ever seen it done. Not bad for a lad no older than you. It worked out to my benefit in the end, and I got a nice buckle out of it, so I bear him no ill will. Well, not much. But when you turned up on the same errand, I assumed you were from the same source."

"No," said Jiaan slowly. "I really do want you to help resist the Hrum. It sounds like you're already doing that, and you're likely to go on doing it whether you want to or not. Wouldn't it be better to do it in alliance with the rest of us?" He probably couldn't trust this man any more than he could the Kadeshi, but at least he wasn't likely to invade Farsala the moment the Hrum were gone. *A young man, working for the Hrum. A man very near his own age —*

"I wouldn't have to fight at all, if Garren had the sense to do what every Farsalan gahn has done for the last thousand years! I wish you'd been a spy, my friend."

Jiaan heard the threat but he was barely paying attention. It had occurred to him that he knew someone, about his own age, who spied for the Hrum.

"A very clever man, no older than me," he murmured. "This Hrum spy, would you describe him?"

Shir's brows rose. It probably wasn't the usual response to a death threat, but at the moment Jiaan didn't care. "You said he was my age," he prompted.

"He was. But a bit shorter than you, and stockier. Wide in the shoulders. Peasant hair—light brown and curly—and a peasant accent. And he had—"

"A crippled hand," Jiaan finished. He had to unlock his jaw to say the words. "His right hand, scarred across the palm. He'll grasp something with it, and then switch it into his left hand to use it."

It was that mannerism that had told him that the peddler the commander had bribed, and the Hrum spy who'd betrayed them, were one and the same man. Jiaan closed his eyes. Blood pounded in his ears. He was still working for the Hrum, the bastard. Trying to undermine potential sources of resistance. Trying to ensure Farsala's defeat.

"It sounds like you know him well," said Shir. "I don't suppose this means you're a Hrum spy after all?"

"No," said Jiaan. He was too angry to do anything except tell the truth. "We only traveled together for a few weeks. Then he betrayed my . . . my master to the Hrum. You should have killed him when you had the chance. Everything he knows about you, everything he heard or saw, he'll tell the Hrum about it."

"Oh, I knew that." Shir lounged in his chair, but his intent gaze was fixed on Jiaan's face. "We had to move our lovely town. Quite a nuisance. I take it he's no friend of yours?"

"He's the man I'm going to kill," said Jiaan. "At least . . ."

"If I let you survive to do so?" The amusement was back in Shir's face. "Hmm. Well, why not?"

"What?"

"Why not let you go? That young spy caused us a certain amount of trouble, and he escaped, which is a bit embarrassing, all things considered." The bandit rose to his feet and began to pace. "If I let you go, you can avenge us, and we won't have to lift a finger. If he kills you, well, that's nothing to me. It's not like we don't have everything of value you carried anyway. And if we should ever need help dealing with the Hrum, then you might be grateful. Wouldn't you, Commander Jiaan?"

Jiaan's jaw dropped. "How? . . ."

"I told you, sailors know everything."

"My army is landlocked."

"Landsmen aren't as good as sailors, but they know almost everything."

Jiaan rose to his feet, meeting Shir's eyes on a level. "I can't promise you aid. Depending on what the Hrum do, we might be too busy elsewhere to come to your assistance."

Shir snorted. "But I notice you don't mind asking for my promise to help you. Oh, don't blush, boy. I don't believe in any man's promises." For a moment, a lifetime of cynicism showed on the young face. Then Shir's expression brightened. "Come to think of it, that's not true. I do trust the last promise you made."

Jiaan frowned. Shir's brown eyes were full of mischief. "What promise? I didn't promise you anything."

"You didn't promise me anything," Shir agreed. "But you made a promise nonetheless. You promised to kill a man, and you meant it. And after all, who am I to stand in the way of another man's promise?"

SPLASHING THROUGH THE MARSH some marks later, Jiaan slowly became certain that the bandit was also a man of his word—Jiaan hadn't been followed, and he wasn't being watched.

It would take him longer to get back to the army without money. He knew that Rakesh would probably return to the place where they'd camped last night, so he would regain the only thing he'd lost that truly mattered, and there was food in Rakesh's saddlebags, along with Jiaan's bedroll. But Jiaan would still have to stop and do a few marks' worth of odd jobs each day, if he didn't want to starve before he reached his army.

For all the bandit's reluctance to fight, Jiaan thought there was an even chance that Governor Garren would be forced to send troops to subdue him. In a fight between the Hrum and Dugaz swamp rats, on their own ground, Jiaan would bet on the rats. So it hadn't been a wholly unprofitable day, despite the loss of his purse and his sword.

And he had learned that the peddler, the *traitor*, was still alive, still spying and lying Farsalans to their deaths. Even using Sorahb's name to do it!

Jiaan realized that his breath was hissing through clenched teeth, and deliberately relaxed his jaw, his shoulders, his back. But he couldn't control the hatred that boiled in his heart—he didn't try. Revenge would have to wait. Jiaan had an army to run, and a war to win, before he'd have time to hunt the bastard down. But once Jiaan was free, he would find him. And nothing would stand in his way then. Nothing.

CHAPTER SEVENTEEN

SORAYA

ORAYA'S FIRST MONTH as a slave hadn't been as bad as she'd feared when she was first escorted to the place where Calfaer had slept. She had known that Calfaer lodged apart from the servants. There were nights, covering her ears to block out their snores, that she thought he had a better situation than the servants did. She had assumed that he had a small room, with a door that could be locked at night to keep him from escaping. The door that led to the narrow slot between the shed's outer wall and the back wall of the goat pen did have a bolt outside, but aside from that . . .

"You're joking," she had said to the soldier

who escorted her to the place where Calfaer had slept. "That's not as wide as a corridor. There's barely room to lay down a pallet!"

The soldier didn't appear to care. "Here's a slave's tunic and britches," he said, handing her a bundle of rough cloth that one of Reevus' clerks had given him. "Put this on and bring your clothes out to me."

Soraya tried to give the bundle back to him. "I'd rather keep my clothes." In truth, her patched skirt and blouse were so worn at this point, that an army slave's tunic might be better. And it wasn't as if she'd never worn britches before—to her father's amusement, and her mother's dismay. But the too-large clothes were soft, worn to accommodate the contours of her body, and they were hers. Or at least, they had been.

"You don't have any clothes," the soldier said. "A slave owns nothing."

Garren had meant it to hurt—watching her clothes and her other small possessions burn in one of the bake ovens. And in truth, losing the carvings Ludo had given her, the hair ribbon Casia had braided, did hurt. When you owned little it became precious. But the confiscation of her meager funds, hoarded desperately for the day she would be able to set out in search of her family— that stung even worse. Three iron mares per week had seemed like so little at first, but she had worked for that money. Her breath had hissed with anger as Reevus passed the pathetically small pile of coins to one of the clerks, to be added to the tally of Hrum loot and then to the camp's general fund. Their equivalent would eventually be sent back to the empire, but all Soraya's worldly wealth was so little that the ledger entry was barely worth their time.

She was also tattooed as a slave. The physical pain of the proceeding made her grit her teeth and blink back tears, but she minded that much less.

FARS—the Hrum abbreviated the name in their square script, and added a horseshoe arcing over it, in memory of the deghans' horses charging toward them at the Sendar Wall. Soraya considered the tattoo a badge of honor—the mark of a Farsalan brave and loyal enough to have resisted the Hrum's invasion. Someday, she vowed, she would earn the right to wear it.

She tried to think of ways to use her position in the Hrum camp against them, but now that she wanted to spy she was too closely watched. Was there some way to fight them with magic? The Hrum's disbelief in any kind of magic was surely a weakness that could be exploited, for Soraya knew that Suud magic existed, even though Brasnian and djinn magic might not. But what could she do with it? Suddenly make Garren's shaving water scalding hot? Even if she dared try to summon another storm, it would be superfluous—the normal, late-summer rains drenched the Hrum camp with dreary regularity.

The only use she could see for her magic was to work on the wood of the enclosure where she was locked at night. No matter how tired she was, she spent some time before she slept seeking out the shilshadu of the wood, persuading it to let damp creep in, to let the rot take it faster. It was uphill work, for the wood's nature was to stay strong, but Soraya kept at it. In time, perhaps she could steal some tool to help her, but for the first few weeks, she had enough trouble simply coping with her new status.

She thought that she had already performed every menial task the camp required, but she soon learned otherwise. As a kitchen maid, she hadn't been required to carry the officers' slop pots to the privies, or to shovel dung from the animals' pens into the reeking midden cart every morning.

She didn't think Calfaer had been required to do these things either—it was part of the animal handlers' jobs, or the officers' own servants. Garren was piling every disgusting task in camp onto her, assuming she would either break under the shame and "confess," or rebel and refuse so he could beat her.

Odd that Hrum law would allow a rebellious slave to be beaten, but not the torture of captured enemies—though in a way it made sense. If you tortured captured enemies they might do the same when they captured you, but everyone knew that slaves had to be disciplined.

Soraya, wielding a shovel in callused hands, smiled grimly. Garren was in for a long wait. About half her current tasks were ones she'd done before—and if she'd traded the lighter duty of serving tables for all the dirty jobs other servants wanted to shed, it also got her out of the kitchen and into the forge, the cobbler's shop, the carpenter's shed. She was accustomed to sweeping floors by now; carrying buckets of charcoal wasn't any harder than carrying sacks of flour; and the fact that her friend Calfaer had once slept there made even the narrow cleft behind the goat pen comfortable — to her heart, if not her body.

Soraya was surprised how much being separated from the other servants hurt. They'd been ordered not to speak to her, though shortly after her capture, Casia, carrying a load of dirty pots out to the wash yard, had paused to whisper, "Are you all right, San — um, girl? We were told —"

"I'm fine," Soraya whispered back. Two soldiers lounged against the fence. Not quite near enough to hear, but near enough to see and report if Casia lingered. There were always two soldiers near her these days — seldom the same men, and most of them very good at not seeming to watch her. But Hrum soldiers were hardly ever idle, and in the midst of the busy camp they were painfully conspicuous. "Don't try to talk to me. You'll only get yourself in trouble, and I'm all right. Truly," Soraya reassured her friend.

Casia, never one for taking orders, had hugged Soraya before going back into the kitchen. Soraya spent the next half mark scrubbing pots, with tears dropping into the dirty suds.

It was good to know that someone cared. But she also noticed that the next day she was set to other tasks, and that Casia scrubbed all the pots—a duty that was usually shared among the kitchen workers.

She didn't know if the order for Casia's punishment had come from Garren or if it was Hennic's own idea, for Hennic was genuinely angry with Soraya. Doing other work, even harder work, was almost a relief since it took her out of range of his slaps and kicks. Most of the other servants were angry with her too—or afraid, as if being revealed as a Farsalan spy had somehow made her dangerous.

Soraya tried to use the strange people sense her shilshadu magic had given her to ease both the anger and the fear, but she failed. She could usually read people's emotions, some more clearly than others, but she couldn't persuade them to change. Maok had said that animals were easier to handle than people—perhaps it was that. Or perhaps, Soraya reflected grimly, it was just that she was a despicable excuse for a Speaker, on whom Maok should never have wasted her teaching.

In her current loneliness, thinking of Maok

and her friends among the Suud brought Soraya to tears. So she stopped thinking about them and avoided the other servants, for she disliked both the emotions that had replaced their friendship — except in Casia, who she was avoiding for Casia's own sake, and Ludo, who she couldn't avoid because he wouldn't let her.

Ludo didn't understand that being a Farsalan spy was a bad thing, though Soraya tried to explain it. She was Farsalan, he said. It was brave of her to fight, though in the end the empire always won. All he really understood was that his friend was sad and lonely, and working too hard. He worked with her when he could, and sought her out whenever he had a free moment, and neither Hennic's furious scolding, nor Soraya's own arguments and pleas could stop him.

Soraya knew she could have stopped him, and perhaps she should. She had only to tell Ludo that she didn't like him, that he was stupid and boring and she didn't want him around. As a child, Ludo had been driven off by cruel children using just those words, and he still cried when he remembered it. Soraya thought that might be why he so stubbornly refused to abandon her to her own hurt.

Even if it might be better for him in the long run, Soraya couldn't bring herself to hurt him. But she didn't encourage him either. At times she longed to praise him for his loyalty and strength, and tell him what a good friend he was. But binding him closer would be unfair at best, and might harm him if Garren took it into his head that Ludo was on her side. Still, she couldn't help welcoming the chance to talk to someone person to person, instead of receiving orders as a slave, to feel friendship instead of anger or fear—both others' and her own. These days, Ludo was the only one who smiled at her.

So when she saw the crowd gathering around him, saw the rare scowl on his face and heard the angry voices, Soraya put down the roll of leather she was carrying to the cobbler's shop and joined them.

". . . don't care if he's simple." Soraya recognized the speaker as one of Marcellus' underlings. "He's got no business spying around my documents! Much less—"

"He works in my kitchen," said Hennic. "One of the cooks probably told him they wanted him to check on some supplies, and he thought they meant the accounts. Was that it, Ludo?"

"No," said Ludo. "I wanted —"

"Well, if he was checking on supply records, what's he doing with correspondence between Governor Garren and the first strategus? Private correspondence, that —"

"If it's so important and secret, then how could Ludo get hold of it in the first place?" Hennic demanded.

"I only left my case for a moment, right outside the door! Tampering with the Governor's corres —"

"Be quiet!" Reevus' voice wasn't loud, but there was an edge in it that cut like a knife. Soraya wasn't the only one who jumped. The ordnancer pushed past her, and the crowd fell back to let him approach Ludo, Hennic, and the ruffled clerk. "What's going on here?"

"It wasn't my fault!" said the clerk, beating Hennic by half a breath. "I've been copying a letter from the governor to the first strategus, and I had to visit the privy. Didn't have time to take my writing case to the record room, so I left it outside the door. Well, you know how small those shacks are. When I got out, my case was open and he" — he gestured at Ludo — "was walking off with a copy of the governor's letter! That's stealing the empire's official correspondence! That's treason! That's—"

"That's your fault, for leaving your case unattended," said Hennic. "You're just trying to shift the blame to Ludo so you won't be punished for negligence. Ludo was probably told to check the supplies, and thought—"

Reevus held up his hand for silence. His expression was so stern that Hennic stopped in midsentence. Soraya shivered. As she well knew, the Hrum took the security of their records seriously. The clerk could be dismissed for such carelessness. But no one could think that Ludo—

"Tell me, Ludo, why did you take the scroll?" Reevus' voice was gentle. As ordnancer, he knew all about Ludo and dealt well with him. Soraya began to relax. It would be all right.

"I took it for a friend," said Ludo. "She needs scrolls from the camp. Real bad. I told her—" He stopped and shook his head. "I don't want to get her in trouble. I'd better not say any more."

Several people gasped, and Soraya stiffened. Ludo went into Setesafon often—he was big enough to carry a heavy load, so they sent him to fetch things. But no Farsalan spy in their right mind would recruit Ludo—he wouldn't know what documents to take!

Reevus held up his hand again. "I think you need to tell us a bit more, Ludo, or there will be trouble. Can you tell me who this friend is?"

Ludo was already shaking his head. Once he fixed on an idea, he was almost impossible to move. "I don't want to get her in trouble."

"But it is a girl," said Reevus. "You've told us that much already."

The dismay on Ludo's face was almost comical, but no one laughed.

"You might as well tell us the rest," Reevus went on persuasively. "What did this girl ask you to look for?"

"I'm not going to say more," said Ludo stubbornly. "I won't get anyone in trouble."

"This is preposterous," Hennic sputtered. "You can't think Ludo was recruited by some . . . some Farsalan spy. He wouldn't even know what to take!"

"Wouldn't he?" asked the clerk. "When I found him, he had Governor Garren's letter to the first strategus in his hand."

Soraya's fingers itched to slap the smug smile off his face. The Hrum expected the enemy to spy on them, to fight back, but for Ludo to do it was treason. He could be executed for this!

"It must have been someone, one of us, who asked for some information," Hennic repeated. "He's just frightened by all the fuss. Ludo, anyone in this camp, I promise they won't get in trouble. This is just a misunderstanding, my friend. If it's a Hrum, they won't get in trouble at all. So you can tell us, all right? So we can straighten this out?"

Ludo set his lips together and said nothing.

"Ludo," said Reevus slowly. "Hennic is right. If it was a Hrum who sent you to get something, no one will get in trouble. Do you understand that?"

Ludo nodded vigorously. He understood. He said nothing. Fear shook Soraya's bones. Some cursed Farsalan she-bitch had recruited him. And Ludo—

Others had reached the same conclusion. Hennic looked around frantically, seeking any excuse, any escape . . . and his gaze fell on Soraya.

"Her! I bet she asked him to do it. She must have! She is a Farsalan spy, but Ludo doesn't understand that—he thinks she's a friend. He'd think she counts as someone in the camp, so you can't blame him," Hennic finished triumphantly.

Everyone stared at Soraya. Her heart was pounding. Even if she denied it, they wouldn't believe her. Garren was looking for an excuse to have her flogged, and this would provide it! They would beat her as a disobedient slave, and then question her as a spy, for answers she didn't possess. Soraya wrapped her arms around herself, trying to still her trembling. If she denied it, they might be sufficiently uncertain to beat Ludo, too. And since she was going to be hurt anyway . . .

"I did ask him to get papers for me." To her own amazement, Soraya sounded calm, almost arrogant. Strange, since her stomach was quivering like jelly. "I was trying to find out where my mother and brother have been sent—"

"You see?" Hennic interrupted. "And you can hardly blame her for that, much less Ludo! He probably got confused about what she wanted."

Was Hennic trying to get her off too, now that she'd supported his lie? If she could sense his shilshadu she might have known, but Soraya's fear pulled her sensing inward. She felt no more

from the crowd around her than she would from
a pile of stones—and that made her feel strangely
isolated, but she lifted her head defiantly and
stared back at them.

"Wait a moment." Ludo had finally tracked
the conversation. "That's not true. She wasn't the
one."

"I told him not to name me if he was caught,"
said Soraya. A strange serenity stole over her. Her
mother would be horrified, that she would sacrifice herself to defend a servant, but her father
would have understood. "I told him I'd get in trouble if he did. That's why he's denying it. He did it
for friendship, because he likes me. He didn't realize that it mattered." Most of which was probably
true—and if she ever got her hands on the girl
who'd abused his friendship so despicably . . .
There were some things even fighting against the
Hrum didn't excuse.

"This must be taken to the governor," said
Reevus. He looked even more worried than he
had before, and Soraya's fear deepened.

Reevus detailed two soldiers to take her to her
"room" and lock her in. She worked frantically at
the boards she'd been trying to rot, shifting them

against the nails that held them, but the wood was still too strong. She tried to weaken them with magic, but she was too agitated to touch the shilshadu of something as alien to her own temperament as the spirit of wood. And if she set it alight, which she couldn't do without a source of fire, the guards would notice. Why hadn't she taken a tool from the carpenter's shed? She'd feared that the tools would be counted after she left, but still . . .

Evidently Garren, or some other Hrum officer, was also thinking of ways she might escape. Just before sunset her guards unlocked the door and took her to the slave pen.

The torches inside had already been lit. "So the night watch can keep an eye on you," one of the soldiers told her as he tied her wrists together. "We're not taking any chances on you getting away." For all the world as if she made a habit of escape, but Soraya didn't say it aloud. If she irritated them, they might tie her hands behind her back instead, and that would be even more uncomfortable. She hadn't even been able to think of a way out of the small slot behind the goat pens, much less this open yard with its open-walled shed and tall, wood-and-iron fence.

At first she could see the men who passed by in the fading light, but after sunset the world outside the fence was a black mystery. In the beginning it made her uncomfortable to be watched by men she couldn't see. But as the night wore on and the camp quieted, she found she could always hear their clanking approach, and hear them leave again. So unless someone was watching her very quietly, and Soraya couldn't think why anyone would, it appeared that she had simply been added to the list of things the night watch was required to check on. They came about every third mark, which might even have given her enough time to escape, if she could only figure out how.

She could probably free her wrists from the rope, tight as it was, but then what? She was agile and desperate, and after a summer of hard work she was strong enough that she might have been able to climb the bars to the point where they curved inward—but not beyond. The Hrum were experts at keeping slaves from escaping; they'd had centuries of practice, after all.

Soraya paced like the leopard cub her father used to call her, but in her heart was none of the leopard's ferocity, only the growing chill of fear. If she had been a spy, with real information, she thought she could have controlled her fear better — she would be steeling her will to resist, to keep her silence at all costs, to protect Sorahb's cause. But to be beaten for information she didn't have . . . She had nothing to protect from the Hrum's harsh justice except Ludo, and while that might help him, it wasn't enough to steady her madly beating heart. She had seen Calfaer flogged. She was afraid of the whip, afraid of the morning.

The night stretched on. Soraya couldn't even think of sleep, but eventually her hands grew numb. At least getting rid of the rope would give her something to do. She might be able to untie the knots with her teeth, but there was a better way.

It was hard to reach the full shilshadu trance, frightened as she was, but the soft discipline steadied her. Once she found the bright, still place in her spirit, she waited until the patroller had passed and then opened herself to the fire of the torch, and thrust her wrists into the flame. Her heart danced with the fire's delight at the new fuel the rope provided, and the flames caressed her wrists like a toddler's patting hands.

How long had it been since she had held Merdas, felt his chubby hands on her face? Almost a full year. He would be three years old now, taller and thinner, talking in sentences. He too would have a slave's tattoo on his small shoulder, and a slave's life ahead of him if Soraya couldn't get out of this, and win him free.

The fire stung her skin—fire didn't feel grief—and she yanked her hands back, breaking the charred rope.

Brushing sparks from her skin, Soraya gazed at the untouched flesh beneath the black smudges. Maok's gift. She danced a few steps, to the joy of magic. Whatever happened tomorrow, she had this: magic, and her goal. She would survive, and go on. If she couldn't escape tonight, well, someday she would and then—

"Girl!" The soft voice came from the other side of the fence, in the corner behind the shed. It wasn't dark—no place in the slave pen was dark tonight, but it wasn't as bright. "Get over here, so we can talk!"

Soraya frowned, even as she moved to obey. She had started burning off the rope just after the watch passed, and it hadn't taken long, so she had some time. Who in the Hrum camp would try to talk to her tonight? Casia? But it sounded like a man's voice. Suddenly aware that someone else might be watching, Soraya slowed her steps and tried to move casually.

"Hurry up," the voice whispered impatiently. "The sentry won't pass for a bit, and they've all gone by on the other side of the pen before, but we've got to . . . You!"

The sharp exclamation was still a whisper. Soraya went up to the fence and pressed her face against the slats, peering into the darkness. The torchlight cast soft bars of light onto the man's face . . . the astonished face of the peddler her father had hired to bring supplies to the croft where she'd hidden all last winter.

"What are you doing here?" They spoke almost in unison.

The peddler snorted. "Never mind. We don't have time for this. Although . . . You're the slave that Ludo got into trouble? I thought you stayed with Golnar and Behras."

"How do you know about Ludo?" Soraya demanded. "About me? I saw you here before—I assumed you were selling things, but—"

"Look, we really don't have time for this," the peddler repeated. "I brought a knife so you can free your hands. You need to—" His gaze fell to her smudged, bare wrists. "How did you get out of the rope?"

"A trick," said Soraya impatiently. "We don't have time for that, either. The night watch will be back soon."

"Right." The peddler drew a steadying breath. He had given her a name once, but she hadn't bothered to remember it—largely because she was certain it was false. "I'm going to let the watch pass one more time, then I'll pick the lock."

"How do you—"

"Will you stop asking questions? I was a smith once. I've helped make locks. But it may take a while, so while I do that, I want you to bundle some of that straw up into a blanket. Make it look like you're still there, asleep. When I get the gate open, head straight for the animal pens. Hide near a place where the midden cart will stop. Do you know where—"

"I've been loading it. It stinks!"

"Who cares? I've arranged for—I've tied a net beneath the cart. It will sag a bit, but it shouldn't be visible as long as no one's looking for it. And that cart is the only thing that will leave camp before they come for you. When the cart stops, get yourself into the net and keep still until you're well away—the carter doesn't know, and we need to keep it that way."

"But won't the carter—"

"There's a bumpy place in the road, just before the second canal bridge, about half a league from the camp. When you reach it, cut the ropes that hold the net. You'll have to cut two of them. Just lie on the road till the cart's over the bridge, then get yourself into the bushes beside the canal. There'll be clothes and food waiting there, and I'll come for you later in the day. But until I come, you hide. Understand?"

"Yes, but why in Azura's name are you—"

The peddler stiffened, listening, then turned and hurried into the darkness. Now that she was listening, Soraya could hear the clanks and clicks that heralded the sentry's approach.

Swearing under her breath, she ran to the shed and lay down in the straw, pulling the blanket over her, leaving just her face showing. The last time the sentry passed, she'd been sitting still to meditate. Now she would appear to be sleeping. When he saw her next, it shouldn't seem odd that she'd rolled over in her sleep, carrying the blanket with her.

Soraya tried to relax, to make her breathing soft and even, but she didn't succeed. She'd never felt less like sleeping in her life.

But why was the peddler, of all people, helping her to escape? He did business with the Hrum. She'd seen him! How did he know she needed to escape? And why did he care? He hadn't known who she was—he'd been as surprised by her identity as she was by his. But whatever his motives, she could hardly be worse off, even if the attempt failed. And that seemed likely. She could probably get from the slave pen to the barns in the darkness, but even though the midden cart arrived at dawn, there would still be some light. How could she get beneath it, unseen, much less get out of the camp without anyone looking under the high cart to see her dangling there like a netted trout? She hadn't missed the fact that someone else had rigged the net, and probably left the clothes and food by the canal for her, so there was at least one other conspirator. And then she had to get out of the net without the carter—who was presumably loyal to the Hrum—noticing her departure! This was far too complicated . . . but it was better than any plan she'd come up with.

She listened as the sentry clanked up to the fence, paused for a moment, and then walked on. She waited until she heard the faint clicks of someone trying to pick the lock before she flung off the blanket and began to gather straw.

Making a straw-filled blanket look like a sleeping human was harder than it sounded and required a lot more straw than Soraya would have thought. She used all the straw in the back of the shed, piling up the straw in front to hide its absence. She was thinking she could use another bundle when a hiss from the gate summoned her.

The iron-barred gate swinging open onto the night was one of the most beautiful sights she'd ever seen.

"It's good enough," the peddler whispered. "You know what to do?"

"Yes," Soraya replied as he quietly shut the gate and snapped the lock closed. From a distance the blanket-shrouded shape looked remarkably like a sleeping person, and she felt a thrill of pride.

"But I'll need a knife to cut the ropes under the cart. And I insis—I'd appreciate it if you'd tell me why you're doing this."

The peddler already had the knife in his hand, but now he hesitated, eyeing her strangely. "You've changed."

Soraya snorted. "Never in my life would I have been crazy enough to insult you at a moment like this."

"It's not that." He handed her the knife, still staring at her face as she tucked it into the waistband of her britches. "At least, not entirely. It's—"

A privy door slammed in the distance. It wasn't the sentry approaching, but it was enough to remind both of them that their time was limited.

"I'll explain later," said the peddler. "I promise. Go now." He gave her a small shove toward the animal pens, then turned and walked away.

Soraya knew he was right, but even as she stepped into the darkness—unable to hurry until her eyes adapted—she wondered what he'd been going to say. Her hands were callused now, but she didn't think she'd changed. Then she wondered if she would escape to hear his explanation, and forgot about trivial questions.

It was very dark coming from the well-lit slave pens, but Soraya had become familiar with this part of the camp over the last month, and she groped her way toward the goat pen without knocking into anything. The goats were out in the pen, but they were familiar with the scent of the person who slept on the other side of the back wall of their shed. They didn't bleat as Soraya felt her way down the fence to the pile of fresh straw that was mounded between the goat pen and the pig sty.

She settled herself between the straw and the fence, but decided not to burrow in and cover herself—it would rustle too much as it was. Still, she could think of no better place to hide. It was all very well for the peddler to say, "hide where the midden cart stops," but the midden cart didn't stop in many places, and all of them were on open streets where there wasn't much cover.

She expected a long, fearful wait, but despite her tension and doubts, there was something soothing about being free. Soraya actually dozed on and off, though the rattle of the cart in the distance brought her jerking awake. She rolled out of the straw toward the fence, and lay watching the street, where she knew the cart would appear.

The sun hadn't risen yet, but the sky had turned from starry black to gray, and the flat light illuminated the world. In early autumn, this time of morning was cold. Soon it would be winter. Soraya didn't want to spend the winter as a Hrum slave. Though if she left now, she would have no way to discover where Merdas and Sudaba had been sent. For a moment her resolve wavered. If she could get that information, it would be worth a beating. But her only chance to see those records had been lost when Garren realized who she was; with the watch he kept on her, she would never be able to reach them. And with a slave's tattoo on her shoulder, her odds of crossing the Hrum Empire to find and free them were vanishingly small.

No, the best thing she could do now was escape, and try to help the resistance keep Farsala unconquered for the remainder of the Hrum's year. In the despair that followed her father's defeat and death, Soraya had thought that impossible. But Mazad had held out for almost six months already, and worried Garren so much that he had suborned the city's governor. When she got free, she must find the men who were using Sorahb's name and warn them. Yes, that was the first thing to do. But she'd have to be careful who she told. She'd seen that peddler dealing with the Hrum; the fact that he was helping her now wasn't . . .

Could this whole thing be some sort of trap? Could Garren plan to let her think she'd escaped, so that in her gratitude she'd tell her rescuer all she supposedly knew? Was he that subtle? He might be. But even if it was a trap—and it might not be—she might still spring it unexpectedly and win her freedom. But she'd have to be very careful with this peddler. Just because he seemed to be helping, didn't mean he was really on her side.

The cart came into view, followed by two yawning men with pitchforks. Soraya watched as they cleaned the corral where the horses and mules were kept. The carter stopped the cart where he always did, and climbed down to help them just as he'd helped her. A methodical man, Azura bless him.

They were too sleepy to talk much, but they grumbled a bit about "that slave girl's" absence, and Soraya grinned. The muscles of her face felt stiff, and strange. Cold? Or had it really been that long since she had smiled? She felt more alive this morning than she had for months—as if her mind, her spirit, had been sleeping and come suddenly awake.

It might have been the excitement, the chance to act on her own, the prospect of escape—but Soraya thought it was also the awkward stiffness of the knife's sheath poking into her belly. She would fight if they tried to capture her, and if she escaped she would fight them in earnest, as a deghass should. As her father would have done. No wonder she felt as if her true self was waking from a long sleep.

They finished with the corral and moved the cart forward to stop beside the goat pen. Soraya took advantage of the noise to extract herself entirely from the straw and crawl around to the other side of the pile. Anyone who came down the street from the other direction would see her, but no one else seemed to be awake.

The cart was still several yards from the straw pile—Soraya had known the cart wouldn't park right next to it since the men needed clear access to the pen. The ox who pulled the cart was near the pile. His nostrils flared as he caught Soraya's scent, and one great eye rolled down to look at her.

But Soraya had been loading the cart herself for weeks now, and the placid ox knew she belonged there.

She waited till the men were busy mucking out the pen, until the carter had climbed down to help them. Then, heart hammering, she crept in front of the ox and down the far side of the cart. She watched their legs as she crawled, moving slowly for silence. If all she could see was their legs, then they couldn't see her. Silence was more important than speed, but she longed to hurry, to get out of sight as quickly as possible.

In moments she passed the first of the cart's tall wheels and could roll —*Quietly, girl!* — underneath. If the net wasn't there . . .

It was! Bound to the bottom of the cart by two ropes that ran through axle braces and crossed in an X. It didn't look like there would be enough room between the tight ropes and the bottom of the cart for Soraya's body, but when she pulled down one edge of the net and worked her way onto the ropes —*Quietly!* — they sagged alarmingly close to the ground.

Small thuds shook the cart as the men cast forkfuls of dung aboard, and Soraya struggled to balance herself on the crossed ropes. The net would catch an arm or leg that slipped, but the weight of her body had to rest on the ropes or she would be dragged . . .

A drop of moisture lit on the back of her neck and ran down the side. What? . . . of course. The midden was damp, and though the slats at the bottom of the cart were well fitted, they weren't watertight. They would leak.

If it meant getting out of here, Soraya didn't care what she was soaked with. Well, she didn't care much. And she could always bathe later.

She hung her ankles over the back ropes, and grasped the front ropes with both hands, with her weight mostly centered on the X, just before the carter mounted and the cart lurched into motion. It moved all of twenty feet before stopping again, to allow them to clean out the pig pen. But that was the last stop before it left camp, for which Soraya was grateful. The hard ropes were already digging into her breasts, hips, and thighs, and more . . . liquid was dripping onto her back and hair. But at its worst, it was better than being flogged.

By the time they finished cleaning the pig sty Soraya wasn't so certain of that, for her muscles had begun to ache and burn. It was a relief when the cart started moving—it actually hurt more, but clinging to the ropes while the cart bounced and swayed took enough effort and attention that it distracted her even from the stench.

The strings of the net cut into her face as she watched the bumpy ground roll under the cart, far too slowly to suit her. At last, here was the turn that Soraya knew would take them onto the road that exited the camp.

Straining her neck muscles, Soraya turned her head and looked to one side. Yes, they were passing the troopers' tents now. She could see the soldiers' legs and feet coming out of the doors, walking past the cart. If the cart had been just a little bit late this morning, she would have been seen on the street and recaptured. But no one paid any attention to the familiar passage of the midden cart.

If she hadn't been so uncomfortable, Soraya might have relaxed. She wasn't even too alarmed when the perimeter guard hailed them.

"Halt the cart."

"Why?" asked the carter. But the cart stopped. "Usually you want me out of here as fast as possible. Especially when the pig shit's aboard."

Another cold drop fell onto Soraya's hair, and she grimaced.

"Yeah, well, we've got new orders today. We're to search everything leaving camp. Some kitchen half-wit almost walked off with an important document yesterday, and the governor threw a fit about security procedures, so . . . new orders."

The guard didn't sound as if he thought much of them, but Soraya's heart beat like a hammer. She freed one hand from the rope and reached for the knife, but the net, and ropes she was lying on, kept her from touching it. Still, its sharp presence against her stomach was as comforting as it was uncomfortable. When they pulled her out she would draw it and . . . and what? Fight several men, armed with swords? She'd do better to hide it under the cart, hoping she might retrieve it later, but she wanted that knife! It made her feel less defenseless, even if the feeling was an illusion.

"Search all you want," the carter said cheerfully. "Dig into every corner. Better you than me, that's all I have to say."

"Are we supposed to stick our lances into that muck?" a soldier complained. "We'd have to wash them."

"Um. I think a close visual inspection will do," another voice replied. "You see any documents in there?"

Soraya prayed that none of them would think to look beneath the cart.

"None I can see from here," said the soldier. "And I don't particularly want to get closer."

The carter laughed. "Well, if your inspection's finished, then I'll be getting on. A good day to you."

The cart rolled forward but Soraya didn't relax, didn't move a muscle, till it passed around the low hill that she knew would take it out of sight. Even then she didn't relax much, for by now it felt as if every muscle in her body was on fire.

The first canal bridge wasn't far outside the Hrum camp, but there was almost half a league between it and the next bridge. Half a dozen times Soraya reached for the knife to cut herself free— if the carter saw her, she would run! But even if she could run, and the way her muscles were cramping that was doubtful, there would be Hrum patrols looking for her the moment the man reported. *No, not yet.* She could endure a little longer.

Then a particularly rough jolt sent pain arcing down her spine. Soraya hissed and twisted herself to one side so she could fumble through the net and draw the knife. This was ridiculous! A beating would hurt less, and she could hide in the fields almost as well as in the brush beside the canal.

She had laid the blade against the first rope, when she heard hoofbeats thundering up the road behind her.

"Halt the cart!"

"What, again?" The carter was stopping the ox as he spoke.

Gazing at the dusty horses' legs that trotted up to surround the cart, Soraya held her breath. Who'd have thought they'd miss her this quickly?

"We're looking for a slave girl who escaped last night," said a crisp voice in Hrum. "We wondered if you might have seen her—she might even have hidden herself in your cart."

Soraya's hand tightened on the knife. If she was caught after getting this far, she would kill someone! Probably the peddler, if she ever laid hands on him.

"They already searched my cart on the way out of camp—for documents, no less. But you can poke through the midden again if you like," the carter added. "If you're all that attached to the stuff, I'll let you keep a bushel or two."

There was a moment of silence broken only by the stamp of hooves, then Soraya thought she heard a soldier mutter, "That stuff stinks!"

"Since you confirm the perimeter guards' statement that they already searched the cart, further search would be redundant," said the officer shortly. "But did you see a slave girl, either back in the camp or on the road?"

"I saw a few women in the camp," said the carter. "I don't know if they were slaves or not, but they seemed to be going about their business. And I haven't seen anyone on the road yet—most folks are just sitting down to breakfast."

"Hmm. So if she came this way, she's probably still ahead of you."

"Or she hid in a ditch as I passed," said the carter. "Or more likely, she's in the city, hiding out with friends."

"Perhaps," said the officer stiffly. "But our task is to search this road till we're certain she didn't come this way. If you see her, you'll report it? There will be a large reward, if she's recaptured."

"How large?" asked the carter. "I haven't seen her, but I can be asking folks to keep their eyes open. A girl, you say?"

"About sixteen years old, small, with long black hair," the Hrum officer told him. Soraya blessed the net that cut into her face, for it also kept her braid from falling to the ground where it might have been seen.

"They haven't decided on the exact amount yet," the officer continued, "but it will be at least fifty gold centirus. Possibly more."

The carter whistled. "I'll keep my eyes open."

He doubtless would, along with every peasant in the area who fancied the price of a new house! Soraya lowered her head onto one of the hard ropes and cursed Garren bitterly as the patrol cantered off. He had turned everyone in the countryside against her. On the other hand, if he was sending out patrols and offering rewards, perhaps that meant the peddler was honest after all. In any case, she would wait to cut herself free until she reached the spot he'd described.

THE WHOLE ROAD WAS so rough and rutted that Soraya feared she wouldn't be able to recognize the "rough place" before the second canal bridge, but when they finally reached it there was no doubt. The cart jolted so wildly that Soraya could hardly cut the first rope, and one ankle had already bounced off its support, so one of her knees now dragged over the dirty ruts despite the presence of the net.

She tried to transfer all her weight to the rope that would remain, but the moment the first rope gave way, the lower half of her body pitched down onto the road. Only her firm grip on the remaining rope, and the entangling net, kept her under the cart as it rolled onward. She'd have thought the carter would hear her being dragged over the ruts, but he was talking to the disgruntled ox, and the cart lurched so much that the shift of her weight was probably imperceptible — but that wouldn't last once they got onto the smoother surface of the bridge! Soraya sawed grimly at the remaining rope with her free hand. Azura be praised for a peddler who sold knives! This one wasn't fancy but the blade was wickedly keen, and it cut through the rope in just four hard strokes.

Soraya hit the ground with a thump and was dragged several more feet as the last rope threaded itself out of the braces. She lay, head and shoulders on the base of the bridge, and watched the back of the midden cart climb up the bridge's gentle slope and then vanish down the other side.

Her gaze swept the nearby fields, thick with the gold of nearly ripe grain and the green of bushy vegetables. No one had appeared yet, but they wouldn't be at breakfast much longer. Moving slowly, as much because her aching muscles demanded it as for silence, Soraya untangled herself from the ropes and net. Then she crawled off the road and into the tangle of willows and tall reeds, dragging the evidence of her escape behind her.

For once luck favored her—the well-worn satchel the peddler had promised her was on this side of the road, hidden from the casual glance, but easy to find once she'd crawled into the thicket.

Soraya was grateful, since she didn't think she could have crossed the road again the way she was feeling. Her hands were so stiff from gripping the ropes that it took several attempts to push the stopper out of the jug, but when she succeeded, strong tea, sweetened with honey, rewarded her.

She made certain no one passing on the road could see her, and then lay still, sipping it slowly, waiting for the ache in her back and neck to fade.

In only half a mark, traffic began to pick up as farmers went to their fields. Once again Soraya was grateful that the midden cart hadn't been later, and that the peddler hadn't chosen a more distant bridge. It wasn't remarkable that a peddler would know the traffic patterns on a main road into a city—he might have walked it dozens of times—but still, his plan had proved sound. Soraya was even more impressed when, beneath the thick sandwiches and apples, she found a shirt, britches, and a brightly embroidered vest and cap, which might have been worn by any peasant boy.

The farmers had all passed now, and there was no one on the road. After careful reconnaissance to be certain no one was working in a field nearby, Soraya waded under the bridge and stripped off the slave's tunic and britches. After a bit of thought she tied them to some willow roots that had protruded into the bottom of the canal. If her knots held, they wouldn't be found until the canal was emptied—probably not till the harvest ended.

It might not matter if they were found, but

"Sorahb" had done such a wonderful job on her escape so far, it seemed a pity to leave the slightest clue as to how it had been accomplished.

She had no soap, but handfuls of sand from the canal bottom made a decent substitute. It felt wonderful scratching against her skin and scalp, scouring away the stench of the midden cart.

With only a small pang, she took the knife and cut her hair short, like a peasant boy's. She watched the long black strands drift downstream and was surprised how little regret she felt—that hair was the mark of a true-blooded deghass. But it had been a long time since she'd felt like a deghass, and given the description the Hrum patrols were giving out she could hardly do otherwise.

When she finally felt clean—or as clean as she was going to get in the shallow, silty canal water—she climbed out and put on the boy's clothes. They were a bit big, as if they'd been handed down from an older brother, but very comfortable. Why were peasant clothes so often more comfortable, or warmer, or more practical than deghass robes? It hardly seemed right.

She coiled the ropes, folded the net, put them

in the satchel, and settled down to enjoy her breakfast. She wasn't surprised to see the peddler leading his mule up the road shortly after she finished.
All the rest of his timing had been perfect, after all.

"Good girl," he said, looking at her short hair
as she scrambled out of the bushes to join him. "Or
rather, good boy. You're the young cousin of some
friends of mine. I'm taking you off to a small village
near Desafon, where the Hrum have already
counted the men, in hopes you can avoid their
draft. Mother's darling, that's what you are. Come
here. I want to make that haircut a bit tidier.
Anyone would think you cut it yourself, with a dull
knife and no mirror."

It was a sharp knife, and unless he insisted on
taking it back, Soraya intended to keep it, but she
couldn't repress a grin. She'd been smiling a lot
this morning. On the other hand . . . "My hair's
still black, and the Hrum patrols are spreading my
description in every village."

He drew his own knife and ran his fingers
through her hair. "That's just what *we're* going to
do," he said, as the damp, dirty wisps started
falling to the road. "We'll tell everyone we meet
about that desperate, escaped slave girl, and the

460

big reward the Hrum are offering. Which will make it even less likely that anyone will connect my friend's twelve-year-old cousin with a sixteen-year-old deghass slave. Though it will be better if you don't talk much, shy like you are."

"I can be shy," said Soraya. "But why are you doing this?" She reached up and caught his wrist, forcing him to meet her eyes. "I've seen you dealing with the Hrum. Why aren't you collecting this reward?"

"Mostly it's because of Ludo," said the peddler. He twisted his wrist out of her grasp and trimmed a few more strands. "There, that'll do. He was so upset about what was happening to you, he might have broken down and talked about what he was really doing, or thought he was doing, and that would have been . . . well, a bad thing. So my friends . . . we promised him we'd get you out."

"Your friends, who sent him to steal papers from the Hrum," said Soraya. "How could they use him like that? As a traitor, he might have been executed! And he was bound to get caught."

The peddler was looking at her strangely again, and she sensed the same mixture of astonishment and suspicion she'd felt before, when he talked about how she'd changed. Then he shrugged and took up the mule's lead. "You think we didn't know that?" He started down the road, and Soraya slung the satchel over her shoulder and followed. It felt strange to walk in the open. "No one asked Ludo to do anything. He was just . . . trying to help because of a conversation he'd overheard."

"A conversation about stealing Hrum documents?" Soraya asked.

The peddler walked on, making no reply. Now that he wasn't focused on her, his emotions were harder to read. It might become easier as she spent more time with him, but she thought he might be one of those people whose shilshadu was difficult for her to sense.

"You're Sorahb, aren't you?" she went on. He could hardly be anything else, but still . . . a peasant? "Or do you work for him?" That would make more sense, but she knew that no distant commander could have come up with that detailed plan for her rescue so quickly. The plan had been his, whoever he worked for.

She owed him an unpayable debt. Not her life, perhaps, but he had certainly spared her a flogging — and probably life as a Hrum slave as well.

Her savior snorted. "Every carpenter's apprentice who spills a keg of nails on the road and doesn't get it picked up before a patrol comes by is Sorahb. But I know folks who've done a few things."

"And you're spying on the Hrum for them?" She found it hard to believe of the man her father had bribed and blackmailed into bringing news from the croft where Soraya had been hidden. But it was that, or he was working for Garren after all, trying to get her to reveal something, and that seemed less and less likely. And if he wasn't working for them . . .

"Are you Sorahb?" she asked again.

"Everyone's Sorahb," he repeated. "Some of them more foolish than I'd ever be. Why? Do you fancy working for the great deghan who leads the resistance? I was planning to take you back to Golnar and Behras. They're working on a farm south of Desafon, but I think they'd take you in."

"They might," said Soraya. She felt a surge of gratitude for it, for the care they'd given her over the last winter. "But I'd rather go to the Suud. Can you take me there?"

The Suud's desert was just across the mountains

from Mazad—she might be able to tell them about the governor, even if the peddler couldn't help her. And she longed to see Maok again.

"The Suud?" The peddler stopped, staring at her until his mule paced past him, pulling on the lead. Duckie, that was the beast's name. What name had the peddler used?

"Why do you want to go to the Suud?" he asked.

"I've got friends there," said Soraya. "And I'll certainly be safe. I'm sorry, I've forgotten your name."

The flash of dismay in his eyes told her that he'd forgotten it too, but he didn't miss a beat. "Garven," he said. "Of Marat, originally, though I've traveled a lot since."

No, she couldn't trust him yet. But it was a long way to the mountains. There would be time to test him—time to learn the truth. Soraya smiled.

CHAPTER EIGHTEEN

KAVI

THE GIRL MADE BETTER TIME on the road than Kavi had expected, walking behind him all day without complaint. Though when they reached the modest inn where he planned to spend the night, she pushed open the door and walked in as if she owned the place, so it seemed she hadn't changed too much.

The inn's mistress stared, and Kavi reached out and smacked the top of her head. "Hey, boy, I know it's your first day on the road, but that's no reason to lose all your manners!"

The girl glared at him, but she had some sense left. She lowered her head and mumbled, "Sorry, mistress. I should've been knocking."

"That's all right, lad. First day on the road? You look worn out with it!" There were shadows under the girl's eyes—small wonder, after the night she'd spent, with a day's walk on top of it. Even Kavi was tired—that she'd held up as well as she had was amazing.

"Come to the hearth, boy, and rest a bit. We've just started cooking, but I know how lads eat. I'll bring you a bit of bread and cheese, to hold you till dinner. What were you thinking, Kavi, wearing the poor boy out so?"

Tired she might be, but there was nothing wrong with her hearing or her wits. Dark eyes, glowing with irony, flashed at him from under the rim of her cap. Then she went to the hearth, sitting on the floor beside it, for all the world like a tired boy. When the mistress brought in bread and cheese, she thanked the woman with an inarticulate shyness that concealed the fact that her peasant accent wasn't very good. Not that she mispronounced anything, but it was too broad, almost a parody. Was that what peasants sounded like to her? In any case, she'd need some coaching—they'd be on the road several days before they reached the mountains, and they didn't dare arouse suspicion. But in the meantime, Kavi had always been able to talk enough for two.

He told his fellow travelers, and a few locals who came in for beer after dinner, all about the slave girl—once a fine lady deghass!—who'd escaped the Hrum, and about the big reward they offered. Sixty centirus, no less!

Some men were interested in the reward, for its size if nothing else. But most men, and all of the women, clearly hoped the girl got free, deghass or no.

Not one of them glanced twice at the boy, sprawling in the shadows beside the hearth with his bright cap and dusty boots. She did look tired.

Kavi sought out the innkeeper and paid a few more foals for a room with a second bed, explaining that the boy kicked in his sleep. The innkeeper pocketed the coins and changed his room, and the girl was asleep within moments of hitting the bed. In fact, Kavi had to pull off her boots and draw the blankets over her.

It wasn't till early next morning that he was able to visit Duckie, and have a quiet chat with the head groom. The food the local farmers had gathered was ready to ship, and there was more than they had hoped. The harvest was beginning, and it looked to be a good one. Many people were willing to empty out their grain and dried vegetable bins to make room for fresh, and even throw in a bit of salt meat, to help the valiant defenders of Mazad. As for news of the Hrum, the man thought there'd been fewer messengers heading for Mazad in the last few months. He'd seen nothing else out of the ordinary except for a patrol that passed yesterday, looking for an escaped slave girl, and they'd turned back at the next village, thinking that a girl on foot couldn't have gotten any farther in just one night.

It seemed she'd been spirited out of a locked cage, leaving a woven straw statue of a girl in her place, so lifelike that by torchlight it had fooled all the sentries. Sorahb was a miracle worker, of course, but this seemed almost like the work of djinn!

Kavi laughed and told the man he hoped the Hrum believed that, but that peasants should have better sense.

Returning to the inn for his breakfast, he found the girl eating fried potato cakes with an appetite that would do a twelve-year-old boy credit. And she thanked the inn mistress in a boy's mumble, without being reminded.

"You make a good boy," Kavi told her when they were on the road once more. They'd enjoyed a stretch of dry, sunny weather lately, and it looked like it would be continuing for at least a few more days. She was doing fine on dry roads, but he didn't think she'd tolerate mud so well.

"I'm pretending I'm Hejir," she told him. "He was only nine, and once he got to know me he talked a lot, but at first he used to mumble like that."

"Who's Hejir?"

"Golnar and Behras' younger son. I took him hunting sometimes, when I was living at the croft. Don't you remember him?"

"I remember the boy. I don't think I ever heard his name."

At the mention of names she sent him another bright, ironic glance, but she made no further comment. And perhaps the bright-faced boy Kavi remembered would have shouldered his satchel and marched down the road without a second thought, but it amazed Kavi that she had.

"Why did you do it?" he asked, and not only

because he wanted to distract her from the subject of names. "According to Ludo, you offered to take a beating for him. He said you were a friend, but that seems to go beyond friendship."

"We were friends," said the daughter of the House of the Leopard, without any hesitation he could see. "But I don't think I'd have offered to be beaten in his place. Hennic accused me of being the one who told him to take the papers. Garren had been looking for an excuse to . . . motivate me to talk, ever since he got the notion I was there to spy for Sorahb. I knew they were going to flog me no matter what I said, so I thought I might as well get Ludo off. And it wouldn't have been necessary if your friends hadn't recruited him in the first place! Not that I'm not grateful that you rescued me. I am. Truly."

Kavi could see that she was, and that it galled her to be indebted to him.

"We didn't recruit Ludo," he told her. "He just—"

"Overheard a conversation, and decided to help out by stealing Hrum documents. Yes, of course," she said coolly.

Clearly she believed that he worked for Sorahb,

and would ask no questions that might cause trouble for the resistance. Kavi decided to let her go on thinking that—it was easier than trying to explain Nadi's penchant for adopting anyone who needed it, be it a simpleminded Hrum servant, or a young peddler whose heart had been more crippled by anger and bitterness than his hand had been by a sword cut. And he certainly wasn't going to explain his ongoing struggle to keep Sim and Hama from trying to actively support "Sorahb." In the future, they'd be more careful what they said in front of Ludo. And the lady Soraya had some explaining to do herself.

"Why were you posing as a servant if you weren't there to spy?" Kavi asked. He couldn't imagine the deghass he'd met less than a year ago acting as a servant for any reason—though he could believe it of the slim boy-girl who walked beside him now, considering whether or not to answer. Had she any idea how much she'd changed? And could the other deghans have changed, have been taught to be better people? Probably not—at least, not by anything less than months of servitude. Which, come to think of it was precisely what most of them were enduring right now. Would they all return competent and steady, and willing to befriend a simpleminded kitchen boy?

Somehow Kavi doubted it.

The girl had made up her mind. "I was there to spy," she admitted. "But not for Sorahb. I was trying to get in to their records, to find out where my mother and brother were sent. I almost succeeded, too. I had the scroll in my hand."

Watching her teeth grind together, Kavi observed that her temper hadn't changed. But in this different Soraya, he didn't seem to mind it.

"Even if you'd learned where they went, you'd likely not have been able to reach them." Was that comforting or not? It was the truth. "They always send slaves far from the country where they're taken, so even if they escape, they can't get home. You've a better chance of seeing them again if Mazad holds out—though your chances there aren't that good either."

Why did that make her look suspicious?

"I suppose you're right," she admitted. "I never found out where they were sent anyway. Never even had a chance to search for my cousin Pari's name. Though I don't know if she was taken

or not, much less where, so that would have
been—"

"She was taken at the Sendar Wall," Kavi
interrupted before she made him feel guiltier than
he already did. "At least, if she's the girl who was
with you when we first met."

The memory of that meeting, where her noble
father had blackmailed Kavi into his service,
roused enough anger to assuage his guilt, letting
him meet her astonished gaze. But still . . . This
was the first time he'd heard the name of the girl
he'd last seen in the Hrum slave pens.

"The Sendar Wall?" said the girl, Soraya,
blankly. "What was she doing there?"

"A lot of the deghans brought their families,"
Kavi told her. "To witness their great victory.
Your father was furious about it, but the
deghans said it was part of their 'ancient and
glorious tradition,' and refused to send them
home."

Pain flashed in the vivid dark eyes at the mention of her father, but most of her attention was
fixed on him. "How do you know all that?" she
demanded, sounding almost like the lady Soraya
of old.

No, he couldn't trust her with any part of his story, much less the whole of it. The Craft Council might have acquitted him, but he didn't think Commander Merahb's daughter would do the same.

"Let's start working on your accent," said Kavi firmly.

SHE CONTINUED TO BE A good traveling companion, sleeping in blankets on the ground with no complaint, and when the fine weather broke and they stopped at another inn, she readily agreed to flip a coin to determine who would sleep in the bed. Under his tutoring, her accent improved to the point that she wouldn't make folks suspicious, at least in casual conversation.

But that one load off his burden of worries was soon replaced by others. Kavi was using this unexpected trip north to check on his arrangements. The gathering of the next food shipment was continuing apace, but the intelligence his people reported was disturbing.

The nearer they drew to Mazad, the more active the Hrum patrols seemed to be. The casks of supplies that had already come in had to be

stored farther from the city than the first shipment, for the Hrum were searching all of the large
buildings in the area on a regular basis. Almost as
if they suspected another shipment was being
gathered, which was absurd since they had no
way to know about the first one.

In a village just west of Mazad, Kavi took the
girl to an inn and left her to eat alone, claiming
that he needed to speak with potential buyers at
another table.

The men he spoke to swore that the searches,
the increased patrols, had started shortly after the
last food shipment. And that the Hrum weren't
looking for Sorahb's wondrous, disappearing
army—not this long after the battle—in other
folks' barns! On the other hand, they didn't seem
to know about the tunnels. Messages still appeared
in the hollow tree, and the occasional guardsman
still came out to contact them. But they weren't
certain a second shipment could reach the tunnel
entrance, not with all these patrols about.

Kavi carried his tankard back to the table
where Soraya sat, wondering how he was going to
get thirty carts of food past all those Hrum.

"You don't look like they wanted to buy many

knives," the girl said softly. Her gaze was on the crowd, not on him. Kavi had spoken to many of them earlier—this close to Mazad almost everyone knew who he was, and what he was doing here. So now, when he seemed to want privacy, they left him alone.

"They don't," he said, erasing the scowl from his face. "But no matter. I'll sell them down the road."

Her expression said clearly that she recognized that for a lie, and a transparent lie to boot.

"They have bought my knives," Kavi protested. And they had, though mostly as an excuse to meet with him.

"That doesn't matter," said Soraya slowly. "What matters is that these people trust you. They respect you too, but trust is the important part."

The flickering light from the hearth, from the candles near the bar, shadowed her face and made her eyes mysterious.

"How would you know what they feel?" Kavi meant it to sound like a joke, but a prickle of unease ran down his spine, for she sounded as if she truly knew.

"That doesn't matter either," said the girl, with the firmness of someone who has made up her

476

mind. "But if they're certain they can trust you, then . . . then I think I can too."

"Oh?" Kavi settled back in his chair and waited. He'd become aware, as they traveled, that she was holding something back. But it couldn't be too important.

"I think that Garren has suborned the governor of Mazad," she said. "I think he's working for the Hrum, planning to betray—"

"*What?*" People all over the room turned to stare, and Kavi lowered his voice hastily. "What makes you think that? Governor Nehar's—"

"A deghan," Soraya finished. "So what? Plenty of deghans were ambitious fools, at the best of times. And this isn't the best of times."

"No, it's not." He watched her intently, but could see no sign of nervousness or deceit. "What makes you think Nehar's a traitor?"

"Some things that Governor Garren said." She was speaking more slowly now. "He'd just found out who I was, and he thought I was spying for Sorahb—I told you about that. What he was most interested in was who Sorahb was, how I was contacting him, that kind of thing."

Kavi felt another chill. If she had made some

bargain, if her imprisonment and the threat to beat her had been a snare, she had certainly made contact with one Sorahb. But surely, that was too convoluted for the practical Hrum. "Go on."

"Well, I said something about Mazad being a bigger problem than Sorahb, and he said he wasn't worried about Mazad."

"So? He likely thinks that all he has to do to overwhelm Mazad is bring in enough troops. Mazad's stuck in one place—Sorahb can be running all over the countryside."

"I know, but he sounded so confident. It just felt wrong. And later, in the same conversation, I said something like, 'No deghan would ever work for the Hrum,' and he said, 'Tell that to the gov—' and then he broke off and tried to change the subject. But I put the two together, and I asked him— accused him, really, of suborning Governor Nehar, and he hit me. I know it doesn't sound like much." Her hands were clenched on the table. "But Garren . . ." She seemed to have run out of words.

"Garren hit you?" Kavi's brows rose. "I'd have said he's not the sort to go hitting folk—more efficient to just tell the arms master to chop off their heads. Anger's not worth the effort, for him."

"How do you know that?" She looked startled, and a bit suspicious. And no wonder, for he'd betrayed a depth of knowledge no peddler dealing casually with Hrum ordnancers should have possessed.

"I know a lot," said Kavi grimly. "But this isn't much to go on. A couple of sentences, in different contexts, that could mean something else entirely."

"But when I reached a conclusion, he hit me," Soraya persisted. "Why would he do that, except to distract me from what I was thinking? To silence me? And why do you think he offered such a big reward for my capture, except to keep me from passing this on?"

Kavi had wondered about the size of the reward. The girl's dark eyes met his without hesitation, as honest and open as any peasant's.

"All right," he said, making up his mind as he spoke. "Can you stay here by yourself for a day or two?"

"Certainly. Just leave me enough money for meals." She leaned back in her chair at last, looking satisfied. Kavi noticed that she was smart enough not to ask questions he wouldn't have answered, but it was a passing thought. Most of his mind was already working on the need to reach Mazad and get in—tonight, if he could.

HE DID GET IN THAT NIGHT, with the help of a local lad who volunteered to guide him across country till he reached the familiar hills near the town. Hrum patrols were everywhere, and they had to waste much of the precious darkness crouching on hilltops, or in the gullies, as the Hrum marched past. His informants were right— they were far more numerous, and more alert, than they had been. Too numerous, and too alert, for thirty large wagons to sneak past them even if he created some sort of diversion.

But a lone man on foot could reach the tunnel's hidden entrance just as the sky in the east began to brighten. The wheel that opened the hatch had been oiled; it still grated a bit, but not nearly as loudly as it had before.

Kavi hurried down the walkway making all the noise he could, for he wanted the tunnel guards to intercept him. It took them a cursed long time, but finally a lance shot across his path, into the water.

"Halt, and remove your—"

"I don't have time for that, and it doesn't matter," Kavi interrupted firmly. "I am marked as a Hrum spy, and the council knows it, and if I know Mazad, every apprentice and kitchen girl knows it too. I need to see Commander Siddas. Now."

IT TOOK A BIT MORE ARGUMENT, but Kavi had never been shy about arguing. He was sitting in Commander Siddas' spartan office before breakfast time. He ignored the two guardsmen who stood by the door, but they made up for that by never taking their eyes off him. They looked quite disappointed when the commander came into the office and closed the door behind him—like a pair of hounds watching a bone they'd hoped for, thrown into the soup pot instead.

"I understand your news is urgent," said Commander Siddas, sitting down behind his desk. Kavi appreciated a man who could get to the point.

"I hope it's not," he said. "By the Wheel, I'm praying I'm wrong, but if I'm not . . ."

He told the guard commander all the girl had said, watching his worried frown deepen. The more Kavi talked, the slighter his evidence sounded. "I know it's not much," he finished. "A few fragments of sentences. But Garren . . . He's a cold bastard. Not the sort to be hitting someone for no reason. Not a man to lash out in anger. If he hit someone, there's a reason for it. Though that girl could enrage stone, if she was trying," he added ruefully. "I expect you think I'm a fool, running all this way with so little, but . . ." But what? Away from the girl's dark-eyed urgency, with the sun shining through the narrow window, the whole seemed nothing but moon wisps.

Commander Siddas leaned back in his chair with a sigh. "I wish I thought you were wrong. This explains some things I've been wondering about as well. But we've no proof, and without it . . . What a flaming mess."

He rubbed the bridge of his nose. He looked tired, though the day was just starting. And he hadn't been running across the countryside all night.

"Explains what?" Kavi asked.

"Shortly after you brought in that food shipment, Hrum activity around the city increased notably," said the commander.

"I saw the patrols on my way in," Kavi confirmed. "I've a second shipment all but ready to move, but I've no idea how to get thirty wagons past all those eyes. Not to mention the swords," he added.

"Yes, well, I found myself wondering why they suddenly became so active," Siddas went on. "It was as if they'd learned that we got the food—just days after we received it—but they didn't know how we brought it in. They searched the area near the city thoroughly—we could see them from the walls. Fortunately the aqueduct entrances are farther out than they thought to look. And they weren't paying particular attention to the riverbank, which made me certain they didn't know what they were looking for."

Kavi frowned. "How could they know about the food at all, unless—"

"Someone told them," Siddas agreed. "That was my thought. We expelled all the Hrum spies before the siege started—and they were easy to find." He gestured to Kavi's shoulder. "So whoever it was had to be a townsman the Hrum had suborned, but not marked. But if it was a townsman, then why didn't he tell the Hrum about the tunnels?"

"Anyone who grew up here would know," Kavi agreed. "It's not something we talk about with outsiders. It's part of Mazad's defenses, after all, but everyone knows about it."

"So the Hrum agent has to be an outsider," said Siddas. "Someone the townsfolk wouldn't talk to. Someone the Hrum wouldn't dare mark."

"But the governor has to know about the aqueducts," Kavi protested. "They were built by that old gahn, with the city's defense in mind. The governor back then probably oversaw their construction!"

"True," said Siddas. "But there've been lots of governors since. Governors who died in office and didn't have time to train their successors. Governors who wouldn't have given a thought to where the water came from, or the sewage went, so long as it worked. Nehar's that type. I doubt any thought of water or sewage has ever so much as crossed his mind. And you may think that the secret of those tunnels is badly kept, but I didn't know you could get into the aqueducts from inside the city till the council told me, and I've been a guard here for almost twenty years. It was townsmen's business, and the guard wasn't town. Not then."

"So you think Nehar doesn't know about the

tunnels," said Kavi. "And he somehow got word to the Hrum that we'd got food in, but he couldn't explain how."

"It would fit with the way they've been acting," said Siddas. "But until now, I thought it was probably one of the guardsmen who are loyal to the governor, not the governor himself."

"The guardsmen who are loyal to him," Kavi repeated. "Would there be a lot of them?"

"Almost a third of the guard," Siddas confirmed grimly. "So just arresting him probably wouldn't work, even if we had solid evidence, and as it stands . . . I can't allow an internal war to break out inside these walls. If it did, the Hrum would be at our gates in moments. We can fend them off now, united. If we were fighting each other, we couldn't."

"So what can you do?" asked Kavi, chilled. "If a third of the guard is prepared to betray you—"

"I don't think the guardsmen themselves would betray us." Siddas sounded as if he was working it out as he spoke. "Not most of them. Not if I had time to explain, and evidence to present to them. So the first step is to get that evidence. For that I have two men I trust, close to the governor.

A gift from the other Sorahb, they were."

Why did that make him smile? "Is there anything I can do?"

Siddas' sober gaze was suddenly laced with amusement. "There are several things you could do for us," the commander said. "Important things. If you care to try."

"What?" Kavi made no attempt to keep his sudden suspicion out of his voice, and Siddas smiled again.

"I admit it's a lot to ask," he said. "But the thing I want most is the next shipment of food."

Kavi opened his mouth to repeat that he couldn't get past the patrols, but Siddas lifted a hand for silence. "And that's not all I want—I want to distract the Hrum from the tunnels, so I want you to bring this shipment in by some other route. And I want the Hrum to know that you've done it."

Kavi frowned. "Except for the aqueducts, the only way into the city I know of is through the front gate."

"Then it will be easy for the Hrum to find out about it, won't it?" said Siddas.

"You expect me to drive thirty wagons

through the front gate in full view of the entire Hrum army? How?"

"I have no idea," Siddas admitted. "But if you could do it, it would not only get us the food and distract the Hrum from the tunnels, it would probably force Nehar to report. If we can find out how he's contacting the Hrum, perhaps even catch him in the act, then maybe we can convince his guardsmen to give him up without a fight."

"But that's impossible!" Kavi exclaimed. "The whole army would have to be asleep on their feet, or . . . hmm."

Siddas waited patiently, but after a long moment he said, "'Hmm' must be promising."

"What? Oh. I wouldn't go as far as promising," said Kavi. "But it's maybe worth some thought. Maybe even worth a visit to the town's apothecary . . ."

HE DID VISIT THE APOTHECARY, and they had a long chat. After he left the city, he located an empty barn outside the area the Hrum were searching, and sent for the scattered supplies.

And while he waited for their arrival, he'd have time to take the girl to the Suud, as she'd requested.

Kavi's informants had told him a lot about the army that young fool had gathered in the mountains, and Kavi didn't want to run into them—if news of the meaning of the tattoo on his shoulder was out, who knew how fast it might have spread, and where? So instead of passing through the croft, he took her down the dizzying trail he, Jiaan and the girl had first used to descend the great cliff to the desert.

The view over the maze of stone spires and twisting canyons was as awe inspiring as ever, and the drop from the edge of the trail as sheer, but the girl paid little heed to either, rushing down so fast that Kavi reached out to restrain her several times. It was good that she wasn't afraid of heights, but still . . .

"I know you're in a hurry to get to the bottom, lass, but the fastest route isn't always the best! Especially not in this case."

"I won't fall," she said impatiently. "This . . ." Her gesture seemed to take in the towering rocks, the open sky, even the heat of the late-afternoon sun reflecting off the barren earth. "This is home."

But she slowed her headlong pace a bit and they all reached the bottom in one piece, to Kavi's relief. "What next?" he asked, scratching Duckie's ears soothingly, though the mule appeared to have no more fear of heights than the girl. "This being your home, and all."

While he was in Mazad, Soraya had purchased a small bag of dried beans to give to the Suud, saving the money from the scant funds he'd left her. When he asked about it, she shrugged. "It's symbolic," she'd said, and added nothing more.

Now she stood with her head cocked, listening. Kavi heard nothing but the soft sigh of the wind—a wind too soft to lessen the heat that was already making him sweat.

"They're here," she said.

"Who's here?" He couldn't see anyone.

"The Suud. They must be posting watchers on all the cliff trails, even in the day." She cupped her hands around her mouth and shouted a string of bouncing, liquid syllables that echoed off the rocks.

"You speak Suud?" Kavi was impressed.

"I had most of the winter to learn it," she said. "Now we wait."

"Wait for what?"

"For night." *You idiot,* her sardonic glance added. It was obvious, now that she'd said it. Kavi knew that the Suud were nocturnal.

"You don't need to stay," she went on. "I owe you more than I can ever repay, for freeing me, for bringing me here. But I'm fine now."

"I'll see you into your friends' hands, nonetheless." Kavi looked around till he found a patch of shade big enough to shelter Duckie, as well as himself and the girl. It was a good thing darkness was only a few marks off, or they'd need more water than they carried. "As for owing, the news you brought to Mazad will more than make up for any trouble I went to. Though I do have a question for you. You know that the Hrum's swords are better than ours?"

Soraya nodded. "Ours break and theirs don't. At least, that's what the soldiers said. There's some secret about the way they make them, but I never heard what it was. Most of the soldiers didn't know."

"Part of the secret seems to be that they're forged in layers," said Kavi. He fished the chip of watersteel out of his purse and turned it in his fingers, feeling its cool smoothness, its strength. It felt different than any other steel, though he couldn't quite tell what the difference was.

"Here." He held it out to the girl. "Take a look."

She reached for the chip of steel, but the moment her hand touched his, she jerked back, staring at him with widened eyes.

Kavi frowned. "It won't bite you. You could cut yourself if you really tried, but it's not going to slice your fingers off on its own."

"No." Her startled gaze narrowed in speculation. She was looking at him, not the steel. "No, I don't suppose it will."

"What's the problem?" Kavi asked. "Did I suddenly grow a third eye or something?"

"No. Well, actually yes, in a sense. Never mind."

She took the steel crescent from his hand. "I see the layers. Is that what makes it stronger?"

"Not entirely," said Kavi. "I've a friend, a sword smith, who's been trying to duplicate this. He can make the layers, but the blade still doesn't turn out like the Hrum's. It takes a better edge than ours, but it's brittle."

"So the layers aren't the secret," she said, passing the watersteel back to him.

"I think they're part of it," said Kavi. "But there's something else, as well. There are rumors that there's some kind of superior ore in the desert.

491

I was wondering, since you've obviously spent time here, if you'd heard anything about it?"

"No." She said it without hesitation, but her eyes flicked away. "No, I don't know anything about that."

It felt like a lie to Kavi, the first she'd told him. But here, with the silent rocks looking down on them, and perhaps Suud watchers listening, he decided not to pursue it. If the desert held secrets, it could keep them, as far as Kavi was concerned.

THEY CAME SHORTLY AFTER SUNSET—far sooner than Kavi had expected them—two dozen Suud, streaming out of the shadowed canyons like pale ghosts. Except that ghosts didn't wear striped robes, or carry such wicked-sharp spears.

The girl wasn't intimidated. She shot to her feet, smiling a welcome as her eyes raced from one face to another until she found the one she was looking for. She ran past the threatening spears without a glance and into the arms of an old woman, several inches shorter than she was, but who hugged her like a mother hugs a daughter who's been gone too long.

Even as Kavi smiled, he noticed that most of the

Suud who carried spears were looking at him. And they didn't look friendly. Clearly the girl was right about being welcome here, and clearly he was not.

Kavi took Duckie's lead rope, nodded politely to the folk with the spears, and led the mule back to the cliff trail.

The moon was just rising, nearly full. He would make camp at the top of the cliff and get on his way tomorrow. It would take several days to get back to Mazad, and he had a lot to do before he could move the shipment.

Halfway up the trail, he turned to look back. The Suud and the girl were gone, as if they'd never been there. It looked as uninhabited, and uninhabitable, as any place Kavi had ever seen, but he wasn't fooled. The spears were there, waiting for any who tried to enter the desert without the Suud's permission. No wonder the miners who went in search of that superior ore never came back. Kavi wouldn't have tried it, even for watersteel.

HIS NEXT MEETING, four days later, was easier to arrange, but reaching a satisfactory conclusion proved harder.

"You mean to poison the whole Hrum camp?" one of his most reliable agents asked incredulously. "I didn't think you were that . . . um . . ."

"I'm not going to kill them," said Kavi. "Just make them sick for a while. And I probably won't be able to get the whole camp—two thirds, if I'm lucky. But that will be enough to force them to bring the patrols in to protect the camp, and we can get the wagons to the aqueduct entrance and get the supplies inside."

"All the wagons except the five that you'll be driving," said his agent. "You and four volunteers, assuming you can find anyone crazy enough—"

"It's not as crazy as it sounds," Kavi insisted, hoping he was right. "Any scheme based on human greed has a lot going for it. But I'll be needing a copy of a brewer's mark. Someone who's been selling to the Hrum. They'll trust casks with a familiar mark on them more than casks from a brewer they don't know."

The agent was eyeing him warily again. "There's no one I hate that much. Even if they do sell beer to the Hrum."

Kavi sighed. He didn't hate them either, although the brewer who supplied most of the beer to the Hrum's camp at Mazad had just suffered the misfortune of losing an entire shipment to a barging accident—courtesy of Sorahb. Kavi couldn't risk the Hrum ordnancer putting his "Sorahb brew" into a supply tent and leaving it there for the next month; it had to be served while Kavi was in the camp. Kavi knew the financial loss would hurt the brewer, but it wouldn't bankrupt him altogether. And as for getting some other brewer killed . . .

"What makes you think I've gone bloodthirsty all of a sudden?" Kavi asked. "I'm going to forge a copy of the brewer's mark you give me, but with several things different. Enough that anyone who looks closely will know it's a forgery. The brewer won't suffer for it."

"No, but you might, if they look too close at your clever, forged mark before they start drinking."

"Until they start getting sick, they'll have no reason to look closely."

"Unless they taste the poison, or—"

"They won't," said Kavi confidently. "My brewer and the apothecary worked together for three days to get it right."

And if the curses of the brewer's assistants had any effect on the Wheel's turning, Kavi was due for a long spell in the Flame. They had been recruited as taste testers.

Eventually Kavi got the information he needed, and promises for the help he'd need as well. But it took more time and argument than any other plan he'd proposed. Admittedly this scheme was wilder than most. But it was the only thing he could think of to accomplish all Siddas' goals. It should work. It had better work, for if it failed, Kavi, and the four other men who'd volunteered to help him, would be taken by the Hrum. And while the other men would be sold as slaves—far from trivial!—Kavi was marked as one of their own. The Hrum had a very short way with traitors.

A WEEK AND A HALF LATER, about two marks before sunset, Kavi drove an oxcart loaded with beer barrels up the road that led past Mazad. Of all the things that worried him, the most pressing was that he wasn't a very good ox carter. The man who'd volunteered the wagons had also agreed to sell them the oxen, but given the likelihood that they'd be trapped in Mazad and eaten, the master carter had offered only his oldest oxen. That was fine with Kavi, since the oldest were also the cheapest. He'd soon discovered another advantage in that the oldest oxen were also the most placid and best trained. The beast Kavi was driving didn't pay much attention to Kavi's commands, but he took the wagon where Kavi wanted it to go and stopped when Kavi wanted him to stop. Well, more or less.

The four volunteers in the other wagons—experienced carters all—had enjoyed a good laugh at his antics as he tried to convince the stubborn beast to do as he wanted, but if he really got in trouble they would come to his aid. Several people had tried to convince Kavi to let them do it all—and he wished he could agree—but Kavi didn't trust anyone but himself to negotiate with the Hrum patrol.

Another thing that hadn't concerned him was finding a Hrum patrol—they'd been so thick around Mazad that Kavi, alone and on foot, had trouble avoiding them. He hadn't been able to get his final message into Mazad to tell Commander Siddas to expect them tonight, but the commander knew it would be soon and Kavi had decided it wasn't worth risking a life to try to send someone else.

So five oxcarts that were looking for a patrol shouldn't have any trouble finding one. Of course, there was always a chance that the officer in charge wouldn't be an arrogant fool, but a bit of rudeness would change that, even if the man wasn't an ass to start with.

All he needed now was a patrol. But since the Wheel never spun as you wanted it to, the small cart train had almost reached the road that turned off to the city before a patrol came marching toward them. A foot patrol, who'd likely been walking all day. Bound to be tired and cross. And thirsty. Kavi suppressed a grin.

"Off the road," he shouted, flourishing his goad. "Make way, make way."

A few of the men started to shift their formation to the side, but the officer, predictably, came to a halt in the center of the road and folded his arms. His men, seeing his intention, dressed their lines behind him.

Kavi began trying to stop the ox, but the ox didn't seem to be interested in stopping. Despite Kavi's increasingly frantic shouts, it lumbered on toward the Hrum commander, who appeared to have made up his mind to let the beast trample him before he yielded the road. Though surely if it came to the test . . .

Trampling the patrol wasn't part of his plans. Kavi jabbed frantically with the goad, but the ox ignored him. The officer was crouching to leap aside when the ox finally braced its feet and came to a stop, right in front of him, huffing hot breath into the man's face through its great nostrils.

The officer settled back into place, warily enough that Kavi suppressed another grin. Then he changed his mind—why not begin as he meant to go on? He'd already made a fine first impression.

"I told you to clear the road," he snapped, just as the officer opened his mouth. "I've a load of fine, strong beer for the mining camps, and I want to make it to the foothills by sunset. So if you'd get your . . . selves off the road, I'd be appreciating it."

He was tempted to make the speech longer, to annoy the officer even more, but he didn't want to overdo it. Judging by the color rising in the man's face, he was close to overstepping that line, so he folded his arms and waited.

The officer, having lost his chance to speak first, made up for it by taking his time to reply, but eventually he spoke. "All carts on this road are subject to search, by order of Substrategus Arus. All citizens of the empire are required to give way to units of the army on the road. In your ignorance, you may not have known this, so I will give you the benefit of the doubt."

His tone implied that Farsalans were ignorant to the point of barbarism, and that Kavi was the worst of the lot. But for all his annoyance—it's alarming to have an ox and loaded wagon rolling down on you like an avalanche—he seemed to be an honest man. Curse him. But Kavi could change that.

"Search?" he sputtered indignantly. "What do you mean, search? You think Sorahb is hidden among my casks? Or in one?" He snorted. "I'd think you wanted to steal a nip, but beer this strong is a man's drink. And I'll not have you breaching my casks—it'd drive down the price. But feel free to search for all the warriors you fear . . . ah, imagine might be there. The sooner you're done, the sooner you'll clear the road."

Several lances, which had been carried at rest,

were now pointing in Kavi's direction. The officer's face was flushed with annoyance, but he only planted his feet more firmly and studied Kavi with insulting deliberation. Kavi returned his gaze, unflinching.

He'd considered, and rejected, the idea of growing a beard or mustache. Almost all Farsalans were clean shaven, and he'd feared it would only make them pay more attention to his features. In the end, all he'd done was to cut his hair shorter than he usually wore it, and darken both hair and skin with walnut stain. His general description already matched half the peasants in Farsala—this just made him match the description of the other half. There were advantages to being ordinary.

The hard part would be to keep them from noticing his scarred hand—but he'd feared that gloves, like a beard, would draw more attention than they diverted.

"We will search the carts," said the officer finally. "And you needn't fear it will affect the price. I'm confiscating this beer for the use of the imperial army."

"What!" Kavi squawked. *Took you long enough.*

"You can't do that! I demand to speak to your commander!"

WITH NEAR PERFECT TIMING, they rolled into the camp right at sunset, so Kavi's negotiations with the camp's ordnancer took place in the dimming light of dusk.

Kavi drew out his protests and negotiations as long as he could—just like any merchant trying to make a profit. If the Hrum had bought his beer in the market, he'd have been able to set the price and they could pay or leave it, like any other buyer. Because they'd confiscated his load, the ordnancer could set his own price for recompense. The price he held fast on was fair, though on the low end of fair. With a pang of remorse Kavi accepted the purse the clerks finally brought out.

When the deghans' armies had confiscated something—and they often did—they had hardly ever paid. Soraya's father had been one of the few exceptions to that rule. Kavi wished that the Hrum would just take the beer—he'd feel less guilt over what he was about to do. But Hrum law insisted that confiscated goods must be paid for.

They were better than the deghans, in every

way but two. And if he'd been taken as a slave, or drafted into their army, he might not think they were better at all. Having all or part of your life stolen was the ultimate confiscation.

So Kavi shrugged off regret, and after the bargain had been struck, he fell into grumbling conversation with the clerks. He was even able to work in his tale that there'd been sickness in the town where he picked up the beer.

"Not serious," he assured them, as they counted the casks and made note of the brewer's mark. That didn't worry him either. In the twilight it looked very like the three hop flowers with twining leaves that a well-known local brewer branded onto his kegs. In the daylight they would soon see that the delicate stems that connected the leaves in the real brewer's mark were absent, and the flowers themselves were smaller, and less well defined. Tebin had done a brilliant job of forging the brand, once he'd been assured that the apothecary's potion wouldn't kill anyone.

"It spreads like lightning," Kavi told the clerks. "One day there's just a few with their bowels disturbed, and the next day half the town's perched in privies, or on their slop pots. The good news is that it's not lethal. At least, no one had died of it when we left, and pretty much everyone was recovering. A couple of my carters had it, and they felt good enough to set out yesterday."

The clerks exchanged glances. "Maybe you'd better talk to the surgeons," one said. "I think a couple of our men were having trouble with their bowels this morning."

"I'd be glad to," said Kavi cheerfully. "Though I can't tell them much more than I've told you."

He'd been delighted when the apothecary told him the chief symptom of his chosen potion—for in any group of thirteen hundred men, a few were bound to be having trouble with their bowels. And if they were worrying about disease, it might take them longer to realize the truth and start searching for the carters.

So even as the strong beer—and it was *strong* beer—was served in the meal tent with dinner, Kavi went to the surgeon's tent to talk about disease. As he crossed the square, he heard several of the men who'd come off duty praising the brew and urging others to try it. He had little hope that those about to go out on night patrol would do so—or at least that they'd drink enough to affect them more than mildly—for the Hrum were as well-disciplined about drunkenness as they were about everything else. But he did have some hope of snaring the officers.

The surgeons showed a fine, professional interest in the disease, speculating on which of several common disorders it might be. Though they made him nervous when they added that contaminated water or food supplies were the most common cause of a sudden, widespread outbreak.

Kavi was still talking to them when the first man stumbled in, clutching his belly and grimacing. It was one of the clerks who'd inspected the casks, and Kavi guessed that he'd taken advantage of the moment to closely examine a healthy draft of the brew. For all their laws and discipline, the Hrum were human after all.

Kavi professed ignorance as to whether this could be the same disease they'd been talking about, excused himself to the surgeons, and slipped off to find his carters.

He finally located them at a table in the meal tent, where they sat with four tankards in front of them that hopefully held something besides the beer they'd brought in. Kavi wondered how they'd turned it down without making anyone suspicious, but they weren't under guard, so they'd evidently succeeded.

They looked up and grinned at his approach. "They're guzzling it down," one of the men reported softly, "like . . . um . . ."

"Like soldiers who've been marching in the heat all day?" Kavi suggested. "We were counting on that. But it'll be acting soon, and those surgeons aren't fools. We'd best be out of sight by the time they figure it out."

The Hrum located every tent in each of their camps in the same position, so Kavi had no trouble finding the laundry tent. It was empty now, the workers off duty for the night, and hopefully drinking beer. Kavi fought down another surge of guilt, as he and his carters traded their peasant clothes for Hrum tunics and scarlet cloaks — long-sleeved tunics to hide their lack of rank tattoos. Azura be thanked, the nights were colder now. They buried their own clothes under a pile of dirty bedding. They would no doubt be discovered tomorrow, but by then it would be too late.

"Should we wait here?" one of the carters asked.

"No," said Kavi. "I want to be ready to load the carts with Hrum supplies and we'll have to do that fairly fast, so we'd best stay near the carts. But not too near. And remember, if anyone says anything to you, just clutch your belly and moan, then head off toward the surgeon's tent. Your accents won't pass."

Kavi was the only one who spoke more than a few words of Hrum, and he feared his accent wasn't the best. But for just a few words, in a night full of chaos and confusion, it should do. At least, it might. It would have to.

They knew it would take several long, unnerving marks for the apothecary's potion to have its full impact. Kavi and his carters found a shadowy nook near the supply tent, where the wagons were still parked. Best of all, if he peered around a corner, Kavi could see the surgeon's tent on the other side of the square. He worried about all of them staying together, but one man produced a small set of the Hrum's battle dice, so they could account for their presence if they had to.

The camp was quiet, however, and they were sufficiently well hidden that the night watch passed them by. At least, the camp was quiet until the potion began to take effect. First a few men, then a handful, then a small stream headed for the surgeon's tent. A surgeon's assistant summoned one of the sentries, who ran off in the direction of the officer's quarters.

"So it begins," Kavi muttered, trying to rub the tension out of his neck muscles. "But will they think it's a disease, or poison?"

That question was answered when another surgeon's assistant trotted over to the supply tent with an armload of empty jugs, and came out a few moments later. But now he carried the jugs as if they were full.

"Fetching samples?" one of the men asked.

"I told you they weren't fools," Kavi replied.

"Will they be able to figure out what we used?" another man asked.

"They might." Kavi shrugged. "It'll make no difference in the end. There's some standard remedies that will help with the symptoms, but the apothecary said there's no cure except to let the stuff work its way through your system."

Many men were going to the surgeon's tent, but still more, Kavi saw, were heading straight for the latrines. Lines were forming, and he didn't think these men would be able to wait.

"So even if they realize it's poison, it won't make any difference," the first of his volunteers concluded hopefully.

"Well, just one difference," said Kavi. "If they know it's poison, they'll start looking for us."

A handful of healthy men lit torches along the main streets, allowing the stumbling, moaning men to at least see where they were going.

Kavi saw several officers, including one he thought was Substrategus Arus himself, being helped to the surgeon's tent by their servants, most of whom looked as if they could use some help too. But there were some men his beer hadn't tempted, and clearly one of them was in charge.

Five men hurried into the ordnance tent and came out with armloads of shovels, which they carried off to the men lined up by the latrines.

The men toward the back of the lines seized them, and took off as rapidly as they could across the small rise behind the latrines. It was far enough from both the camp and the river not to contaminate anything—at least, assuming they made it over the rise. The way they were walking,

Kavi wasn't sure they would. It had been dry for several days now, and though the nights were growing cooler, it wasn't so cold that a night on the ground would kill anyone, even a man too sick to make it back to his tent. The apothecary had promised that no one would die from this, so Kavi suppressed his sympathy. A task that became easier as four of the night watch came into view.

When Kavi had seen them before, they'd been patrolling on their own. Now they stayed together, and while two of them carried torches, which they used to look into the dark alleys between the tents, two carried drawn swords.

"Looking for us?" one of his men murmured.

"Most likely. It may be time for us to split up, my friends." But instead they huddled closer, to Kavi and each other, and he didn't order them to scatter. He wasn't looking forward to wandering through this bedlam, trying to pass himself off as a Hrum soldier—and *he* spoke the language.

The watch searched the empty buildings as well as the alleys, so their approach was slow. But Kavi was drawing a breath to order his men to leave this secluded trap when a group of five soldiers caught his eye. They were clearly healthy for they moved rapidly, almost running across the square . . . straight for the supply wagons.

Kavi's breath hissed through his teeth as one of them mounted the first wagon and goaded the ox into motion. His whole plan depended on stealing those wagons back! The soldier guided the ox forward and stopped it in front of the supply tent, where his comrades had already gone in. Now they began to emerge, rolling beer kegs in front of them.

It was a perfect chance . . . if he dared take it. Kavi took a deep breath, which did less than he'd hoped to quell the shivering in his belly. "Follow me."

He strode out of the alley, trying to look as if he'd just used it because it was the quickest route, and went up to the soldier who'd driven the wagon.

"Our tactimian sent us to help you," he said. "To take over, if that would be better. We didn't drink any beer, so we're working tonight." He tried to sound like a soldier roused from sleep to deal with a minor emergency—half excited, half disgusted. He tried to sound like a Hrum, and to his own ears didn't quite succeed. But after all, there were many lands in the empire and many soldiers had accents.

The soldier he spoke to didn't look suspicious. "Good. We're to help the surgeons when we're finished, but they could use us now. They could use five of each of us. Great Lokkar, what a mess. Do you know where to dump the stuff?"

"Out of camp, away from the river," said Kavi. "That's all I was told."

"Out in the farmland," said the man. He pointed toward the fields, now rank with weeds, that surrounded the suburbs of Mazad. "Hey! Head on over to the surgeons and make yourselves useful. These men will handle the loading, and get rid of this stuff."

"And good riddance to it," said Kavi. "Have they thought to bring in the patrols yet?"

"Almost a mark ago," the Hrum confirmed, to his great delight. "They should start coming in any time. Though I think if someone was going to attack us, they'd have done it already. At least, goddess be praised, they're still coming after us and not the hidden camp."

"I think you're right," said Kavi. "They won't be attacking us tonight." *Hidden camp? What hidden camp? And where, and why?*

The man was turning away—how to phrase it!

"But I think we're every bit as important as the hidden camp. Probably more. After all, they'll not take Mazad without us." His urgency made his accent slip. He held his breath.

"Yeah, but we won't be able to get past those walls without the siege towers." The man was moving off, his reply barely audible. "So they're every bit as . . ."

He was gone. "Keep loading the beer," Kavi told his men sharply. "At least until the search has passed. Then start hauling out food instead. But only the stuff that's stored in barrels."

Siege towers. Kavi had never seen such things, for Farsalan deghans never used them, but he'd spent enough time with Hrum soldiers to know what they were. As if Mazad hadn't trouble enough! But that was for tomorrow—assuming he survived the night.

He helped load the carts, trying to pay attention to his task and not the torches of the watch, drawing nearer and nearer. But he did make sure he was the one coming out with a keg when the search reached them.

The watch commander glanced at the tent, noting the sounds of activity within. "Getting rid of that cursed brew, are you?" he asked.

"Orders," Kavi confirmed. "Though I think it could have waited till morning. What harm will it do, sitting in the kegs?" He must have gotten the tone right, if not the accent, for the man only shrugged. Odd, for Kavi would have sworn the pounding of his heart was audible ten feet away.

"They probably want to be sure no one gets into it by accident. I don't suppose you've seen the Farsalan men who brought it in?" The commander waved his men past the tent.

"I never saw them," said Kavi. "So I don't know what they look like."

"Neither do I," the commander snorted. "But that didn't stop them from ordering me to go find the bastards."

He followed his men to the next alley, but Kavi saw him glance at the brand on the barrels as he passed.

"Start loading other goods," he told his men. He managed to keep his voice from shaking, though he wasn't sure how. This was different from firing the warehouse. This was a job for some soldier-hero, like that young fool leading the army. So what was a sensible man like Kavi doing here?

But he knew the answer to that, and his debt

was still unpaid. If it took a fool-hero, then a fool-hero he'd be. And fool-heroism had worked . . . so far.

They loaded the wagons hastily, not paying much attention to what food they stole, for anything would be welcome in Mazad. And if some of the barrels were different sizes, and all had different marks, that couldn't be helped.

Kavi mounted the lead wagon, praying that the perimeter guard would be less alert than the night watch. Praying that when the patrols had been called in, the real shipment could get through. Praying that the cursed ox would move when he told it to!

It took him several attempts to get the beast walking, for it seemed to be unnerved by the darkness and the torches. But once in motion it kept moving, and turned when Kavi told it to, and all too soon brought him to the perimeter of the Hrum camp.

The road between the camp and Mazad glowed in the moonlight. It looked rough and ill tended, but it was better than the blackened rubble that had once been a prosperous suburb.

Kavi had known people who'd lived and

worked in those buildings, and a sudden surge of anger steadied him.

"Halt! What are you doing, heading out of camp at this time of night?"

"We're supposed to take the poisoned beer out in sight of the walls," said Kavi. "And pour it on the ruins. It's supposed to symbolize something, or something. As long as I don't have to get within arrow range, I don't care."

"This couldn't wait till morning?" One of the perimeter guards eyed him suspiciously. There were only two of them, Kavi was relieved to see, though he had no doubt that more could be summoned swiftly. Assuming they weren't all lined up at the latrines.

"I guess they want to be sure no one else gets into it," Kavi told him. "I thought the same as you at first, but then I realized that by daylight their archery is likely to be better, and changed my mind."

"But why drop it on the ruins at all?" the guard persisted.

"Like I said, it's supposed to symbolize defiance or something," said Kavi, trying to sound impatient instead of frightened. "Personally, I think someone's brains were affected as well as their bowels, but all I know is what they told me to do. It's away from the camp and the river, so it hardly matters, does it?"

"Hmm." The perimeter guard stepped forward, looking at the mark on one of the kegs.

Kavi swung his ox goad, catching the man on the face, and he staggered back with a cry of pain. Blood, black in the moonlight, poured through his fingers.

"Go!" Kavi yelled. He jabbed the goad into the ox's hindquarters, harder than he'd dared before, again and again. "Go, go, go!"

The ox was too large to shy like a horse, but it tossed its massive head and set off down the road at a lurching trot.

The others were already in motion behind him. The other guard drew his sword and leaped toward them, but when the heavy oxen charged down on him he leaped out of their way, and the other carters' whistling goads kept him at a distance.

The guard Kavi had struck was also standing back, already shouting for help.

Kavi didn't think it mattered. The great city gate was only a few thousand yards from the camp, the road before them open and empty. They would reach the gate long before the Hrum could gather enough healthy men to stop them.

But he kept the lumbering ox to its trot, though his jabs with the goad were no longer so savage. Looking back, he could see men running to the perimeter, bringing horses, the flash of armor. On horseback they'd cover the distance to the gate in moments, and would be able to escape as swiftly, but the gate was looming before Kavi now and would open any time. Any time now, so they could charge through without a check. Any time!

The ox lurched to a stop in front of the closed gate, breathing in puffing gasps.

"Open the gate!" Kavi shouted. "The Hrum will be after us in just a moment!"

He heard men moving on top of the wall, then a man in the helmet and tabard of the guard leaned over and peered down at them. "You look like the Hrum to me. What if this is a ruse?"

Kavi started to scream at him, realized it would do no good, and tried to sound reasonable instead.

"We're not the Hrum! We're the food shipment Commander Siddas told you to expect."

At least he'd better have told them to expect it! Kavi looked over his shoulder. Some of the Hrum were mounted already, but others were still bringing up their horses.

"Not tonight," said the guardsman. "The commander said he'd warn us when the shipment was supposed to arrive, and he didn't say anything about tonight."

"He didn't know it would be tonight because the patrols were too thick for me to get the message in, you . . ." Kavi stopped and took a deep breath. "You were told we'd be coming, and here we are. Flame take you man, they're mounting up! Let us in!"

The guardsman scratched his chin thoughtfully. "I don't know. The shipment was supposed to be delivered by Sorahb's men, not Hrum soldiers. Suppose you're Hrum, who caught Sorahb's men and took their place. And after we open the gates you block them with your carts, and all those horsemen charge right through. Then what?"

Kavi clutched at his hair. It did no good to scream, he reminded himself. Though when he got his hands on this fumble-wit . . .

"We had to put on Hrum clothes to get out of

their camp," he said, as calmly as his furious frustration would allow. "If it makes you feel better, we can take them off."

"I don't know. I think I'd better wait for the commander."

"Look, there's no time for—"

Hoofbeats drummed on the road behind him. Kavi gave the charging Hrum horsemen one frantic glance and screamed, "Open this gate right now you feather-witted, moronic, incompetent, shit-for-brains! Who put you in charge of the gate? You couldn't manage a butter churn! I'll see you reported to the craft master, and the guard commander, and . . ."

The gates swung open and the portcullis rattled up. The ox didn't even need the goad—it charged through at a brisk walk, which was as fast as an ox pulling a loaded cart could charge. But it was enough. The cart rolled through, with the other four behind it and the gates slammed shut, right in the teeth of the charging horses from the sound of it, but Kavi was too busy slowing the cart to look.

The ox stopped without much argument, which was good, because the way Kavi was shaking, the beast might have won. He listened to the twang of bow strings, and told his racing heart it could slow down. Any time now. He was still sitting on the wagon when Commander Siddas strolled up, with an embarrassed-looking man walking behind him.

Kavi glared at him.

"Sorry about that." The stranger spoke first. His voice was familiar—the gate keeper. Kavi wanted to climb down and hit him, but he wasn't certain his wobbling legs would support him. He transferred his glare to the man, instead. "Really sorry," the guardsman continued. "But Commander Siddas wasn't sure what night you'd be coming, or exactly how, and he told us to be wary about opening up."

Kavi had said he'd let them know when to expect him, but still . . . He moved his glare back to Siddas.

"I'm sorry too," the commander repeated. "But in truth, I wasn't sure you could bring it off. I'm impressed, lad."

"The rest of the shipment is coming in?" Kavi asked, diverted from anger.

"They've unloaded all the supplies into the

tunnel and the wagons are headed back. By the time the Hrum recover enough to send out patrols, they'll be well out of range."

Elation bubbled through Kavi's blood. If his legs would have supported him, he might have climbed down and danced.

"It almost didn't come right, at the end," he grumbled instead. "What made you finally decide to let us in?"

"The way you were cursing me," said the gate keeper promptly. "Sounded just like my old master, when I messed up some simple task."

Had he been in the habit of messing up simple tasks? How reassuring.

"And the way the Hrum were charging after you," the man went on. "And the fact that we'd finally gathered enough men to handle things if all those kegs had proved to be full of Hrum soldiers."

"Oh." Kavi looked around. There were a lot of armed men present. Perhaps the man was more competent than he'd seemed. On the whole, that was a good thing, so Kavi regretfully abandoned his plan to kill him. Mazad would need all its soldiers soon.

"You may be needing more men," he told

Siddas grimly. "I heard something tonight: The Hrum are building siege towers, in a hidden camp somewhere."

Siddas didn't look as dismayed as Kavi had thought he would. "I was expecting siege towers eventually," he said. "In fact, I'm surprised they haven't used them before now. I think they may be counting on . . . other things."

Kavi hoped that his actions tonight would let the commander bring down Governor Nehar— because Kavi wasn't doing this again! Still . . .

"I expect it would be useful," Kavi said slowly, "to find out when those siege towers are likely to be finished." And even more important, where they were being built.

"A great help," said Commander Siddas. His tone made it clear that he was speaking of tonight, as well as the future, but it was the future that filled Kavi's mind, as a new plan began to form. He'd need more information than he currently had, and probably some help from that foolish half-deghan and his amateur army, and, oh yes, lots more information . . .

WITHOUT MONEY, SORAHB *could no longer wander aimlessly. He had to stop in a town or village, for a morning, or a day, and work for his meals and a few coins to take him down the road.*

One morning, after a night of storm, he came to a prosperous-looking farm.

Perhaps the storm has caused some damage, *he thought.* If it has, then surely these folk can pay for my labor.

Indeed, as he approached the farmhold he found an old woman, struggling alone to rebuild the fence that surrounded a large pen. Inquiring, Sorahb learned that the woman's ox, affrighted by the thunder, had broken from the pen, shattering timber and uprooting the posts she was trying to replace.

Sorahb offered his services, and in return she offered to pay him a silver falcon if he would mend the pen and find her ox.

Sorahb's brows rose, for that was pay for a month's labor, not a few days. But he agreed, although he warned her that the beast might have come to harm.

In fact, the ox wandered back to the farm only a few marks later, and Sorahb finished rebuilding the pen by late afternoon.

"I'll take less than you offered," he told her, "since the second half of the task you set proved unnecessary."

Her ancient eyes glittered. "You're an honest man, stranger," she said. "But I said I'd pay a falcon, and pay it I will. For a bargain is a bargain, just as an oath is an oath."

Sorahb, remembering the oath he had abandoned, frowned as he followed her into the farmhouse.

She opened a chest and pulled out a heavy purse, which she set on the table before him to extract his wage. Looking into the bag, which he could do without effort, Sorahb saw it held many silver falcons, and several gold eagles as well, and his frown deepened.

"Mistress, I would never offer you harm myself, but not all men think as I. You shouldn't show such wealth to strangers."

Her smile was as old as time and as new as sunrise. "Your honesty is a gift to me, young man. But you should know that it's a gift to yourself as well. Not because an honest man can't be cheated—that's a deghan's fool fancy—but because an honest man will never cheat himself."

CHAPTER NINETEEN

KAVI

KAVI WISHED HE COULD be in the Hrum camp at Setesafon when the report of what had happened at Mazad reached them, but instead he took over a week to make his way there. The journey usually took four or five days, but despite the dyer's promise that just a few washings would remove it, the dark dye lingered on his hair and skin. He didn't dare face Patrius until he was certain that no change in his appearance could arouse suspicion.

"I didn't hear anything about that missing girl," he told the tactimian. It was a decent excuse for the visit. "And I traveled out on the road to the north and came back on the road from the east. But she might have gone south or west—or still be hiding in the city for that matter."

Patrius shrugged. "By this time she's well away, wherever she is." He didn't sound sorry about it. "I doubt she brought Sorahb too much information," he added. "In fairness to the man, Governor Garren isn't one to discuss sensitive information in front of servants."

Neither was Patrius, but Kavi had cultivated the acquaintance of several soldiers who would gossip over a tankard of beer, though whether any of them would know the location of the "hidden camp" was another matter.

"I also heard about what happened at Mazad." Kavi tried to sound consoling, though it was hard. "At least, I heard the rumors." In fact, he was the one who'd started the rumor, but it had spread like wildfire, without any help from him. "The reality likely isn't so . . ."

Patrius was staring at him in astonishment. "What happened at Mazad?" he asked.

"You don't know? I'd have thought . . . Ah, well, what I heard was that Sorahb poisoned the whole camp, and while they were clutching their bellies and groaning, he loaded twenty wagons with their own supplies, drove them right through Mazad's front gates, and then escaped before the Hrum could get saddled up to chase him. But likely that's all exaggerated. You know how rumors are."

In fact, he'd only claimed eight wagons when he started the rumor, but the next time he heard the tale, the number had risen to fifteen, and the last number he'd heard was forty, with three quarters of the garrison dead into the bargain. But he didn't want to alarm Patrius unduly.

"I haven't heard any of this," said the tactimian. "Are you certain it's true?"

"Not at all," said Kavi. "But the way folk are talking, it sounds like something happened." Why hadn't Arus reported—

"But why hasn't Substrategus Arus reported it?" Patrius asked. "I need to check into this. Would you mind staying here, in camp or in the city, for a few days?"

Kavi rubbed his chin, trying to look as if he was doing calculations instead of gloating. "Not at all," he replied. "Not at all."

A COURIER WITH A GOOD MOUNT could reach Mazad in just three days, so Kavi was half expecting it when, in the late afternoon of the sixth day, Patrius summoned him to meet with the governor.

In truth, he'd gotten restive by that time. The soldiers were aware that siege towers were under construction somewhere, but no one seemed to know where. It was being kept secret, they said, for fear that Sorahb might attack the place. Garren's army was already stretched thin trying to intimidate the towns that were threatening to rebel in the west, and having to suppress the rebels at Dugaz — they couldn't afford to put additional forces into the hidden camp.

So why didn't Garren send for more troops? The soldiers were asking that same question, with even more intensity than Kavi.

Kavi brought up the subject in a conversation with Patrius, and the tactimian's lips pressed tight. "He won't summon more troops."

Not "he can't," Kavi noted. But not "he doesn't want to," either.

"I've gathered that he's not doing it," said Kavi. "I was wondering why? Seems to me you people could use them."

"We could," said Patrius. "But he won't. We'll make do with ten tacti. We'll—"

He broke off, but Kavi thought he knew how the sentence would have ended. *We'll have to.*

This was information worth passing on to Commander Siddas, but it occurred to Kavi that Soraya had spent months in the Hrum camp, as invisible as a mouse in the corner. She might know something about why Garren wasn't sending for troops, maybe even something about where this hidden camp might be. If she didn't, Kavi could put out word along the road that "Sorahb" needed to know. He was certain the local people would know of the Hrum's presence at this secret place, though they might not know what was being built there.

He hesitated to do that if he didn't have to—the wider the word of his interest spread, the more likely that the Hrum would hear of it too. If they did, the number of guards in that camp would double, despite the shortage of troops. Yes, he needed to talk to Soraya first, and his desire to set about it made him wonder if the Hrum's fast courier had taken root somewhere.

At least the delay had let him go into Setesafon and spend some time with Nadi, Hama, and Sim. Kavi wanted to make sure that they'd convinced

Ludo that the conversation he'd overheard had to do with something else, and that they had no interest in Hrum documents.

Still, Kavi was more than ready as he accompanied Patrius to the governor's quarters that evening—though he was always careful in Garren's presence. No one took that man for a fool.

Dozens of other officers had assembled as well. Kavi couldn't be sure, but he thought there was a tense, resentful air about them—like a staff of journeymen and apprentices who expect to be rebuked for some failure in the shop, which might or might not have been their fault. Sign of a bad master, that. But Garren had always struck Kavi as a very bad master indeed.

The governor entered abruptly from the door to his private room and looked around till he found Patrius.

"You first, Tactimian," he said. "Let them know how I learned of an attack on a unit of this army."

His voice sent a chill down Kavi's spine. Garren might not lash out in anger, but that didn't mean he didn't feel it.

"This man is a peddler," said Patrius in Faran, "who sometimes brings us news. He came to me some days ago, to report a rumor he had heard."

He gestured to Kavi, who drew a breath and stepped forward. "I heard in the countryside that someone had poisoned the army besieging Mazad." He spoke in Faran too, since he wasn't supposed to know Hrum. Though he thought that by this time several of the men present suspected that he understood some of the language, at least, and Patrius knew he did. "Rumor claims that someone then drove a shipment of food into the city, though reports vary widely concerning how many wagons there were."

He nodded humbly and stepped back. There. Clear, concise, and true—for he saw no need to enflame Garren's temper by mentioning either Sorahb's name, or how heartily the country folk had laughed.

"This," said Garren into the silence that followed. "This is how the Hrum high command learned of the attack—from rumors spread by peasants, days after the fact. Which is why I'm ordering Substrategus Arus' return. He can take a few deci and chase after those bandits in the swamp. If he captures them, he may redeem himself in my eyes. If not . . ." He shrugged, and several officers winced.

No one in the room, Kavi noted, seemed particularly disturbed by Arus' fall from grace.

A red-bearded substrategus whom he'd noticed before stirred. "If you want Arus to bring any of his men back, you'd better give him a few centris, instead of a few deci. Besides, it's time we did something about those bandits."

Garren's lips tightened, but he nodded assent.

Kavi wasn't sure if he was pleased or not. Arus was fairly incompetent, which had been good for Mazad. On the other hand those Dugaz cutthroats would run rings around him, which might also be good. But best of all, Garren showed no sign of ordering Kavi out of the room now that his part was done. Kavi tried very hard to become invisible.

"I'm sending Tactimian Laon to replace him," Garren went on. "At least until we're ready for our assault."

By the sour look on Patrius' face, Laon was no improvement on Arus, but . . . *Ready for our assault?* Did that mean, when the siege towers were complete? Was there any chance the man would announce a date?

"Sir, might I ask what happened at Mazad?" The man who spoke sounded a bit more timid than a substrategus should, in Kavi's opinion.

"What happened at Mazad?" Garren's mouth tightened. "A patrol confiscated five wagonloads of beer that turned out to contain some strong emetic, which afflicted a large portion of the camp. In the resulting confusion, the Farsalans who drove the wagons disguised themselves as Hrum soldiers, loaded their wagons with our supplies, and drove straight through Mazad's front gates. So even if Mazad had been starving, it wouldn't be now."

"But it wasn't poison—or at least, not strong enough to kill?" another officer asked. "The garrison survived?"

"No one was killed," Garren confirmed. "At least, according to that . . . to Substrategus Arus."

"Didn't their ordnancer check the casks?" a female officer asked. "I thought all purchases from local merchants were supposed to be carefully examined, and tested if necessary, to prevent this kind of thing."

Kavi barely controlled a start of surprise. This was the first he'd heard of that. His whole plan would have toppled like a pile of blocks if —

"Sometimes those precautions aren't taken," another man admitted reluctantly, "as a matter of common sense. If grain is drawn from a bin, for instance, when the merchant had no way to suspect we were about to make a purchase. Or if it's a merchant we've dealt with often, who's proved reliable."

Garren's brows rose. "That's interesting," he said mildly. "Arus' ordnancer offered similar excuses. The mark on the casks was familiar to him, though close examination proved it a forgery. And since the load was confiscated, he assumed there was no reason to test it for poison. But neither of those excuses stopped me from ordering the man flogged for his negligence. So I advise you, Ordnancer Reevus, to start obeying our policies, which were instituted for a reason, and to send out an order for other ordnancers to do the same."

Kavi winced. Was this his fault? Garren's? Both?

Patrius' spine straightened, and he drew a breath. "Sir, isn't that . . . extreme? If the forgery was a good one, and especially since the load was confiscated, the ordnancer had no reason to be suspicious."

Garren looked steadily at the tactimian. "Do you question my right to discipline this army as I see fit?"

Several officers stiffened at the words, though Kavi didn't know why. "No, sir," said Patrius stubbornly. "But surely—"

The officer who stood behind him reached out and gripped his elbow, hard. Patrius paused, then drew another breath. "No, sir."

"Good." Garren's voice was very soft, but Kavi wasn't the only one who shivered. "Substrategus Arus, his ordnancer, his whole command, are really guilty of the same error, when you come to the root of it: They underestimated the enemy. We've all been guilty of that, gentlemen, even me. And in time of war, that's the most dangerous, most fatal mistake an officer can make."

His gaze moved over the room, meeting men's eyes. Kavi looked down. He wouldn't draw Garren's attention now for a whole right hand, and the secret of watersteel thrown into the bargain.

"That stops here," Garren went on. "Work on the siege towers is behind schedule, for they haven't enough men, so every tactimian in the army will order twenty of their carpenters to report to that project. What goes undone because of their absence goes undone. I realize that most of the soldiers' cabins are still unfinished, but Hrum armies have wintered in tents before, and can do so again. When the towers are completed, the assault on Mazad will begin—and I have no doubt of its success."

If Governor Nehar's men opened the gates for them, Kavi didn't doubt it either. Even if the governor was taken out of the game, those siege towers might do the job on their own. Kavi considered following the carpenters to the hidden camp, but the odds that he could remain undetected, day after day, were low. If he had to, he could probably follow their route by asking in the towns and villages if they'd passed through, and in which direction they'd departed. He wouldn't know where they'd gone after they left the road, but once he was in the vicinity of the hidden camp, the local people could probably help him find it.

"We might also consider sending more men to

Mazad," said Red-beard. "Siege towers still need men to man them, and if Sorahb continues to attack the garrison . . . If they'd been ruthless enough to use real poison, there would no longer be a siege at Mazad. And I don't understand why they didn't attack the camp while the majority of the men were ill. It would have given them a powerful advantage."

There hadn't been real poison, or an attack, because Kavi didn't want more deaths on his conscience—he was still trying to redeem himself for the last lot!

"They may have planned just that," said Garren. "But the centrimaster who took charge when Arus was incapacitated had the good sense to recall the night patrols to defend the camp. Because they were on duty, they hadn't drunk the poisoned beer, and they probably returned too swiftly for Sorahb to take advantage of the situation. But that brings me to the final thing we must accomplish." Garren's voice was hard. "I've heard some say that Sorahb is no more than a nuisance to us, but it's a nuisance I will tolerate no longer."

His gaze swept the crowd again, and settled

on Patrius. "Tactimian Patrius, how many centris are left in your tacti?"

"Only four, Governor." If Patrius resented it, it didn't show in his voice, but Kavi blinked. He'd known Garren was splitting units off from the tacti for different duties, but over half of Patrius' command was gone.

"Hmm," said Garren. "Still, it should be enough to handle this. In fact, a small, elite strike force might be better."

Might. Kavi felt a pang of pity for his friend.

"Your task, Tactimian, is to hunt down Sorahb. Capture him if you can, but kill him if it's necessary."

You will criticize the governor in public meetings.

Patrius had too much discipline to flinch. "May I recall at least part of my tacti, sir? I know the estimates of the force that first attacked the garrison at Mazad weren't reliable, but their best guess was that Sorahb had almost a full tacti himself."

"Yes, but they were also pathetically unskilled fighters," said Garren. "With the result that the garrison, though badly outnumbered, killed or captured almost two hundred of them. Are your men less well-trained than those of Substrategus Arus?"

"No, sir, but I'm not sure it's safe to assume that Sorahb hasn't done any training, or replaced those men in the last three months. I would not wish to underestimate my enemy."

Kavi wasn't the only one who winced, but Garren only scowled.

"Very well, you may recall two centris. That should be more than enough to take care of this amateur army . . . when you find them."

The question of how Patrius was to do that seemed to hang in the air, almost visible, but Patrius only nodded. "Thank you, sir."

He likely could do it, Kavi thought grimly. The croft was well hidden, and the folk who knew of it had kept the secret, but too many knew of it. One of them was bound to get greedy. Young Commander Jiaan would have to be warned.

Kavi felt a flash of guilt at the idea of betraying Patrius to Jiaan, for Patrius had dealt fairly with him. Treated him better, and more kindly, than the deghan's bastard had. On the other hand, there was a limit to how often a man could change sides, and Kavi had likely surpassed it already. Jiaan must be warned.

Even if it meant Patrius' death?

But perhaps Kavi could prevent that some-how. After all, Jiaan would owe him for the warn-ing, for his help with the siege towers, and for freeing his half sister—though when Kavi had seen them together, they didn't seem to be close.

Should he take the girl with him, as a charac-ter witness, when he approached the new com-mander of the Farsalan army? Jiaan couldn't know what he'd been up to . . . unless he was in closer contact with Mazad than Kavi thought he was.

Garren had gone on to discuss some situation with supplies, leaving him free to think.

Yes, he needed a character witness. The girl had seen him trading with the Hrum. If Jiaan accused him, he could say that it was known that he traded with the army, and that those who resented folk who sold to the enemy had blown everything out of proportion—not knowing that he only did it so he could spy on the Hrum! Yes, that would do. There was still some risk, but not much, and he would need both Jiaan and Soraya's help to find the hidden camp and take out the siege towers. He would set out for the Suud's desert tomorrow.

CHAPTER TWENTY

SORAYA

MAOK POKED HER HEAD into Soraya's hutch shortly after sundown. "That peddler who brought you here wants to see you. He's set himself at the bottom of the twisted trail, and he's waiting, meek as a hopping mouse. Wake up, girl! Anyone would think you were a day dweller."

Soraya turned a yawn into a grimace, and rubbed her eyes. She'd only been living with Proud Walking clan for a few weeks, and making the transition to sleeping days and waking nights took a while.

She still wasn't sure whether to be annoyed or amused that in all the time she'd spent with them last winter, the clan hadn't told her their name. Maok said it was because they weren't sure she'd come back. But now that she had, they had told her—making her part of the clan in a way she hadn't been before, no matter how well treated she'd been as a guest.

But if she was now part of the clan, what about Sudaba and Merdas? No, Soraya wasn't here to stay this time either, no matter how welcome she felt, or how glad she was to be with them. She could discard the trappings of a deghass, but the core of it, her duty to her family, to Farsala itself, couldn't be cut off like excess hair. But right now, there was a peddler to attend to.

"Did he say what he wanted?" she asked. "Could the watchers understand him?"

The Suud tried to make sure that at least one of the watchers they posted spoke at least some Faran, but not many tribe members did, so it wasn't always possible. And they didn't speak a word of Hrum.

The chill that swept over Soraya at that thought had nothing to do with the cool night. When she first heard that the Farsalan army intended to hide in the desert, she'd been angry at Jiaan for endangering the Suud. Then she'd heard Maok's reasons for agreeing, and anger gave way to fear, and a furious resolve.

She would not let the Hrum come here. They had done damage enough in Farsala, where the people had a roughly equivalent level of mechanical sophistication. The Suud, fighting with wooden spears against those accursed, watersteel swords, would be destroyed.

Thinking of watersteel reminded her of something else. "This is the man I told you about," said Soraya. "The one who spoke to the shilshadu of the watersteel."

It had been so startling—for a moment, brushing his hand, she had tapped into the open channel between his spirit and the steel. But unlike the peddler, she knew how to follow that channel, to wholly sense the steel's crystalline song.

Yet when she held the fragment herself, its shilshadu was closed to her. Soraya thought she might have found it, if she went into a full trance and searched for a month, or two, or three. And she might not find it either. Yet she knew that the peddler, who could open that channel without even realizing he'd done it, hadn't sensed nearly as much as she had.

"I thought you wanted to talk to him," she added.

"Of course I want to talk to him." Maok came into the hutch and sat beside Soraya's bedroll. "Since we teach our own people to search for the shilshadu of things from the time they're children, we seldom get the chance to meet someone who does it instinctively. Naturals, they're called. It was people like them, people who were particularly attuned to some creature or element, who eventually became the first Speakers! There are dozens of questions I'd like to ask. But I can't ask them without telling him about our magic, and that's always dangerous. Especially now, when your people are groping so desperately for weapons."

"You're probably right." Soraya sighed. "But I owe him a lot. Giving him magic would be a fitting repayment." She knew she could never repay Maok for giving it to her. Her teacher had been startled by how much her control had improved in just one summer, and even more surprised at the way her shilshadu had opened to people, which Maok said usually came upon Speakers only after many years of study. She then discussed with Soraya a long list of rules about its use, and its abuse, and started teaching her how to suppress the sensing unless she consciously chose to use it. Soraya sighed again. She hadn't thought of her ability to read the feelings of those around her as an invasion of their privacy, but she knew she wouldn't want someone looking into her shilshadu without permission.

"Maybe after this war ends, things will change," said Maok consolingly. "Naturals aren't that rare, though mostly it takes the form of openness to a particular species' shilshadu. Generally it's horses with you people, but once I met a hunter who was open to the shilshadu of all kinds of animals. He had no idea why he was so successful, why he always knew what direction a startled gazelle would jump, or where to place his snares."

"Didn't you want to tell him?" Soraya asked. "To help him open his shilshadu fully to his creatures? To teach him to Speak to other things as well?"

"A part of me wanted to," said Maok. "But his life was already set. Magic might have been an intrusion—or even destroyed it! He made his living as a huntsman. What would become of him if he opened his spirit so fully to the spirits of his creatures that he could no longer kill them?"

Soraya knew that this was why the Suud, also hunters, so seldom spoke to the shilshadu of animals.

"The peddler," she said slowly. "He told me he was a smith once. Is that why he has an affinity for steel?"

"Very likely," said Maok. "Or perhaps that affinity is why he became a smith in the first place. That's one of the things I'd like to ask him. But why is he a peddler now?"

"Something happened to his hand," said Soraya. "There's a scar on his palm, and it's not very strong. He never said so, but I think that's what stopped him from being a smith."

If that was true, then teaching this man to sense the spirit of the steel he could never shape might be a cruel punishment instead of a gift. Maok was right—she had to learn to think about the effect of magic on people, and the world, instead of just using it.

"Well, right now your peddler is getting bored

with waiting." Maok rose to her feet, though she had to bend under the hutch's low ceiling. "Get out of bed, girl. You'll waste all the moonlight!"

For Soraya that was a serious consideration, and she scrambled out of her blankets and went to wash. The Suud, with their eerie, wide-dilating pupils, could see well enough by starlight, but after the moon set, Soraya would be all but blind outside the firelit camp.

Fortunately the moon was waxing now, and would set about four marks before sunrise. That would give her plenty of time, for Proud Walking's current camp wasn't far from the bottom of the twisted trail.

As they ate breakfast Soraya tried to convince the clan council that they didn't need to send an escort of warriors with her and Maok. "I don't know what he wants," she admitted. "But I've never seen him do anything violent. He's the kind who thinks his way out of things. And the trail watchers say he's alone, so even if I'm wrong, the four of them will be more than enough to come to our aid."

Soraya knew the council's concern was for the safety of their best All Speaker, not for a mediocre hunter and a Speaker just beginning to learn magic. But the council had also learned the futility of trying to coddle Maok, and in the end, Soraya and her teacher went to meet the peddler alone, though Maok did insist they talk to one of the watchers first.

"He's just been waiting," the watcher confirmed. "Patient as can be, though he calls out every now and then. I like the beast that's with him. It has a mind of its own."

Soraya, who had helped drag the reluctant mule out of several duck ponds on the road north from Setesafon, grinned. "You don't know the half of it."

IN FACT, IT WAS DUCKIE who noticed their presence, picking up Soraya's scent and whickering a greeting.

The peddler followed the mule's gaze and his bored expression brightened. "You made good time."

They actually hadn't hurried, but he didn't know how close the camp was, and Soraya wasn't about to tell him.

"This is Maok," she said instead. "My . . .

my . . ." *Teacher, counselor . . . mother?* "My sponsor among the Suud. Maok, this is the peddler Kavi, whom I told you about."

The peddler grinned. "Nothing too bad I hope," he said confidently.

"Maybe yes, maybe no." Maok's serene smile made Soraya wince — her teacher loved cutting the overconfident down to size. "Depends on how you think of bad, but mostly you're not big enough for bad."

Even her rough Faran got the point across. The peddler stopped grinning. "Ah, um . . ."

Soraya took pity on him — anyone fool enough to cross swords with Maok needed all the help he could get. "Why are you looking for me now?"

"Ah . . . After I left you, I . . . did some things."

"You poisoned the Hrum garrison and took food into Mazad," said Soraya impatiently. The Suud had a surprising number of contacts in the villages near the foothills. They traded foodstuffs and knives for Suud baskets, and added gossip into the bargain for free.

"Yes." He had almost adapted to the level Maok played on. Though Maok had abandoned the conversation to make Duckie's acquaintance, stroking the mule's soft nose and whispering in her ears. Duckie didn't make a sound, but Soraya had the unnerving impression that the mule was whispering back.

"Anyway," the peddler continued, "I learned that the Hrum are making siege towers to use against Mazad, in a hidden camp somewhere. I wondered if you'd overheard anything that might give us a clue where the camp was."

"Siege towers? I never heard anything about—no, wait a moment." Soraya thought carefully. "I do remember one comment. It was almost two months ago. A couple of men in the meal tent were talking about how the camp for 'the project' would have to be located where there was timber readily available. That means somewhere in the mountains, doesn't it?"

"That it does," said the peddler. "And in the higher mountains, where the straight pines are, not the scrub around Mazad."

"I'm sorry," said Soraya. "I can't think of anything else. It wasn't long after that that I got caught, and people started watching what they said in front of me. It doesn't help much, does it?"

"It helps some," said the peddler thoughtfully.

"Assuming this project is the siege towers—and even if it's not, they'll still need timber—then we should start looking in the mountains near Mazad. They won't want to ship something that big very far, even if they aren't completely assembled. But more important, if they hadn't even set up the camp two months ago, then they likely won't be finished for a while yet, even if Garren does send more men. We have time to find them."

"How do you plan to search all the mountains around Mazad?" Soraya asked. "And what will you do if you find them?"

At one time, even a few weeks ago, that question would have been sarcastic, but not anymore. Even allowing for the exaggeration that plagued all rumors, what she'd heard about his raid on the Hrum garrison was impressive.

"Yes, well, that's the next thing I wanted to ask you about. I have a few ideas what we can do about those towers, assuming we find them in time."

"How will you find them?" she asked again. "Those are big mountains."

"Oh, I won't go searching up and down the hills myself." He sounded almost shocked at the prospect. "Duckie prefers roads. I'll just talk to the men in the mining camps. No one could establish a base in the mountains without the locals knowing about it—though they likely don't know what the Hrum are doing there, or they'd have passed the word on already."

"One man established an army in the mountains, without anyone noticing." Soraya felt a bit smug, knowing something he didn't.

"If you mean Commander Jiaan," said the peddler, "the local folk knew all about it—they just didn't tell the Hrum. But that's the other thing I'll need when the time comes, the help of some first-rate archers. And the young commander has the only archers I know of who aren't Hrum. But I'm afraid he might have heard I've traded with the Hrum, and not be knowing the real reason. According to the local folk, he's packed up his army and vanished, so I was wondering if you know where they are, and if you'd be willing to introduce me, you being . . . um . . ."

Jiaan was known to be her father's bastard, though no one had ever been so rude as to say it in Soraya's presence. She stood silent, watching him fumble with it.

Perhaps fortunately, Maok came to his rescue. "I don't know if the stubborn girl will speak for you," she said, turning away from Duckie. "But the army is here."

"Here?" the peddler asked, looking around as if he expected them to spring out of the rocks.

"In the desert," Maok went on. Soraya wondered what her teacher had sensed, that she spilled that secret so easily. "They began making their camp several weeks past, and just came there. We will send for the commander to meet you."

THE ESCORT MAOK HAD SENT to fetch Jiaan whistled to warn the camp of their return.

Soraya went to the mouth of the canyon where she knew they'd emerge. The rocks were a black-and-silver sculpture under the light of the near-full moon. Her father's bastard son had come into his household as a page at the age of ten, but Soraya had never known him well. It was beneath a deghass' dignity to befriend servants. But the boy had grown to look startlingly like her father — she'd have to brace herself for that.

The peddler came up to join her, along with

the spouses and children of the Suud who'd gone to find Jiaan.

The last time all three of them had been together—

The peddler noticed her sudden, indrawn breath. "What?"

"Nothing," said Soraya. "Just that . . . just a thought."

The last time all three of them had been together, her father had been alive.

But he was dead now, Soraya told herself firmly. And he'd had small patience with people who wept and moaned forever, instead of getting on with their lives.

So get on with it.

The small party came around the bend in the canyon, Jiaan walking with them. He hadn't brought any of his own men—a sign of his trust in the Suud, in Maok, who had summoned him, without telling him why.

His eyes widened as he caught sight of her. She found she didn't mind his resemblance to her—their—father as much as she'd expected. She had, after all, known him for most of her life.

"Lady Soraya!" he exclaimed, stepping forward. "What are you doing here? I thought you'd gone with . . ."

The peddler had stepped up beside her, and Jiaan's gaze fixed on him. Color drained from his face, then surged into his cheeks in a feverish flush. What—

She hadn't even time to complete the thought. Jiaan took three running steps and hurtled into the peddler, knocking him flat, pounding his fists into the peddler's body, his face.

"What are you doing?" Soraya shouted. "Stop this! Stop it at once!"

But Gorahz, the djinn of rage, had fully possessed Jiaan—he didn't even seem to hear her.

The peddler tried to defend himself, to fight back. But few of his blows landed, and Soraya could see that he was already losing.

The Suud from the camp were running toward them, but Soraya ran the other way, to the stream where she snatched up an iron kettle, which earlier that morning she'd scrubbed out with sand. It took several long moments to fill it in the shallow water, but the shouts of the Suud, and the thud of blows, told her the fight still went on.

With muscles made strong by a summer of

hard work, she hauled up the heavy kettle and staggered back to the fight. By now she'd had so much practice changing water that it took only a moment of connection, of disciplined yielding, to reach its shilshadu, to remind it of melting snow, icicles, and cold running streams. A part of her heart shared its joy in changing, even as she ran up to the struggling men and hurled the icy water over the two of them.

The peddler had stopped fighting and had raised both arms to protect himself, so some of the water was deflected onto his chest and the ground. But the freezing cascade caught Jiaan full in the face, and he swore and lifted both hands to wipe his eyes.

Three Suud hunters, two of them the biggest men in the tribe, and the last the reckless Abab, caught Jiaan's arms and shoulders and dragged him away. A fence of spears lowered between him and his victim. They also pointed spears at the peddler, but he showed no sign of leaping to the attack. In fact, as battered as he looked, getting to his feet might be beyond him for a while. His mouth and nose were both bleeding.

Soraya turned to Jiaan. "What was that

about?" Her voice held an arrogant command that would have made both her mother and her father proud.

Jiaan staggered to his feet, still staring at the peddler. He started forward, only stopping when half a dozen spears pricked his chest and abdomen. He finally looked at Soraya.

"What are you doing here? With him? He killed our father! He's a Hrum spy!"

"Are you mad? Our father died fighting the Hrum." He had to be mad, or possessed, or at least mistaken, for Jiaan had fought in the same battle.

"Oh, he didn't do it personally." How had the peasant boy she remembered learned to put so much contempt into his voice? "He's too cowardly to fight face-to-face. He kills by sneaking, and spying, and lying. And betrayal. You don't believe me? I can prove it. The Hrum mark their spies, just like they do with slaves. Watch."

He started toward the peddler, who had risen to his knees, but the spears stopped Jiaan. He looked past Soraya's shoulder, and she turned in time to see Maok nod consent.

The spears withdrew and Jiaan stalked forward, drawing his knife.

Soraya opened her mouth to protest, but Maok's hand on her shoulder stopped her, and she subsided, watching. Watching, and dropping the mental shield that blocked her people sense. She had to know what was happening here, invasion of privacy or not.

Jiaan's knife reached toward the peddler's neck and Soraya stiffened, but he only slid the blade into the collar of the peddler's tunic, and slit the fabric over the shoulder and down the sleeve.

Cloth fell away, showing a series of black diamonds running around the peddler's upper arm, like half of a bracelet.

"There!" Triumph laced the seething fury she sensed from Jiaan. "That's the mark of a Hrum spy. And that . . ." His knife flicked toward a thin, pink scar at the top of the peddler's shoulder. It barely missed cutting the skin, and Soraya sensed the peddler's flash of fear. He was harder to read than Jiaan, but she knew he was afraid. Afraid and angry.

"That," Jiaan went on, "is the scar left by an arrow I fired at a Farsalan traitor who we saw passing information to the Hrum. He escaped then."

The sudden flare of guilt and grief didn't show in Jiaan's face, but Soraya felt them.

"It was later that I realized I'd seen the traitor start to reach for his payment with his right hand, and then switch to his left. And I remembered whose mannerism that was, and I remembered that this peddler had been snooping around the camp, all curious and innocent. He's the reason the Hrum knew our plans! He's the reason they were able to ambush our archers!"

The peddler, still on his knees, drew a breath. "That's true," he admitted. "Well, the bit about the archers. The Hrum's long lances would have destroyed that army, and your father would still be dead, even if I'd never met the Hrum. But I don't expect a deghan to let a little thing like truth stand in the way of beating a peasant!"

His anger was different from Jiaan's, sullen and slow burning as a forge fire, and perhaps the hotter for it. But if what Jiaan said was true . . .

"You don't deny you're a Hrum spy!" Jiaan shot back. "You don't deny that you gave them Farsalan battle plans. You don't deny that you scouted the Dugaz rebels' camp for them, and probably other things as well!"

"Wait," said Soraya. She had to come at the truth of this—and there were some things she knew that Jiaan didn't. "That can't be right. He's been working against the Hrum! He's the one who poisoned the garrison, and smuggled food into Mazad. And he helped me escape from their camp."

Where he'd been welcome . . . and trusted. She faced the peddler, who was wiping blood off his chin with his sleeve, and opened her sensing as wide as she could. "Explain," she demanded.

The peddler snorted, splattering fresh blood onto his face. "What for? Yes, I sold Farsalan battle plans to the Hrum. And yes, I've been working against them since." He was telling the truth. He had sold her father's battle plan to the Hrum. A chill began to grow in Soraya's heart. Hatred, but cold rather than hot. Cold as steel.

The peddler wiped his face again. "But deghans never care why a peasant does anything. So instead, I'll tell you something you might care about—you can't beat the Hrum without my help. The country folk trust me, and they won't trust you. Not with their lives. You can't find the camp without them. You can't sabotage the siege towers without them. You can't—"

"Siege towers?" Jiaan interrupted. "What siege towers?"

"The ones the Hrum are building in a hidden camp, to take Mazad," said the peddler. "The siege towers you wouldn't have known about till they rolled up to the walls, if I wasn't spying on the Hrum for your Flame-begotten cause. But you won't care about that, either," he finished bitterly.

It was true, Soraya realized over the cold boil of her own anger. If it hadn't been for him, they wouldn't have known about the siege towers. If it hadn't been for him, she might still be looking for a way to get word of Nehar's treachery to Mazad. If it wasn't for him, she would still be a Hrum slave, with scars on her back, and perhaps a broken spirit to go with them.

And compared to the fact that he'd had a hand in losing the battle that killed her father, none of it mattered at all. She wanted to kill him, to smash him with her fists like Jiaan had, to go on and on until he was obliterated, and her father's death was obliterated, and the whole nightmare was gone, and she was home and safe.

But killing him wouldn't bring her father back.

"I don't believe you," said Jiaan. "You're playing a double game—winning Mazad's trust so you can betray them too!"

"That's not true." The peddler's voice was almost calm.

"He is telling the truth," said Soraya. How could she sound so remote, so dispassionate, when she hated so much?

"How do you know that?" Jiaan demanded.

A reasonable question. Soraya shrugged.

"Whether I'm telling the truth about that doesn't matter," said the peddler. "Because I am telling the truth when I say you can't get the Hrum siege towers without me. You can't even find them."

And that was also true. Even Jiaan knew it, but he covered his sudden doubt with bluster and anger. "I don't care. We'll find them somehow, and destroy them somehow. When they're being taken to Mazad! We can attack them on the road!"

"Now, there's a deghan's answer if ever I heard one," said the peddler. "You'll sacrifice half your army—maybe more, since every man Garren can spare and some he can't will be guarding those towers by then. But they're just peasants, after all.

What are their lives, compared to a deghan's vengeance? And you'll likely lose, and those towers will bring down Mazad, and all its folk will be shipped off as slaves. But what's that, compared to a deghan's vengeance?"

Even Jiaan fell silent.

If her father had had scant patience with weeping and moaning, he'd had nothing but contempt for those who wasted life in vengeance. Unlike Jiaan, she could sense the emotions behind the peddler's words. His hatred, his bitterness. His own outraged anger, as deep as hers. As justified? No.

But that sensing let her work past her anger, to clear thought.

"He's right," she told Jiaan. "You can't kill him. We need him."

A year ago she would have taken Jiaan's knife and slit the peddler's throat without a second thought. The peasant was right—it was a deghan's answer. But this deghass had a baby brother who was going to grow up as a Hrum slave. She would do anything she had to, to change that. And that meant defeating the Hrum, and to do that they needed the peddler, so

. . . "You can't kill him," she repeated. "And you know it."

He did, and that knowledge was even more intolerable to him than it was to her. Jiaan backed away a step, then another, and then turned and fled into the moonlit shadows of the canyon.

CHAPTER TWENTY-ONE

JIAAN

JIAAN'S IMPULSE WAS TO RUN, to run until the whole situation disappeared. That way he wouldn't have to make an impossible choice. He couldn't let the peddler live — he couldn't!

But in fact, he hadn't run more than a few hundred yards before his feet slowed. It was a foolish impulse; choices couldn't be outrun.

His anger, his desire to see the traitor's blood pouring onto the desert sands, still burned. If he'd used his knife instead of his fists, it would all be over by now! If only he'd been wearing his sword . . .

But the Suud were allies, and uneasy allies at that. Wearing a sword to visit them had seemed both foolish and discourteous. And what if he'd killed the traitor, and then discovered that they needed his help to defeat the Hrum? Then what?

Then they'd have found another way! The thought of letting him live was intolerable enough — the girl wanted Jiaan to work with him?

No. Not ever.

Not even to defeat the Hrum?

The girl was right. He could all but hear his father's voice, complaining about deghans who thought with their honor instead of their brains. Still . . .

"When the world's been kicked this hard, it's not easy to know who to trust, is it?" The old woman's voice was the first sign of her presence, but somehow Jiaan wasn't surprised.

"I know who not to trust," he said, turning to face her. "And that filthy traitor is at the top of the list. We'd have to spend every moment watching for a knife in the back — and sooner or later, there'd be one."

"Hmm," said Maok. "Maybe, maybe not. To me, he seems like a young man who has reasons."

Jiaan didn't care. "I just hope you didn't leave him unguarded. He'll sneak off in an instant — and he already knows too much."

Maok smiled. "Sneak from camp, maybe. Sneak from the desert before we could stop him? I don't think he'll try to go, even from camp. I think he wants to stop the Hrum, to save Mazad, as bad as you do. Maybe more."

Jiaan half believed that she might know. "Why do you think that? What makes you so sure?"

For a moment he thought she would shrug it off, as Soraya had, but instead she said, "I've heard some things that happen in the old land, on the other side of the mountains. By what I heard, he's done much to fight the Hrum."

"You think he's Sorahb? There are dozens of Sorahbs. He's probably claiming credit for what they did."

But there was one other Sorahb in particular, the one whose plans were so economical, so successful, so . . . sneaky. Jiaan had been certain that that Sorahb, the one he'd wanted to meet, had been in charge of the last strike against the Hrum garrison. It had felt like his work. Soraya said the peddler was behind that, said it as if she knew. If that was true . . . could the peddler be that Sorahb?

No, surely not. And even if he was, it wouldn't stop Jiaan from killing him.

Maok must have seen his expression harden, for she sighed. "I see. But you may not kill him here. Your father didn't fight us, and he didn't fight others in our camps. If you wish to stay in the desert, to keep our trust, you must take the same path. You may not kill him while he is under our protection."

But if the peddler escaped, it might be years before Jiaan found him. If he fled Farsala, Jiaan might never see him again!

"You talk about my father as if he was here for some time," said Jiaan, trying to gain time to think. His army needed this desert base.

The woman studied him for a moment, then nodded. "It was a secret we kept, for fear he would find trouble from it. But he is safe from trouble now, and it is time for you to know.

"A tribe of miners came to the desert, to search for the good iron they say is here. They captured many of our people, and forced them to dig for them. But the clans of the people they captured attacked and freed them—those who had not already died. Then the miners sent to your gahn and asked for soldiers to protect them, and so your father came to the desert."

Jiaan frowned. "I thought he went to look for a group of miners who'd gone missing."

Maok smiled. "That's what the miners told him to say, because they didn't want word of what they found to be known. And that is a secret you must keep," she added firmly. "But when your father came, the miners were mostly alive. We played tracker with your father's men for a time, but whenever he met our hunters, he greeted us, and treated us well. Not like the miners at all. So one night we crept into his camp and woke him, and he followed our warriors into the desert alone, not telling his men where he had gone. We spoke to him then and told him what the miners were doing."

The old woman's smile was full of amused respect. "He was a smart man, your father, and a good one. He made his men look for a time, and then said the miners must be dead, and sent them out of the desert to wait for him. When they were gone, he came to us. He helped us fight the miners. He killed several of them, even though he was sent to protect them. He said Farsala law wouldn't punish them, not for killing us. And though I don't know it, for our tribe was not doing much with this, I think those miners maybe called your father 'traitor' too."

"But . . . but he had good reasons for what he did." Jiaan's mind was spinning—he'd never heard a word of this! It sounded like his father, though. Especially the part about him following his enemies alone into the night to parlay. And sending his men out, so if one of the miners survived to accuse them, his men would be safe.

Maok's smile widened. "I think traitors mostly have reasons."

She turned and walked back to camp, leaving Jiaan torn between outrage and the fact that he couldn't immediately think of an argument. How could she compare his father to that . . . that contemptible peddler! Yes, what his father had done was probably, technically, treason, but he'd seen a terrible wrong and known there was no other way to right it. He'd had good reasons . . .

Could the peddler have reasons that seemed good to him?

Jiaan thought about that for a moment and decided that he still didn't care. But Maok's story had reminded him of something else his father believed: that there were things more important than the deghans' code of honor.

The deghans had always put personal honor, personal glory, first—and it had crippled the Farsalan army. Was putting personal vengeance first any better? Jiaan knew what his father would say.

He walked back to the Suud camp. The peddler sat by the central fire, pressing a damp cloth gently against his face. The lady Soraya stood nearby, watching him with the intensity a leopardess bestows on a threat to her cubs. She'd cut her hair, Jiaan noticed. She looked stronger, and far tougher, than when he'd seen her last. For a moment he almost pitied the peddler. Almost.

He walked up to the fire, stopped in front of his enemy, and folded his arms. "All right," he said. "I'll accept your help in destroying the siege towers. I'll accept your help to fight the Hrum, until their year is over, and they're either gone or here to stay. But then I'm going to kill you."

The peddler lowered the cloth and stared at him. His lower lip was split and swollen, and

Jiaan was pleased to see that he had the beginnings of a magnificent black eye.

"You want me to work with you for six months, and then you'll kill me?"

He looked at Soraya, who nodded.

"I'll help him," she agreed, with something that might have been enthusiasm if it hadn't been so cold.

The peddler snorted. "You're certainly knowing how to motivate a man."

Jiaan shrugged and watched him think it over.

"But you'd work with me for those six months?" the peddler finally asked. "I'd be in no danger from you, till the Hrum's year is over?"

"Yes," said Jiaan. The girl nodded.

"Done," said the peddler. "At least, the working together. You'll understand that I don't agree to the killing part at the end."

Jiaan expected him to resist that. In fact, he was looking forward to it with a savagery even he found appalling. But that was what he felt.

"Done," he agreed bleakly.

Soraya echoed it. "Done."

None of them attempted to clasp wrists to seal the bargain. It would be intolerable working with someone he hated, and worse working with someone he didn't trust. The peddler could never go unguarded, never be allowed to know their secrets. But they needed him, and he seemed to need them, so for six months Jiaan would endure it.

Until Farsala was free.

SORAHB WANDERED ON, *until one morning he saw a man with only one leg, hobbling down the road on crutches. Sorahb urged his horse to a faster pace, thinking to assist the man. But when he drew near he saw that the man wore the tunic of a Hrum soldier, though his scarlet cloak had been replaced by one of drab brown.*

Sorahb hesitated then, but the road was rough and muddy, and he had known Farsalans who had lost a leg in the war. He would hate to see them struggling alone on the road.

He offered the soldier a ride to the Sendar border, and the man gratefully accepted. It took some effort to mount him behind Sorahb, but soon they were able to set out. The soldier told Sorahb that his horse had pulled a tendon, and he had sold it to a farmer who could give it time to heal while he went on, for his eagerness to reach his home was too great for delay.

As the marks passed they fell to talking of war, as soldiers will. "I lost my leg, but we won the battle," the soldier told him. "I count it small loss, when all is said, for I've my life, my wits, my hands, and my pension into the bargain."

"Then you are more fortunate than I," said Sorahb. "I've kept my legs, but all my battles have been lost."

The soldier was seated behind Sorahb, so he did not see the man's eyes, which were suddenly far too old for the young face that surrounded them.

"Then you have been given a gift," said the soldier. "For only when the last battle is lost, only when he's desperate, will a man discover new ways to fight."

SORAHB LEFT THE SOLDIER at the Sendar Gate and returned to the army he had abandoned.

"I'm sorry I left you," he told them. "But at the same time I am glad, for walking in the world I found wisdom. The deghans' ways have failed, and only a fool such as I would have tried to use them again. We must find new ways to fight, ways that will work where the deghans' did not. We will take them from Kadeshi raiders, from Dugaz swamp rats, even from the Hrum themselves. But first, I ask you to teach me your ways, peasant ways. Now is the time for you to speak, and for me to listen. For we will be able to defeat even the mighty army of the Hrum, once we have learned to work together."

Don't miss these favorites from Newbery Medalist

CYNTHIA VOIGT

"Entertaining, interesting,
and well-written."
—*New York Times Book Review*
WINNER OF THE
EDGAR ALLAN POE AWARD

"Beautifully written . . .
miraculously convincing and
moving."—*Publishers Weekly*

"Enjoy this one for the
pure pleasure of the creepy
goings-on."—*Booklist*

Song of the Lioness Quartet

*Discover how it all began
in Tamora Pierce's
Song of the Lioness quartet.*

THE
IMMORTALS

MAGIC LIVES ON IN
THE KINGDOM OF TORTALL.
Experience all of its legends!

THE IMMORTALS QUARTET

Wild Magic (Book I)

Wolf-speaker (Book II)

Emperor Mage (Book III)

*The Realms of the Gods
(Book IV)*

Crowsnest Community Library
Date Due